MARIE MCFALL

The Roda Odyssey

Traversing The Mist

First edition

ISBN: 978-0-9991474-4-3

This book was professionally typeset on Reedsy.
Find out more at reedsy.com

To The Creator of All,
Thank you for placing the people in our lives that helped make our dream come true.

Aunt Kathy is inspired by Kathy Chapman.
We hope you can read the final product in Heaven.
Your beautiful soul is missed here on Terra.

Contents

Acknowledgement

Our family who supported our dream and stepped up to help where they could, Matthew, David, Mom, Jonathon, Joi, Kortney, Meredith and Pam.

Irreplaceable editing skills of Debbie Smith, Meredith, Matthew and Pam! Your never ending patience with these grammar, punctuation, sentence structure challenged writers is priceless!

The amazing cover art by Jeff Brown Graphics, www.jeffbrowngraphics.com

Beginning story line edits Andrea Hurst.

Content editor Ashley Kelley, www.terraincognitamarketing.com

Awesome Dragon names at:
  www.fantasynamegenerators.com/dragon_names.php

Author's photo by the incredible Misty Terrell.

Chapter 1

Kolob

Tucked away at a small pool at the Sacred Temple Mount, the coolness of the crystal floor was welcoming on Kerberos's bent knees. His head leaned forward in a slight bow with his feathered wings folded tightly to his back. The pool was a private oasis, secluded from prying eyes and daily routines. Here there would be no one calling out his name, or My Liege, to get his attention just solitude. Staring into the pool seeking clarity, he struggled to control his racing mind after so many sleepless nights.

Pressing his fingers to his temples, he tried once again to remember the dream The Creator of All had giving him. Rather than finding clarity, he was met with the vivid memories of the same physical reactions. He always woke violently, heart racing, vaulting from his bed, grasping the handle of his sword to unsheathe it in an instant.

"What was it about? What happened?" he thought as he slowly pressed into his temples aggravated at his lack of progress. No matter how hard he searched it was just out of his grasp. "Augh!" he burst out in frustration. "This will get me nowhere," he chastised himself and took three deep calming breaths.

Rubbing his temples he thought, *"Start with the core knowledge. Nephilim were created to serve. We are the guardians of the worlds of Terra, Eirenic and Agon. We are built to maintain the balance of good and evil that exists in all beings. All are precious to the Creator of All but none more so than the humans of Terra. The reason why the Creator of All favors them is unclear, but it is not for* a Nephilim to question the Creator's will, only to serve," he paused a moment, then blinked his eyes several times to moisten them.

"The Creator of All blessed few Nephilim with interactions with the human populations on the three worlds. Only humans of great importance were blessed with guidance from a Nephilim. I have watched the Terran girl Dani grow into a bright, beautiful young woman. In those moments I have been able to give her gentle guidance. Even though the portals are closed, I feel a strong connection with her. My interactions with Dani are a source of comfort and bring a spark of light to the murky life around me. What is Dani's importance is for the future?" He puzzled. His sense of failure at not remembering his dreams crept into his consciousness. Failure was not an option.

Closing his eyes, he could barely hear the whispered words of his own prayer. "I do not understand what I am to do, but I know something must be done. Something evil comes and action must be taken. Creator of All, you have blessed me with the opportunity to guide Dani on Terra. I feel you have made this unprecedented connection for a reason, but I know not why. With the Axis Mundi sealed the Nephilim are unable to watch and guide the other worlds as you intended. If all worlds are as imbalanced as Kolob, then all are faltering in their paths. Please, Creator of All, hear my prayers and give me guidance. Give…me…a…" He felt the strength leave his body as he slumped over sideways, landing on the pristine hard white crystal floor.

Lying there he could not move his limbs or wings. His eyes refusing to open, he was left in darkness. The sensation of his spirit leaving his body set his teeth on edge. He was fighting the urge to struggle against it. Taking a calming breath, he steadied his resolve. If this was the Creator's will, let it be done.

Blurred images started flashing before his eyes, growing in focus until they were sharp and clear. A moment later he felt his spirit settle on solid ground. Rising to his feet looking around, he recognized the smaller vegetation on the world of Terra. A slow drizzle from the dark gray cloudy sky soaked everything around him. He noticed emaciated humans with dirty rags hanging from their unwashed bodies, lined up in rows, shivering. Mud caked and splattered up their legs almost to their knees from the saturated ground.

They were pale and gaunt, with their bones clearly visible, protruding under their unwashed skin. Their hair hung in filthy matted clumps on their heads.

Needing answers, he called out to the closest humans. "What is happening? Why are you standing here? What are you waiting for?"

Looking at the humans for some sort of response he was dismayed when they did not even blink or acknowledge him. Frustrated with no response, he opened his wings and flew into the drizzling sky. Drops of rain ran down his feathers, as he pumped them for lift. He sought the head of the line to determine what was happening. A shiver ran through his soul at what the cause of all this depravation might be.

A gut-wrenching need to find Dani hit the pit of his stomach. It was not an option; he had to find her. From his high vantage point in the sky, he could see for miles in every direction. Rows and rows of malnourished humans stood, moving only when the person in front of them did. He hovered a few seconds in shock at what he saw. Leaning forward, he raced to the front of the lines, hoping to find answers.

Drawing close to the front, he saw the ancient remains of a civilization long since passed. The remains of stone buildings and walls lined the narrow, muddied roads. In two archways still intact, he could see the raised markings on the inner stones indicating their true purpose: portals that led into the Axis Mundi. The shimmering of their vertical, watery surface clearly indicated they were open and operational. Here, the multiple lines of humans merged into one line. Eirenician guards, easily identified by their clothing, stood at the head of the line.

The guards were sorting the humans into three groups. Humans were either being shoved into one of the two portals or pushed off to the side into a holding pen. As he flew closer, he noticed a pattern. The portal on the right, almost exclusively, had young females shoved into it. The portal on the left had mostly males shoved through, young and old. Occasionally a large-framed female was included. The group sent to the pen looked to be very old, sickly, or children. Searching the dirty scared faces of each Terran female, he found himself growing more desperate to locate Dani.

The sound of a female's shrieking sobs hit his ears. Without thought, he

3

raced to the scene. Several guards were attempting to part a young female from a male. She was crying and screaming to go with him. A large male guard, who seemed to be in charge, grabbed the female's arms, shaking her violently while yelling, "You will learn your place Terran or suffer. It makes no difference to me."

The guard shoved the female into the portal on the right. Throwing his full weight forward Kerberos lunged in after her, knowing that she would be unable to keep herself from falling from the guard's violent push. Expecting to feel the hum of power normally felt when traveling through a portal of the Axis Mundi, confusion clouded his mind when instead a cool wisp of air moved over him. Darkness clouded his mind for just a second, causing him to slightly lose his focus. In moments, he stumbled through another portal, without even being aware that he had traveled the passageways of the Axis Mundi.

Quickly righting himself, he looked around for the accosted female. Confused at not seeing a line of females that had been shoved through he thought *"Where could they have gone and where am I?"* Taking a calming breath, he took a moment to collect his thoughts. *"I am still in the vision the Creator of All has given me. I must follow it to the end."*

Looking farther in the distance he recognized the royal palace on the world of Eirenic. He needed to find answers to what was going on and those answers would be at the palace. Flying in the crisp clean air felt good on his skin and feathers, after the decaying conditions on Terra. It troubled him that he had not found Dani. He would have to try and go back to search for her. For now, he would find out what he could from the palace on Eirenic. As he grew closer to the palace, the sound of raised shouting male voices filled the air. Quickening his wings, he flew to a large open field at the back of the palace.

The field was overflowing with Terran females, shabbily dressed, and huddled in small groups. In the middle of the field was a large, raised platform with a deep pit just off to the side of it. On the platform were ornately dressed males in long silken and fur lined robes. In their midst he could just make out a couple of females. He suddenly stopped his forward momentum to hover in the air over the platform, looking in shock at what he was seeing. The ornately dressed males parted to show an emaciated, filth-covered Dani. Her once beautiful long brown hair hanging in matted clumps around her ashen face.

The sight of her caused him to take a sharp inhale of breath. Dani's broken voice barely filled the air as she said, "It was me, and me alone, that made the decision to stand against Erabos. Please take me and let the others go," Dani weakly sobbed.

An older male with heavy gold chains around his neck spoke. "You dare, even now, to call The True Light by his given name. You are nothing but filth and you cost the lives of your family and all those who dared stand against The Light." The male sneered down at Dani's broken body.

Dani looked up and he could see tears running freely down her dirty face as she questioned, "Cost the lives? You have already killed them?"

The male laughed and then the others joined in. "Yes, you pathetic excuse of a being. I wanted to make you watch, but The True Light showed mercy I would not have given. We are the perfect race; you are not even worthy as a slave."

Dani hung her head. He was just about to dive onto the platform when he froze, seeing Dani lift her head again and start to speak.

"I failed. I chose not to become what I was meant to be; now I have nothing left to lose," Dani choked out. She took a deep breath and continued in a stronger voice, "Erabos is evil and by following him, you choose evil. You think you are perfect. You are, perfectly evil. The Creator of All made us equal. It is by your hands and actions that you have destroyed all that is beautiful and good!"

The ornately dressed male screamed, "How dare you! Executioner, be finished with this thing and throw it in the pit with the others. Let the Creator of All judge her soul's worth."

A battle cry erupted from deep within Kerberos as he dove grabbing and unsheathing his sword desperate to stop the executioner, but before he could reach Dani, her spirit was gone. The executioner had done his master's bidding. He flew right through the executioner as if he did not exist, watching in horror as Dani's frail body was thrown over the side of the platform into the large rectangular pit.

Lunging forward, he reached trying to catch Dani's body before it fell into the pit, discarded like garbage. A staggering thought raced through his mind: he had failed her. As he flew past the edge of the pit, unkempt human males and females shoveled dirt from a mound that must have been created when the pit was dug, covering the mangled dead bodies below.

"Noooo!" he howled. The emaciated face of Dani, her eyes staring blankly into space, filled his vision. The Creator of All had honored him above all other Nephilim, to help guide her. He had failed. Diving into the pit, his eyes fixed on Dani's death-masked face covered with the next shovel full of dirt. His wings involuntarily snapped shut on his back. He desperately tried opening them to stop his downward dive into the pit, to no avail. All his muscles clenched tight; his teeth were locked together as he strained to open his wings. As the ground raced towards him, he closed his eyes and braced for the impact with the ground. His shock was brief when he did not impact the earth, but instead flew through it into darkness. In his despair he began to pray. *"I know you have more to show me Creator of All, but I do not know if I can handle more."*

Slowly he became aware of sounds and smells filling the air around him. He was now laying on his side on a hard cold surface. He could hear heavy booted footfalls not far from where he lay. He groaned when he tried to pull first his hands free and then his feet of the heavy chains that bound him. *"What do you wish for me to see now?"* he thought, and barely slitting opened his eyes to look around.

"I am home, outside the Hall of Equality, but why am I chained?" he thought. Slowly moving his head so that he could look down his body he barely held in the gasp at what he saw. *"I guess that explains the pain,"* he thought as he took stock of the multiple of wounds actively dripping blood onto the crystal floor. He tried to take a calming breath and shuttered at the lancing agony that raced through his chest. Tilting his head farther downward, he could see dark raised welts across his chest. *"Broken ribs, no doubt".* He quickly closed his eyes when footfalls came closer and stopped on either

side of him. He could not hold in the groans of pain as he was lifted by his chained arms. Opening his eyes briefly, he knew he was being carried into the Hall of Equality. Gritting his teeth, he closed his eyes to concentrate while attempting to control some of the pain racking his body.

When they reached what he thought must be the center of the speaking floor, his captors dropped him onto the cold crystal floor, where he landed on his side again. He did not even attempt to hold in the sound of pain when he was unable to keep his head from slamming into the crystal floor. Dazed, he laid there taking shallow breaths to clear his head. Gritting his teeth he lifted his head, opening his eyes.

"I will face what the Creator of All has to show me, for I do not know how much more of this I will be able to withstand." When he was able to focus his eyes, he whispered out in shock, "Of all that is Holy, what has been done?" He looked around in dismay at what his vision took in.

There were several tiered levels of black crystal in the middle of what had once been a single level pure white crystal floor. Looking up, he knew his mouth fell slightly open at the sight of what sat at the top of the black crystal. A throne of black crystal rose high into the air. A maniacal laugh reverberated off the walls. *"I know this voice"* he thought, and it could only mean one thing. The Evil One, Erabos was on Kolob to start his reign of terror and darkness.

A noise to the left caught his attention. Turning his head, he saw a Nephilim with a black hood, striding towards him with a large axe dripping with fresh blood. The guards who had carried him into the hall lifted him into a kneeling position and forced his head over a blackened crystal stone whose sides were streaked with fresh blood. He looked up watching in horror as waves of black rolled from the high throne. It was as if the unadulterated blackness of evil was seeping up into the pure light of the crystal around him, suffocating it. The sound of the axe whistling through the air, heading toward his neck, was the last sound he heard.

Complete and utter nothingness surrounded him. He was not even sure whether his eyes were open or closed. He could hear nothing, not even the sound of his own breath or heartbeat. Drifted in the void of nothingness he had no concept of time. In desperation he started to pray in his mind, *"I have failed you Creator of All. I have also failed Dani. I have failed to bring back the balance to all the worlds. Without restoration of the balance, all the worlds will fail. I know this now. I know they are not as you intended for them to be. I know Dani is a key component to your plans, but I do not know why or how."*

Lost in anguish and despair at not getting a response, he started repeating a prayer he had learned as a youngling, for the Creator of All to help him. Just there, floating, somewhere in between with no concept of time passing he felt the presence of something slowly moving towards him. It was as if he was seeing a bright light off in the distance in the darkest of nights. *"I am here Creator of All, tell me your will,"* he said in his mind as his heart started to race.

As the sensations of something drawing near intensified so did the feeling of overpowering waves of pure white light. As it drew closer, he was able to distinguish not one, but three different beings. One being's presence encompassing the other two so completely he had not noticed the other two at first. The beings stopped their approach and he lay there observing them. One was larger and he could only look at the edges of its pure light. The other two were just as pure in light but not as overpowering to him to try and look directly at. His heart raced with uncertainty as he called out again, *"Creator of All, please guide me to your will,"* hesitating a moment in true fear at who the three could be he added, *"Protect me from that which tries to defeat your purpose for me."*

One of the smaller beings started moving and drew closer. As it did, he felt the pure light of its presence surround him and penetrate deep into his very soul. If he could have thrown himself on the ground with his arms wide in reverence, he would have. Unable to do so, he listened with his entire being as it spoke.

The voice was not male or female, it just was. "All worlds Terra, Eirenic, Agon, and Kolob's futures are intertwined. Change must happen, the people of all worlds must choose to become what they were created to be, or all that you have seen will come to pass. Evil will rule where the true light of salvation is unknown or has been extinguished. You are one of my most faithful children, your hour approaches. You will be one of the pillars to bring about the change that is needed to bring the balance of light to all worlds."

Chapter 2

Terra

Dani could barely sit still while she waited in the conference room. She was buzzing with excitement as she waited for Mrs. Avery, the office manager, to interview her. The room had a long oak table with leather corner pads placed in the middle and a cow hide rug on the floor. Pictures of rodeo scenes hung on the walls. Riverton, Wyoming was a small rural community, and everyone knew everyone. She had attended school with several of the doctors' and Mrs. Avery's kids. This has been her doctor's office since birth. She took a deep breath knowing her interview would feel a little awkward. She had known them all for years, and they felt like family so to add layers of formality felt out of place.

"Sorry about the wait, Dani," Mrs. Avery said as she hurried in and took a seat across the table from her.

"No problem at all, Mrs. Avery. Thank you for giving me this opportunity," she replied.

Mrs. Avery smiled at Dani. "You have my permission to call me Linda."

She knew if she could see her own face, her smile would be awkward looking. Mrs. Avery was always going to be Mrs. Avery no matter the circumstance. Calling her Linda was just too weird.

"How about you tell me a little bit about why you want to intern here for your senior high school project," Mrs. Avery said.

Taking a deep breath Dani launched into her well-practiced speech, "I would be glad to. I know most students don't start their senior projects until the first part of their senior year. I am applying early because I want to have it completed before my senior year. By starting early in my junior year, I feel I will have a better shot at scholarships and getting into the universities I am applying for."

"Isn't your dad still a professor at the University of Wyoming?" Mrs. Avery asked.

"Yes, he is. He is now the head of the supercomputer department," Dani replied. She smiled, thinking about the picture of her dad in the recent UW journal. With his pocket protector in his right front pocket and glasses that at times did have tape on them, he was "the picture" that popped up on your computer screen if you searched "computer nerd."

"So, you should get a good break on tuition then. That will be nice," Mrs. Avery said with a smile.

"Yes, if I go to the University of Wyoming. I want to get into medical research." She tightly smiled back. "They do not have a top ranked program for it there."

"Jeez, just because her dad worked there and almost everyone in Wyoming went to UW didn't mean she wanted to." She didn't see her dad as much as she had when she was younger. The "every other holiday and summer months track" had ended sooner for her than for some kids with divorced parents. She really did not want her college experience to include having her dad looking over her shoulder. He was set on her going to medical school to become a doctor. That was not what Dani wanted. Getting into medical research was her goal.

Mrs. Avery gave her a small smile. "Why don't you tell me why you want to do medical research?"

Taking a calming breath, she continued her pitch for the internship. "I want to get into a research program geared towards the cure for cancer. My goal is to one day help people like my Aunt Kathy. If it weren't for the amazing research that led to the new treatments she had eight years ago, we wouldn't still have her. I want to make a positive difference in people's lives. To help them live the longest, fullest lives they can." She had rehearsed that pitch in the mirror over and over and hoped she had pulled it off.

Mrs. Avery smiled at her. "I think you will be an excellent addition to our team here. I can tell by the bright smile on your face that you are excited about working with us. I know everyone here will be happy to have you."

Dani smiled even wider if that was possible.

"Besides, by starting so early, we will be able to pick up another student when you are finished here. Maybe someone in your class wants to be a doctor, who knows," Mrs. Avery commented. "I will be right back. I need to get the paperwork you need to sign before starting," Mrs. Avery said and stepped out of the conference room.

Leaning back in the chair, Dani let her body relax a little as she thought about all the things that had brought her to this moment. It had scared her down to her soul to know that Aunt Kathy could have died. Aunt Kathy was her rock and go-to sounding board. Her relationship with both her mom and dad was complicated. Each had their own ways, and rather than fight with them she just went with the flow to try and keep her life as peaceful as possible. She loved them both and knew that in their own ways they loved her to.

"Mom was great and all", Dani thought, *"but Mom and Brooke have more in common. They have the perfect slender bodies, and believed hair and makeup was a must for any occasion. Both are extroverts who love any social event and retail therapy. I just want to get in and get out."*

Going clothes shopping with her mom and sister was not at the top of her list of fun things to do.

"What is the big deal about trying on twenty different outfits just to pick the first one you tried on?" she thought. *"I just don't get it, but it is just one of the many things Mom and Brooke love to do that I do not. I tried the whole cheerleading and dance thing. I really did. It just isn't my thing. It's kind of hard to compete with Brooke's perfect face, hair, body and coordination anyway,"* she mused to herself.

The waiting seemed like forever and her thoughts continued to drift back to the argument she overheard between her mom and dad. Her dad's voice carried when he was mad even on the phone. "Dani is wasting her time on things that are not going to grow her intellect", that was all she needed to hear to give her the excuse to quit.

Even though it was what she wanted it still stung a little to hear her mom give into her dad so easily without consulting her first. *"It really doesn't matter,"* she told herself. So, she tagged along to cheer and dance events to watch and "support her sister" as mom put it. She really didn't want to spend her weekends that way. When her mom took noticed and asked if she would just prefer to stay with Aunt Kathy, she jumped at the chance. Time with Aunt Kathy was far better than being drug around to all the different cheer and dance competitions each weekend. She felt everyone would be happier that way.

Aunt Kathy always made it fun for her at the cabin. They cooked together and made cookies, which she never got to do at home. Her mom worked, and when she was not working, she was doing something for Brooke, so her alone time with her mom was limited. She thought it was cool that they had that special bond. She envied it when she was younger, but now, she was happy Mom had Brooke to do all the things she had no interest in. It meant she had more time with Aunt Kathy and that was perfect!

Sometimes, her mom would get snarky and ask if she just wanted to move in with Aunt Kathy. To be honest, she had thought about it. Some days she was tired of being the third wheel to the "Mom and Brooke" show. Deep down she knew her Mom loved her, but there were times when she did not feel accepted or wanted from her mom or sister. Never wanting to rock the boat, she just kept her mouth shut and tried to ignore how they made her feel on occasion. After all, she had Aunt Kathy.

Looking around the small conference room, she brought her mind back to where she was and what she was going to have the opportunity to do. Her excitement came bubbling back. So much was coming together. It was going to be a year to remember, she just knew it!

Tomorrow, they would be leaving for Aunt Kathy's cabin for their annual end-of-summer get together. Her sister, Brooke, and their friends Brandi, Heather, and Jamie would be seniors. She was a year younger and felt like an outsider at times, but the cabin was the great equalizer. Their mothers and Aunt Kathy had all grown up together in Dubois, Wyoming, so it was more of a family event than camping with friends.

She could feel the tension in her body start to fade just taking a deep breath and smelling the cedar wood that lined the walls of the conference room. Aunt Kathy's cabin was made of cedar and the smell permeated the entire cabin. Anytime she even got a hint of the smell of cedar no matter where she was always brought a smile to her face. The old pictures in the hallway reminded her of how long their families had known each other. Pictures of all the girls growing up were scattered throughout the cabin. Aunt Kathy took pleasure in pointing out the really old pictures like the one of Dani's great grandmother.

Aunt Kathy would always say, "You look so much like her Dani. She was a wonderful woman, ahead of her time. She didn't take a back seat to anyone, even her husband. Back in those days, that's saying something. Always spoke up for what she felt was right and true. Especially when treating someone else. She would always say, Jesus never said only love those who believe exactly like you do. He said to love everyone and treat them as you want to be treated. I see the same fire in you." The old pictures on the walls and the stories Aunt Kathy told made her feel like she really belonged.

On every trip to the cabin, she made a point to walk or ride a borrowed horse up Dinwoody Canyon or just sit by the pond by the cabin. No matter the problems life had for her; school, parents, friends, she always felt better after her time at either place. She never felt alone. It was like someone, or something was with her, listening to her as no one else did. She remembered the time Aunt Kathy caught her talking out loud and she jokingly explained that she was talking to her guardian angel. Aunt Kathy's response always brought a smile to her face, "Our guardian angels are smart beings. The world would be a better place if more of us would talk and listen to what they have to say."

She knew it should creep her out, but Aunt Kathy's words made it feel right. She always left feeling calmer than when she arrived, and with a clearer direction. If that added to her strangeness, she was fine with being her quirky self. She had no overblown ideas about being a super star. She had worked hard for everything she had accomplished so far.

The click of the conference room door pulled her from her thoughts.

14

"Alright, let's get started," Mrs. Avery said as she shut the door and returned to her seat. "We are all looking forward to your internship with us and having you as part of our team. Let's get the paperwork out of the way."

When the paperwork was complete, she got up from her chair with a big smile and with a pep in her step said thank you to Mrs. Avery. It was official: she was now an intern at Riverton Family Medical!

Turning to the door to leave feeling excited she thought, *"YES! It's all coming together."*

Her dream of medical research was *looking good* if she did say so herself. She was so excited it was all she could do to not break out in her happy dance.

Pulling the door of the conference room open she heard the whoosh of another door down the hallway. As she stepped into the hall, a little past the door frame, she froze. Aunt Kathy stepped out of one of the other doctors' offices several yards away. Frozen in her spot she watched as Aunt Kathy stopped and attempted to shake the hand of the doctor, who engulfed her in a hug. He embraced her for a few moments and released her. She knew by the way Aunt Kathy held herself, stiffly nodding at what the doctor was saying to her, that it was not good news.

Her mind raced as to what this news might be and who the doctor was. She knew all the regular doctors in the medical office building. She did not recognize this one, so he was probably one of the specialists who saw patients in Riverton but had his main office in a larger city. From the distance she couldn't hear what was said, but as her aunt turned in the opposite direction, she saw her wiping away tracks of tears that flowed down her pale face and thought this could only mean one thing.

"No," she quietly gasped from the doorway. The reality of what she had seen sank into her as her excitement vanished. Mrs. Avery had walked up behind her and leaned over her to see what she was seeing.

"You know everything you see and hear around here is confidential, right?" Mrs. Avery said as she placed her hands on her shoulders and gently turned her around to face her.

"Yes, yes, I know" she quietly said back, even as she was screaming *"NO"* at the top of her lungs in her head.

"Give your aunt time. She will tell you when she is ready," Mrs. Avery said

She turned back around to leave the office, nodding her head so Mrs. Avery knew she heard her.

"No, no, no," seemed to be the only coherent thought and mantra running through her head as she left the medical building and headed for her car. She just managed to get into her car and slam the door shut when she started to pound her fists on the steering wheel. She wouldn't say it...she couldn't say it... oh forget that...this was just...SHIITAKE *MUSHROOMS!* Aunt Kathy would not be impressed if she started yelling cuss words in the parking lot of the medical clinic. She took a deep shuttered breath and let it out. It was back!

"Oh, dear God," she desperately prayed once she could breathe again, "Please watch over my Aunt Kathy."

She had to pull herself together. She could not say anything to anyone about what she knew was true. Aunt Kathy, the sweetest, kindest, most generous person she knew, her rock, was out of remission. She knew in her heart; the cancer was back.

Chapter 3

Kolob

Kneeling on the floor of his private sanctuary, Kerberos began his ritual meditation. Several days had passed since his vision at the Sacred Temple Mount. With his thoughts even more turbulent than before his vision, he began to whisper a prayer.

"I beseech you, Creator of All, to let me know your will. What would you have me do?"

The sound of his own rough deep voice echoing around the small room was all he heard. His muscles coiled tight from the stress of his internal thoughts and struggles.

"Creator of All I have found more disturbing information about the Nephilim forefathers. Long ago they chose to manipulate things that only you should influence. I believe their choices have sent a ripple through time and is the main contributing factor to the devastating chain of events leading to all worlds now standing on the brink of annihilation. At least Eirenicians and Agonians know their worlds are in peril; Terrans knows nothing," his voice paused at the mention of the Terrans. The horrific visons haunted him. The sight of Dani's lifeless body being thrown into the pit caused a cold shutter to run through him. He gave his head a small shake as if to dislodge the gruesome pictures from his mind.

"Creator of All you have gifted me the high honor of providing guidance to the young one Dani. I know that I am blessed with it because you grant this opportunity to few. She must be of great importance to the future. I pray that you lead me in my guidance of her to do your will."

His interactions with Dani the last few years were his only respite from his tedious searching of the past. He guessed the Creator's true purpose for Dani would stretch her to her limit and she would need all her inner strength for the task at hand. He prayed she would be ready when her hour came.

Quickly turning his thoughts from Dani to the current state of all worlds, frustration crept back into his prayers. He desperately sought direction on how to bring the balance back between the worlds.

"I know you have a plan for all. I know that simply killing the Evil One, Erabos, will not restore the balance. There is more that needs to be done, but would it not be a good start to rid the worlds of such evil? Why have you shown me the terrifying visions? Why Creator do you not guide me more directly now?" He sighed out in frustration gathering his thoughts and calming his mind before whispering, "All that must be done will be revealed on the Creator's timeline.Nothing of my making alone will bring balance."

Rising from his prayers, he took a few short steps into his living chambers as he continued to contemplate. *"I need to find more information about the past actions of my people, but the more I learn, the more I struggle to place all the information in order."* Irritated at his lack of progress, he walked over to the small worktable. Grabbed his sword from it resting spot next to his bed, drew it from its sheath and pulled a sharpening stone and oil off the worktable. Sitting down on the backless chair next to the table, he began rhythmically running the blade over the edge of the sharpening stone mentally sifting through the information he knew.

"My Liege," a younger male's voice he knew like his own sounded from the doorway.

"Enter," he called out as he set aside the sharpening stone and picked up the polishing cloth. He ran the cloth over his sword, admiring the frosted small intricate patterns that wove their way across the center of the iridium blade. He was not one for ostentatious jeweled adornments. His only concession was the hardened, carved bone handle peeking out of the very end of its leather-wrapped grip.

He preferred physical battles, where he could wield a sword or an ax, to sitting and waiting. His mind knew how to study and analyze an opponent's attack, find a weakness, and utilize it to his best advantage. His muscular, toned body was molded and shaped to do the will of the Creator of All. He turned slightly looking down at his waist to fasten the sheath of his sword to his side.

"There you are my liege." He did not look up from his task to identify the warrior speaking; he did not need to. Zopyro would be dressed much like Kerberos, as all Nephilim dressed, short open-backed tunics, so as not to restrict their wing movements, with leather balteus straps depicting their rank hanging from their belts. Their sword sheaths, hanging off one hip, held blades sharp enough to remove a head from its neck. A series of straps reached across their chests and connected at the neck.

"Yes, here I am," he replied dryly.

"Judging by the shine of your sacred crystal and sword, you have been in a contemplative mood this morning," Zopyro teased lightly.

Kerberos reached up and touched the sacred crystal and asked, "What is the purpose of a sacred crystal?"

"I see we are going to start early this day," Zopyro chuckled, "A sacred crystal is a vessel that holds an intelligent, consecrated living power inside of it. As such the crystal knows who we are at our core and our intentions when we attempt to use its power. We do not fully understand the dynamics of the living power within it but know that it is a blessing from the Creator of All. To use a sacred crystal, one must be pure in intentions. To use something so pure in light for anything other than that which the Creator of All would bless, will damage, or even kill the sacred life force inside of it.

A sacred crystal affects each living being differently. For Nephilim, the crystals channel our power to overcome physical obstacles, like having to dwell for short periods of time on other worlds not meant for our physiology. The crystals also enabled us to control the opening and closing of the Axis Mundi with the blessing of the Creator of All."

He listened to Zopyro recite the information and thought of his next question. Maybe in their daily teaching something new would work its way through his thoughts, "What is the purpose of the Nephilim race?" he asked.

Zopyro replied in the same even tone, "We are here to do the Creator of All's will. There are two different cast of Nephilim. Warrior Nephilim are the gatekeepers of the Axis Mundi portals. We open and close the portals with the blessing of the Creator. The Creator also calls upon us to battle and restore the balance in times when great evil spreads on any world. To the humans we are considered giants. We are significantly taller and stronger than humans because our bodies need to be in top physical shape to withstand the strains of being on other worlds, we are not physically compatible with. No army in history has withstood a sanctified, united Nephilim purge of evil," Zopyro smiled broadly.

The thought of a united Nephilim army brought about a sad smile to Kerberos's lips as he thought of the current situation. Zopyro took a breath and continued.

"The Scholar Caste of Nephilim stores the histories and seeks to serve the Creator of All with enlightenment through research and science. They are shorter in stature and not as muscular," Zopyro paused then asked. "Have you found more information from the sacred scrolls, My Liege?"

"Continue with the information you know now," he answered. He hoped by Zopyro reciting the information, even though he had not shared it all with him, that a connection or some pieces might fall into place in his mind.

"As you wish," Zopyro continued, "Through many generations, the Scholars have manipulated the genetic makeup of the humans they were charged with protecting and have cleverly hidden this information. You suspect the Scholars have also done something to the Nephilim genetic makeup as well. The Scholars failed to predict the accurate outcomes of their manipulations, causing devastating cascading events through history which have culminated in the current state of all worlds. The imbalance of male to female birth rates on Eirenic and Agon are a direct result of this manipulation. Exactly what is occurring on Terra, we do not know. We surmise the female to male ratio might be the opposite of Eirenic and Agon. In your research, you found hints that the Scholars intended Terran females to be the genetic incubators for the children needed on Àgon and Eirenic."

Kerberos stood silently going over the information he knew by heart then pressed on. "The great war?" he asked.

Zopyro did not hesitate, "Was the doing of Erabos' evil ideologies that fractured the Nephilim world, much as they did the other worlds. In the Great War brothers, sisters, mothers, and fathers fought against each other. Families were forever shattered on all worlds. So many lives lost. It is unknown if any of the worlds can recover, especially with the birth rate issues on them."

Pausing only a moment Kerberos pointedly asked, "How do you think it was so easy for Erabos to spread his lies?"

Zopyro stood silently for several moments. Kerberos waited, knowing the only conclusion the younger male could come to, was the same one he had. When Zopyro spoke it confirmed his thoughts, "The short-sightedness of the Scholars manipulations brought forth the rise of Erabos, and his followers. The people easily fed upon their fears of never finding their chosen one and their extinctions." Zopyro stood staring at him as if shocked by what he had just said.

"Yes, we the Nephilim are to blame for all that has happened to the perfect balance the Creator of All tasked us to keep." Kerberos said, paused then added "Now all the worlds suffer. Some suffer in silence, feeling abandoned. Most have no knowledge that their suffering was brought about by our actions. And how do we fix it? The endless debating in the Hall of Equality leads not to action, but to more divisive and debates. Today will be the same as it was yesterday and so many days before." In his mind he added as he thought back to his vision, "*We will all pass from this existence if something does not change. If a movement or force did not start a new ripple across the pond of their existence soon, it would be too late for us all.*"

As the two exited the chambers, Kerberos turned the yellow light crystal so that it no longer glowed brightly. His eyes noticed the glistening marbled gray and white walls and his thoughts turned inward. "*How long have I walked these halls never noticing how the light plays across the smooth surfaces, causing fragments of colors to appear and disappear in the crystal domain?*" He slowed his pace to take in the beauty of the outside world as they passed a window and attempting to soothe his troubled mind.

On Kolob there was a constant mist, hugging the land in some areas as a blanket. In other areas, it thinned and lifted high enough to allow a view of the lush greenery of the many plants that dwelled below. Sharp cliffs gave way to verdant valleys that flowed down towards the dark blue seas. Few places offered the breathtaking views of Kolob like the Crystal Fortress. There was only one other place higher, the Sacred Temple Mount. It had been built on Kolob's tallest mountain. The Sacred Temple Mount's clear crystal beauty was unmatched by anything on any world. The wind drifted through and around it, sweeping across skin and feathers as if the gentle hand of the Creator of All was caressing you. Peace and reverence were felt by all who entered its sacred halls. He longed to stretch his wings and find solace in the wind and fly to the temple, seeking peace for his turbulent thoughts.

"Is there any new information from the scholars on how Erabos got into one of the most secure places on Kolob and stole the Light of Amun Crystal?" Kerberos asked.

"No my liege, after the amount of time that has passed since it was taken, I doubt they ever will...," Zopyro answered and the pause in his voice indicated that he wanted to ask something.

"What is it you wish to ask, Zopyro?" he asked.

"Is it true that the Light of Amun Crystal gives the user untold power over everything?" Zopyro asked.

"Everything?" Kerberos paused then continued, "Not Everything. The Light of Amun, like all sacred crystals, enhances the user's inner abilities. The difference between a normal sacred crystal and the Light of Amun is the enhancement is far beyond any other crystal known, except for one. Erabos is an immensely powerful Elemental, able to manipulate the environment around him. What he lacks is the connection to The Creator of All. The Creator of All gave us free will. Unlike normal crystals that must be used with purity of intentions, the Light of Amun Crystal allows one to exercise the users free will however they choose without causing damaging to it. But without purity in purpose and more importantly the connection to The Creator of All, Erabos will never find fulfillment in his actions and his greed will consume him," he said with a sad sigh before continuing.

"As you know the Creator of All made the Axis Mundi and its corridors with the doorway portals connecting the worlds of Eirenic, Agon, and Terra to be the passageway for beings to travel between them. This was to ensure a balance could be maintained between world populations. Erabos using his heightened Elemental gifts used the Light of Amun crystal to traverse the Axis Mundi on his own, but only after a Nephilim opened a portal for him.

Those who opposed the Evil One, Erabos, united to seal the Axis Mundi's portals so that he could no longer freely travel between worlds bringing death and destruction. We surmise he used his increased powers from the Light of Amun to create a vortex around himself to survive here the few times he came to our world. He is the only human ever to be able to do so. The sacred Light of Amun Crystal should have been protected from everyone. Made untouchable so that those without pure intention could never use it as Erabos has," he said.

"It seems with all things, not all is what it should have been," Zopyro said. "You mentioned there is another sacred crystal just as powerful as the Light of Amun on Eirenic. Shouldn't we be concentrating on it, to retrieve it, even with the sealing, so that it does not fall into the Evil One's hands as well?"

Kerberos replied, "With the Axis Mundi and its portals sealed to contain the Evil One on Agon, there is currently no known way to open a portal for us to pass through. The crystal is well hidden on Eirenic. It remains undetected by the Evil One and his followers or we would all have felt the power of it being used. Very few even know of its existence. Its exact location is kept secret for its protection."

Walking down the hall thinking about the legionnaire beside him, Kerberos's mind drifted *"Zopyro was young but had proven himself in battle during the Great War. The Great War,"* he sighed mentally, *"as if it were over,"* He retorted in his mind. *"No, it was not over, only locked behind sealed portal doors, still a simmering, seething, evil force, building, just waiting to strike again."*

Turning his head slightly he caught their reflection on a polished wall and noted their differences. Where Zopyro was fair haired, he was dark.

Zopyro had yellow eyes while His eyes held the colors of the portals they fiercely protected. A lighter color blue haloed his pupils and faded to deep blues the further it went towards the whites of his eyes. Heading further down the corridor he heard raised voices.

"They are quite vocal today, my liege," Kerberos heard Zopyro saying as they headed down the corridor past one of the giant pillars that stood outside the Hall of Equality.

Glancing in, he saw several Nephilim on the speaking floor at once, each one trying to shout over another. Bored with the scene that was all too familiar of late he glanced around. The Hall of Equality was a sight to behold, as was the crystal fortress itself, but he had no tolerance for it today.

As they continued past the Hall and cleared the corridor heading down carved stairs to the field of practice, he noted his Legionnaires were working hard, he finally spoke. "Report on training?"

"Sir, the men are in their exercise and sparring routines as you can see. All seems to be going well, with minor injuries," Zopyro smirked.

As they approached the field of training, he was again disappointed in the lack of other lieges' colors present. The Nephilim legionnaires are the Creator's warriors. When the Creator calls, they will go and battle the evil that is ever-present in all the worlds they protect. They had to strike quickly and with decisive action because there was a limited amount of time they could exist on the other worlds. He thought, *The other two legions would not be in their peak physical form with the only workout they were getting was in the Hall of Equality trying to out shout each other."*

When the Axis Mundi and portals had been sealed, he had allowed himself to be drawn into the bickering in the great hall. He soon learned nothing was going to come from the endless debating. No plan of action, no decisive way to turn. No, they would go in there, like they have for far too long, and fruitlessly debate what to do. They grew weaker day by day as time was running out. All worlds hung on the brink of annihilation. The Creator of All would be calling him to action and his legion would be ready.

Plans started shifting through his ever-calculating mind with different scenarios playing out. He knew Dani was a crucial element to any plan.

While it was still unclear what her part would be, he was certain of this, Dani was central to any plan he made and if the Nephilim were going to uphold their sacred duty, they had to be ready. He was chosen by The Creator of All to propel the drop of water that would start the ripple of change through time. He mentally prayed to the Creator for continued guidance for his role as well as any others that had been chosen. Let the Creator's will be done throughout space and time.

Chapter 4

Terra

Dani sat at the kitchen table listening to the conversations of the moms, Aunt Kathy, and the girls around her. She had to find a way out of going on the ride to Dinwoody Canyon. The problem was that everyone knew how much she loved that ride and stopping to admire the pictographs and the petroglyphs on the canyon walls. To know that someone carved or painted them hundreds of years ago still amazed her. Ancient spiritual places had always fascinated her. So much was unknown of why they were made or who had made them. But she could still look and wonder at the beauty and mystery of them all. Ancient sites had their own feel, their own vibes, as if they too had once been a living thing, just waiting to be reawakened.

The only reason she was willing to miss it, was to get alone time at the cabin. She needed to do some snooping through Aunt Kathy's office and see if she could find any information about her cancer diagnosis. Her stomach was giving her fits from worrying about Aunt Kathy. At least now when she told everyone she wasn't feeling well, it would be the truth. She still felt a little guilty for what she was planning to do.

Heather's voice drifted over to her from across the table, "I love the cabin. It's so tranquil. I love spending time here before starting the chaotic pace of a new school year."

Heather was smart, genius-level smart. Her Native American heritage was evident in her long, thick, black hair and beautiful tan skin.

Dani looked around at all the moms now seated at the table with them.

They were all divorced for one reason or another except Aunt Kathy who was a widow. It wasn't easy for everyone to come out and have girl time.

Dani's mouth started watering as she smelled the bacon, but she just pushed it around her plate. She had to keep up her story until someone noticed. It didn't take long when Aunt Kathy spoke, "Dani you Ok? You're not inhaling your bacon like you usually do?"

"I think I might have over done it on the marshmallows last night. My stomach is a little off. Think I might stay here and chill for the day," Dani answered.

Lynn, her mom, reached over placing her hand to her forehead, "You don't feel hot." She announced. "Anyone you know having any stomach issues? Maybe you caught a bug somewhere."

Aunt Kathy spoke next, "I can stay here with her Lynn, if you're concerned."

"Great" she thought, "No, no I really am fine. Just ate one to many of those giant marshmallows last night. No worries really."

"If you're sure," Aunt Kathy said.

"Yep, I'm sure. Go enjoy the morning." Dani tried to sound reassuring to make sure her aunt went on the ride. It would ruin her snooping if she stayed behind, and she would have missed the ride for nothing and more importantly not get the information she desperately wanted to find.

Finally, everyone left. The adults were driving part way and then hiking the rest. She hung out on the couch just to be sure no one doubled back when she made a dash for Aunt Kathy's office. Dani had a feeling her aunt would cut the morning hike short to come and check on her, so she had to be quick. Her internal dialog was driving her insane. One minute she was determined to find out all the information and treatment options, and the next she was fighting back the overwhelming sense of defeat like it was pointless and too late anyway.

"Nothing I do will really matter. I am going to lose Aunt Kathy no matter what I do." She shivered, feeling lost and alone in the wilderness with an avalanche barreling down the mountain towards her as she went through files. *"How am I going to cope without my rock, Aunt Kathy?"* Shaking her head determined to shake out the negative thought she focused on what she had

just found. Reading the name of the cancer on a letter from the clinic, she searched the internet. *"Normally a slow growing non-aggressive cancer."* she took a steading breath, *"There is still time to find a cure and fight this,"* she thought. *"We are going to fight this and win no matter what!"* she said in her mind with conviction.

"I wish I could just freaking ask her," she sighed out with frustration knowing she couldn't. Numbering off the reasons why she couldn't in her head, *"First, I can lose my internship. Second, I really don't want my worst nightmares to come true and find out that Aunt Kathy could not do chemo, or it was not going to work or something. Nope, I am going to hold my tongue and deal with my fears. It's not my secret to tell. But this confidentiality crap sucked worms."*

Being sure to put everything back the way she found it, she headed back to the couch and flopped down. A bible verse Aunt Kathy used the few times Dani was having a really hard time with someone came to her mind, *"Do not gloat over me, my enemy! Though I have fallen, I will rise. Though I sit in darkness, the Lord will be my light,"* she felt some comfort. *"Whatever happens we got this, with Jesus,"* she thought.

Her prediction that Aunt Kathy would cut the hike short was confirmed with her crew cab truck pulling in the driveway. The afternoon flew past with lunch and then dinner. Before she knew it, they were all sitting outside at the fire ring again.

"Alright girls, quiet down, we have a surprise for you," Aunt Kathy said.

Dani shifted in her seat and looked back to Aunt Kathy. She had tried to stay close to her and help where she could without seeming too obvious. Did Aunt Kathy seem to tire more easily? Maybe she had lost some weight she hadn't noticed before? How advanced was the cancer? *"Oh, I need to get a grip on myself"* She thought.

Aunt Kathy continued speaking. "So, as you know all of you but one will be graduating this next year," everyone turned to look at Dani, as if she did not know she was the one not graduating. Cue the eye roll. "We wanted to give you all a special trip for your graduation present."

"Well, except Daniella, she will be getting hers early," Dani's mom said. "But I am sure Daniella won't mind. She will simply be happy to get to go."

Dani's mom insisted on using her full first name at the most annoying times and she groaned to herself. She looked over at her mom with a pasted-on smile. Her Mom knew it annoyed her, so why did she keep doing it? Probably because she had opted out of helping the cheerleaders get all their gear sorted and checked out for the school year a week ago. Her mom had told her Brooke was up for Prom Queen and would most likely make it, so she needed her help because Brooke would be busy.

Dani told her mom, "Brooke is the cheerleading captain and had adoring fans and admirers. Let them help. What is the use of all those guys hanging around anyway? Why not put them to work?" She knew she should have helped but didn't like how it was asked.

Aunt Kathy's excited voice brought her back out of her internal thoughts.

"Ok, so you are probably wondering why this year we let you bring a computer of some sort. Our gift to you girls is, we are taking you all on a worldwide graduation celebration trip next summer!" Aunt Kathy said.

The girls sat in stunned silence, not even a breath. She looked over at Brooke, Brandi, Heather, and Jamie. Each had the same stunned look on their faces.

Brandi broke the silence first. "So, we are *all* going on our senior trip around the world?" she yelled as she jumped to her feet. Brandi was an athletic phenomenon and smart on top of it. She was super competitive, but kind. She had a dark chocolate complexion and shoulder length hair that made her stand out in their community. Brandi sometimes muttered about her hair and how long it took her to keep the kinks out and not frizzy looking. That was when it was not up in some amazing looking braids. She really was a big overachiever in almost everything she did.

Aunt Kathy answered Brandi's question, "That depends on where you young ladies pick to go."

The adults all looked so pleased with themselves, and she was lost as to what they were trying to tell them. Aunt Kathy must have understood because after the briefest of pauses she continued.

"You see, we wanted to do something special with you. You know, one last group get- together. Who knows when we will get the chance to do it after everyone goes off to college? I hope you don't mind if us old people come along," Aunt Kathy said. "We want each of you to pick a destination."

Jamie spoke up next, "We get to pick anywhere?" Jamie was smart and so artistic. Her creations won first place in anything she entered. She, too, had long wavy hair that just seemed to go with her flowing clothing. When she walked, she seemed to glide.

Aunt Kathy smiled and said, "We do have a few parameters to go by. It needs to be somewhere that is not currently in social unrest. You need to keep in mind that we will spend about three days at each stop. Depending on where you all pick, we can all talk about it more if you feel more time is needed at your destination. We are requesting no places like amusement parks. Try and think about historical or ancient places you have always wanted to see. We will need to know your picks by Christmas, at the very latest, so we have plenty of time to book our reservations and get passports before we leave at the beginning of June."

Looking around Dani could tell the rest of the girls were as excited about their surprise as she was. In the excitement she got the old familiar feeling again, like her guardian angel was near. At first she thought it was probably due to all the excitement building from the surprise trip announcement, her getting the internship, and the looming "C" with Aunt Kathy, but as the other girls ran to get their laptops she felt the urge to go talk with her guardian angel.

When the girls had returned and settled around the fire, Dani got up and walked out to a small rise that let her see into a deep pool section of the lake. The shimmering moonlight reflected from its tranquil surface. She appreciated the slight breeze that kept the biting bugs away but did not disturb the calm surface of the water. So many thoughts ran through her mind at once, first and foremost being Aunt Kathy's condition. As she stood by the water she sensed that someone was near, listening to her so she started whispering.

"Surely the chemo must be able to work if she plans on being able to go on the trip," she paused as her thoughts raced in another direction. *"Aunt Kathy could also be viewing this trip as her last big adventure before...,"* Dani could not

finish the thought. She stared down into the water, lost in her emotions. *"Please God. Help Aunt Kathy. I don't know what I would do without her."* A single tear ran down her cheek followed by another then another.

She continued staring down into the water. Her mind bounced from Aunt Kathy's cancer to wondering what place she would pick. Fading laughter and a door closing let her know the others had gone into the cabin. There were so many places she wanted to see, so many possibilities. As images of several ancient places shifted through her mind, she whispered again, "Where would you go?"

As if a person on the other side answered her, images of ancient stone walls came to the forefront of her mind. She felt a strong pull towards the site as if someone or something was guiding her towards it. A sense of excitement washed through her. She recognized the images at once. She had always wanted to see the intricate layered stone walls and structures of Tiwanaku City and the surrounding areas. As if still talking to someone she said, "Thank you, that's a great idea. Maybe I will finally get to meet you there," she laughed out loud.

Brandi called out from the window in the loft, "Hey Dani, get up here. Come see what we have found so far, we are going to need your mad linguistic skills to decipher some of these."

She quickly wiped the tracks of tear off her cheeks away. She had a fascination with other languages and could easily decipher words in several different languages. Latin was easy for her to speak and read which lent it to deciphering Spanish, French, and other languages that evolved from it. She didn't know where this adventure would take them, but she was excited for the journey. Standing up she called back, "Sure, be right there."

Chapter 5

Kolob

"Wait outside the entrance", Kerberos ordered to the guard as he entered the sacred pool room.

"As you command Liege Kerberos," the guard said saluting by thumping his fist over his heart and left the room.

Staring down into the clear water Kerberos let his mind ponder, "*So many questions still lay unanswered,*" he thought, "*Why am I being given the blessing of seeing and interacting with the human Dani? What purpose does she have in the Creators Plan? She is so young, what could she possibly do to bring about the balance of worlds? I have helped guide her to a portal. I must trust the Creator of All to guide me, even if I do not understand*" Taking a calming breath he watched as Dani headed into the dwelling.

"My liege, I hadn't expected to see you here," Zopyro called from the darkened doorway behind him.

Jumping slightly, and spinning towards the voice, hand at the hilt of his sword, he faced Zopyro biting out, "Why should I not be here? Is it not my sacred duty to be a guardian? The sacred pools are now our only link to the other worlds, as you well know. We cannot be remiss in trying to find out what is occurring beyond the sealed portals. Who knows when The Creator of All will bless a viewing?"

Stating at Zopyro, he berated himself in his mind, "*What a fool so engrossed with guiding Dani to Tiwanaku City, I did not even hear Zopyro come up behind me. In the not-too-distant past, that lack of focus on one's surroundings could have gotten me killed. Who am I jesting, it still can. I cannot draw attention to myself. There is a reason I have not shared the full extent of my interactions with Dani. Someone might find out what the Creator of All has planned for me to do and try and stop me. That, I cannot let happen."*

Taking a calming breath, he looked at Zopyro who was standing at full attention not meeting his gaze. He did not mean to snap so harshly at him. Mentally he justified his actions, *"I do not like being caught off guard and was unnerved,"* he reasoned in his mind. *"The Creators plan involves the use of a much larger sacred pool. I must keep up my routine of visiting other pools not to draw suspicion. I need to defuse the situation with Zopyro, so the listening ears of the guard don't perk his interest more and he wags his tongue to others."*

He questioned in a low calm voice, "Zopyro, what do we use the portals for?"

"Before or after the sealing my Liege?" Zopyro formally asked.

"Start with before," he replied.

"As you wish," Zopyro paused then continued, "Before the sealing, Nephilim could use their crystal to open a portal with the use of a sacred pool. There are three different ways one can use an open portal. First, you can view only, second view and speak to one another and lastly physically travel through to another world. All the pools on Kolob are large enough for a Nephilim to travel through to the other worlds if the Creator of All calls them to do so. Our people are not limited to the corridors of the Axis Mundi when we leave our world to travel to the other worlds as the humans are. The Creator of All guides our alternative one-way routes so that we come out where we are needed. Once on the other worlds we must use the portals set up there to return through the Axis Mundi and on to Kolob."

"Are all interactions blessed by the Creator of All," he asked.

"No, but to do so without pureness of heart in your actions, you would kill a sacred crystal," Zopyro replied.

"After the sealing?" he prompted watching as Zopyro's body started to relax the more he spoke.

Zopyro quickly replied, "After the sealing the portals to the other three worlds have been mostly closed. To my knowledge it is unheard of for a Nephilim to be granted even a viewing to another world. I know of no other

Nephilim granted this gift since the sealing other than you, my Liege."

Leaning in slightly and lowering his voice to whisper as he spoke, "As such do you not think it prudent to not bring unwanted attention to these rare glimpses to the other worlds? One never knows who is listening or watching." He said looking over Zopyro's shoulder to the doorway leading out where the guard stood. He looked back just in time to see the understanding hit Zopyro.

"Yes, my Liege, forgive my lack of judgement," Zopyro said thumping his chest with his fist and slightly bowing.

"Let us go then," he gestured towards the door where the guard for the sacred pool stood at attention, waiting to be let back in

As they walked down the corridor, he thought of the viewing and interactions he had been blessed with. Thus far, they had been centered on Dani alone. He knew she was unique and special. He sensed, though, that she did not see herself as anything special or worthy of note by her peers. He did not understand this but thought it might be due to her young age. He did know that Dani and her family would be at a portal site, a site that he had guided her to. How that played into the Creator's plan, he did not know. Uncertainty was not something that sat well with him.

"I presume you had a reason for seeking me out," he said.

"Sir, Liege Dionysius has requested your presence in the Hall of Equality," Zypyro said. He managed to stifle a groan at this news, but just barely.

"And Liege Burkhart?" he asked. *"Maybe there was a way out of this yet,"* he thought.

"He said, and I quote him on this one, if he has to be present then you bloody well better be there too!"

He didn't miss a step as he chucked slightly. There was not much to find joy in the days that preceded this one. He was relieved he had not lost the ability. As soon as he and Zopyro could be seen by the gathered Nephilim, silence descended throughout the hall. They continued walking across the pristine white crystal floor listening to their footfalls echo around the oval shaped hall. He knew everyone in attendance could see them from the raised seating area.

Liege Burkhart and Dionysus were standing in the middle of the speaking floor and had turned to watch as they progressed towards them. Not needing to raise his voice knowing that the curved shape of the hall's walls and ornately carved dome ceiling would allow all to hear what he said clearly. He spoke, "You had need of me." He stated.

A rustling of feathers and fabric from the seating area showed that not all were pleased with his blunt tone towards the other two lieges. Shifting his eyes, he noted males and females were in attendance watching and listening to their every word and move. The uneasy movements had come from Burkhart's section. Glancing back towards his destination the nightmarish vision of what the hall had looked like caused Kerberos to pause in his forward movement with a moment of unease. Shaking the vision from his mind, he continued in.

"Will you address the hall my Liege?" Zopyro quietly whispered.

"That is not my intention," Kerberos answered in his normal voice that carried throughout the hall. "If you wish to, be my guest. You know anyone who wishes to be heard can speak. The only formality is who chooses to lead the discussion. As Liege Burkhart and Dionysius are both here perhaps one of them is a good choice. I have found that the usefulness of stimulating conversations has turned into a useless commentary of voices shouting over one another and nothing be accomplished."

He looked up again at the assembled Nephilim. He noted that the divide between the three legions seemed to have grown over the years since the sealing. The seating was starkly divided by legion colors. His, being red and gold, sat above the right side of the main floor.Dionysius' green and white were located clearly in the middle and Burkhart's blue and yellow were to the left.

"So good of you to join us, Kerberos," Burkhart grumbled sarcastically.

Very few would dare goad Kerberos in such a way. He was the youngest liege ever appointed. He was also one of the largest, quickest, and most accurate of the Nephilim warriors ever. His mood still sour from his lack of attentiveness, he did not need Burkhart's sarcasm to add to his irritation.

"You did not bring me here to poke at me. What need do you have of me?"

he replied sharply with little patience.

"As always straight to the point," Burkhart countered just as sharp.

"My fellow Lieges, if we could," Dionysius gestured for them to locate seats in the raised seating section.

Kerberos did not want to sit down, his frustration barely contained.

"What is it this time, Liege Dionysius? We have beaten this debate over and over for years now. Nothing changes but the volume of the voices speaking," Kerberos irritably stated. "Something needs to change, or we are dooming not only ourselves to extinction, but also the worlds we vowed to protect. Nephilim are ultimately responsible for the way things are now. I have little doubt that it was our race that brought about the chain of events that spiraled out of control to bring all our worlds to the brink of extinction," he lifted his arms to include the entire hall.

The Hall of Equality had become deathly quiet. The acoustics of the great hall allowed his voice to travel with crystal clarity. Why those around him chose to shout was beyond him. He did not need to shout; everyone could hear and know in their hearts what he said was true.

"What would you have us do?" Burkhart retorted. "Open the portals and let the evil that we barely contained free once more? To finish what it started in ruling us all in his tyrannical fist?"

Zopryo quickly interjected, "Why can we not open some of the portals through the Axis Mundi, but not all of them? So that we may see what is happening on the other worlds. Aid the humans like we use to do if the Creator of All calls us to do so again. Yes, it is a risk of allowing the evil one and his followers to communicate, but would it not be better than just sitting here waiting and dwindling away?"

Burkhart shouted back, "We cannot open even one portal without it affecting the magic that sealed them all. You invite death and evil to rule all if we do."

Dionysius moved to the middle of the small group on the floor. With his hands raised, palms out, he spoke calmly, "We need more prayer, guidance and research. We cannot do this on our own. We need to ask the Creator of All for his divine wisdom and direction, clear guidance before we risk making things worse than they already are."

Zopryo acted as if he had not heard Dionysius and shouted back at Burkhart, "It was due to our meddling in the first place that this all happened. Are we sure the Creator meant for us to restrict the movement of the humans between worlds at our discretion? If our opening and closing is pure and of his blessing, why did we close them? Or was it that we became arrogant and greedy for power over others?"

"Enough!" Kerberos snapped. His low rumbling voice rang throughout the hall, and silence reigned. "If we do nothing then we die as a race along with the other worlds. You all have valid points. I believe in your assessments and analysis to a point. Everyone has a right to be heard." He took a controlled breath in in and let it out trying to regain control of the emotions he rarely let show. *"Same old debate, nothing had changed,"* he thought to himself.

Kerberos took another deep breath and spoke again. "We have been debating this issue for so long now. Yes, we took more control of certain portals that led directly to Terra. Did we close them permanently? No, that is not the truth. The influence on the culture and peoples of Terra was becoming too extreme with the presence of some of Agon's and Eirenic's self-serving citizens. Some allowed and others demanded that Terrans worship them as only the Creator of All should be worshiped. They left us little choice but to limit their access."

"Did the great evil, Erabos," a collective inhale was heard at the name, but Kerberos pushed on, "take advantage of this fact and twist it to do his work? Yes! By the statements just made, his ideas are still here eating away at us. Some feel the Great War is over. I say we have just put off the inevitable. We either open the portals and finally deal with what has been wiggling and seething behind them all these years, or we condemn to extinction not only our race but the worlds we were created to protect and provide balance to. We need to be accountable for what our forefathers did in altering the beings on the worlds we were charged with protecting." He paused to let his last words sink into the minds of those around him.

Taking a deeper breath knowing what he was about to say would not be received well by all, Kerberos continued, "Our forefathers caused the imbalance and enabled the evil to come in its current form to the perfect worlds the Creator of All had made. We either take action to bring the Creator's worlds back in balance, or we all die. We must stop this incessant debate that gets us nowhere. If we do nothing, the Evil One will win. He is not sitting idle behind sealed portal walls. He is planning for action. I would rather die with my sword in my hand, in support of the goodness in these worlds and ours, than die behind a locked portal gate having done nothing to end the evil that was brought about by Nephilim actions." His deep voice echoed unchallenged by any other as it ricocheted off the walls.

Kerberos waited for the stunned listeners to react. It did not take long. It was like a wall of rolling, combusting voices that had been released from their restraints all at once. It was done. He had said what he had ached so long to say. The unimaginable truth that his people had caused the wave of evil to roll and increase through all their worlds, caused him great anguish.

"May the Creator of All bless my actions for the benefit of all," Kerberos silently prayed in his mind. He needed to finish the plans that he was positive the Creator was guiding him to. Making his way to the nearest exit point, he glanced back over his shoulder at the chaos left behind. He looked around briefly and saw Nephilim in all manner of heated debate: in the air, seated, and some spilling over onto the floor level of the Hall of Equality. Shaking his head slightly, he turned and strode out into the corridor.

"You know how to leave a discussion in chaos." Kerberos turned to see Dionysius frowning to match his tone, and Burkhart waiting just on the other side of the door, out of view from the hall floor. They must have taken a side passage to get in front of him when they saw him leaving.

"It needed to be said. All Nephilim deserve to know our dark history so that we do not repeat it," Kerberos responded flatly, trying to take a path past them.

Burkhart moved aggressively to block his path and shoved his barrel chest into Kerberos before yelling, "You will do nothing without our consent. We all lost those we love to the great evil. I for one do not want to repeat that!" Burkhart snarled.

He knew Burkhart had lost his Chosen One, the one the Creator of

All makes to complete you, as well as two of his three children. The one remaining, Burkhart sheltered beyond what was normal. "I see and hear your pain Burkhart. You are not listening to the entirety of the information I have given," he said trying to placate the old Liege.

Thinking to himself, *"Rumors of what the ancient ones have done are abundant and have circulated for eons. I have uncovered a small number of the facts. I must find out the complete truth of their meddling. I cannot let the extent of what I am truly doing in the ancient archives come to light or there are some who will try to stop the truth from coming out."*

Kerberos tried to soften his next words, "Would you have your child watch over the years as everyone around her slowly disappears from this existence, so that all that's left are her fleeting memories? She would never get the opportunity to know her Chosen One as you did. She would never hold her child in her arms."

Burkhart's sharp intake of breath was followed by his brisk, seething reply, "I would have my daughter never know the pain of losing a child she watched come into this world. To watch the light leave her Chosen One and know there will never be another by her side for the rest of her existence. She would only know despair and loneliness await her the rest of her days at their loss. I would spare her this."

Light footfalls echoed across the hallway, approaching them. Kerberos turned to see Jodoc walk to her father's side. It was not uncommon for females to participate in the hall discussions. So, her appearance was not surprising.

"But father, to never know, I would miss one of the greatest gifts the Creator of All has blessed us with: love." Jodoc placed her small hand on her father's arm. "I, for one, agree with Liege Kerberos. We need to open the portals again."

Kerberos watched the play of emotions run across the older Nephilim's face. Jodoc was beautiful, wearing a delicate tunic with a gilded leather balteus hanging from her waist. The small sword hanging from her side looked out of place on one so angelic.

Kerberos had known Jodoc his entire life. She was everything a cultured elevated status female was meant to look like. It was Jodoc's cold demeanor towards those that worked for her that he disliked. She did not blatantly treat those serving her badly, but the aloofness she showed was telling enough. She apparently had no doubt in her mind that she was better than those around her. With Kerberos she presented a sickly-sweet, demure persona that grated on his nerves. Jodoc was the only surviving member of Burkhart's family. Burkhart's protectiveness towards Jodoc bordered-on obsession. He had no affections for the female and if it took forever, he would wait for his Chosen One.

Burkhart looked from his daughter back to Kerberos. "I know you are keeping things from us. Mark my words, Kerberos, you do nothing without our consent, or there will be a reckoning," Burkhart snarled and then turned, walking away with his arm wrapped protectively around his daughter's shoulder.

"Do you really think opening the portals is the answer?" Dionysius asked from Kerberos' side, watching the pair walk away.

"I do not know," Kerberos sighed, rubbing his hand through his hair in frustration. "What I do know is if we keep doing nothing, we will all die. We will all grow old and pass from this existence leaving no one behind to carry out our sacred duties. What solution do you have, Dionysius? What, in all these years of conversing and debating, are the answers you have found?" Kerberos turned and looked straight into the eyes of the older man.

"Nothing definitive, you know this." Dionysius said. "Acting, just for the sake of action, is an unwise choice. Time and prayer for guidance are what is needed now. Not rash actions," Dionysius said and turned, walking away.

Kerberos had listened to the words of the great debater of his time, but words had not fixed the dilemma all these years. Dionysius was the leader of the Scholars. All Nephilim history and scientific journals were at his disposal.

He wondered, *"Learning of the sins of the past Scholars should be at the front of Dionysius mind. I truly hoped the current Scholars are not following in their forefathers' footsteps. I most proceed with care when digging for the truth. There is no one on any world that held onto a bit of information tighter than a Scholar;*

especially information that did not put them in a good light."

In some ways, Kerberos felt completely alone and exhausted from the constant mental battle to gain more knowledge and understanding from Dionysius and the Scholars without revealing details of the actions he was being guided to take. Drawing in a deep breath, he let it out slowly. He was not alone. His prayers were being answered by the Creator of All as he solidified the plan of action he would take with Dani and her family. He had to have faith to follow the path set before him.

This plan could not simply be talked into a favorable position. No, action was needed, so he prayed in his mind that the plan taking shape would put them all on the right course to end the Great War once and for all. To put the evil out of their lives and fix the imbalance his people started long ago. He prayed for Dani and her family that they would have the courage and strength to endure what they would be going through. May the Creator of All bless them and guide them to become who they were meant to be.

"Alone at last," Kerberos thought and turned in the opposite direction, walking down a side corridor towards a sacred pool that very few knew about. Its entrance was obscured by the weight-bearing column directly in front of it. The hallway to the sacred pool also contained several large storage areas. These areas were used less and less as the Nephilim population had dwindled. He had used the small pool room multiple times and felt confident that no one would disturb or discover him.

The last few weeks had shown him that Dani and her family were the central point to the plans the Creator was guiding him to. He needed to be vigilant in his observations over the next few weeks, in order to not miss the signs the Creator was showing him. What he was planning would require the full support of the Creator of All or it would fail. If it failed while Dani and her family were traversing the mist of the Axis Mundi, it would prove fatal for them all. He had to keep watch to be sure he caught the family at the right place and time. He was very cognizant of the fact that if nothing changed in the worlds, they were all doomed anyway. *"I will not be the direct cause of Dani's demise or of her family,"* he resoundingly said to himself.

Chapter 6

Terra

"Where did the time go? The school year went by in a flash and we are already done with our third stop," Dani thought as she leaned back in her airline seat and closed her eyes. Tired from all the travel but excited about their fourth stop, her chosen destination, Tiwanaku City, and the Puma Punku Archeological sites. The girls had all been given journals to write in and she had just finished her latest entry from Easter Island. Brooke had chosen that stop and the island had a vibe about it. It was like it was alive and trying to tell her something. Thinking about it, all the stops so far had that same energy vibe. Getting up close with the colossal statues carved from solidified volcanic ash had been amazing. Chichen Itza, chosen by Jamie, had been their second stop and, wow, just wow. The thought of primitive people managing to build the large pyramids, with all the perfectly spaced steps to the top was mind-blowing. The pyramid complex at Teotihuacan, Mexico had been their first stop and Heather's pick. They could have spent a week there and not seen everything it had to offer. More of the complex was still being discovered. It had been fun watching Brooke, Heather and Jamie being so excited about their places, they had each beamed with excitement. Dani was looking forward to her pick and hoped everyone liked it.

"Hey, you still awake?" Heather asked from the seat to Dani's right.

Dani opened her eyes and turned her face towards her. "Yeah, what's up?"

Heather said, "I don't know, maybe I am hallucinating, or maybe I'm tired from all the travel. Have you been getting the feeling we are being watched?

42

It is totally freaky."

Dani looked at her for a moment, thinking back to each stop. "Yeah, I did. But it didn't feel creepy to me. I get the same feeling when I go to Dinwoody canyon. I guess I am used to it by now, so it doesn't bother me." Dani saw Heather's eyes get wide.

"You feel like someone is watching you at Aunt Kathy's place? Why haven't you said anything?" Heather asked concerned.

"Did you feel threatened by the feeling you got? Like whoever was watching you was going to hurt you in some way?" Dani asked.

Heather thought for a moment. "No, nothing like that, it was just the feeling we were being watched but not in a creepy way."

Dani smiled at her and watched as Heather had settled her unease.

"Okay, you got me there. But what about the shimmering water thing?" Heather questioned, and then continued. "That is very strange. If it happened in one place, we could play it off. But it has happened at all our stops so far. At Teotihuacan it appeared in a doorway leading under the pyramid."

Jamie spoke next from across the aisle, "At Chichen Itza, it was in between the arches at the top of the pyramid."

Brooke spoke next from her seat next to Jamie, "Are we talking about the strange reflective stuff? At Easter Island it was stretched between two of the heads still partially buried. I couldn't get to it. Jamie and I asked our guide about it. He didn't give us a straight answer. At Chichen Itza the lady looked at us like we were crazy. I don't think they were seeing what we were seeing. I don't know about you but if we see it again I think we should get a closer look at it." Brooke said.

"I agree, I don't think they saw what we were seeing either," Heather said.

"Don't you mean, IF, it happens again?" Jamie asked, looking at Brooke.

Brandi spoke from the window seat next to Brooke, "Nah, I'm with Brooke. It has happened at every stop so far. It will happen again, so I'm for checking it out and finding out what the heck it is."

Their conversation ended when the stewardess announced their descent into La Paz, Bolivia. After grabbing their luggage they were met by a guide and a large passenger van. Dani was excited to visit Tiwanaku City and looked for it as their driver drove them to their hotel. Looking out the windows of the van, Dani had the feeling that not much had changed in the landscape in the last 100 years. After arriving at their hotel, they settled into their rooms, two by two, and then headed down to the hotel restaurant for lunch. Dani's roommate this time was Heather.

"So, you excited to show us your pick?" Heather asked as they headed down the stairs to the first floor and turned into the hotel restaurant.

"Yes…" was all Dani got out before…

"SURPRISE!" everyone yelled at once.

Dani jumped what felt like a foot into the air and took in a sharp breath.

"HAPPY BIRTHDAY!" Everyone was saying over the top of each other.

"Holy moly," Dani muttered. "I just lost ten years of my life," she said as she placed her hand over her heart. Heather chuckled and headed to an empty seat. Dani sat in the last empty seat at the table between her mother, Lynn, and sister, Brooke. It was her 18th birthday and she had not thought they would make a big deal of it on the trip.

"Here, you need to try the Charque De Llama," Brooke said in her best Spanish-accented voice as she tried to pass her a piece of the jerky-style meat. That went a bit too far outside Dani's comfort zone. Llamas were cute, even if they could spit a green slimy ball at you if you irritated them. She and Brooke had gotten along well enough, but the llama jerky was pushing it. They ate amazing authentic food from each location on their trip. There moms had insisted it would add to the experience so at each place, they would order different things, and everyone would share, but for Dani Llama was off the table.

"So, Dani, where are we going today?" Aunt Kathy asked with a tired smile from across the table. Dani could clearly see the dark circles under her eyes.

"We are going to go to Tiwanaku today. If we don't finish exploring it today, we will come back tomorrow to finish up. We will then go see the ruins at Puerta del Kalasasaya. Both are large complexes. The grounds are fairly flat, with a few stairs here and there. So, it will be much easier than the hillsides of Easter Island," Dani said.

She had been keeping a close eye on Aunt Kathy throughout the trip. The group had made a pact that no one went anywhere alone. They always stayed with at least one partner. Dani was pretty sure Aunt Kathy would have stayed behind a few times out of exhaustion, but she and Dani had chosen to be partners when out and about. Aunt Kathy often slept in whatever vehicle they were traveling in. Dani was glad she had selected a hotel close by, so the trip to both sites was short. They could go and have a good time, retire early for the night, or maybe even check out the swimming pool.

"Great, we load the van in 15 minutes everyone, eat up," Amanda, Jamie's mom, barked out.

Dani saw everyone roll their eyes at that one. Amanda was a force, for sure. She and her mom had issues. Who didn't at times with their parents? But Jamie was one of the most easy-going people she knew. Her mother Amanda was a driving force. *"God makes everyone different. I am just very thankful, Heavenly Father, for the mother I have,"* she thought.

"I am looking forward to finally figuring out what that shimmering water is," Brandi said as they headed down the hallway towards the van.

"I'm just glad we have our guardian angel watching out for us," Jamie added.

"Oh, you feel it too?" Brandi asked.

They looked at each other, all of them nodding their heads yes.

"Dani says she gets the feeling all the time at Aunt Kathy's," Heather said.

All four of them turned to look at Dani.

"Hey, not in a bad way, I just think like Jamie, that a guardian angel is watching over us," Dani said, trying to downplay it.

"Let's hope your angel knows what he's doing and can help us with the water thing," Brandi grinned, stepping into the van.

The drive to Tiwanaku was only about 10 minutes from their hotel. From the parking lot, the ancient complex did not look like much. A large hill stood out in the distance in the otherwise unassuming landscape. Grass and weeds could be seen poking through the hard orange clay soil here and there. They got out and started walking down the graveled pathways towards the hill that rose in the distance. As they wandered around the ancient site, Dani noticed several large rectangular excavated sections that were each lined with smooth carved stones that fit perfectly together. Complex drainage systems could still be made out around the ruins. Large stone carvings of men in some sort of costumes were found in a few places. In odd places, archways made from enormous blocks of carved and etched stones still stood while the structures around them had crumbled into history.

"This is so cool. Nice pick, Dani," Brandi said as they made their way around the site.

"Thanks, it was a site featured on that alien TV show. I have been fascinated with it ever since," Dani said, trying to push some of her loose strands back into her long braid. "Come to think of it, all the places we have gone to have been mentioned on that show," Dani commented as they continued to explore.

Dani looked down at the orange, hard-packed clay path. What little grass there was, grew off to the sides where people did not walk. Out in the distance Dani saw a small herd of llamas grazing near one of the far puzzle pieced stone walls.

Dani called Brooke with a teasing look, "How could you eat something that cute?" She pointed over to the herd.

Brooke looked where she pointed and smiled. "They are kind of cute, aren't they?"

"Until they spit a green loogie at you," Brandi piped in. All of them laughed at that.

As they got closer to one of the large stone walls, Dani was amazed at the construction. Tons of intricately placed stones were positioned precisely on top of one another. The walls looked like a gigantic jigsaw puzzle. Dani stood thinking about what it must have taken to build the wall, *All the edges of the large stones lined up to perfection. Some of these stones must weigh several tons. The ancient builders had to have had very advanced knowledge and concepts to get all the walls completely flat and level using all the different shaped stones. But how? The ground is not completely flat, and the rocks they used were perfectly puzzled in.* Not coming up with an answer she walked on with the rest of the group.

After a couple hours of amazed, leisurely exploring, and good-natured calls in greetings to the llamas wondering about, Dani could tell several of the moms and especially Aunt Kathy were lagging. Looking around, she realized that they were the only group left at the site. Even the workers were nowhere to be seen. Their guide had called them together asking if they were through for the day. Dani looked at the sky in the distance and noticed clouds starting to roll in. It looked like it might rain soon. Amanda sent their guide ahead to get the van ready as they made their way back through the complex towards the parking area.

"Hey everyone, can we get one more picture of us in the archway with the colossal statue on the platform in the background? PLEASE," Brooke asked in her little pouty begging way.

"I'm sure everyone would love that," Lynn replied quickly. "That is all right with everyone, isn't it?" It was not really a question as the pair headed off without waiting for answers. Dani was fine with it. It seemed everyone else was to, because no one complained or objected as they walked back towards the archway. In fact, everyone was walking with quick purposeful steps despite their lagging moments ago. Maybe it was the thought that after this, they all got to chill for the night at the hotel.

"Ok, here we go. Everyone group together behind me. I have the selfie-stick as far out as it can go so everyone squeeze in. Everyone say ... llama," Brooke said in a sing-song voice.

Everyone said llama and Brooke took the picture, and then looked at the screen on the camera to check the picture. "Strange, it is all blurry. We need to try it again. I must have moved." This time small grumbles could be heard.

"One, two, three, llama," Brooke looked at the next picture on the screen. "Ok, that is just weird. Look, there," she pointed, holding the camera so people could see it. "Look at the funny light, and how the colossal guy looks all blurry."

Everyone crowded around and jockeyed for position to see the small screen better. "Ok, last time. I am getting a strange feeling just being here," Brooke said.

"Yeah, me too." Brandi chimed in.

Dani could feel it to and looked back up through the archway. She blinked her eyes several times and still could not believe what she was seeing. The colossal statue was gone. There was an undulating vertical wall of what looked like water filling the archway and blocking the view of anything behind it. The watery surface was reflecting the last rays of light back at her. She was about to say something when Brooke must have noticed and turned to see what caught her attention.

"What the Heck? There it is again!" Brooke exclaimed.

Dani heard the shuffling of feet as everyone turned to look back through what should have been the archway up to the colossal statue. Stunned silence quickly fell on the group. Even the bugs had gone quiet.

"That's so weird. It is that same shimmery thing we have seen at the other sites," Brooke muttered. "I am going up to see what that is, you all coming or what?" Brooke called, as usual not waiting for replies. She walked up to the white rope stretched across the steps to the archway and stepped over it.

Brandi, Heather, and Jamie followed her over the rope. They stood at the top of the stairs a few feet away from the shimmering wall.

"You girls get back here right now. That area is off limits, hence the rope," Amanda said in her no-nonsense voice.

Dani hung back with Aunt Kathy, off to the side of the group of moms. She kept thinking that the moving surface reminded her of the lake at Aunt Kathy's cabin. It was the same undulating movement, as if alive, when she would talk to her guardian angel. Dani saw the set of the four girls' shoulders change and knew the exact moment they had made up their minds to try and walk through the vertical wall of water. They looked at one another and two by two stepped forward, vanishing from sight.

"Jamie, you get your butt back here right this instant!" Amanda demanded.

"All of you get back here!" Theresa, Brandi's mom, yelled next.

"Jeez mom, chill, we are right here. We can see you; can't you see us?" Brandi's voice sounded a little muffled.

"No, no I can't," Theresa said. She then stepped over the rope and rushed up to the shimmering water, the other mothers hot on her heels. "Can you still see me?" she asked.

"Yep, and you gotta come see this. It's some sort of tunnel" Brandi's voice sounded in awe.

Dani stayed with Aunt Kathy at the base, looking up at the group and yelled "I don't know about this Brooke someone went through a lot of trouble to try and hide it. We have no idea what's on the other side!"

"I think it would be best if you girls came back this way. You're probably in a maintenance area or something like that, so it's hidden for a reason" Dani's mom's voice shook with unease as she spoke.

"Oh, come on mom. So, the worst that can happen is we find a storeroom. You really have to see this. There is a light up ahead. I am going to check it out. You can stay there or come through, up to you, but the rest of us are going to investigate." Brooke's voice had started getting more muffled as she spoke. Dani was guessing she had already started walking farther in.

Jamie's mom did not hesitate. She walked right through, muttering something about teenage girls thinking they know it all. Heather's mom, Wendy, hesitated only briefly before heading through. Theresa turned, looking down to Dani and Aunt Kathy. "Are you two coming?" Not waiting for an answer, Theresa turned back around and walked through.

Dani and Aunt Kathy looked at each other and shrugged. Then they stepped over the rope and up the stairs, looking up at the strange rippling water wall. There was a slight mist coming off it. Dani could still hear the murmurs of the others' voices from the other side. She could feel her heart pounding in her chest. She and Aunt Kathy stood side by side just inches away from the shimmering surface. Dani reached her right hand out in front of her, expecting to feel wetness. Instead, all she felt was a cool tingling on her hand.

"I guess we'd better follow them. No telling what kind of trouble they can get into unsupervised, hopefully it has an air conditioner" Aunt Kathy said with a tired chuckle.

"Yeah, here goes nothing," Dani said as she followed Aunt Kathy through.

Chapter 7

Axis Mundi

I t took Dani a moment to get her bearings after stepping through the misty, watery wall. Passing through it had felt like a silk scarf brushing over her exposed skin with a slight tingling sensation. She was now standing in a dimly lit tunnel whose walls and ceiling were perfectly pieced together, just like the walls of the ancient complex. The tunnel had to be 20 feet tall and at least that wide.

"Oh holy cow, you could drive a semi-truck through here" Dani exclaimed.

Everyone else was moving farther down the tunnel, except for Aunt Kathy who was only a few feet in front of her. A muted light from farther up the hallway lit their way as they took a few tentative steps forward. She watched as Aunt Kathy turned around and looked back the way they had come.

"Well, I guess it is only onward and upward from here," Aunt Kathy quietly said with a slightly wide-eyed expression.

Dani turned around and looked behind her at what Aunt Kathy was looking at. Standing in shock at what she saw. Where a shimmering wall had just been, she now saw a rock wall. On the verge of panic reaching up she moved her hand over the surface, pushing here and there, and feeling for any movement. Her heart skipped a beat at the firm, immovable stones beneath her pressing fingers.

"There has to be a way to open it," Dani said

"I'm guessing there should be maybe a lever or something close by," Aunt Kathy replied.

"Yeah, I guess so," Dani said quietly, letting her arm drop back to her side as she turned back around and looked into Aunt Kathy's wide eyes.

Dani felt and pushed along the wall trying to find some lever or button to push. There wasn't one. Turning she looked over to Aunt Kathy who had been doing the same thing. Both shook their heads no.

"Let's not start a panic with the others. Maybe there is another way out up ahead," Aunt Kathy said.

"Good idea," Dani replied, and they slowly headed down the tunnel after the others.

Walking further down the hall the material used to make the walls, floor and ceilings started to change. Jigsaw style, pieced-together stone wall turned to white and gray swirled granite with sparkling crystal in it. She looked further down the hallway trying to see where the others had gone and noticed a shining brighter light up ahead. She could almost feel it beckoning them on. The tingling sensation she had first felt walking through the watery wall had not gone away and Dani shook her arms as if trying to shake it off. She was also feeling a slight energy boost, like when she tried one of Brandi's energy drinks, all jumpy inside.

"Aunt Kathy are you feeling alright?" she noticed, walked slightly behind Aunt Kathy, that she had started shuffling her feet.

"Just a little tired, that's all," Aunt Kathy sighed. Dani cringed a little at Aunt Kathy's weary voice and the sounds of her shuffling feet. Keeping a close eye on Aunt Kathy as they made their way down the tunnel, she continued to feel the strange tingling all around and through her. It was getting stronger the farther in they went. The walls, ceiling and floor had changed from gray granite with a sprinkling of crystal, to crystals with a little gray granite woven in. Then in the span of two steps, everything was made of white crystal. Light permeated through the walls, ceiling, and floor. Listening closely trying to understand the whispered voices of the others in front of them Heathers loud excited voice jolted her slightly.

"Oh, holy cow!" Heather exclaimed.

Dani now had a hold of Aunt Kathy's elbow, adding her support to keep her moving forward. She had a nagging feeling that it was critical that they quickly get to wherever they needed to go. That feeling grew stronger building inside her. They needed to keep moving and even pick up the pace. Accompanying the building drive to move forward was the growing anticipation that something important was up ahead of them.

Aunt Kathy gasped in awe as their next steps took them into a large circular crystal chamber that had to be about fifty feet across. Dani felt her mouth fall open standing at the threshold of the chamber looking around in wonder.

"Wonder where those tunnels go?" Aunt Kathy asked.

Dani looked across to see two dark tunnels branching off on the other side of the room.

"I don't know, they seem to be evenly spaced out from the one we are in," Dani replied.

"You guys gotta come and see this," Brooke called out.

Dani looked to her and saw that everyone else but her and Aunt Kathy stood around a raised column in the middle of the room. She and Aunt Kathy walked towards them.

"Hey, there is something floating in the air," Brandi exclaimed.

"Dani hurry up, isn't that the all-seeing eye up there at the top?" Heather called out.

Dani looked up above the heads of the group as they got closer and could just make out what looked like a glowing all-seeing eye floating in the air. Looking directly above the glowing eye there was a dark hole in the ceiling. The closer she and Aunt Kathy got to the center, the others moved to make room for them around something that looked like a well that was at least eight feet across and stood about three-foot-high.

"Look at the rows of raised carvings. Those are so detailed," Jamie said. Dani looked at the intricately carved rows going around the well.

"The very bottom row looks creepy. Those creatures look evil to me," Jamie said.

Dani looked closer. Some were tall and hooded while others had evil monstrous heads and long claws. Just looking at them gave Dani a foreboding feeling. "I agree, those give me the creeps too." Dani said.

Dani quickly looked at the next row up were different types of animals where depicted.

"What the heck do you think that is," Jamie asked.

"I don't know. Wow that one has beautiful wings and this one clearly has fur," Dani said and then took a quick inhale, "Holy cow, that one is unmistakably a dragon." Dani stared at it for a few seconds before adding, "Lots of cultures have dragons in their history, I guess why not here."

"These are easy to identify," Heather said now standing to the left of Jamie. "Horses, elephants, whales, and cows,"

Dani shifted her focus to the next row up from there and said, "These look like the row two down only they seem more refined in some ways, slighter in build and not so heavy."

"Yeah, I agree the ones lower are a lot heavier looking." Jamie said.

Heather exclaimed, "Wow look at the top row."

Dani looked at the top row were the carvings of enormous, winged men and women could be seen. They were in warrior clothing with Roman or Greek style helmets, and swords drawn. Straps hung from a belt around their waists and a strap ran across their chests. They looked to have a type of kilt under the straps around their waists.

"They look like warrior angels," Heather said.

Dani and Jamie shook their heads in agreement. Dani looked up above the well, where a floating three-dimensional model of some sort, slowly spun midair.

Brandi called over to them from across the well, "What do you make of it?"

Dani took a moment to study it. The model was made up of several different-colored orbs all the same size that were connected by glowing tubes coming out of a central yellow shining orb. She looked to the bottom of the model where a very dark black orb was about a foot directly below the central yellow one.

"I don't know why but that dark one just gives off an evil vibe to it," Dani said.

"I agree with you," Aunt Kathy said from Dani's right side. Dani looked over to her when she felt Aunt Kathy leaning a little more on her as Dani still supported her with a grip on her elbow. Aunt Kathy looked so tired.

"What do you make of that one above the yellow center?" Brook asked.

Dani looked back to the model to what Brook was talking about. Another orb was about the same distance the black orb below was only it was directly above the central yellow and right below the all-seeing eye that Dani had noticed from across the room. Looking down to the middle of the model, three more colored spheres seemed to orbit around the sides of the central yellow. The entire thing reminded her of the shape of a spinning top toy.

Dani looked back down to the lowest black orb once again stunned at what she noticed next, "Wow the surface is moving and undulating. Like a mist is slowly spinning inside it."

"Yeah, I see what you mean," Heather said.

Leaning over a little Dani looked down farther into the blackest hole she had ever seen, straight down in the center of the well. A shiver ran up her spine.

"It's as if the light just gets absorbed by the dark," Dani whispered.

"Yes, creepy," Jamie said from beside her.

Dani quickly looked back up to the dark sphere and it gave her the same foreboding shiver she felt looking at the bottom row of raised inscriptions on the sides of the well and the darkness in the pit of the well. Quickly averting her eyes, she followed the glowing tube that connected the dark orb to the yellow center. Half-way up on the tube she noticed a strange symbol.

"Doesn't that look like a Celtic symbol? Like one you might see from Scotland?" Brandi asked.

"Yes, I think your right. It has a very strong similarity," Dani agreed.

She followed the glowing tub from the yellow center outwards towards the middle orbs. Brook spoke next, "Hey look a different Celtic symbol is on this tube. The orb at the end of the tube looks like it has white wispy clouds with some green areas."

Dani leaned in and looking closer at the orb Brooke was talking about as it passed her and said, "Those green areas looked like land masses," she pointed to a blue area and said, "I think the blue areas are water."

As another orb rotated into her view, Dani took a sharp breath in before saying, "There is no mistaking what that orb is," she pointed to it, "That is Earth. Look the brown and green land masses are the right shapes for our continents. The white north and south poles with white clouds floating around are in the right places too."

The last of the three middle orbs slowly rotated into her sight. She looked closely at it.

"Look this one has reddish brown land masses, and greenish blue water and white clouds," she called out. "Oh, my, gosh, worlds! We are looking at different worlds." She said in astonishment.

"What would a map of different worlds be doing in the basement of an ancient Incan temple? Maybe it is just the different hidden chambers around here?" Brandi said. But she didn't sound too convinced with her own words.

After a few more moments of studying the rotating scene in front of her, Dani looked up to the white, swirling-mist world directly above the yellow center.

"That one is really pretty," Jamie said looking up to where Dani was looking.

Dani answered, "I agree it is beautiful with the white mist thinning in places, you can faintly see lush green shining through, and with deep blue of what must be water. It is connected by a glowing tube coming from the yellow center, too. Look it has a different Celtic style symbol on it partway."

Dani looked farther up to the brightly glowing symbol of the all-seeing eye. It hung high above everything and seemed to radiate shimmering waves of light to the worlds below. Following the waves down the model, she noticed as the light reached the dark world on the bottom it was extinguished.

Looking back up, she noticed an outline going around the opening to the tunnel in the ceiling above The All-Seeing Eye. Squinting she could just make out the same winged men and women that were on the top row of the well. Evenly spaced between the figures was the same Celtic symbol that was on the tube connecting the white top world above the yellow center. Quickly turning to look at the tunnel they had just come through she found rimming the entrance were the same pictures she had recognized as the animals of Earth, alternating with the Celtic symbol from the tube connecting Earth to the yellow central. Wanting to confirm her suspicions she quickly looked to the other two tunnels across the well from her. Matching them the same way she did Earth and the white mist world from the top.

"It's a map," Dani said quietly. "From what I can tell, I think we are standing in the yellow center."

Aunt Kathy gripped her arm leaning towards her. "Shhh, I think you are right, but right now might not be the time to point it out to the others."

Dani looked at the people around her. The girls looked to be more excited than nervous, but the moms were definitely stressed. Shaking her head yes, she let it drop.

"Hey, come on, you guys. We need to get moving," Brooke said from across the room. Looking her direction, she saw one of the two tunnels across the chamber from her had started to glow with light and Brooke was heading to its opening.

"Yeah, I think so too, but that's not the tunnel we came through," Brandi said with a slight shake to her voice. She was standing right next to Brook looking across the center room back at the tunnel they had all originally come down. The moms were hovering off to the sides of the girls. They were having a quiet conversation between them.

"I agree Brandi, it's not. Let's go back the way we came," Amanda said walking forcefully across the room. As she was getting closer to Dani, she could tell Amanda was shaking slightly.

"I am sorry, but the way we came is no longer an option," Dani said as Amanda came closer.

"What do you mean not an option? We can walk right back the way we came," Amanda snapped, now standing by the well.

"No, we can't. When Dani and I came through, the watery wall disappeared and a very firm wall, like the ones around the complex, was left," Aunt Kathy stated.

"We looked for a lever or knob or button to open it again but couldn't find one," Dani added.

Everyone was now talking over the top of each other as panic started to set in.

Suddenly, Dani felt the presence of what she had come to call her guardian angel. She softly whispered, "A little help would be nice." As soon as the words passed her lips, the light in the tunnel across from her, where Brooke and Brandi stood, shined brighter.

"Look!" Dani shouted over all the panicked voices and pointed to the tunnel. "I think that is a sign we need to head that way."

"We don't know where that goes," Amanda said, but she started walking towards the brightly lit tunnel with a firm grip on Jamie.

"I know, but we can't stay here. The way we came is blocked. It is either that tunnel or the one to the right of it, which is dark. I for one would rather walk down a lit tunnel than a dark one," Aunt Kathy firmly stated from beside Dani. Reaching over Dani gave Aunt Kathy's hand a squeeze, thanking her for the support.

The group stood around looking between the light and dark tunnels. Heather, Jamie and Brandi now stood not that far away from Dani and Aunt Kathy.

Dani spoke, "I am getting the feeling we needed to get moving."

Heather, Jamie, Brandi, and Brook walked to the entrance of the lit tunnel. The moms formed a semicircle behind them. Dani watched as the girls looked at each other and nodded their heads once.

"I am guessing if there is a way out, it is down this tunnel. Come on mom, let's get going," Brooke said grabbing their mom's hand and pulled her in the lit tunnel, going first.

Brandi and her mom were next, followed by Jamie and her mother. Dani grabbed Aunt Kathy's hand and arm walking towards the tunnel as well. She was not going to give Aunt Kathy a chance to think about stopping. She could hear the other girls giving words of encouragement, or in Jamie's case pleading for her mom to get moving. It worked. Each pair headed down the lit tunnel. Dani gave a brief sigh of relief. Now all she needed to do was get Aunt Kathy moving faster as well.

The tingling sensation she had felt the entire time had started to build even more in Dani's body. As she got closer to the lit tunnel the tingling would decrease. If they stalled in their forward movement, it would build again, and if that was not enough, a low hum started to fill the room and grow in intensity.

"Aunt Kathy, we need to get moving," Dani said as she switched her grip on Aunt Kathy's hand. With her free hand, she grabbed right above Aunt Kathy's elbow, pulling at her wrist with one hand and pushing with the other. Looking up at that lit tunnel entrance, she saw that only Heather and her mom Wendy were in sight. Heather had a tight grip on her mom's hand, pulling.

Heather mouthed, "You guys coming?"

Dani nodded her head yes and gestured to Heather to go on. The hum was making conversation impossible, except with someone right next to you. Aunt Kathy had again stopped walking forward and they were only halfway from the well to the tunnel entrance.

"You go ahead, Dani. I think I am meant to stay here," Aunt Kathy said, sounding exhausted. Aunt Kathy turned as if to go back towards the well.

Taking a close look at Aunt Kathy, she noticed how pale she was and clearly in discomfort panting slightly. Not willing to give up Dani moved closer to her, despite the feeling of urgency to move forward. In stark contrast to Aunt Kathy, Dani felt a boost of energy. It was as if every little physical ache or pain was no longer bothering her. Her body had been a little achy from dragging her suitcase all over for the past 15 days. Now, it felt perfectly fine, better than perfectly fine. She felt she could run the steps of Teotihuacan and not break a sweat.

Then it hit Dani. What if the chamber or the light was what was overwhelming Aunt Kathy? Whatever was giving Dani the energy rush of a lifetime, maybe was causing the opposite in Aunt Kathy. Dani knew in her heart, if Aunt Kathy stayed there, she would die. She did not know how she knew; she just knew.

"You listen here, Aunt Kathy. Where I go, you go and if you stay here then I will too. I think we both know if we do that, we are not going to make it. So, you need to get your feet moving so we can catch up with the others and get out of this place. The tunnel we came in was not that long. I bet this one isn't either," Dani said forcefully.

"I don't know if I can, Dani. Please, just go without me," Aunt Kathy exhaustedly said.

"I don't think so!" Dani said.

She changed her grip, throwing Aunt Kathy's arm across her shoulders as she wrapped her arm around her waist, dragging Aunt Kathy step by step. They needed to leave now. The light in the chamber and the tunnel had started to grow dimmer as the hum grew in intensity. Dani's heart began to race, and she thought, *"Please don't let us run out of time."*

Dani whispered frantic prayers as they reached the entrance to the tunnel and took labored steps into it. Finally entering the tunnel, she could just make out Heather and her mom's shapes several feet in front of them. Just as she saw them they vanished from sight.

"Heavenly Father, please help us. Please help me get Aunt Kathy out of here. Please!" Dani pleaded. It was her mantra as she pulled her aunt along. After a few more steps, Aunt Kathy almost collapsed, her legs beginning to buckle.

"You have to go, Dani; I am dying anyway. I know you know this. Just let me go," Aunt Kathy pleaded. They had made it partway down the tunnel and Dani was desperate to keep Aunt Kathy moving forward.

"If you don't go, I won't either, so don't even go there!" Dani gritted her teeth, barely holding on. Tears welled up in her eyes as she saw the anguish on Aunt Kathy's face. The tunnel was almost dark now. "You would say this verse to me this when things get hard. Do not goat over me, my enemy! Though I have fallen, I will rise. Though I sit in darkness, the Lord will be my light."

Dani breathed in and desperately pulled Aunt Kathy. "You never let me give up. Now I refuse to let you." Dani blinked back tears, before saying, "I don't know if you can hear me or not, but a little help right now would be awesome," Dani begged.

The light ahead suddenly flickered brighter. Dani was not entirely sure that the light was a sign someone or something was listening to her, but she had nothing to lose by praying for help. Down the tunnel a flash of light caught her attention as it rushed towards them. Instinctively she braced herself quickly tightened her grip on Aunt Kathy.

The light engulfed and seemed to wrap around them and a force of energy hit them from behind. Out of the corner of her eye, Dani caught a blur of bright red and orange behind them. A screeching cry, like a large bird of some sort, quickly followed. She could have sworn she heard the ruffle of feathers and the beating of wings as she felt the energy propel them forward. Intense heat radiated up her back as if something hot was brushing up against her, as it pushed them forward. Inside her head she heard a deep male voice.

"You need to get out of the Axis Mundi quickly." The deep male voice rumbled through her head above the annoying hum. She didn't know who the voice belonged to, but he sounded familiar, so she put more effort into pulling and dragging Aunt Kathy down the tunnel.

Wave after wave of light energy pulsed at them from up ahead. Step by step they made their way farther down the tunnel. The walls had not changed from the crystal back to the stone or clay like the tunnel they first came down, but she knew they were making progress. The beating of wings from behind was steady, giving them added strength to continue. But the intervals between the waves of energy were getting longer, and their progress slowed.

They came to an abrupt stop at what they saw ahead of them. Not wanting to completely take her eyes off it, Dani turned her head slightly so she could see Aunt Kathy out of the corner of her eye. Aunt Kathy's mouth was slightly open, and Dani had no doubt Aunt Kathy was looking at the same thing she was. The arched ceiling was no higher than before, but now they could see through the crystal. Up ahead of them in what must be the outside sky, the shape of a winged creature suspended in the air. As if she were looking through an antique glass, an opalescent light-blue dragon with his massive wings beat rhythmically, hovered. A soft blue shimmer ran across his scales as he moved. He opened his mouth and bathed the crystal with glowing white light energy. He was breathtaking.

Watching the dragon beat his massive wings, she could tell he was getting tired as another blast of light energy hit them, propelling them on. His enormous head hung a little lower with each blast. It was then that she could see the horns that rimmed his forehead. His fatigue and exhaustion became more apparent the longer she watched.

"That must be why the intervals had slowed down," Dani thought. He, and whatever was behind them, was propelling them forward. They were giving them their energy to make it through the tunnel. But it looked like it would not be enough. Aunt Kathy was ready to collapse again. Tightening her grip, she was just about to call out for help again when she saw them.

"Holy crap!" Dani stared in disbelief.

As if it was not enough for her befuddled mind that there was a light blue dragon on the other side of the crystal wall, now another one flew up behind him. The shine coming off this one's scales was a rainbow of colors. He beat his wings with strong forceful strokes. She didn't know why, but she guessed he was younger than the light blue dragon with sharp spiked horns circling his head in the shape of a crown.

Floating on waves of warmth through her frantic mind as she watched the light blue dragon, she heard a voice she did not recognize say a name, Sir Goirves Protector of the Weak. Shifting her eyes to look at the bright rainbow dragon, the same voice said in her mind, Lord Xadrayrth the Gifted.

Trying to keep what little sanity Dani had left, she tried to make sense of what was happening in front of her and in her mind. Right now, she just did not have the mental faculties to deal with it all. So, she shortened the names told to her into things she could manage. Light blue dragon was now Gordy, and the bright rainbow dragon was Xad. The names just clicked in her mind and stuck to the dragons in front of her.

To her complete and utter astonishment, more dragons came up behind Xad. There were six on each side of him, spaced far enough apart to allow their wings to beat freely. They came in all different tones of red, blue, and green. Each had a slightly different shape, and none had the pronounced number of horns the first two had. Trying to look closer, she noticed each had a person on its back, seated right where the top of their wings met the base of their necks.

"Oh, holy cow, what is going to happen now?" Dani thought still not able to completely wrap her head around the sight before her. Really hoping that

whatever voice spoke into her mind did not try to connect names to the other twelve dragons.

"Aunt Kathy, I know you see what I see," she said, hearing a slight shaking in her own voice. "I think we are about to get a major jump start. Hold on, ok, you've got this." Dani looked at her aunt's face. It was damp from perspiration. She just had time to look back up through the crystal wall when the first massive wave of light energy hit them.

"Wow," Dani gasped out.

She felt like she was absorbing pure energy. It was like drinking a thousand espresso shots all at once. The pure energy flowed thickly down the tunnel, energizing them with each blast. Looking over at Aunt Kathy, she saw her surrounded by a bright concentration of light energy. In her peripheral view she caught glimpses of large glowing red and orange wings shimmering like waves of heat.

The wings redirected the energy that would have passed them. Instead of continuing past them and down the tunnel, the energy curled back towards them, and pushed them from behind. It propelled them forward so quickly they almost lost their footing and fell. If she wasn't so desperate to keep her footing and get them out of the tunnel, she would turn around to see what had to be a magnificent creature that was helping them from behind. The way it was she looked up just in time to see the twelve dragons blowing white energy into Xad. He then blew an even brighter force into Gordy. Gordy then blew the concentrated energy into the crystal tunnel they were in. All of this seemed to happen in the blink of an eye. Over and over this pulsing, pushing field of energy was directed at them.

Stumbling forward with the overpowering force of energy, Dani caught sight of a watery shimmering vertical wall to their left. It looked just like the one they had come through before. Relief flooded her.

"There!" she said, pointing to the left. "Aunt Kathy, there is the end. You've got this. Just a few more steps," she said and gave one large pull on Aunt Kathy, propelling them through the watery wall. Cool air hit them as they stumbled through the opening and collapsed on the ground.

"We made it Aunt Kathy, you did it!" Dani croaked and let her head fall to the ground.

Chapter 8

Kolob

Sitting in the room by the sacred pool, panting Kerberos struggled to catch his breath. All had come together over the last few weeks. It was his legion's turn to guard the sacred pools during the summer solstice celebration. It was easy for him to place himself as the sole guard at the Temple of the Sun sacred pool. The plans the Creator had guided him to, getting Dani and her family through the Axis Mundi had come together efficiently. The Creator of All had to have given his sacred crystal the power it needed to open a portal between Terra and Eirenic, despite the sealing magic. The glow from it had been almost blinding.

As he caught his breath his thoughts spun over the events that had happened. He needed to get them straight in his own mind before the others showed up to question him, *I had no intention of being so involved in Dani and her family's journey through the Axis Mundi, but it was clear that the sick older one would not have made it through without my intervention. The healing process was not always successful if the one journeying through could not recover from the onslaught of physical changes. I am in awe of the strength of spirit Dani showed refusing to leave her aunt behind. The same spirit shone brightly in the dragon when, sensing the aunt's failing health, it desperately started pushing its energy into the Axis Mundi to save her,* he rubbed his hand over his head continuing his internal thoughts to solidify why he had acted to help.

"I could not stand by and not help the desperate attempts of the dragon pnēvma synergáti. The Creator of All creates the sacred bond between pnēvma synergáti and humans. The dragon pnēvma synergáti bonded with the older females Chosen

One did not have all the power needed to get them through. I had to act. Dani and her aunt would have died had I not helped them traverse the Axis Mundi," he reasoned out.

"I had no conscious thought of what the combined infusion of power would do, and definitely had not anticipated the fierce fire phoenix appearance. I recall saying a quick prayer for guidance in helping Dani and her aunt make it through as I pushed energy into the Axis Mundi, as the Creator of All guided me to do. Dani had a strong, self-sacrificing, glowing spirit that she does not see in herself. Still, I am somewhat surprised that the Creator has partnered her with a phoenix as her pnēvma synergáti. It so rare, I have only heard stories of only one other in history." Kerberos thought.

"Dani will be a formidable Chosen One for some lucky male," Kerberos mused out loud. Before thinking again, *"I would feel honored to have Dani as mine, but no matter my admiration for her spirit, I cannot be her Chosen One or her mine. Humans cannot survive on my world, and I can only survive for short durations on the human worlds of Terra, Eirenic and Agon. I will enjoy watching Dani and all the females grow and adapt to their new home on Eirenic. Please Creator of All let your will be done, and the females are somehow the answer to the problems that they did not know existed. I know the females will learn quickly, especially Dani."*

He heard, long before he physically reached him, the beating of Burkhart's dark gray wings. Burkhart's leather-clad feet hit the stone floor with a forceful thump. Waiting for the deluge of condemnation that was sure to follow for what he had done did not concern him much. Everyone and everything connected through the Axis Mundi would have felt the force of energy that had been poured into it. He would stand by his actions and pray that the ripple he started would finally bring about the events that would end the Evil One's effects on all.

"What have you done?" Burkhart's voice boomed through the Temple of the Sun as he raced inside.

The center of the sacred pool shined for a moment and then went clear, again showing the pillared crystal walls surrounding it.

"What had to be done," Kerberos said bluntly.

Dionysius came in at that moment as each Liege stared at the sacred pool. All could feel the magic that had sealed the portal had been damaged. They watched as the faint blue of the magic seal was now trying to re-form over the portal but could tell that it was much weaker than it had been.

Suddenly Burkhart rushed at Kerberos, swinging his large fist at his face. "Traitor," he yelled as he swung.

Kerberos easily ducked to the side avoiding the punch.

"I do not wish to fight with you, Burkhart," Kerberos said flatly.

"You will be beaten nonetheless," Burkhart growled as he swung towards him again.

Easily blocking the next blow, he stepped outside the older males reach again. Burkhart was formidable, but aged. They both knew he was no match for him, but Burkhart was not thinking with a clear mind.

"Enough Burkhart, this will solve nothing," Dionysius pushed in front of Burkhart.

"He has doomed us all!" Burkhart shouted.

"All he has brought about is change. How we deal with this change is what defines us," Dionysius tried to placate.

Burkhart's rage was barely contained as he started pacing the temple.

"Clear the temple," Dionysius demanded; looking toward the doorway where a crowd of Nephilim Legionnaires from all three regiments were jockeying for position just inside the arched doorway to see what was happening.

The temple cleared, save the three Lieges. Dionysius turned to Kerberos.

"What exactly has been done, Kerberos?" Dionysius sighed as he rubbed his temple.

"With the blessing of the Creator of All, I opened a portal between Terra and Eirenic to allow some females to pass through," Kerberos replied. He was never one for elaboration in speech.

"There was more to it than that or we would not have felt the energy pulses that we did. Tell us what you did!" Burkhart roared.

"I told you what *I did*," Kerberos said.

"Ok, so what else happened while the females were traversing the mist?"

Dionysius asked, continuing to rub his graying temple.

"There was a middle-aged female that was clearly in poor health. Her Chosen One's pnĕvma synergáti sensed her failing strength and came to her aid, pouring its life energy into the crystal…" he was interrupted by Burkhart.

"That does not explain the amount of energy we felt, and you know it," Burkhart seethed.

"If you would stop interrupting me, I will tell you the rest. Or would you prefer to try your hand at me again?" Kerberos's patience with the older Liege was nearing its end.

"Patience is needed here from both of you," Dionysius held up a hand towards each of them. "Continue, please," he said to Kerberos.

"The older dragon did not have enough power to accomplish his task and would have failed had he not received help. The true king of Eirenic and his pnĕvma synergáti rose with his guards to provide the additional energy needed to bring the two females through to Eirenic," Kerberos said.

Burkhart's face turned red as his anger grew before he yelled out, "Two females? What specific two females are you speaking of? How many females did you send through? Dionysius, he still holds back what he did. Maybe he is in league with the Evil One and is trying to bring about the fall of the protections on all the portals. We cannot trust him!"

As he spoke his arms slashed through the air working himself up even more. Kerberos knew Burkhart would most likely not see reason in his current state, but he still had to try.

"I am not holding back information. My crystal still shines clear; the Creator of All guided my actions to open the portal. The female with the older one refused to leave her behind. She was the one who ultimately saved the older female. If she had not been there to drag her onward, no amount of energy would have saved her," Kerberos said.

"You sound as if you admire this young female," Burkhart's condescension was evident.

Patience with the older Nephilim now gone, Kerberos could not hold back his quick reply. "I hold in high esteem any that would sacrifice them self for another. One who would stand up to an unknown force and conquer it instead of hiding away waiting for it to finish them and everyone else off!"

Dionysius quickly spoke up, "What is done is done. We must now determine what effects opening two portals and pouring that amount of energy into the Axis Mundi has had on the magic used to close all the portals. Arguing here will accomplish nothing. Shall we go and study the effects or stand here doing nothing constructive but firing insults at each other?" Dionysius looked between the two as he spoke, his hands outstretched to keep the others apart.

Burkhart stormed towards the door and left. Dionysius sighed, sweeping his hand in a gesture for Kerberos to walk ahead.

"My friend, I hope you fully understand what you have started," Dionysius spoke quietly as he walked beside Kerberos.

They had just made it to the arched doorway when Burkhart's booming voice could be heard shouting for all to hear. "Liege Kerberos, on his own volition, has opened a portal. It is up to us to find out how his actions have damaged the magic that has sealed us all from the evil that resides on Agon!"

The two exited the temple to a multitude of voices in the courtyard. Crowds of Nephilim Legionnaires were all talking at once. Some praised Kerberos's action, while others condemned him.

"Legionnaires, fall into your formations on the practice field and wait for instructions from your Liege," Dionysius' commanding voice ordered. Slowly the masses took to the skies and all that was heard was the beating of hundreds of wings.

Chapter 9

Eirenic

Sprawled on the ground with their limbs still tangled around one another Dani and Aunt Kathy laid there for several moments exhausted from their ordeal. Finally rolling to her side, Dani looked over to where she thought the dragons should be in the air, but they were gone. The sound of footsteps rushing towards them and lots of voices caught her attention next.

"Daniella, Kathleen, are you two all right?" Dani's mom said.

"What the heck just happened?" Amanda demanded.

There was complete confusion. Dani watched as Heather tried to go back in the tunnel, but the shimmery water would not give. Brandi and Jamie were pointing at something off to the side. Before Dani could get her bearings, she heard a deep male voice she did not recognize.

"Here, let me help you up," looking toward the unfamiliar voice, she saw a man kneeling next to Aunt Kathy.

"I am fine, just give me a minute," Aunt Kathy said with labored breath as she and Dani continued to untangle themselves from each other.

"Take the time you need but we have much better resting places at the Palace," the man said and kneeled on the ground next to Aunt Kathy. Dani watched as the man looked at Aunt Kathy and then around at them.

"What was with the light show? Did you guys see that while you were still inside the tunnel?" Brooke asked.

Brandi started speaking almost over the top of Brooke, "Yeah that was crazy. We didn't know what was going on. Then these guys walked up to us

69

from down the hill." Brandi gestured to the men standing with them and the one kneeling next to Aunt Kathy.

Dani looked over the group that now stood in front of her. There were four strange men standing in their group. Her mind still spinning, she managed to notice that each was dressed decidedly differently from the others. She and Aunt Kathy stayed lying on the grass right outside the arched doorway they had just tumbled through. Looking around, she noticed it was sunset and the colors of the sky were starting to turn a dark shade of blue, with a few faint twinkling stars. Where were the clouds she had noticed before going into the tunnel gone?

Peering through legs, Dani could see they were on a little outcrop on the side of a crystal mountain. Wanting a better view of her surrounding she stood slowly. Looking down the green hillside she saw a large meadow with a large pond to one side. The meadow was bracketed by a forest of tall trees all around it. Not sure why she was doing it, she started looking around for the ruins of Tiwanaku but did not recognize any landmarks. The arid desert was gone, replaced with rolling hills and lush thick forest. She knew they had not walked far, but to get from the desert to this environment they would have to have traveled several hundred miles. She also couldn't help scanning the sky looking for the dragons. She was certain what she saw through the crystal was indeed dragons. She didn't want to say it out loud yet and was looking for confirmation from the others.

"You didn't see what was lighting up the tunnel?" Dani asked, looking around.

"No, we just saw the whole mountain light up in pulses. Did you guys see something?" Brandi asked.

"I don't know. It was a little strange in there," Dani said. She looked down at Aunt Kathy still sitting on the ground.

"Yes, it was a little strange," Aunt Kathy agreed.

Dani figured neither one of them wanted to talk about the dragons right now. Too many other pressing questions needed to be answered.

The main question Dani had was where the heck were they? She looked back to the group still standing around them. All the girls and moms seemed to be doing the same thing Dani was. Trying to figure out what just happened and where they were. The stress and worry was plane to see on the pale faces, creased brows and down turned lips on all their faces. Each was trying to hold it together as best they could. Looking around again, she got an uneasy feeling something was not quite right.

Looking back to the trees she noticed they were not just tall, they were gigantic. From her vantage point partway up the mountain they were huge. Even the undergrowth of plants was larger than anything she had ever seen. Looking into the darker sections, she could start to make out iridescent glowing outlines of plants.

It suddenly hit her, and she reached over to grip Aunt Kathy to get her attention without the others noticing. They were standing around quietly talking to each other and looking around anxiously. Dani did not want them to hear what she was going to say, "Aunt Kathy I think that is a three-dimensional floating map. Look at the rings of inscriptions of animals on the well below. They are all so different from anything I have even seen pictures of. Could we have traveled to another world that was on that map? We are clearly not in Bolivia anymore."

Dani also grasped the realization that if she didn't know exactly where she was, she couldn't figure out how to get back home the way they came. She chose to not say that out loud. Aunt Kathy was about to say something when Amanda called out.

"So, anyone want to tell me where we are and pardon my rudeness, but who are all of you?" Amanda asked, rubbing her neck with one hand, and holding Jamie's hand in a death grip with the other.

The man kneeling next to Aunt Kathy spoke. "I am sure you are all disorientated by your journey. I would prefer to make introductions at the Palace," he paused for a moment looking at Amanda's face then continued, "I see it will not wait."

"Please do," Amanda said in a sharp tone.

"I am Zidicus." He pointed to his right and introduced the men in order going from right to left around the circle of people. "That is Ballene, Barbar, Filtiarn, and Azmer." Each man inclined his head as his name was called.

All the men kept sweeping their eyes around their surroundings. Clearly, they were not comfortable being there. Dani could see the concern on their faces as they talked among themselves and gestured toward the watery wall.

The rigid posture of all the moms and the way they kept themselves between the men and the girls spoke volumes to Dani. They were now in overprotective mode. Brandi looked from her mom to Dani, Aunt Kathy and Zidicus. The look of, "now what?" was plainly written on her face.

As if on cue trying to defuse the tension, Zidicus prompted, "May I ask your names as well?"

Seeing a look of confusion on her mom's face, Brandi replied, "I am Brandi, and this is my mom, Theresa."

"It is a pleasure to meet you both," Ballene said from beside Theresa. He leaned over, reached for Theresa's hand, and placed a kiss on top of it. A flush went up Theresa's face. A glowing crystal, hanging from a chain around Ballene's neck, fell out of his shirt as he leaned over. As he straightened back up, the light of a shimmering tattoo with multiple circles briefly flashed on his upper chest. The design looked somewhat familiar, but she could not put her finger on it. There were too many thoughts running through her head taking her in too many directions at once. Glancing at Theresa she looked as shocked as Dani was at what Ballene had done.

Ballene let Theresa's hand go and Dani took a closer look at his appearance. He was interesting looking, to say the least. Not ugly or anything, just different. He had on form-fitting clothes that almost had a rubbery look to them. The seam of his shirt ran horizontally across his chest.

"How in the world is it held together," Dani thought.

It was folded open so that the same patch of his deeply tanned skin showed as the other men's, at the base of his neck. His hair was shaved close to his scalp. The color, from what she could make out with the fading light, looked sun bleached.

Theresa managed to stutter, "Pleasure to meet you too."

"Guess it's our turn," Heather said awkwardly. "I am Heather, and this is my mom, Wendy."

"I am honored to meet you both," Barbar said and reached for Wendy's hand. The same actions that Ballene had just done were repeated. The same glowing crystal and tattoo showed on his chest and neck. Barbar's hair was long with sections of braids pulling it back from his face. He was wearing loose-fitting pants and an open vest for a shirt. Not only had the shimmering tattoo showed, but also dark bands encircling his upper arms. They looked almost tribal with tiger stripes in them. He had a dark complexion, so it was hard to make out, but the swirling circular tattoos on his neck and chest looked raised up on his skin.

Jamie spoke next, "Hi, I am Jamie, and this is my mom, Amanda." Filtiarn reached for Amanda's hand. He placed a kiss on the back of it, not taking his eyes off Amanda. A subtle blush swept up Amanda's face. It was amazing to see the dominant mom at a loss for words. Filtiarn had dark brown hair that was kind of shaggy. He was wearing dark colors of brown and green. He wore a deep "v" shirt that was made of a noticeably lightweight material that moved with him.

"Okay, we are up. I am Brooke. This is my mom Lynn and that," Brooke thumbed over her right shoulder pointing to Dani, "is my sister Dani."

It was Azmer that took her mom's hand and repeated the sequence, placing a kiss on her hand. His flowing golden hair was striking with lighter streaks showing throughout it. It almost looked like a mane. He was deeply tanned and wore loose clothing in light browns.

Zidicus spoke as Azmer released Lynn's hand. "And you are?" he asked softly, looking adoringly at Aunt Kathy. Zidicus' clothes were also loose fitting, but the material looked to be made of a finer woven, more expensive cloth. His vest-like top was long, not stopping at his waist but falling almost to his ankles. He had a gold rope belt that held the long vest together at the waist. The vest was a creamy white that shimmered with shades of blue; his pants were a light blue.

"I am Kathy," Aunt Kathy said.

"It is truly an honor and a privilege to meet you, Kathy," Zidicus said and took Aunt Kathy's outstretched hand. Instead of kissing the back of it as the others had, he turned her hand over and kissed her palm.

Looking more closely at each man Dani started cataloging what she knew.

It looked like they all had the same tattoo, but each had one circle shaded differently from the others. The chains around their necks were different, but it looked like the same type of crystal was worn by all of them. They were all so differently dressed. She wondered what it meant and why each of them kept eyeing their surroundings with unease.

"Now that the introductions are complete, can you tell us where we are, and how we get back home?" Brooke asked in her *"I am so done with this"* voice.

Looking at her sister, Dani almost wanted to laugh despite the anxiety she was feeling. Her sister, who prided herself on looking perfect no matter where she was, was definitely out of her comfort zone. Her usually perfect hair was sticking out in areas, while other pieces stuck to her face and neck. Her eyeliner had run in some spots and her clothing was rumpled and dirty. She tried to stifle her chuckle at the sight.

Brooke looked over at her with the *"I am going to kill you"* look. Before she could act on it or Dani could do anything else to provoke her, the unmistakable sound of beating wings was heard by all.

The moms shifted further in front of their girls as they all looked in the direction of the sound. Dani stood up straighter, looking between heads and bodies trying to see more clearly. Stepping closer to peer around her mother, Dani noticed some large animals at the far end of the meadow below, but as intriguing as they looked, she wanted to find the source of the beating wings. Whatever it was, it was getting closer. It was also getting louder; something large was approaching and getting ready to land. Blinking her eyes several times, she tried to make sense of what she was seeing.

"Holy crap!" Brooke shouted.

Four dragons flew in and landed halfway up the hillside. Men could be seen getting off two of them. Two, rider-less, dragons landed a few feet away from the two already on the ground. If she was not mistaken from this distance, one of the rider-less dragons was Gordy, the light blue dragon that had pushed the energy at them in the tunnel. All the dragons looked huge, even from this distance. Strangely, she did not feel threatened by them. In a way, Dani was relieved that they were real, that what she and Aunt Kathy had seen through the crystal was not a hallucination.

Looking back to her family and friends, she saw they were all clutching onto each other, the lines of strain visible on their blanched faces. It would not take much more for them all to lose what little remained of the control they had on their emotions. Looking down at Aunt Kathy who had reached over and grabbed her pant leg, her face told her she was holding on by the same thread, as was everyone else.

Two of the riders dismounted their dragons and started walking up the hill. They had on what could only be described as military uniforms that looked remarkably similar to what the warrior angels wore on the raised carvings on the well under the floating map she had seen earlier.As they got closer, she could tell the material was the same rich-looking kind that Zidicus wore. They came to a stop a short distance from the group. Each placed a fisted hand over his heart and bowed at the waist.

"May we be of assistance in getting the females back to the palace?" The first one spoke behind his gold, intricately carved helmet. His face was mostly hidden. Only his eyes and chin could be seen. The helmet looked Greek or Roman in its design.

"We were just about to get moving," Zidicus spoke as he stood.

"We are not going anywhere but back through that crystal passageway…" Theresa's voice trailed off as she completely turned around and, with wide eyes, looked back at the passageway they had just come through. Seeing the look of shock on her face, Dani turned quickly around.

"What the Heck! You open that up right now! We are going home!" Brooke's voice wobbled with emotion, "I want to go home." The last words trailed off into whispered whimpering.

Staring at the solid wall of crystal that once had been the doorway, Dani mirrored her sister's desire. The archway could still be seen, but it had been completely filled in.

Slowly reaching over she took Brooke's shaking hand. As soon as their skin touched Brooke latched onto her hand like a vise. Looking around all the girls and their moms were holding onto one another. The men were clearly trying to comfort them as best they could.

"We are not going anywhere until you tell us where we are. Then we will decide if we are going with you," Amanda's sharp tone was edged with panic.

"Amanda, we will explain everything once we reach the palace. I swear on it. We need to move from this place," Filtiarn spoke.

Dani could hear the tension in his voice for the first time.

The women all looked to one another. The unease in their group had not dissipated since they figured out, they could not go back the way they came in the tunnels. Watching the men look around and shifting from side to side gave the clear impression they too were not comfortable with where they were. She could clearly see lines of strain on their faces and watched as their eyes darted around the small clearing they were in, and at the crystal mountain they had come through.

Looking at Aunt Kathy's exhausted face Dani leaned over to squeeze her knee, reassuringly. An unspoken message passed between the two. They both understood that they had no choice, really. They could hang out by the side of the crystal mountain or go with the men. Looking again at the men standing next to the moms she noted they were tall and muscular. Not an ounce of fat showed on any of them. They also seemed to be about the same age as the moms. She could not guess the two new men's ages, as their faces were covered by the helmets.

As Aunt Kathy shifted to stand her shirt gaped open at her neckline and Dani got the shock of her life. On Aunt Kathy's neck was the same shimmer-inked tattoo the men had. Dani sucked in a breath and looked up to Zidicus and back to her aunt's neck. Zidicus followed the line of sight to Aunt Kathy's mark. He shook his head ever so slightly as if asking her not to point it out. He looked pointedly to the other women. Dani immediately got it. If she pointed it out now, it might just be what sent everyone over the edge.

Aunt Kathy needed someplace to rest clearly exhausted. Looking back at Zidicus, Dani gave a quick, small nod to indicate she agreed. She accompanied it with a look that she hoped he got that she was going along with it for Aunt Kathy's sake. He nodded back and seemed to physically relax a little. Her aunt's needs are a lot higher up the priority ladder than figuring out what is up with the new body art.

Looking back to Aunt Kathy looked like she could curl up and sleep on a stone bench if they had one. Someplace nice to rest, with food and answers, was what they all needed now. It was clear they would get none of that here.

Dani understood the anxiety of her group. They had no idea where they were and who the heck these guys really were. Glancing back over to Zidicus, her gut instinct told her she could trust him. He looked like he really cared about Aunt Kathy. Looking at the other men, she got the same sense of caring from them towards the moms. Each has significant size to them, towering over the women. If the men wanted to, they could force them to go. The women were definitely outmuscled. Taking a deep breath, Dani went with her gut, trying to defuse the situation and get them all moving to whatever palace the guys spoke of.

"So, how far away is the palace?" Dani asked.

"It is not far for the pnẽvma synergáti. They will carry us." Zidicus said, exhaling in a sigh of relief when none of the other moms or girls protested.

"Ok, what is a pnẽvma synergáti? If I remember my languages, I think it is a spirit partner, right?" Dani asked him.

Zidicus smiled at her "You are correct, little one. Those are our spirit partners." He gestured toward where the dragons were and then to the large animals that were moving up the hill towards them. All the women turned at Zidicus' gesture and an audible intake of breath could be heard from all. The other animals continued moving closer, up the hillside. They now stood beside the dragons.

"Oh, holy crap!" Theresa exclaims.

"Mother! You yell at me for my language." Brandi snickered. Brandi quickly turned, making eye contact with Dani. Dani tilted her head towards Aunt Kathy and winked. Dani smiled and gave a nod. Brandi was helping get them off the hillside.

"Cool, which one do I get to ride?" Brandi asked as she started to walk down the hill. Dani, Brooke, Heather, and Jamie followed.

"Girls do not just walk up to…" Amanda called after them. It was almost comical to listen to the pause in her words as she tried to figure out what to call the creatures in front of them. "…animals you do not know."

The girls were about halfway down the hillside when they stopped several yards away from the animals. The animals, who had also stopped moving up the hill, could be seen more clearly now. All of them were huge, their bodies bigger than a bus in most cases. She tried categorizing them as animals she knew in her mind, *"Dragons were the easy ones. They were.... dragons. Why the heck did that sound so normal compared to some of the others?"*

"Ok, so we have lions, tigers, wolves, and dragons that all look like they took way too many steroids early in life." Brooke said, trying to do the same match in her mind as Dani was.

Ballene walked over to a beautiful turquoise dragon. It was sleek and built longer, like a whale only with wings and a long slender neck. Its wings were tucked securely under a flap of skin on its back and its massive, clawed feet were webbed. Ballene turned towards Theresa, beckoning her forward. To Dani's surprise Theresa hesitantly walked up to the dragon. The giant dragon slowly lowered its massive head so that Theresa could touch it. Dani could see the shivering of the scales and the slight upturn of the dragon's lips as Theresa tentatively rubbed its snout. Clearly, the dragon was enjoying the attention from her.

While Dani was watching Ballene and Theresa, she had not noticed the other moms moving. Looking around, she saw that Barbar and Wendy were by the enormous saber-toothed tiger. Filtiarn and Amanda were by the enormous dire wolf. Azmer and Mom were at the lion, and Zidicus was helping Aunt Kathy onto the back of Gordy. All the pnēvma synergáti, as Zidicus had called them, looked incredibly pleased by the moms' tentative touching, and petting them. Dani looked back around as all the moms were now seated on the animals with the men closely behind them.

"So what do we get to do, walk?" Brooke said in a frustrated voice.

All the moms turned towards the girls and started to voice their concerns all at once. Some were trying to get off.

"Please calm yourselves. We will take the young ones with us," the guy with the gold helmet said.

"Like heck you will!" Amanda firmly stated, "Jamie comes with me, or we do not go anywhere," Amanda again moved to get off. "Why can't the girls ride with us? Nothing against you guys, but we don't know any of you from Adam and I for one am not willing to put my daughter's life in a complete stranger's hands," Amanda forcibly stated. The other moms quickly agreed. Filtiarn wound his arms around Amanda and lean over to say something that only she could hear. She saw Amanda shake her head no, and then a reluctant yes.

"My apologies to you all for not introducing them sooner," said Zidicus as he gestured to the two dragon riders. "These males are part of the royal palace guard. They will guard the young ones with their very lives," Zidicus said from the back of Gordy.

"Guard them from what?" Theresa asked sharply.

"We will take them straight to the palace, my ladies. No harm will come to them. I swear it," the guard with the gold helmet assured them. His voice sounded strained as he bowed slightly with his fisted hand over his heart.It was clear the men did not feel safe where they now were.

Filtiarn lifted his head from Amanda's ear. Amanda was clearly still not happy by the look of her expression, but she nodded her head again to whatever he said. The stress of the day, that had eased somewhat just a short time ago, was now etched on all the moms' and girls' faces again. None of them liked the idea of being separated.

Watching Zidicus and Aunt Kathy made up Dani's mind for her. Aunt Kathy was leaning into Zidicus. He had his arm wrapped around, supporting her. Aunt Kathy was exhausted and pale. Dani caught Zidicus' eyes, and he gave her a pleading look. With a short nod and a hard look that clearly stated, "You'd better take care of her."

"You will need to clear the area so that the other guards may land," The gold helmet guard said to the group.

Turning Dani started the short walk back up the hillside to the ledge they had tumbled out on. They clearly needed to get moving and that was not going to happen where everyone was currently standing.

Dani called back as she walked, "Come on let's go cowgirl up! First one there gets to pick their dragon ride."

Dani knew a small challenge was all it would take to get Brandi moving.

Brandi looked over to her with wide eyes. It was clear Brandi was not comfortable with the situation. Dani nodded at her, communicating the need that they had to get moving. The others would follow, not wanting to be left behind. Brandi sighed and started up the hill and as Dani predicted the others following.

Looking back down the hill Dani could see the moms looking back and forth between themselves, the girls, animals, and guys. They were clearly not happy about their current situation. The men had their arms securely wrapped around them.

"What could they do? They were in a strange land with even stranger mythical animals, for crying out loud. The men seem honest enough," she thought.

The guard with the gold helmet acted quickly to get the moms moving.

"The young ones are clear for you to take off," he said loudly.

Before any of the moms could so much as utter a sound, the animals were off. Dirt flew from the feet of the ground animals as they bolted for the trees, the men holding the moms tightly around the waists. The two dragons were the last to take off. With one enormous downward thrust of their wings, they were in the air. A blast of wind hit her as the force of their wings downward thrust swept the air past them. Squeals and gasps could be heard from all the moms as they left the clearing. If Dani wasn't mistaken, Theresa was saying a few colorful phrases before she got out of earshot. The speed with which the creatures moved was amazing and in moments they were all out of sight.

The sound of multiple wings beating, getting closer, was unmistakable as eleven more dragons and their riders landed in the meadow halfway up the hillside. There were now thirteen dragons on the meadow that was moments ago filled with the large animals their moms rode away on. Dani and the other girls stood in silent awe, looking below them at the now overflowing meadow filled with dragons.

Dani looked from dragon to dragon when one caught her attention. It was white with a crown of horns around the top of its head. When the fading light hit it just right, a rainbow effect shimmered on his scales. The horns looked much smaller in size than she remembered seeing through the crystal when she and Aunt Kathy were fighting for their lives. The dragon also seemed not as brightly colored, as if it was dimming itself but Dani just knew it was the same dragon.

"Xad!" she thought. Ignoring the other girls' calls, as she walked down the hillside to the gigantic dragon, barely noticing as the rider slid off its back.

Reaching Xad quickly Dani looked up at his enormous head and said, "Thank you, Xad, for the energy that saved my Aunt."

She then reached up touching his beautiful scales just as the dragon lowered its massive head.

Xad was amazing. He looked so regal, and warmth radiated off him. His scales were small around his eyes and nose, then fanned out larger as they went down his neck. Xad put his head down until it almost touched the ground, and she was looking into his kaleidoscope of colors around pupils that slit upwards like a cat's. Reaching out, she gently stroked the scales to the left of his eye.

"I will take this one," called the guard who slid off the dragon. Dani jumped a little and turned towards him. Looking back to Xad, it hit her. This was her ride. She was going to ride on the back of this amazing rainbow dragon.

Chapter 10

Kolob

Standing off to the side of the speaking floor, Kerberos watched the spectacle of the inquiry into his actions, opening the Axis Mundi for Dani and her family to travel through. The Hall of Equality was overflowing with Nephilim. A pompous show was taking place on the main floor. He had yet to be called forth to give his account. The proceedings here meant little to him. He answered to only the Creator of All.

Thinking to himself, *"At least this was a change from the never-ending carousel of "what should we do?" Now it was not about whether the portals to the Axis Mundi should be opened, but what actions the Nephilim would take now that the magic sealing them was weakening."* Kerberos sighed inwardly.

He had things to do and plans to make other than listening to the biased drivel flowing from Loquacious' mouth. Loquacious was a legionnaire of Burkhart and in his inner command circle. Burkhart looked like his head was on a swivel, the way it bobbed up, down and around agreeing with all of Loquacious' accusations.

"Kerberos, please explain to us why you chose to act alone and open a portal, allowing several women to traverse the Axis Mundi from Terra to Eirenic. In doing so you pushed so much energy into the Axis Mundi that it has irreversibly damaged the magic used to seal the portals. The very magic that is the only thing keeping the great evil on Agon. You have now opened all worlds to the Evil One and his followers once again." The voice of Loquacious rang with pageantry and flare. Not waiting for a reply to his questions, Loquacious continued.

"Kerberos, if you could enlighten us as to why you saw fit to act alone and against direct orders from Liege Burkhart," Loquacious waved his arm to the filled seats in the Great Hall.

Kerberos had had enough of the show and stepped into the center of the floor. "First let me make one thing perfectly clear. I have never, nor will I ever, take orders from Liege Burkhart. I answer to the Creator of All. My actions have been and forever will be in direct response to the Creator's will, placed upon me. Secondly, you will address me by my title as Liege. It is the rank given to me by the Creator and you will use it."

His deep, powerful voice floated across the floor. He did not need his voice to be loud to make his point. He could wield it like a blade at any volume. The hall erupted, and he saw Loquacious swallow and take a small step back. He felt the volume of voices from the overflowing seating area hit his ears all at once. A few were easy to pick out. In the seating section that Burkhart's legionnaires sat, one stood and yelled, "Traitor."

Motion to his right caught his attention and he watched as Dionysius placed a hand on Burkhart. Burkhart's face was flushed red and flailing his arms about in frustration.

"You will submit to this inquiry!" Burkhart yelled.

Kerberos flexed his hands, not realizing he had been holding them in tight fists at his side watching the chaotic scene. He knew there would be an inquiry into his actions. Actions he never questioned. He knew in his heart that the Creator of All had been and was continuing to guide him in his plans for the future. Looking back to the seating area he saw a few of his Legionnaires trying to make their way to the one who had shouted traitor.

Making eye contact with Zopyro and then nodding in the direction of his Legionnaires, no other explanation was needed. Zopyro quickly flew over and stopped their forward motion towards Burkhart's males. He had little doubt that his males would have prevailed in the altercation, but calmness was what needed to prevail.

He also knew he had to be careful what he divulged. There were those on every world not to be trusted. Erebos, the Evil One, had devoted, fanatic followers, on all worlds, and it was impossible to know who they were.

He walked a tightrope on how much to divulge about the events that had led up to the portal opening. If he divulged too much, he could put Dani and her friends in danger. He could not give the evil faction any sliver of information they could use against the Creator's plans.

"Liege Kerberos," Dionysius said over the crowd. The other voices died off. "Could you please let us know how the Creator guided you in your actions?"

Kerberos inclined his head with a small smile. *"Always the politician,"* he thought.

"I have long prayed for guidance on an action to take to resolve the issue of the evil that hides on Agon," he stated. "In my meditation and prayers, the Creator showed me what would happen to all worlds if we did nothing. The destruction and deprivation shown was horrific even for my battle-hardened eyes. I could do nothing but watch as unspeakable horrors were committed. All worlds descended into a blackened pit of despair and evil. I was entrusted with the knowledge from the Creator of All that if nothing changes, this was what would come to pass."

Kerberos paused to let what he had said sink in, then continued, "After the vision I prayed for guidance on the actions the Creator of All wished for me to take. He guided me to a group of women on Terra. The Creator continued to show me this same group over time as they planned a trip on Terra to several ancient portal sites. It was in my prayers and meditation over several moons that he guided me to do his bidding. I know that alone, I could not break the seal and open a portal through the Axis Mundi. The Creator of All, through me, opened the portal and let these women go through to Eirenic with his direct blessing. I know not why, nor the purpose for which those women were chosen. As for this inquiry, I ask you," he waved his hands to the Nephilim around him, "has my rank and name been stricken from the Holy Book that is in the Sacred Temple, given to us by the Creator? The Holy Book that is one of the most sacred connections we have to the Creator of All."

"No" shouted from the hall.

"My sacred crystal," Kerberos pulled the glowing stone from his chest and thrust it out. "Glows brightly with the pure sanctified actions I took on the Creator's behalf." He gently laid his sacred crystal back against his chest. "I say, let us be done with this nonsense. I have followed and always will follow the will of the Creator. We need to stop this endless bickering and determine how much longer the magic that seals the portals will hold. Then we need to plan for not only our future, but the futures of Eirenic, Agon and Terra. We need to plan to deal with the inevitable fall of the magic seal. This fall will allow the Evil One and his followers to travel through the Axis Mundi. We need to plan on upholding our sacred duty to the Creator of All and be the guardian Nephilim he entrusted us to be. We need to plan our victory over the Evil One once and for all!"

A battle cry was heard throughout the hall as the Legionnaires in attendance were finally stirred into action. Saying what he needed to say, Kerberos turned and headed for the archway leading out of the great hall. Only a few feet into the hallway, he felt the unsettling presence of another creep across his skin. Careful not to give away his knowledge, his only deviation in movements was to slow the swing of his arms always keeping the pommel of his sword close to his hand.

"Kerberos, look out!" Jodoc's scream sounded from behind him moments before he heard the swish of a blade through the air. Kerberos dodged to the side, pulling his own sword, and faced the assailant.

"So, the evil wasted no time letting itself be known," he taunted.

"I will deal with you next, whore." The assailant's voice was directed at Jodoc, but he did not take his eyes off Kerberos.

"Hmmm, that would imply you will still be living, and I will not." He taunted again, to keep the assassin's attention on him as he moved sideways, mindful to keep himself between the assassin and Jodoc.

The high grating voice of the assassin said, "You think you are above us all. You are an empty shell, and I will return you to nothing. When the portals open, we will be ready."

"Again, you assume too much," he said as he swung his sword through the air. The sounds of clashing metal on metal echoed off the crystal walls. "I will be here and you, evil one, will be dead. May the Creator have mercy on your soul, for I will give you none."

It was not much of a battle. Slicing into the assassin's arm and next his thigh Kerberos crippled the male. The assassin's sword dropped, and he slid down a pillar to the floor. Kerberos kicked the sword across the crystal floor out of the assassin's reach. He would not kill him. No, he needed answers only the assassin could provide. Turning slightly, he looked towards Jodoc to be sure she was unharmed keeping the assassin in his peripheral vision. A multitude of footsteps and beating wings could be heard rushing towards them.

"Thank you for the …" was all Kerberos got out before he heard the whistle of a flying knife that had him dodging to the side. A grunt of pain sounded beside him. He turned to see Zopyro several feet away looking toward the assassin. Turning his head to the assassin he saw Zopyro's short blade embedded in his chest.

"Zopyro! He was in no shape to cause harm," he snapped, quickly leaning over the assassin to check if he still lived. There was a heartbeat, but it was weakening.

"He was about to throw this, my Liege," Zopyro said, kneeling as he grabbed a knife out of the assailant's hand.

Kerberos took the knife held out towards him. He noticed a strange look flash across the assassin's face as he looked beyond him. He turned to see where the assassin was looking and saw Jodoc leaning on a column staring back at the assassin with a cold hard look on her face. Jodoc made brief eye contact with Kerberos before dropping her eyes to the floor. She quickly masked her face into one of relief before speaking.

"Zopyro, thank the Creator of All you saw the knife just in time," Jodoc said as she rushed over to them.

"Jodoc what in the mist are you doing here?" Burkhart yelled from the doorway leading out of the Hall of Equality. "By all that is holy, what has happened here?"

"That male was trying to murder Liege Kerberos." Jodoc said. He watched as Burkhart took Jodoc by the arm and led her to two of his Legionnaires. Looking at the older Liege's stiff posture, he could tell Burkhart was not happy to find his beloved daughter there. Through with the scene before him, Kerberos headed down the hall, pondering the event. *"The Creator of All had blessed all creatures with free will. What they did with that will was up to them. Why some chose to waste their will on following the Evil One is beyond me. What is to come will come. It has begun."*

Chapter 11

Eirenic

Glancing at the guard standing next to her, Dani noticed him staring at her hand as she stroked the dragon's warm scales. She was in awe of the magnificent creature. Looking back to her hand she could not believe she was standing next to a living, breathing dragon, let alone rubbing it. She could hear the slow thudding of its massive heart and feel warmth radiating off him. Xad's presence and rhythmic breathing were soothing to her frayed nerves. She felt a slight pressure on her hand as Xad leaned ever so slightly towards her, responding to her touch. A warming sensation filled her from within that she didn't recognize. Focusing back on Xad, he appeared to be enjoying her attention. So many questions ran rampant in her mind. Where were they, and how had they gotten there? Looking back to the guard watching her she thought she saw a strange look in his eyes. It was kind of hard to tell with the helmet on.

"I am sorry, did I do something wrong?" she asked pulling her hand away from Xad's face.

The guard tilted his head and answered, "Not at all, it is just that he doesn't warm up to most people that quickly. Dragons are ancient intelligent creatures that do not trust so easily," the guard said and then gestured to Xad's front leg, "Shall we? I will show you how to mount."

The guard stepped up onto Xad's cocked elbow. As he did so the dragon lifted it slowly, so the guard was almost level with his back. The guard then gripped two of the spikes protruding from the dragon's neck. Pulling himself up and onto a leather saddle between the spikes at the base of Xad's neck where it met his massive body. Dani looked up trying to get a closer look at the double rows of spikes. They appeared to be closer together side to side with a larger gap front to back.

She stood there looking up at the guard now seated on Xad's back, her heart started racing. The words of their mom's protest rang in her ear, *"You don't know any of these guys."* Her nerves and reluctance must have been showing on her face because the guard reached down at her and she thought smiled.

"Come, I will help pull you up," the guard said reassuringly as he reached farther down for her.

"That is a long way up," Dani thought looking up to where the guard sat.

"Ok, I got this," Dani whispered. "Just like riding a horse, only bigger." She looked up and down trying to judge the size of the dragon. "A very, very large horse," she muttered.

Trying to reason with herself in her mind she said, *"Don't really have much of a choice, not really. Aunt Kathy, Mom, and the other moms are already gone. The only way to them is to ride the dragon. Cowgirl up!"*

Looking over her shoulder she tried to see the other girls. Concern for the small group of people she considered family weighed heavily on her mind. Looking back to the guard's eyes she pleaded, "Swear to me that no one is going to be hurt if we go with you."

The anxiety she was feeling was unmistakable in her slightly shaking voice, the guard quickly answered.

"I swear on my honor that no harm will come to you or your family." The guard placed his hand over his heart with a thump and a slight bow of his head.

She took a deep breath trying to steady her nerves. Turning again, she looked to see how all the other girls were doing. Each was standing next to a dragon and a guard. She could tell by the gesturing of the guards that they were trying to talk the girls up onto the dragons. Turning back to Xad, she walked over to his bent leg and looked a long way up to where her foot would have to be placed.

"How the heck am I going to hike my leg up that high," she mussed to herself.

The guard was at least a foot taller than she was, and there was no way her leg would lift that high.

"Darn long-legged guys," she muttered.

"What was that? I didn't quite hear you," the guard said.

She could tell by the tone in his voice he was chucking behind his helmet, and she gritted her teeth. Her pride got the best of her as she thought, *"I will get up on that dragon if it is the last thing I do."*

"Nothing," she called back. Sighing, she knew she had to figure something out. This was her only ride. *"Think Dani, you have fallen off horses before and there wasn't someone there every time to boost you up."* That was when she thought of her solution spotting it at the edge of the clearing.

Patting Xad's leg, she looked up into his eye that was focused on her. "Would you mind walking closer to that tree, Xad?" She turned her back to the dragon, pointing to the tree so he knew where she wanted to go. "I will just climb the tree and then onto your back. That way we save your leg and I save my diiig…" She squealed in surprise. "What the heck!" she yelled.

Dani felt the firm grip of the dragon's warm lips on the back of her neck as he latched onto the back of her shirt and backpack lifting her into the air. She was lifted and placed into the outstretched arms of the guard. The guard quickly grasped her at the waist as she was lowered and put her feet on the dragon's neck in between the spikes. She could clearly see now that the double ridge of spikes was spaced about three feet apart, front to back, and about a foot apart, side to side. There was plenty of room between the pairs of spikes for a person to sit comfortably.

"Just like riding a horse," she thought, *"except for the spikes. Only problem now, I'm facing the wrong way. No problem, I'm sure everyone has this problem their first time on a dragon,"* she mused to herself.

The guard's chuckle was unmistakable, and she figured he was guessing her disgruntled thoughts.

Pulling herself together she said, "Xad, a little warning next time, if you don't mind," she said over her shoulder. A long hot tongue ran across her cheek.

"Oh, come on, did you just lick me?" she swung around to look at the dragon's face and almost lost her balance. The guard steadied her by grabbing more securely at her waist. Xad swung his head back forward and she could have sworn she felt him vibrate through her feet. It felt like he was laughing. The guard holding her at the waist *was* laughing out loud now.

"I am sorry, little one, but he definitely has taken a liking to you. What is it you call him?" the guard chuckled as he asked.

"Xad. I shortened the name I think is his. I don't know, it just came to me. Am I wrong? Should I be calling him something else?" She asked still shocked by the giant tongue licking her.

"No, Xad is a much shorter version of his name. I am just surprised that you knew it. Lord Xadrayrth, or any other dragon, do not share their names with just anyone," the guard said.

"I don't know that he gave it to me. I think his full name just kind of popped into my head when Aunt Kathy and I were in the crystal mountain getting all that energy pushed towards us. I remember that it was really long and with everything going on, I knew there was no way I would remember it all. I just shortened it, so it was easier for me to remember that way," she said.

She knew she must sound a little crazy, but it was the truth. She had no idea who the voice belonged to that spoke in her mind and didn't want to point that out now. Quickly she turned around and sat facing forward. Xad's massive wings unfolded from his sides, and he started to flap. As they launched swiftly into the air, her stomach bottomed out in her big toes. Gripping the spikes in front of her, she held on for dear life. Once they leveled off, the steady up and down motion of Xad's wings rocked her soothingly and she began to relax a little.

She was surprised that the wind was not as forceful as she thought it would be. It felt like cruising down the road at about 35 miles an hour with the windows down. Still, she was glad her hair was being held back with a tie as she looked around. Behind her, she saw that the rest of the group had also mounted and were in the air following them. Xad was the first to take off and in the lead the others carrying her friends were behind them in pairs, two by two. The dragons without girls were in the back and off to the sides.

Looking more closely to check on her friends and sister Dani smiled when she saw Jamie, the quiet introvert. Jamie had a smile stretching across her face, ear to ear, squealing in delight with her hands up in the air like she was riding a roller coaster. Heather was smiling but did not appear to have any intention of letting go of the spikes in front of her. She could just make out Brandi, as she and her dragon were behind Jamie's. Brandi looked like she was shouting over at Brooke, who was flying next to her, to let go. Brooke was pale and looked slightly green, with a death grip on the spikes in front of her. Apparently riding a dragon was not one of her sister's many talents.

She tried to make sense of what she was seeing as they flew through the cool early evening air. Below them, the vast forest they had been in was starting to thin. She caught glimpses of iridescent glowing plants flash in the darkness as they sped past. She wondered what it would be like to walk around the forest and see it all up close.

Dani's mind started to race, thinking about everything that had happened in the last few hours. Had it been hours or days? She had no clue how long it had taken them to get through the crystal mountain. Where were they? How would they get back home? She shied away from putting an "if" they could get back. It was all too much for her overtaxed emotions at this point.

"What exactly had happened in the crystal mountain? What was the animal that had directed the energy to push her and Aunt Kathy forward?" she asked herself.

None of the spirit partners she had seen so far looked like what she guessed was some kind of large red bird.

Questions kept coming in her mind, *"Who was the deep-voiced man she heard in her head telling them to quickly get through the Axis Mundi? Was that what they went through, some sort of axis? Axis of what exactly? What was the other voice she heard telling her the names of the dragons?"*

She placed her right hand on her throbbing temple, rubbing slightly. Taking a deep breath, she tried to calm her spinning-out-of-control thoughts.

"Just keep breathing, it will all work out," she said to herself.

As she continued her regimented breathing in and out, she looked at the sky in front of her. It had a slight glow that she thought indicated a more populated, well-lit area was ahead. The trees below them gave way to open lush green hills with lines of trees scattered here and there. The ground seemed to slope away as they continued across the sky.

Looking down Dani could tell that some of the land was cultivated by the strait rows going across the fields. She could just make out more large animals moving about in the shimmering halo of lights when the first buildings that came into view. The buildings resembled barns from home. So far, the animals she had seen up close were ten times the size of their counterparts from home. Heaven only knows what animals must be walking around in the barns. Dani's mind clicked back to seeking answers to her endless questions. She decided to start with the dragon she was currently on and how it helped save her and Aunt Kathy when they were in the tunnel.

Dani started with one of the pressing questions she had running through her mind, "Why did you and Xad help us?"

The guard stiffened behind her then said, "It is quicker this way for all and safer to get you to the palace as soon as possible. The other pnêvma synergáti could have managed, but with us here, it is less weight for them to carry," the guard flatly said.

Dani had a feeling he was trying to avoid her real question. She did not know why but she was determined to get a clear answer. She turned and made direct eye contact.

"You know that is not what I was asking," she said.

The guard sighed. "I would ask that you not tell the others what you think you saw."

She snorted a little. "What I think I saw, really, that's your answer?"

The guards' placating voice sounded from behind the helmet, "Please, what was done, was done to get you and Zidicus' Chosen One through the Axis Mundi. Not all make it through, and I could not stand by, and watch Zidicus' mate die in the passageway between worlds. If I may ask, what the flash of red I saw as the energy reached you and Zidicus' mate?" he questioned.

All Dani heard was the word *mate*.

"Mate? What do you mean mate? My aunt, mom, or any of the other moms for that matter, are not mates to anyone. My Aunt lost her husband in an auto accident before I was even born. The other moms are divorced, but wait, is that why you brought us to ..." Dani waved her hands around. This cannot be happening. They were some sort of breeding stock. "You want us to be your mates? Soooo not happening! We are not brood mares. Where is my mom, Aunt Kathy, and the other moms? I want to see them now!" Dani shouted.

She was trying to turn completely around to give him a scathing look, but she couldn't get her leg over the large spikes she was sitting behind. Dani twisted and turned, almost losing her balance. So worked up she had forgotten where, and on what, she was riding.

"Calm yourself, little one," The guard said in a low soft voice, and he placed his hands firmly on her waist again. "To fall from this height would surely kill you." His grip tightened as he spoke the words.

Dani stopped fighting him and looked down at the faint outlines of hillsides below them. She took several shuddering breath thinking, *"Yep that was a no-brainer. No bouncing back from a fall like that."*

The guard started speaking again, "We will be at the palace shortly, but to your questions, WE did not bring you here. The Nephilim, an ancient race chosen by the Creator of All, control the portals in and out of the Axis Mundi. The portals were sealed in the Great War. Or so we thought. Few had come through in many, many years even before that. Yes, the portal brings to the Eirenicians their Chosen Ones, or a Chosen One can be found here. In our history, almost all came from beyond on Terra."

The guard took a deep breath and continued, "Please understand, Chosen Ones are the completions of our souls. There is no one held as precious as one's Chosen One. There will never be another for an Eirenician or Agonian after their Chosen One has been found. It is not this vulgar thing you are thinking of. Chosen Ones, once they find each other, have an instant bond to one another. Their souls know they have found their other half. Your mothers will be cared for by their mates as the most precious thing gifted to them by the Creator, even more so than their very lives," the guard said pleadingly behind her.

Dani sat silently, taking in all he said. Turning her head as far as she could to look at him, she said, "Let me get this straight." She paused; she really needed to wrap her already-taxed mind around the new information. Letting go of the spike in front of her with one hand, she rubbed her aching temple again.

Dani finally said what was running around in her mind, "An ancient race of beings called Nephilim opened a portal into the Axis Mundi that we walked through that brought us to you. My mom, Aunt Kathy and the other moms are the Chosen Ones of the men who were waiting for us when we tumbled out of the crystal mountain. You all have spirit animals that are way beyond anything I could have ever imagined. One such animal is a dragon that I am riding now. Who are taking me and my friends to meet up with our mothers and Aunt Kathy at a palace? What's next? Is a mouse in a tux going to step out and start dancing with his girlfriend?" Dani knew she was losing it and desperately began taking calming breaths again.

The guard sighed behind her. "I do not know what your reference of a mouse has to do with this or what a tux is. I know you have many questions. This must seem unreal and overwhelming to you and your family. I give my word: all your questions will be answered. Let us get to the palace so that it can be explained to all of you at one time."

"Fine," Dani mumbled and turned completely back around as her mind raced a hundred miles an hour again. *Where the heck did he say they were, Eirenic? What was this about portals, Axis Mundi and Nephilim? Chosen One's are mates here not husband and wife? Oh man, my head is going to explode just thinking about all this.*

Dani tried to calm her whirling thoughts, looking down at her hands as they gripped the spikes of the dragon. She almost broke out in hysterical laughter. *Yep, calming your mind is really going to work right now,* she thought.

Taking her eyes off her hands she looked ahead. The sky was lit up more brightly and she knew they must be getting close to the palace, or at least to civilization. One way or another, answers would be provided. She dreaded the realization that her senior year of high school and the others' freshman year of college was not going to be exactly as they had planned.

"Holy cow," Dani exclaimed as they came over a hill to the magnificent viewed of a brightly lit city, stretched out along a bay in the distance. The land continued to gently slope away from them, all the way down to the bay.

Xad started a large circle of descent towards what had to be the palace. It was a huge building several stories tall. It sat at the point where the bay opened on a vast expanse of water. She guessed it was an ocean, due to the salty smell in the air. She could make out the white tops of waves rolling towards the shore. Dani could see large channels of water running into the palace itself at several different locations from the bay as they circled around to the other side. A large field sat between the palace and the tree line as they came around the backside. The large field stretched from the backside of the palace to a gentle sloping hill that rolled up to the trees.

Getting closer, Dani still could not tell what the palace itself was made of, only that it was huge, and multiple stories tall. She could just make out the cream color in the muted light of the many windows lit from within on the bottom floors. The top floors of the palace were mostly dark. Vast balconies jutted out from large, windowed doors on all the floors. On some of those balconies she saw large shadows of animals that seemed to be resting.

Looking over the palace again she thought, *"It really is a monstrous building,"* she started counting floors, *"at least ten stories tall, and that's just the lit windows. It was hard to tell the number of floors that were above that,"* she mused.

The guard behind her slightly increased his grip on her waist as they approached the ground. Dani wasn't nervous about landing, as it was a necessary step closer to answers. She was more anxious about what they would learn once they did land. Dani loved a good mystery, but not one that involved her and the lives of all the others in her group. It was clear they would be landing on the open grassy field behind the palace. That should have been a no-brainer because there was nowhere else that could hold thirteen dragons.

As they now glided closer, she could make out people moving about on the ground. Xad landed softly on the grassy field, and she heard the others landing behind them. She took a big breath to settle herself and started to lean over, trying to figure out the best way to get off.

"Hold on a moment and someone will be here to help you down," the guard said.

Looking down she saw that Xad had crouched down and again placed his front leg as a step, the way the guard had gotten on and off before.

"No worries. I think I can slide down on my own," she said and tried to swing her leg over.

Keeping her hands firmly gripping the spikes she rotated her hips to swing her offside leg over. She was doing great right up to the point her jeans got caught on the darn spike.

"Crap!" she muttered as her leg was jerked back by her jeans. Her hands slipped from the spikes and the rest of her fell over headfirst.

She would have fallen to the ground if it wasn't for the guard grabbing her flailing arms and pulling her back up. He then unhooked her jeans and lowered her onto the dragon's waiting leg. She felt her legs wobble a little and would have fallen on her back side if it had not been for Xad placing his snout at her back to steady her.

"My hero, again," she said. Then slowly turned around and stroked the dragon's nose. She heard the guard jumping to the ground behind her.

"You should not have let her attempt to dismount on her own, guard." An unfamiliar, grating female voice snipped behind her.

Dani turned around to scowl at the face of the condescending woman. Knowing she was tired, hungry and beyond any sort of rational thinking she kept her mouth from saying the words she really wanted to, but just barely. She did not need someone giving the guard a hard time for keeping her from doing a header off Xad.

Sliding off the dragon's leg she faced the annoying woman. Her voice was one of those whiny high-pitched ones. Dani did not know quite what to make of her, but that voice was grating on her last nerve. The woman was dressed to the hilt. She had on flowing fabrics, jewels, and a face that had to have taken her all morning to plaster on. Not to mention the hair.

"Jeez, who wears their hair up like that anymore? It looks like a giant termite mound," she mused to herself.

Looking more closely she noticed the woman's dress was designed to show the tattoos she had. Hers was not filled in like Aunt Kathy, the moms and their guys had been, but still had the same design. The same type of crystal also hung from a very thick gold, ornately carved chain around her neck. The woman was dressed so over-the-top Dani wondered how she managed to walk. Taking a step away from Xad, she placed herself between the guard and the annoying women.

"Thank you for your concern. It was my fault. The guard thankfully kept me from falling on my head," Dani said, trying to draw the women's focus to her and off the guard who had helped her. An awkward silence fell between them.

Turning her back on the women to face the guard who was standing beside Xad's front leg Dani spoke to the guard, "you said something about my mom, aunt and the rest being here. I would love to see them now and thank you for saving me, again, from falling on my face." She could have sworn the guy was holding in a laugh as the woman behind her started sputtering.

"I believe Lady Eulalios will be taking you to them," the guard leaned over slightly as if to bow and she saw a sparkle of a gold necklace peek out from his rounded collar.

"So that's the annoying ladies name," she thought.

"If we are through being rude," Lady Eulalios quipped, "follow me."

Dani rolled her eyes and thought, *"This lady clearly did not wake up on the right side of the bed. Kill them with kindness, Aunt Kathy always said."*

"How very kind of you to offer your assistance," Dani turned and beamed a fake smile at the woman.

Lady Eulalios stared at her, with her mouth opening and closing like a fish. Dani had tried to keep the sarcasm out of her voice. She wasn't sure she had succeeded. Hearing footsteps approaching, she looked over and saw that the other girls were heading their way. Looking from face to face they all looked tired, and were clearly holding on by a thread, as she was. They all really wanted to see their moms and Aunt Kathy. The other girls walked up and stood next to her, so they presented a united front to the annoying woman.

"If you would be so kind," Dani gestured to Lady Eulalios again.

"Follow me," Lady Eulalios snottily said.

Lady Eulalios turned, not looking back to see if they followed, and continued talking. The girls looked at one another, shrugged, and followed.

"A great feast has been arranged for you. It was no small feat to get it all coordinated. The other mates with their escorts showed up all at once. Really, who would have thought the nation's rulers would have all shown up, with not one of them letting us know they were coming. You are all honored guests of the beloved Regent Ruler Democritus. He is as wise as he is fair to his people. You should feel honored; not every *mate* that comes through the portal is given this honor. But then again, you all do not have *mates*, do you? So maybe it would be wiser to show more respect for the one who sleeps next to the Regent Ruler and who will help decide your fates." Lady Eulalios finally paused in her ramblings, turned, and looked down her nose at her.

"I decide my own fate. You can keep your favors. Thanks, but no thanks," Brandi chimed in.

Not taking her eyes off Dani she said, "We shall see, we shall see. Come along." Lady Eulalios turned back around and walked towards a huge set of double doors.

The men stationed on either side opened them as she got close, bowing to her. Dani made the decision there was no way she was going to let this woman make any decisions for her life or anyone in her group. Looking to the girls around her, she saw the same determined look on their faces. As one they walked together and stepped through the doors.

"Where are we going?" Brooke whispered to Dani.

"To find our moms and Aunt Kathy and apparently eat a grand feast," Dani replied dryly.

"Food will be nice, but I want answers, too," Heather said.

Lady Eulalios called back to them. "Please do try and keep up. I do not have all night."

Chapter 12

Kolob

Standing at a sacred pool by the Hall of Equality, Kerberos watched as Dani and the others interacted with the Eirenicians. He knew that the Creator of All had a plan that he was not privy to. He had to trust that all would be reviled in time.

Pondering to himself he said, *"Why has the Creator place the unmatched females on Eirenic? Clearly Dani and the others are going to play a key role in the battles that are coming. They are all so young and inexperienced. What could they, or more importantly, Dani, possibly contribute to defeating the evil plaguing all their worlds and bringing balance to those worlds? Dani had courage and inner strength that I admire greatly, but she is not a trained warrior. Even with the incredible strength of her pnēvma synergáti to help her, she would not fare well in physical combat."*

He would keep a close eye on the group, looking for any clues or signs of what the Creators plan might be. He was beginning to mentally formulate ways to prepare the young ones when his thoughts were interrupted.

"Watching again, I see," Dionysius said from the threshold to the room. "I have never before noticed you being blessed with so much time to watch. I wonder…what has changed? Why does the Creator show you this group of females? I wonder if you are truly sharing with us all the times you have been granted this blessing." Dionysius walked over to Kerberos, stopping beside him. He tapped his chin, looking contemplative. "Blessed often enough that it could set off Burkhart again and risk possible contempt of some fellow Nephilim." Dionysius did not wait for replies in his ramblings. He gazed into the sacred pool and continued speaking.

"They are fair, to be sure, all unique. Their mates will one day have their hands full," Dionysius said laughingly. "The older ones you spoke of? They will fit into the Eirenic society more easily than the unclaimed daughters. It must feel like a windfall for the Eirenicians to have so many females come through at once and only five have Chosen Ones waiting. It is unprecedented to have unchosen females come through. I cannot imagine the chaos this will bring to their Regent Ruler. Born second, he was never meant to rule in the first place. This should be stimulating to watch. I think I will join you." Dionysius leaned over placing his hand on the side wall of the viewing pool.

"I was just leaving, Dionysius," Kerberos said.

For some reason he felt the need to steer Dionysius' interest away from the group and from Dani in particular.

"The task given to me was to bring them through, that is all. To start to bring hope, life, and balance back to our worlds and finally have an end to this stagnant existence we created for all. I do not question the wisdom of the Creator of All that he continues to bless me with these viewings." Kerberos said waving his hand over the pool and the images of the females walking into the palace faded away.

Having Dionysius observing Dani and the other females had brought about a foreboding feeling in the pit of his stomach. Dionysius was cunning and wise to question the number of times he had been blessed with his connections to Dani. Some Nephilim prayed in front of sacred pools for hours and were not given access at all to view other worlds. Others received only fleeting glimpses of the worlds beyond. The sealing had brought to a halt their interactions and abilities to influence the human races. His interactions with Dani are the only exception he knew of. His connection to these females and specifically Dani was still clearly in the Creator's plans. He did not question the Creator's will, but his mind could not stop whirling with the unknown possibilities and outcomes that lay before them all.

"As you say. I need to attend to what Burkhart has been stirring up again." gesturing to the arched doorway. "Shall we?" he turned and started forward, wanting to focus Dionysius' thoughts on something else.

"Some results have come back from the evaluations of the magic securing the portals. Burkhart has called a meeting in the Hall of Equality," Dionysius stated, following him to the door. Nodding at the two guards standing at attention just outside the sacred pool room they walked into the hallway. One guard would stay and guard the room. The other would follow him.

Dionysius continued, "The magic sealing the portals has been damaged. As far as we can tell, it is irreparable. In fact, the last analysis reveals that the magic is slowly weakening. We cannot seal the portals again just from Kolob. It was only successful the first time only because so many had collaborated in the effort. Beings from all four worlds had joined forces in the sealing of them."

Kerberos already knew the information Dionysius was telling him, so he interrupted, "Yes, some had willingly sacrificed their ability to return to their home worlds in order to seal the portals on other worlds. On Terra a select number of Eirenicians and Agonians had made such a sacrifice. They had been battling the Evil One's followers through several different time periods on Terra. They chose to stay behind to not only seal the portals around Terra but to eliminate the Evil One's followers who would be trapped there. As you know, I did not agree with the decision to seal the portals. It was a decision made in haste after a series of fierce battles. A reactive decision not thought through by the ones who made it," he said. "I should have argued more firmly that a different solution be found. Burkhart had been the strongest advocate of sealing the portals."

Dionysius cut in, "He had just lost his Chosen One. Having already lost both sons, he was not thinking rationally. I cannot condemn him; it had been a desperate time in the Great War. We had lost some advantage to the Evil One and his followers. With the Evil One's possession of the Light of Amun Crystal, things had taken a downward turn. In desperation, the plan was carried out."

Kerberos felt a pang of sympathy for Burkhart's loss but was glad that Dionysius had brought up the issue of the Light of Amun Crystal.

"Yes, he lost much, as did so many others. You mentioned the Evil One's use of the Light of Amun Crystal. What has been discovered about how the

Evil One got it out of one of the most secure places on our world? The vault under the great library is controlled and guarded by your Legionnaires, is it not?" Kerberos questioned.

Dionysius sputtered, "You know this. How does the Evil One do anything? Through his followers as he always has. You cannot say that you have no followers of the Evil One in your ranks."

Kerberos countered, "I have taken precautions so that there are checks and balances for each guard position my Legionnaires have. I do not believe you can say the same. Did we not just leave only one of your Legionnaires on duty guarding the sacred pool we just left?"

Clearly frustrated with the turn of the conversation, Dionysus said, "With the sealing of the sacred pools, there is no need for more than one guard. Some even question the need for that. You are the only one so far who is granted access to another world. Are you saying we should double your guard?" Dionysius gestured to the guard now following them, "Should we be questioning your intentions?"

Unphased, Kerberos answered the absurd questions, "Zopyro feels a guard is necessary after the Evil One's assassination attempt on my life. Those still loyal to Erebos will still make the choices to do the Evil One's bidding. He clearly still has far-reaching influences. We need to plan for the future that lies before us. We need to focus on the possible outcomes," he said and then added in his mind, *"I need most of all to plan and prepare Dani and the others. The magic sealing the portals is slowly fading and eventually the Evil One will be loose again."*

"Is there any additional information on the Evil One's assassin?" Kerberos asked. He had been doing his own digging but wanted to find out if Dionysius would divulge anything new.

Dionysius answered as they continued walking down the hall. "Only that he was a lower legionnaire of Burkhart's. Burkhart was still questioning the people who knew him. I am sure he will provide us with additional information at this meeting. I wonder if it is a coincidence that all this is happening only now, after you were the one chosen to guide the females through the Axis Mundi."

"I do not believe in coincidences," Kerberos stated.

"Indeed, neither do I," Dionysius answered.

Kerberos thought of Dani and wondered again how she fit into the Creator's plan. He hoped and prayed that she could remain a pure light that she did not even realize shone brightly from her soul. He also prayed the evil that surrounded them all did not take notice. He would do everything in his power to shield and guide her away from the evil that was rising again. A thought of a passage from the Terra holy book entered his mind that he had heard Dani say, *"Do no gloat over me, my enemy! Though I have fallen, I will rise. Though I sit in darkness, the Lord will be my light."* He prayed the darkness remained ignorant of the light that shone through Dani.

Chapter 13

Eirenic

Dani heard the gasps from the others as they followed Lady Eulalios through the massive corridors of the palace. She was feeling so many things all at once: apprehension, awe, and fear seemed to want to fight for dominance in her. She tried to appreciate the opulent splendor of the palace and not dwell on what the future might hold for them all. She knew she would feel some relief once they got back with Aunt Kathy and the moms.

"The walls have to be at least two stories high, and look at the arched ceilings," Heather whispered. "The tapestries are beautiful."

"Look at all the massive paintings," Jamie said.

Dani tried to take it all in as the girls around her pointed out the different people and all sorts of large animal in the paintings and woven into the tapestries.

"Some of these resemble the religious paintings from old churches in Europe," Brandi said. "Mom and I took a trip there a few years ago."

Dani looked up to the pictures Brandi was pointing out. One painting had the same winged men and women in gladiator or Roman style clothing as those in the ceiling frescos. It dawned on her that they appeared to be the same people depicted on the top row of raised markings on the well inside the crystal mountain. In these paintings, a crystal glowed around each person's neck.

"Young ladies, please keep up. We have important people waiting on us," Lady Eulalios said snidely, quickly walking ahead of them.

"Patience is a virtue," Heather whispered.

"I don't think she was blessed with that virtue," Brandi smirked back to Heather.

Dani had not realized she and the other girls had slowed down to take it all in. They all quickened their pace to catch up with the very impatient, annoying woman. There was still so much to see. Dani did not want to miss any of it, not knowing what would happen when they caught up with the adults.

One pair of large paintings caught her attention. One had a breathtakingly beautiful scene of a misty, lush green world with a crystal temple shining above it all. The other large painting, had an imposing looking winged man holding a sword. He had a gold-trimmed red cape that seemed to be blowing in a breeze strapped to one shoulder. Even from her great distance, she could see he had a commanding presence. A slight tug on her arm from Jamie had her following Lady Eulalios once again. Lady Eulalios had continued making irritated sighs that they all heard echoing down the enormous hallway. Anyone they passed would stop and move to the sides of the halls, staring at them.

The girls continued down the hall, trailing the now fast-moving Lady Eulalios.

"Really, you would think that one's so young could move faster. Children these days! No sense of value for those older and wiser than them and their constraints on time," Lady Eulalios exclaimed back to the girls from some distance ahead of them.

Ignoring her snide comment, Dani looked more closely at the intricately carved pillars evenly spaced down the hallway. She got the feeling this was an ancient palace. A timeless palace that looked like it had stood the test of time for centuries if not longer. Lady Eulalios continued walking farther ahead of them, loudly sighing irritably. It started to grate on her nerves even more. Looking to the others, she could tell they were all feeling the same way. So, they did what any reasonable teenager would do. They stopped completely as they passed over a large bridge that spanned a water channel. She remembered seeing channels coming in from the bay, during her flight earlier. They all leaned over the sides, staring down like a bunch of tourists looking with amazement at what was below.

"Holy Crap, are those men riding on the backs of giant killer whales?" Brandi pointed in her excitement.

"What the heck is that Dragon doing in the water with them?" Jamie gasped.

"All will be explained to you, if you would just follow me," Lady Eulalios said with an air of impatience some distance away. She turned and walked off down another hallway, calling over to one of the guards that had flown with them. "Be sure they make haste. The Regent Ruler does not like to be kept waiting and neither do I." Eulalios continued down the large hallway out of sight.

Dani figured she must have gone ahead to the banquet without them. She hadn't realized the guards from the mountain had been following them. The guard who offered help in getting them to the palace sighed, "My Ladies, if you would continue on, we can take a tour after introductions. Maybe a hot meal and a chance to rest first would be a benefit?"

Looking over to him, she saw that his uniform had a golden braid over one shoulder that she had not noticed before.

"Do you promise?" Dani asked.

The brief overwhelming grandeur of the palace they were walking in was subsiding some. Dani really did want to get to Aunt Kathy and the moms. But she also wanted to be sure that they would get to come back and walk around to see it all in not such a rushed state.

The other girls chimed in with approval at Dani's question. It was hard to imagine the guards' faces or tell any of their ages behind the helmets. The guard who had spoken seemed to have kind eyes and a strong jawline. Like all the other men they had met so far, he was tall and muscular. His uniform did not cover his arms or legs. Funny, that seemed to be a theme here and in all the paintings and carvings. She wondered if she would ever get to see the winged men and women who appeared in so many of the paintings, especially if the one with the red and gold trimmed cape was still alive.

As if sensing her study of him, the guard took off his helmet and smiled.

He was maybe a little older than they were, but not by much. His hair was shaved close to his head on the sides but was longer on top. It was held in what looked to be a braid. She could not be sure because he was so darn tall and facing her. She looked at the other guards who had fanned out around them. Her unspoken request was clear. She wanted to see them without their helmets as well. The guard that had ridden with her looked around the corridor, as if to check for people watching them. As if satisfied they were not being watched, he nodded for the other to take their helmets off.

The guard Dani had flown to the palace with had piercing blue eyes and dark long hair. It was shaved at the sides but clearly went down his back in a long braid. The braid must have been tucked inside the helmet in some way because she had not noticed it before. But really, she had seen only the front of all of them so far.

"Oh my, do they have any ugly guys here?" Dani thought looking from guard to guard.

They were all striking in their own way. Footsteps could be heard approaching from the hall Lady Eulalios had headed down. The guards quickly put their helmets back on. Dani was a little disappointed. With their helmets off she felt more at ease. With them on, it was a blatant reminder that she was not touring an ancient site from home.

Looking to see who was approaching them, Dani saw Zidicus, the man who had met Aunt Kathy and her at the entrance of – what had it been called? The Axis Mundi walked over saying, "Perhaps a tour could wait until after they are reunited with their mothers?" Zidicus said.

He stood in between the lead guard and the one that had ridden with her. "The aforementioned Mothers are most eager to see their daughters and are quite vocal about seeing them quickly. Shall we?" Zidicus gestured down the hall he had just come down.

They did not dawdle this time, quickly walking down the large hallway. As they got farther down the hall the sounds of raised voices grew louder. Glancing around, Dani saw the opulence factor had increased a ton. Gilded embellishments were everywhere on the walls and paintings. The over-the-top gold kept increasing the farther down the hall they went. At this point,

Dani thought the decor was way over the top. She chastised herself for being so judgmental. Who was she to judge how these people lived?

Finally, they stopped when they reached a set of large ornately gilded doors. The muffled sounds of shouting could be heard through them. They waited for the guards posted outside the doors, who were polished and shining in their armor, to open them. Dani could hear her mom, Aunt Kathy, and the other moms' strained voices shout back at someone through the door. It sounded like chaos on the other side, and she glanced to the other girls who all had the same expression.

"I really want to see my mom but also do not want to go in there," Jamie whispered.

As if sensing that the girls were going to bolt, the guards quickly opened the doors, ushering them and Zidicus in. Dani figured they had probably been waiting for a sign from within telling them it was okay to open the doors, but decided to forgo that and just got them in. The sound of raised voices blasted them like a shock wave as soon as the doors fully opened. She could have sworn that they all took a step backwards.

The girls had made it just inside when the doors were closed firmly behind them. Amanda was the first to turn and see them yelling, "They are here!" Standing so fast she knocked over her chair and took off running towards Jamie with outstretched arms.

Dani watched as Jamie flinch when her mom grabbed her in what must have been a bear of a hug. She braced herself as the other moms rushed to them and grabbed anyone and everyone in succession. She was relieved to see them all in one piece. Even if she thought their reactions were a little over the top. She wondered if it had something to do with whatever they were fighting about before they came in.

"We thought maybe your guards got lost on the way here. What took you so long?" her mom asked.

"I told you they would be here shortly. Even dragons take time to fly," Azmer said in a placating voice.

"We were kind of gawking at all the decorations once we got inside. It slowed us down a bit," Dani replied.

As the moms calmed down, Dani turned to look around the room. The largest rectangular table she had ever seen sat before her. The black polished table had to seat at least fifty people. On the opposite side of the table from where she stood, was Lady Eulalios talking with an older, ornately dressed man. He was wearing a dark cape that was fastened by an expensive looking gold and jewel encrusted chain. There were several other people around the table that she did not know. The men who had met them as they exited the tunnel stood with the moms.

"Ladies, if you would please retake your seats by your... by the males you came here with, and your daughters can fill in the spots around you." The ornately dressed man gestured from his seat to the table.

Following the moms back around the side of the table, Dani arrived at the only open seat beside her mom. She stepped to the side and gestured for Brooke to take it. She had noticed during the hugging fest the dark circles under Aunt Kathy's eyes and wanted to check up on her. So, she sat with Aunt Kathy on her right and Brooke on her left side.

Once everyone was seated the older man continued to speak, "Before we get back to our previous discussion, I would like to welcome your daughters to Eirenic. I am Democritus, the Regent Ruler. It is with great pleasure that we welcome you to our homes. The males seated around this table that you do not know are the rulers of the nations on Eirenic." He gestured towards the end of the table opposite end from where they all sat. "Now, before we get on with all the questions you must have, we shall have a fine meal." He rang a small silver bell located on his carved chair's armrest.

Panels on the walls slid open and men dressed in cream-colored tops and dark blue pants came in, their arms laden with overflowing plates of food. Dani assumed that they were platters to be placed in the center of the tables, but she was wrong. Each person received their own overflowing plate. She had not realized how hungry she was until the rich aroma of the food hit her. Her stomach growled loudly, and she started to reach for her fork. Aunt Kathy reached over and squeezed her elbow.

"What the heck?" she thought and looked over at her.

Aunt Kathy shook her head ever so slightly, keeping her eyes directed down the table. Her hand had not made it above the tabletop, so she reluctantly dropped it back into her lap. She turned her head and followed Aunt Kathy's gaze to the Regent Ruler.

Democritus and Lady Eulalios looked up and down the table as if checking to be sure everyone had received their food. Clearly, they knew that each person had their own waiter stationed behind them and everyone had gotten their food at the same time, so what was the big deal? Then it hit her, this was all about control. Democritus took a bite of his food and then Lady Eulalios followed.

"Please, enjoy your meals," Democritus said. Dani guessed that was the cue that everyone else was now allowed to eat.

Rolling her eyes, Dani looked across the table, making eye contact with Heather. Heather rolled her eyes as if in agreement, and then looked down at her heaping plate. Dani looked at hers, trying to decide what to try first, but gave up and just dove in. The murmur of small quiet conversations started up around her. She was too hungry to try and listen in. Most of the food on her plate tasted like things from home, but just looked different. What she guessed went for potatoes were a purple color. The red meat served was tender and delicious and had the slightest hint of a gamey taste. She guessed maybe some kind of deer.

What felt like moments later the plate that Dani thought was way too loaded down with food, now sat three quarters of the way empty. Looking up from her plate and around their small traveling group, she noticed the girls trying to question their moms. Thinking this was a great idea she tried as well with Aunt Kathy.

"Aunt Kathy, do you know what is going on?" Dani whispered.

The voice she heard came from down the table and was not her aunt's but that of Democritus, the Regent Ruler. Sighing inwardly, anxiously rubbing her now stuffed stomach Dani thought, *Now we get answers."*

"Young Ladies, with the indulgence of our other guests," the Regent Ruler grandly gestured around, "I will repeat the information I have spoken of already with your mothers." His head tilted towards the mothers.

"Really dude, just get on with it already," Dani thought.

"A Portal was opened on Terra, or Earth as you call it, and you traveled through the Axis Mundi to Eirenic, our world. I did not open this Portal nor did any other Eirenician. The portals are controlled by a race called the Nephilim who live on Kolob, the mist world. There is one other world connected to us that we do not normally speak of since the Great War. It is called Agon. Agon is where a great evil has been trapped. The gateway you came to us through has been sealed once again by the Nephilim. We have no control of the opening, so do not ask us to send you back to Terra. It is out of our hands," Democritus paused slightly.

Dani was about to raise her hand, like she was in school, when her aunt reached over and placed her hand on her arm again, holding it down. She got the message even if it irritated her: do not interrupt the Regent Ruler.

"The Portals leading through the Axis Mundi were sealed many years ago. We used to travel somewhat freely between our worlds, with the blessing of the Creator who guides all of us. I will not go into a long-drawn-out discussion or debate as to what led to the sealing. It was necessary at the time. Most of the people traveling between worlds were connecting with their Chosen One, the one who completes them. A significant number of females from Terra are Chosen Ones for Eirenicians as you can see." He gestured to the moms sitting beside the men who met them at the exit point.

Dani leaned over looking at her mom, then aunt, eyes wide.

"Holy cow, what the guard said was true then? What the Heck, you just come through and poof, you have a "Chosen One"? That is just bogus," she thought.

"Before you get worked up, ladies, your mothers and Chosen Ones will show their décolletage scribes," The Regent Ruler said and paused, looking at their moms and Aunt Kathy.

She looked at her aunt, searching her face. *"Why did she need to look at the base of everyone's neck? Did it have to do with the tattoo-looking thing?"*

As if reading her thoughts Aunt Kathy pulled open the top of her button-up blouse. She could hear the gasps from the girls around her.

"What the Heck?" sounded from Brandi across the table.

She had seen the tattoos on the guys and the one on Aunt Kathy at the crystal mountain. So, they did not surprise her. She was very curious to see them closer and get an explanation to their meaning. It must be significant because everyone she had seen on Eirenic had one. Just like the crystals that hung around their necks.

Looking more closely, she could see what looked like iridescent oil had been penned on her aunt's skin. It reminded her of a three-dimensional drawing. Studying it she would have sworn if she reached out and touched her aunt's skin the image would move and revolve around. The intricate design took her a moment to figure out. Her eyes flew wide when she put it together. It was designed to look like the three-dimensional map above the well in the Axis Mundi.

There was one circle on the left side of her aunt's tattoo that was shaded darker. Inside this circle a swirl of light blue, turquoise and green could be seen. Zidicus leaned and placed his hand on Aunt Kathy's arm. Aunt Kathy leaned back so that she could see him. Zidicus held his vest open wider and the exact same tattoo was on him. More noticeable, he pointed to the circle on his left side.

"It is colored exactly like Aunt Kathy's, swirls of colors and all!" Dani thought.

Her mouth dropped open. Dani had not noticed at the crystal mountain that the colored-in areas were matching. She had a sudden, startling thought and quickly reached up opening her shirt, looking down. Why it shocked her that she had the same tattoo, she did not know, but it did.

"What the Heck?" she thought.

There it was the same outline that all the others had. One difference stood out: hers did not have any circles colored in. Thinking back, she recalled that Lady Eulalios' was not colored in either. Confused, rubbing her hand over her tattoo, Dani looked to Aunt Kathy for clarification.

"We are told that yours will not fill in until you have met your Chosen One," Aunt Kathy said gently.

"Oh, heck no, I am not being told who I am going to be with, chosen or not!" Brandi screeched from somewhere down the table. "This is bull crap! You cannot do this to us. We want to go home. Take me back to the portal thing, now!" Brandi ranted.

"Dear, lower your voice and observe, yours is not colored in. You have nothing to worry about, *yet*," Lady Eulalios coldly chided.

Dani reaffirmed her strong dislike for the woman at that moment. She looked down the huge table and noticed that there were very few women other than her group. All the men had open-fronted shirts, and only the ones sitting next to the few other women had a colored-in circle. All the colored-in circles matched with a person sitting next to them.

"When you meet your Chosen One, you both get colored in the same way? By who," Dani puzzled. Her thoughts were cut short by Brooke's question to the witchy Lady Eulalios.

"Yours is not colored in, why not?" Brooke snapped towards Lady Eulalios.

Lady Eulalios gasped audibly and placed her hand over her tattoo.

"That is none of your business, insolent brat! How dare you come to my home and …" Democritus' voice cut short what was sure to be an interesting string of insults from Lady Eulalios.

"I see you are tired. Shall we adjourn for the evening?" Democritus cut her off.

Looking over to Aunt Kathy Dani still had questions she wanted answers to, "I still have tons of questions. Why can't we get a hold of these Nephilim guys and get back home? What does all this mean for us? What does it mean for you, Mom and the others? Can we really not get home?" she paused when a man from the nation-ruler side of the table spoke. She turned to see who it was.

"Where will the young ones be staying?" a man dressed in tight plastic-looking clothes, like Ballene, questioned.

"Orcnians, I know you are set on returning to Atlantis tonight. But we simply cannot divide the young ones up right now," Democritus said.

Then all heck broke loose. The moms and, in turn, their Chosen Ones were up, all talking at once. Dani looked across the table to the other girls. She was done with this scene and looking for a way out. The adults could fight all they wanted. She was not going to be divided from anyone. She still had so many unanswered questions. Right now, she needed a quiet place to wrap her head around all the crazy information. Dani made eye contact with the other girls across the table. They all nodded slightly and started slowly moving out of their chairs and towards the door. Dani had just stood when Aunt Kathy reached out and grabbed her hand.

"Where are you all going?" Aunt Kathy questioned.

"Just out to catch our breaths. This is all a bit much right now," Dani answered.

Aunt Kathy gave her a comforting squeeze then said. "Please do not go far."

Nodding her head yes, she and Brooke walked to meet the other girls at the large double doors they had come in.

"I am so out of here," Dani muttered.

"I hear that," Brandi replied.

There is nothing like the feeling of everyone talking about you and not to you. Dani knew her mom, Aunt Kathy and the other moms loved them and would do all they could to keep them together. That was fine for now. After everything that had happened, she would have a strong opinion on where and when she went anywhere. Looking at the determined looks on the other girls, she knew they were all thinking the same thing.

All the adults were still shouting behind them when the girls opened the double doors and started walking out. The guards who had flown them there were still waiting outside the doors, along with the two guards stationed there. Brooke, the last girl to make it out, tried to shut the door quietly when it was blocked by a hand. She inhaled sharply, wondering who it might be and if they would try and stop them.

Zidicus' head pushed through the parted doors. "Perhaps this would be a marvelous time for that tour," he said to the guard with the gold braid and the one she had flown with. When they both nodded, he ducked his head back into the chaos of the room and closed the doors.

Chapter 14

Eirenic

Dani's mind whirled around like a Tilt-A-Whirl at the fair. The nations' rulers wanted to split her and her friends up. There was no way for them to get back home. No one was speaking. Dani was certain the others were on the same crazy ride she was. The walls that had taken her breath away earlier now passed by without her even noticing them. She felt depressed and numb, staring down at the carpet as she walked across it. Only looking up when the guards in front of her stopped. They stood at the foot of a set of stairs wide enough to accommodate a couple of trucks driving side by side.

"Jeez, did they do anything small here?" Dani glumly thought.

She had no way of knowing where they were going and, at the moment, she really didn't care. She just blindly followed the head guard up the stairs. Her mind was running in too many directions all at once to even try to focus on any one thing. As they approached another floor, she noticed the guard she flew with lean forward and speak to the head guard. At the top of the stairs, they turned and walked a short distance down the hall. The guard she flew with and the one with the gold braid stopped at a set of double doors and pulled them open for the girls.

The girls walked out onto a small balcony. It was not one of the massive ones Dani had seen from the air. She was grateful this one seemed private and secluded. Chairs were scattered in groups and the girls, not even needing to speak to each other, each grabbed one and pulled them together before flopping down. They sat in silence for several minutes. The guards had stepped back, their backs against the wall. She guessed it was an attempt to give them privacy.

"Oh, holy cow Toto, we are not in Kansas anymore," Heather said.

"You can say that again, Dorothy," Brooke replied.

"Do you all have *"the tattoo"*? Brandi asked, pointing at the tattoo on her chest.

Everyone pulled open or down the collars of their shirts, showing their new tattoos to everyone else.

"Well, Crap," Brandi breathed out.

"At least it is classy and didn't hurt to get it," Jamie quietly said.

"True, I always planned on getting one, but darn. It turns colors when we meet our *Chosen One*, what's up with that BS?" Brandi questioned.

They sat in silence for a few minutes, each poking and rubbing at their tattoos. Unable to sit any longer Dani stood and walked over to the railing, looking out. She could see and hear the waves crashing in the distance. The city was off to her left. It must be late, because most of the glowing lights she had seen before were now dark.

"At least we get a choice, maybe. Our moms didn't even get that," Brooke lamented.

"Come on, did you see those guys? They are *all* easy on the eyes, even the old ones," Heather said.

"True, I don't think they do *ugly* here," Brandi said.

"That doesn't mean they are nice people," Jamie quietly added.

"I still have so many freaking questions," Brooke said.

Looking back towards the group huddled together on the chairs Dani knew each was barely holding on like she was. Shifting her eyes, she looked at the guards. They stood quietly but still close enough to hear the conversation. Not saying a word, not defending or clarifying anything, just letting them process and vent. She wondered if this had happened so many times in the past that they had a system worked out for new arrivals. Or maybe they were just as lost about what to do as they were.

"I have been told that to be a Chosen One means you are cherished and loved above all else," Dani called out.

"Who told you that?" Brooke asked.

She looked over to her sister and answered, "The guard I flew with. Did any of you get any information on your flight over here?"

"No, I was too busy holding on for dear life and not throwing up," Brooke replied with a groan.

Jamie spoked next, "Despite everything that was happening, I was having the ride of my life. That was so cool, can we do it again?" Jamie looked towards the guard that must have flown with her. His smile was easy to see below his helmet. He gave a nod yes.

"Sweet!" Jamie replied. "If I am stuck here, at least I get to fly on dragons."

That sobered them all up. A depressing silence settled around them.

A very depressing thought hit her, *"Are we really stuck here now?"*

Not willing to dwell on that thought now Dani called over to the guards, "So, what is going to happen to us now? Thanks for the privacy, but you all can hear everything we are saying anyway. You might as well come on over. At least then we can get some answers to *our* questions."

The head guard and the one that had flown with Dani looked at each other and then walked over. The others just moved in tighter on their formation, but still hung back.

"For the ease of conversation, I would like to properly introduce myself," the head guard said and removed his helmet. The others followed. "I am Fraener. This is Herodion," he pointed to the guard next to him that flew with her. He then continued with the other guards, pointing each one out, "Ladon, Nidhug, Ormr, Pachua, Tatsuo, Veles, Longwei, Apep, Askook, Lodecus, and Ryuu." Fraener looked back to the girls.

Each girl took turns trying to pronounce the guards' names. It helped cut some of the tension in the group because some of their names were very hard to pronounce.

"Wow, your names are like going to an all-Latin mass and trying to say prayers," Jamie muttered. "Sorry, I know I am butchering them."

"You are doing fine. We appreciate your efforts. As to your question, what is to happen to you now? I cannot say for sure. What would you be doing at home?" Fraener questioned softly.

"Well, the four of us were heading off to college and Dani was starting her senior year in high school. Guess that isn't going to happen now," Brooke said with a sad grumble.

"Can we really not get home?" Jamie asked before he could speak again.

"The opening and closing of the Axis Mundi Portals are in the Nephilim hands. We have no way to open them. I am sorry," Herodion answered.

"So, get us in touch with the Nephilim," Dani said.

Herodion looked to Fraener. "There was a time when I would have gladly done so. After the sealing of the portals, no contact has been made from the other worlds. Before you ask, yes, we have tried, hundreds of times. That is, until you all came through," Herodion said.

"Well, this just sucks," Brandi burst out.

They sat quietly for a few moments. Dani felt her mind spinning through random things. Much like the conversation they were having. One minute happy to fly on dragons the next not knowing their future.

Dani sat thinking, *"If what Herodion said was true, none of them would ever see anyone from home again. I will never see Dad again."* her heart was breaking. *"Sure, we have our issues, but to never see him again?"*

Tears started forming in her eyes and as she looked around the group the others were either already crying or trying hard not to.

"I am sorry," Herodion finally said. She saw him look to Fraener with a panicked look. She guessed it was universal, guys really do not know what to do when girls cry.

"What is college?" Fraener blurted out. The slight color rise in his cheeks, gave away that he was grasping at anything to stop their crying, poor guy.

"It is where you go to continue your education after high school. You probably don't know about our education system," Brooke said, looking over to Dani for help. Dani had always been the go-to for the group to add clarification or to be a sounding board.

"We get a formal education from five years of age until eighteen-ish. Depending on your age when you start," Dani said. "You can then choose to go on to higher education after you graduate high school or twelfth grade. Some people don't, and just get jobs."

"Ah, so it would be like our School of Knowledge," Fraener said.

"Do you move away from home to attend the School of Knowledge?" Brandi asked.

"Yes, when it was in session, you stayed there in the domiciles," Fraener said.

"That is great, maybe in time, when we figure all this crap out, we can go there?" Brooke chimed in.

Dani could tell they were all looking for some way to feel like they had some control of their futures and something to look forward to.

"The school was closed soon after the Great War began. The leaders of the different nations started keeping their young adults, especially their females, home. The attendance dropped to so few it was pointless to keep it open," Fraener said.

"What is it with you guys and females?" Brandi snapped irritably.

"You must understand," Fraener said in almost a pleading voice. "For every 20 males born, we are blessed with only one female child. Most chosen pairs are lucky to have a child. To have more than that, is rare. It is the same on the world of Agon. Without Terra, our people will become extinct. We *are* slowly becoming extinct. That is why the leaders of the nations were all arguing to get a chance to bring you to their nation. It is in hopes that your Chosen One would be among their people.

"You five are unheard of for our world. You were brought through and your Chosen One was not called to you for some reason, only the Creator of All knows," Fraener said, rubbing his hands over the back of his neck. "We also, in the distant past, would go to your world and find our Chosen One. Never have females been sent through the Axis Mundi without their Chosen One being called to meet them," Fraener said.

Everyone sat in silence for a few minutes chewing on that information.

"So, you have been to our world?" Dani asked.

"Me personally, no. Eirenicians and Agonians did long ago. It was one of the causes, some say, for the Great War," Fraener said.

"How so?" Dani asked.

Fraener looked over to Herodion. Herodion nodded and spoke, "I will not go far back in our ancient history, but only to the more current events that are relevant to us where we currently are," he paused looking at Dani if that was okay. Dani quickly shook her head yes for him to continue.

Herodion continued, "The Great War started, some believe, because the Nephilim began limiting our access to Terra. Some of our people and some Agonians went through with their pnēvma synergáti and let it be believed that they were gods. They encouraged the Terrans to worship them as gods. Understand that when we go through the Axis Mundi to Terra, time changes. You can go through and find yourself one hundred years in Terra's past or even a thousand. Either the Nephilim or the Creator of All chooses the time in Terra history you arrive. We do not know which, as we have no conclusive evidence either way. What we do know is that some Eirenicians and Agonians were on Terra masquerading as gods and were called home. Do you not have any history of such things?" Herodion asked.

Dani thought for a moment and said, "We do, but in the very, very distant past. In fact, all the places we visited, or planned to visit, on our trip were ancient civilizations that had myths about different gods."

"I would hazard a guess that we are speaking of the same things, just from different viewpoints," Herodion said just as his stomach growled loudly. Pink tinted his cheeks as he placed his hand on his stomach, "My apologies."

"You guys haven't eaten yet?" Dani gasped.

"It is of no concern; we shall eat later," Herodion quickly said, still looking embarrassed.

"That is not cool. You guys have to follow us, right?" Brooke chimed in.

"Yes," Herodion answered hesitantly.

"Good, where is the kitchen?" Brooke asked as she and the others stood up.

"I assure you we will take care of our hunger at a later time," Herodion tried again.

Brandi spoke up just then, "Sure, sure. I need dessert though. I cannot think on a sugar-depleted stomach, how about you ladies?" All the girls agreed and started toward the door. Herodion and Fraener put their helmets back on. They all entered the hall and stopped.

"So, you going to show us, or do we get to wander the halls and waste away from sugar deprivation?" Brandi teased.

"This way please. I am guessing you do not want to rejoin your mothers at this time?" Fraener asked.

Everyone answered "no" at the same time. Dani understood none of them wanted to go back into the adult craziness. Besides, they were getting more answers this way.

"Can someone let our moms and Aunt Kathy know where we are going? That way, when they are done with," Dani wove her hand in the air, "that mess, they can catch up with us?"

"Of course, Ormr will inform them. We will be going to the guest suite you will be staying in for the night. We can order substantial proportions of sugar to be delivered there?" Herodion's humor was unmistakable.

"Sure, but I get to do the ordering." Brooke beamed her beauty queen smile at him. Dani rolled her eyes. She did not think Herodion had a clue what he was up against when Brooke flashed that smile.

"Fine, but do you know what Aliter Dulcia or Dulcia Domestica is?" Herodion countered.

"No," Brooke's tentative answer came.

"Then perhaps you would give me the honor of guiding your choices," Herodion smiled back. Dani smirked.

"Touch big guy, touché. Apparently, there is more to you than just being eye candy," Dani thought.

The two of them headed over to a small table and she saw Herodion writing things down as he asked Brooke questions. He then handed the list to a man dressed like the waiters from dinner, who must have been nearby. He quickly hurried off down the corridor with the list.

Chapter 15

Eirenic

Dani was impressed by the suite of rooms they would be staying in. Each had their own bedroom and bathroom off a communal living room and formal dining area. The guards had warned them they were not sure who was staying in each suite of rooms. Apparently two sets of suites had been made ready for their group.

Food arrived soon after they toured the rooms, and the girls and guards all sat around a large table eating and getting answers to their millions of questions. Dani knew each girl was trying to wrap their minds around all that had happened to them and not feel completely overwhelmed.

"Okay, so let me see if we have got this straight. Eirenic is the name of this world," Dani said and looked over to Fraener, who nodded, yes.

"It is divided up into several different nations. Like countries for us," she continued. Again, Fraener nodded yes.

"The men and women at the other end of the table from us at dinner were the rulers of those nations, right?" Dani questioned.

"Yes, you seem to have a grasp of it," Fraener answered.

Brandi added to the exchange, "Those rulers compose a type of assembly that is governed currently by the Regent Ruler. The former king and queen died in the Great War and their son, the guy who should be king, is being a pansy and not ruling now. Even though he is old enough to rule, he is letting his uncle do it until he decides to man up and do it himself."

The guards around them sputtered and some almost spit out the remaining bite of food or drink they had in their mouths.

123

"That is not exactly what I said and involves much interpretation," Fraener said, wiping at his mouth with a napkin to be sure he got all the juice he had spit out.

"I would say, he is waiting for the right time to take over as ruler when he feels he is wise enough to do so," Herodion said stiffly.

Dani looked over at him and the rest of the guys, wondering why they took offense to the comment. She guessed it was frowned upon to speak ill of their future king.

"Sorry, I didn't mean to offend anyone," Brandi said.

"Offend who?" Aunt Kathy asked, walking through the doorway that led into the dining area. The guards immediately got up and left the table, placing their helmets back on their heads.

"Thank you for sharing a meal with us, Ladies," Fraener said bowing slightly.

"No, thank you for all the information and letting us pick your brains. I hope we can do it again soon," Dani said.

"We will be guarding you ladies for the foreseeable future. It would be our pleasure to take a meal with you when not on duty," Fraener said. With a slight bow, he left the dining area.

Aunt Kathy spoke next. "Just to give you girls a heads up, I think your moms are going to want you to stay in the same suite of rooms they are. This has all been a bit much for us all."

Groans could be heard from all around. "I get it, I do. We are all a little on edge right now. This is a lot to take in," Aunt Kathy said.

"Where is the other suite of rooms?" Dani asked.

"It is just down the hall, kitty corner from your door to the right heading out. Why do you ask?" Aunt Kathy asked.

"Well, I was hoping if they were close enough, we could convince them we are safe where we are. They can have their space and we can have ours, maybe?" Dani replied.

"I like that idea. Let's see if we can get it to fly with our moms. Everyone in?" Brandi asked. All the girls nodded their heads in agreement.

Zidicus, who had been standing next to Aunt Kathy, left to speak with the two guards now standing on either side of the door. The others must have left or were waiting in the hallway.

"Aunt Kathy, what happened after we left?" Dani asked.

Before she could answer, the door to the suite opened again and the moms entered the room. Hugs were given all around again.

"Why don't you ladies all sit down. I will get us something to drink," Zidicus said as he entered back into the room. He walked over to a cabinet that when opened, revealed several jars filled with different colors of liquid.

In my current mood I think the underage people as well as the adults, could use a good stiff drink, Dani thought.

"First and foremost, I want to be sure you all know we are not going to let them take you anywhere. You will be staying with us, no matter what those idiots think," Amanda informed them.

Dani smiled at the fierce scowl on Amanda's face. Looking from mom to mom, she saw that they shared the same determined look. With all that had happened, she was so thankful to have the moms and Aunt Kathy here with them. She was positive if it had just been the girls, the adults at that dinner would have forced the issue of breaking them apart.

Zidicus came around handing each one of the moms a drink, then handing the girls a glass with a different color drink, Amanda spoke up. "That does not have alcohol in it, right? They are too young to be drinking."

"It is very mild sedative made from a root grown here, Amanda. It will help them sleep after all the trauma of the day. If you would like to taste it first, I will give you a glass," Zidicus said.

He then walked over and handed Amanda a glass. Amanda sipped it and then nodded that the girls could try it. Dani took a sip and decided it tasted remarkably like a cough medicine she liked.

They all sat quietly, sipping their drinks. It was strange seeing the men that had met them at the portals hanging out in the entryway. Every so often one of their heads would peek into the room. Theresa was the first to start the yawning. Soon everyone was copying it.

"We have two suites with five rooms each. I was thinking Lynn, Brooke, Dani, Jamie and I in one suite and Brandi, Theresa, Heather, Wendy and

Kathy in the other." Amanda said after a big yawn.

"We were kind of hoping to stay here together and you guys could have the rooms down the hall," Dani said.

All the moms started objecting at once. In the end they all agreed to a compromise. The first few days they would try it the moms' way, then reevaluate. At this point she was so tired she could have just curl up on the couch and sleep for a week. Who knew what tomorrow would bring? Right now, she needed to crash. Tomorrow would just have to wait. She just hoped it was dull and boring. There was no way she could handle another day like today.

Chapter 16

Eirenic

Dani did not know if she could handle seeing another day passing with no decisions being made about what was going to happen to them. They had spent the first two days getting tours all over the palace and the surrounding city. Their group was stared at wherever they went. It made them all feel like a circus exhibit. It became overwhelming at times. Nothing felt normal. For the first time in her life, she was measured for clothes. All clothes on Eirenic were hand made. No more running to the store to pick something up. They could not keep wearing the same clothes from home every day. Funny how those clothes now had a sentimental value to them. She now treasured each piece and the connection to home.

She was the only one who had something other than the clothes they were wearing and cell phone when they went through the portal. It was her backpack and a lightweight jacket she kept in it. Dani knew once the Eirenic clothes were made, she would still wear a piece of clothing from home here and there as a tangible reminder of her life from before the Axis Mundi. She firmly believed if the Axis Mundi could be opened to let them through, it could open again to bring them home.

They all had their phones with them but no way to charge them. The girls would turn their phones on now only when they felt desperate for a visual connection with home, finding comfort in looking through their photos. The battery life of their cell phones mirrored their hope of ever getting home. The lower the battery level went, the more depressed they seemed to get. At least they had the familiarity of each other living together in the beginning to help them all cope with the crazy changes in their lives.

Things had gotten uncomfortable quickly though when, on the fourth morning. Dani got up and walked out to grab breakfast wearing only a long night shirt and underwear that had been made for her. She was greeted by Azmer and Ballene, already seated at the dining room table. Feeling the blood rush to her face with embarrassment, she rushed back to her room and got dressed before returning to the dining area. The other girls were complaining of similar situations. By the end of the first week, everyone agreed that it was time to move all the girls to their own suite.

By the end of the second week, Dani was ready to pull her hair out. She was bored out of her mind. The other girls were, too. Frustration with their situation was boiling over. They had to rely on others for everything they needed. None of them liked not having a path toward a productive future. They had no idea how to fit into the culture they had been brought to.

"Not only no, but a Heck no, was the resounding opinion on becoming baby-making machines for a living. We all had dreams of future careers and self-reliance." Dani thought.

Not knowing what to do was weighing heavily on them all. Not only that, but they were still coping with the realization that they could never go home. Never see their fathers and friends again. Each of them was grappling with their losses. They were all desperately reaching for anything to bring some sense of control back to their lives. She prayed nightly for some hope and a way out of their current situations.

One evening, the moms were having solo dinners with their Chosen Ones. It was a nice break in her mind from watching Dani's mom and Azmer get better acquainted. She had never seen her mom take an interest in a man before. Watching them interact was awkward. In a late-night conversation with the other girls, it was shared that they all felt the same with regards to their moms and Chosen Ones.

None of the men pushed a relationship with the girls. They were all very respectful and genuinely seemed to care for the entire group. All the girls agreed that it was still simply weird. They wanted to establish a little distance, so they did not have to watch the intimate details of the relationships unfold. These were their moms, after all. The girls decided to invite their "guards" to dinner again. They were always trailing them around and it seemed like a nice way to say thank you for putting up with the craziness that was their current lives.

Dani was sitting at the dining room table listening to the conversations around her when she felt an internal pull from across the room. Turning her head to see where the pull was coming from and saw a large map. Standing she walked over to it as the others continued to talk. The conversation was heading into the chit-chat phase, and she did not really enjoy that. She wanted to process what she had learned so far. Looking more closely at the map, she noticed a large complex located just across the bay from them.

"What is this?" Dani called out, pointing to the map.

Herodion stood and walked over to her. "That is the School of Knowledge," he said.

"So, all the facilities are all still there, just waiting for someone to reopen it?" Dani questioned.

"Yes, I think so. There are caretakers assigned to the facility to keep it maintained. Why do you ask?" Herodion asked.

She had no doubt she was being led to something. Now she just needed to figure out what. The reality was that they could not get back home. As depressing as that was, the girls still needed to figure out what to do with the reality that was their lives. What was leading her to the School of Knowledge? Something pushed at her, just beyond her grasp. Ideas started to form in her mind. She knew the other girls were probably feeling like she was, desperate to have some control of their future.

"How hard would it be to open it back up?" Dani asked.

"Not hard, I would think," Herodion answered from beside her.

"We need to learn how to live in this place. What better way for us to do that than at your School of Knowledge," she said to him. A warm peaceful sensation pulsed through her, and she placed her hand on her chest. It was the same type of feeling she would get when she was at Aunt Kathy's cabin talking to her angel. Funny that she would get it here.

"Do you really think it is possible that we can reopen it?" Brandi asked, now standing behind her and Herodion with the other girls.

"I do not see why not," Herodion said.

The girls all shared a moment, looking from one face to another. This was the straw they would grasp to try and cope and deal with the lives they had now. Dani felt this was their way forward to take some control of their futures.

"We are going to go to college after all," Heather excitedly said.

"Heck yeah!" Brooke raised her hands to Brandi's that were already in the air ready for a high five.

"Guess you get to go to college early, Dani," Brooke high fived her.

"Not like you haven't been taking college classes since your sophomore year of high school anyway," Jamie called over to her.

No one had heard the entry door open, with all the celebratory high fives going on. The guards had just stood back, grinning, and watching the girls.

"Here I thought I would find a bunch of depressed young ladies again, not a celebration going on," Aunt Kathy said from the hall. The guys all quickly put their helmets back on and moved to stand in the entryway as Aunt Kathy and Zidicus entered the room.

"What are we celebrating?" Aunt Kathy asked.

"We are going to open the School of Knowledge and go to college," Dani said excitedly. All the girls nodded their heads in confirmation.

Zidicus looked around the room at the girls then said, "Not to put a damper on your current moods. I understand your desire to become self-reliant and find your purpose here. But the facility has been closed for many cycles. It will take some work to get it operational and we will need to find knowledgeable instructors for you. That could prove a lot more difficult to do than getting the facility ready for learning."

Dani was quick to reply, "We don't seem to have anything else to do, so we can get the grounds and buildings ready ourselves. If you wouldn't mind, could you look into the staffing, Zidicus? You seem to know a lot about it," she asked. "With all of us working together we can have it up and running in no time, I just know it."

All the girls exclaimed enthusiastically, "YES!"

Aunt Kathy placed her hand on Zidicus' arm. He turned and looked down at her smiling face. "I think that is a perfect place for them to learn everything they need to know about living on Eirenic," Aunt Kathy said.

"As it seems I am outnumbered, I will put forth the idea to the Regent Ruler in the morning," Zidicus said with a slight bow.

"Why do we need his approval?" Dani questioned.

Brandi said, "I don't like him very much and I definitely do not like that prissy, entitled, witch, *Lady* Eulalios. Whoever put *Lady* in front of that woman's name has a vastly different idea of what a lady is than I do." The girls all started agreeing. A couple of loud coughs, covering up laughter, could be heard from the entryway.

Zidicus answered, "Indeed, but the Regent Ruler is the one who currently controls the funding for the school, so we will need his consent; and antagonizing Lady Eulalios is not advised at this time, even if I might agree with your assessment," Zidicus said, smiling.

"If he says no, maybe we can find the real king and get him to man up with the money," Brooke said.

Zidicus arched his eyebrow and said, "I see you have had quite the education these last few weeks," Zidicus looked towards the archway leading to the guards. "Perhaps we should keep that to ourselves and not threaten the Regent Ruler with the loss of his power to rule just yet," he said placatingly.

Brooke looked embarrassed by her statement and shrugged.

"We leave it in your hands, then, Zidicus, thank you," Aunt Kathy said.

The moms walked into the suite with their respective men in tow. Looking closer at their faces Dani could tell the adults all looked a little uneasy about something.

"Hey girls, how about we have a conversation in the living room?" Lynn asked.

The girls all looked to one another, knowing something unpleasant was up. The girls and moms moved into the living room and found seats.

"We are thinking that eventually we are going to have to move out of the palace. I mean, we cannot stay here indefinitely," said Theresa. "We wanted to give you girls fair warning that when we do go, we will be going as families and heading to different parts of Eirenic. I know it is not what you want to hear or do, but we don't know of any other way. I'm sorry, girls."

Dani looked around to the other girls. All had the same look of unease. No one wanted to be the first to talk about the plans they had made. She took a deep breath and let it out.

"This ought to be fun," Dani thought in a sarcastic tone.

"Thank you for thinking of us, but we kind of have a plan on what we want to do," Dani said quietly watching the moms look at each other, confused.

"How could you have made complete thought-out plans in two weeks? What exactly are these *plans*?" Amanda questioned in a domineering tone.

"Wow, Mom, relax a little will ya? Just hear us out," Jamie quietly said.

"I will not let you be separated from me, Jamie, and that is final," Amanda barked.

"I was going to go to college out of state in the fall, Mom. I would have been separated from you then," Jamie said.

"This," Amanda waved her hands around adamantly, "is not going to another state. This is an entirely different world that I know little to nothing about," Amanda snapped.

"Let us hear what they have to say," Wendy said.

Amanda sighed but remained quiet. She looked over to Jamie, who had grown a little pale. Jamie was the least confrontational person she knew. It had taken a lot out of her to speak up to her overbearing mother. Amanda had no problem getting what she wanted. Standing she squeezed Jamie on the shoulder as she passed her, heading over to the large map on the wall.

Pointing to the School of Knowledge, Dani told the moms about their ideas to open the school. All the moms started asking questions and voicing their objections, the volume of voices started to rise. All the girls started trying to argue their points. As she was trying to convince her mom that they had solid ideas, she saw the moms' Chosen Ones and Zidicus walk into the room.

"Fine, if this is what you all want, I guess we will just live at the palace indefinitely," Amanda infuriatingly said.

"You know that is not an optimal solution, Amanda," Filtiarn said, placing his hand on her shoulder.

"And leaving my daughter is?" Amanda snapped.

Zidicus spoke, looking at Amanda then the rest of the moms. "I know you are not comfortable yet on our world. It would be pointless for us to assure you that they will be perfectly safe. There are several obstacles in our path to getting the School of Knowledge up and operational. I suggest we all let it lie tonight. We are all tired and a good night's sleep always brings clarity."

The moms and Aunt Kathy gave everyone bear hugs before they left. Zidicus and Aunt Kathy were the last ones heading for the door. She placed her hand on Zidicus' forearm.

"You will still check into getting what we need from the Regent Ruler, right?" Dani asked quietly.

Zidicus looked over her head and she turned to see where he was looking. All the other girls stood in the entryway with expectant looks on their faces.

Zidicus replied, "You need to give your mothers and Aunt Kathy a measure of understanding. You are the most precious thing to them. All of them stood up and fought hard the night you arrived. I have never been so in awe of the strength and courage they all displayed going up against males twice their size. All of whom are used to getting their way."

Aunt Kathy placed her hand on his, intertwining their fingers. Zidicus turned and they just looked at each other for several beats. Zidicus sighed, "I will look into it."

A chorus of "thank you" was called out to him. Dani made eye contact with Aunt Kathy and mouthed the words, thank you, to her as well. She had no doubt it was Aunt Kathy that swayed Zidicus to agree with their request. Dani knew it was the place the girls were meant to be. She knew she had been guided to the idea. Now they just had to convince their moms and everyone else.

Chapter 17

Kolob

Kerberos smiled thinking back to his viewing of Dani and her friends he was blessed with this morning. After the inquisition into his actions opening the Axis Mundi and the assassination attempt on his life, he did not have much time to interact with her and was glad he was blessed with it now. The School of Knowledge was an answer to their prayers. The girls wanted choices for their future, and he wanted Dani and the others to be someplace where they could learn and be protected. He had guided and nudged Dani to look at the map. He had also helped her inquire about opening the school again. Dani and the others would need to learn how to live in a strange new world without the aid of their Chosen One.

The School of Knowledge would be the perfect place for Dani and the girls to learn how to interact with their pnēvma synergáti and eventually be presented with their sacred crystals. Dani would need a good foundation and training to deal with her fierce spirit partner. At the school, they would be protected by the strong males around them and nurtured in their learning. He did not know how much time they had before the evil found them.

The Creator did not grant him access to others on Eirenic so he could guide through the process of opening the school. Kerberos had faith in Zidicus and the true king to help make it happen. He did not concern himself with the convincing of the mothers. The love they shared with their daughters would bring them to support them in their desire to have some control over their futures. This was where the girls were meant to be, so it would happen.

Kerberos's more pressing issue was to do more research into the ancient forefathers. He needed to completely understand the actions of the past so that he might correct those mistakes for the future of all their worlds. He knew he was being watched closely by others now. After the assassination attempt, Zopyro had tried to reason with him to always keep a guard with him. Kerberos had refused at first. He finally relented knowing that no one could always watch every angle around themselves. Still, he did not want others to know his movements throughout the day. Always having a guard with him would limit his ability to move about the Crystal Fortress undetected, especially in the ancient archives of the Hall of Records and Library. But he would find ways to limit the guard's ability to watch him by leaving them in doorways to guard a room.

Walking out of his doorway, his guard fell in step behind him.

"We are going to The Hall of Records," he stated.

"Yes, my Liege. Was there any particular section you wished to visit? I can send someone to notify the scholars, and have it prepared for when you arrive." The guard said.

"The section I will be visiting is several stories underground. I do not feel the need to notify anyone of my comings and goings." He stated and the guard fell quiet.

The location he would be going to was designed to keep the collection of irreplaceable manuscripts at the optimum environment for preservation. The very nature of the location gave limited access to all who entered. The parchment manuscripts dated back to the first words written by a Nephilim. In these ancient accounts of Nephilim history lay the clues that he needed to put together. He needed to find the dark secrets of the Nephilim's meddling in the human genes on the other worlds.

Flying in the damp morning air he thought to himself, *"Dani and her family must be a key component to bring about the change needed in the gene pool of Eirenic and Agon."*

The Hall is slightly down the mountainside from the Crystal Fortress. Landing on the wide front steps he walked in and walked down the spiraled stairway that led to the lowest levels several stories below the main library floors. He stationed his guard on a landing in the stairs several stories above the vault he would be visiting, trying to slip in undetected.

Walking in he noted a scholar head out the door as soon as he entered. He would not have much time to search before someone disturbed him. Walking towards a back wall he pulled several rolls of parchment down and flipped through the tags that labels that described what was located on them. In no time he felt the presence of someone watching him. It was not an unfamiliar feeling to him now. It seemed his research into the past was making the scholars very nervous. He did not raise his eyes from his current scroll when an all too familiar voice called out to him.

"I trust you have found some of the information you are seeking," Dionysius said, coming out from a row of ancient texts.

Lifting his eyes, he stood still and watched as Dionysius took the last few steps to stand beside him. Dionysius in many ways was like the ancient archive they now stood in. Thousands of stored documents no doubt overflowed the figurative tall shelving units in Dionysus' mind. The same smell of ancient parchment books and ink would waft towards you, filling your sinuses, when near him. Like the ancient room, you never knew what might lie in wait. What information you could find that might change the course of future events. He never quite knew where Dionysius stood on the ancient forefathers' meddling. He was, after all, one of the head scholars as well as a warrior.

"There were times," he thought, "Dionysius supports all that the scholars had done in the past. Of course, he never came right out and said this. No, that would be too clear and direct a statement to come from the master politician." These thoughts, along with others, reminded him to keep his reasons for searching to himself.

"Yes and no," Kerberos answered, and tried to walk away. Several different scholars had offered him assistance each time they found him in the stacks of ancient texts. He had no doubts his every movement was being watched and reported back to Dionysius.

"If you would enlighten me as to what you are seeking, I may be of assistance," Dionysius said, stepping in front of him.

"As you have been so kind as to send scholars to offer assistance daily, if I required any I would have asked one of them," he replied. Standing there, he watched the play of emotions over the older Liege's face, irritation being a prominent one.

"I was just on my way to get refreshment from the cart," Dionysius swept his hand to the gilded cart only a few feet away. "No matter the amount of care taken, dust seems to sneak in and onto anything that sits for too long," Dionysius said looking down at the dust coating his brown clothing. "It appears I am one of those things," he said as he patted at the dust, trying to remove it. "The scientists have more data on the extent of the degradation of the magic sealing the portals," Dionysius continued talking as he walked to the serving cart.

Kerberos knew Dionysius was attempting to manipulate him into a conversation by leading with information the sly one knew he would want. He had followed the older Liege out of the shelves and was determined to cut the conversation short.

"I look forward to hearing it put forth in the Hall of Equality," he said, trying to end the conversation and turn back to his research.

Dionysius looked back at him after pouring two crystal goblets full of liquid. "Come now, no harm is done by our discussing the findings now," Dionysius said, handing a goblet to Kerberos.

Kerberos had two choices: take the crystal goblet or refuse it. He decided to take it and hear Dionysius out. He never knew what information he might glean from the manipulative Liege. The hard part was being sure he did not divulge anything in return.

"Let us sit and have a peaceful conversation," Dionysius gestured to the plush padded seating situated around a large glowing crystal that provided heat. Tables were expertly placed to provide function as well as distance if small groups wish to converse without disturbing others who occupied the same space.

"As you wish," he said and walked across the short distance sitting on an ornately carved stool. He then sat his drink down on the table beside him.

He had not wanted the drink in the first place. He used to enjoy the juice in his younger years but had found that it was too sweet for his liking now. He looked at Dionysius, waiting for him to speak.

"The magic sealing the portals is slowly diminishing," Dionysius said with a flourished sigh. "One day it will fail altogether."

"You are not telling me anything new," he stated.

"Yes, yes, ever the impatient one," Dionysius said sitting quietly for a moment. "Have you thought about what the failing will mean?" Dionysius prodded.

"It was my understanding that you had new information on the magic sealing the portals. If I was mistaken, I will take my leave, so that you may get back to your day," Kerberos said irritably and started to stand.

"Oh, for all that is holy. Would it kill you to have a normal conversation for once? One where you actually spoke freely to those around you," Dionysius said exasperated.

Lifting his eyebrow at him was the only response he gave.

Dionysius sighed and continued, "I see that it is. The new data shows that it may soon be possible to directly interact with the other worlds. The timeline on when this will be possible is in direct correlation to the degradation of the sealing. We are measuring its decay constantly. The rate of the decay is inconsistent at this point. We are hoping that with time we can better calculate the exact rate and be able to predict its inevitable demise," Dionysius said with exasperation.

A choking sound followed by a thud off to his right made Kerberos look to see what made the noise. Jumping to his feet Kerberos ran to a Nephilim scholar who now lay twitching and seizing on the floor with foam erupting from his mouth. A crystal goblet lay next to his hand on the floor, with juice spilling out of it. He leaned down to see if there was anything he could do to help, when the young scholar stopped moving altogether. Reaching out he pressed his fingers on to the scholar's neck checking for a pulse. There was none.

Kerberos looked up to Dionysius who stood by his side. Several other Nephilim came rushing over to them.

"Seal the hall. No one enters or leaves unless it is approved by me. Bring me all the refreshment carts, and be sure to mark where they came from," Kerberos ordered.

When all the carts were lined up, Kerberos went to each, holding his sacred crystal above the juice pitchers one by one. As he suspected, only one had a swirling of black that showed from the pure light of the crystal. It was the one that Dionysius had used for their drinks.

"We could have been killed," Dionysius said with over-the-top shock.

"Indeed, we could have," Kerberos answered.

After questioning and checking everyone's whereabouts, no one could be found with the poison on them. The murderer had been thorough in covering his tracks.

Burkhart came storming through the doors. "What is going on?" he demanded, looking at the now covered body of the dead scholar.

After hearing the events that had happened, Burkhart announced, "Anyone could have drunk from that pitcher. Be glad you had not yet taken a drink from your filled goblets. That poor scholar was in the wrong place at the wrong time."

Kerberos could not counter the other Liege's reasoning. He did not believe in chance, though. Something did not sit right in Burkhart's assessment.

"Dionysius, I see that you did not drink your juice. Why is that?" he questioned.

"I admit I have never liked the juice even as a child, finding it too sweet. The only reason I took a glass this time was out of social correctness when offering some to you. Normally the refreshment pitchers contain only water. This is to safeguard the ancient scrolls and artifacts. Spilled water is easily dealt with; sweet sticky juice is not. Why did you not drink yours?" Dionysius asked.

"In my younger years I loved the juice. As for the last few years, I have found it too sweet for my liking, so I stopped drinking it," Kerberos stated.

"Lucky for you that you did," Burkhart said.

"Yes, lucky for us both," Dionysius answered.

A stillness from within him filled his body and Kerberos had no doubt the poisoning was meant for him. He was making someone or someone's extremely nervous with his digging. The secrets of the past deeds by the scholar forefathers had been efficiently vaulted away eons ago. His keen interest in not only Nephilim history but of the other worlds they guarded had shown him unnatural evolutionary changes in the humans they were meant to safeguard. The more Kerberos researched, the more the scholars became interested in what he was doing.

The scholars made it clear they did not like him poking into the ancient texts. As a Liege, they could do nothing to stop him. He was watched constantly by one or more scholars while in the archives. So, he had adapted his tactics to throw them off. He would spend time in sections of the shelving that he needed nothing from. It left scholars wondering what he was up to, and that pleased him. This new assassination attempt proved he was getting close to the information he sought.

Chapter 18

Eirenic

Dani sat on a large couch picking bites of cut up fruit out of a bowl she had next to her. She wore a loose-fitting lounge outfit she had found in a drawer. It was midmorning and none of the other girls were up yet. The day and especially the night before had been rough. Too many thoughts and emotions were still running wild in her mind. She hugged a throw pillow to her chest to try and comfort herself. She had struggled the day before to keep it together around the others. What bothered her most was she could not figure out why. They were trying to get the School of Knowledge going. The girls now at least had a direction to go, so she was unsure why she was feeling so emotional.

The day before, the girls, their moms, Aunt Kathy and all the guys had met for breakfast and had been together the entire day. She enjoyed getting to see more of the palace and walking on the beach. It was still so overwhelming to have so many people following them around. The guards at least tried to be discreet, standing back from their large group. Everywhere the group went, people made way and stared long after they passed. She thought the novelty of her group would have worn off by now, but apparently not yet. Everywhere they went she saw very few women. It just felt so surreal to her.

Thinking about it more while hugging the pillow, something occurred to her. She was still feeling kind of like breeding stock when conversations turned to the School of Knowledge. The girls all being in one place, on display in some ways for male students from the regions to come and get to know them. What other choice did they have if they wanted to try and gain some control of their futures? Maybe trying to open the School of Knowledge had finally made her see that they were never going home.

Just then a door opened down the hall, followed by others. Soon all the girls were sitting around the living room, most with red rimmed puffy eyes like hers. Dani looked from face to face as each gave a small, resigned smile.

She thought back to the conversation she had started the night before. The following hours had flown by, each girl taking a turn talking about what they would miss and not miss from home. They laughed and cried at little things they mentioned, like French fries. Each of them took turns letting out their emotional turmoil that was overwhelming them from within. They had cried the hardest at the mention of their dads. Brooke had little contact with hers, but he was still her dad. It was the thought that even if she wanted to, she could not get in touch with him. That sent them all into a big crying spell. Jamie and her dad were the closest of all of them. Jamie had just sat and sobbed for the longest time.

Now Dani sat staring off at nothing, thinking of the night before and looking through a window. A large shadow crossing the balcony caught her attention. Leaning forward and looking up, she saw a dragon circling overhead. The sun was behind it; she could tell it was a dragon only by the dark shape. She sat there with wide eyes, not sure if she would ever get used to seeing something that massive, let alone that it was a dragon, flying in the sky. The slow beating of its wings and gliding brought it closer and closer.

Dani watched as it landed at the far side of their balcony. Standing and setting the pillow down she walked to the doorway, opening the door she looked out. She instantly recognized the dragon and walked out on the balcony and over to Xad and Herodion, her half-eaten piece of fruit still in her hand, as Herodion stepped off the dragon's leg.

"Good afternoon," Herodion said.

"Hey, how's it going?" Dani replied quietly.

"We are doing well. I came to check on you and the others," Herodion stated with concern. She looked at him, a little confused. How could he know they had had a rough night? The only ones around them were the guards stationed in the hallway outside their door. The answer occurred to Dani. The guards must have heard them through the door. She turned a little red at what they might have heard.

"We are doing as well as can be expected, I think," Dani said a little defensively.

Herodion took a small step towards her before he spoke, "I am not here to judge you or the others. It was just that Ladon and Askook were deeply concerned and came to get Fraener and me. We did not mean to eavesdrop on your conversation but just wanted to be sure you all were safe. I can only guess at how hard this is for all of you. You do not have the benefit of your Chosen Ones to help you adjust. If there is anything we can do to help, please, you only have but to ask," Herodion said sincerely.

"Thank you, we appreciate it," Dani said. "I think it's just going to take us a little time to absorb all of this. The tour yesterday was great, but do we have to walk around with so many people with us? How long do you think it's going to take for everyone to stop staring at us? It is kind of creepy at times."

Herodion smiled slightly and said, "I do not know how long that might be. If we can get the School of Knowledge open and running it will be easier on everyone, I think. It is in an isolated section of the bay so few people will be there other than students and staff."

"I sure hope so," Heather said, walking out onto the balcony followed by the others. Each one plopped into a chair. Dani saw a look of concern cross Herodion's face as he looked at each of them.

"Speaking of the school, Zidicus has requested you all attend his proposal presentation to the other leaders when council is in session this afternoon. You have a few hours to get ready. I will send for some food and beverages for you all. Your Aunt Kathy told us of a stimulus drink you all love. I believe you call it coffee," Herodion smiled as they all groaned in pleasure.

"You would be my hero if you can get us the largest pitcher of coffee you guys have," Brooke said.

"With cream and sugar please," Heather added.

Herodion looked from face to face. "If I had known that was all it took to get so much hero worship, I would have done this the first night," he smiled and turned, entering their suite. Dani heard the front door open and then close a few moments later. Herodion then came back out onto the balcony addressing them all.

"Right, it should be here in just a short while. If you have need of anything else, please do not hesitate to ask. We will do all we can to help," Herodion bowed slightly, and walked over getting on Xad. Dani stood and walked to the ledge a little distance from them. The dragon leaped into the air and dove over the side, opening his wings once he was clear of the balcony. A gust of wind swept up against her as he started to flap. She couldn't help but smile at his thoughtfulness. If he had started flapping on the balcony, he could have blown the rest of them off.

Food arrived just as Herodion said it would, with an exceptionally large pot of what passed for coffee here. The girls finished eating and were ready early, sitting in the living room waiting for the call to head out. The doors to their suite opened and all the moms and Aunt Kathy came in with the men. After a long and tenuous conversation two days ago about reopening the school, the girls and Aunt Kathy had finally won the support from the moms. There was no doubt in her mind that had been the real battle. When they got their moms and Aunt Kathy on their side, nothing could stop them.

Since then, the adults had been a little tight-lipped on their presentation to the counsel for opening the school and their plans on where they would be living. She could tell that the men wanted to go back to their respective homes. Dani knew the moms were torn between wanting to stay with them and heading off to their new homes in their Chosen One's nation. All the girls still agreed it was definitely an awkward situation all the way around. They did not want to be the third, or in Dani's case fourth, wheel while their moms got better acquainted with their "mates."

Just saying the word "mates" regarding my mom, is simply weird," Dani thought.

She didn't know if she or any of them would get used to that any time soon. The girls were all for their moms finding love again, just not right in front of them.

"I see by the nervous energy you all enjoyed the capulus drink," Zidicus smiled.

"If you mean the coffee drink, yep, that was freaking awesome," Brooke said with a wide smile, bouncing from one foot to the other. Dani felt jittery and she had consumed only two cups. She had lost count of how much the others had. Zidicus chuckled warmly.

"You might want to drink it in more moderation. Capulus seems to carry more of a punch than our coffee from home," Aunt Kathy chuckled. They all laughed heading out into the hallway and then down a flight of stairs to stand in front of large double doors leading into the Council Hall.

Dani felt a jumble of nerves, and it wasn't the capulus drink, as the doors opened, and they walked into the decorated hall. Like everything else she had seen, it was covered with intricate carvings, tapestries, and paintings. The Regent Ruler sat in a large, cushioned chair raised up slightly higher than the rest of the chairs. Only two other chairs, unoccupied, sat higher than his, and there was no mistaking what they were: they were carved, high-backed thrones. She had no doubt that had to be where the king and his Chosen One, the queen, would sit. Their group sat in plush seats down at the front, waiting while Zidicus was called forward and began to speak.

"We all agree that we have never had females traverse the Axis Mundi and not have their Chosen One called to them. To say we have no precedent to go by is puzzling, at best. We have been blessed by the Creator of All in sending us the five young ones. His purpose in this, is still unknown by all. We need to think with clear heads. The young ones need to find their place in our society. To do this, they need to learn our ways and customs. I can think of no better place to do that than the School of Knowledge. It is where our brightest minds from across our regions have come together to teach our young for generations."

As Zidicus continued to make their case, she smiled. Zidicus was brilliant and had most of the leaders swayed towards opening the school in no time. *"Some, still seemed to be holding out, based on the questions they were asking, and objections they are making,"* Dani thought. She racked her brain on to how to turn the other nation's ruler's minds in their favor.

At a moment of pause in the debate, Dani nervously stood up. "If I might have a moment of your time," she said.

She stared at the Regent Ruler who seemed to be preoccupied with people coming and going, whispering in his ear, and then leaving after he would comment back. He would occasionally speak to the assembly but only when pressed by one of the Nation Rulers or Zidicus. Other than that, he watches the door his people walked in and out of on the side wall, clearly waiting for more information. The Regent Ruler must have sensed everyone looking at him because he scanned the room, looking a little confused, before finally looking at Dani. He nodded once.

"Pretty sure he has no clue what he just nodded, yes, too," Dani thought before saying, "We have all decided we will not be separated, divided up like cattle, and paraded around your nations," she said and heard gasps and the sputtering of the others trying to comment. "Hear me out, please. That is how we think of it. Try to put yourselves in our place. Try to understand how this has affected us." She paused gesturing her hand to the girls in the seats next to hers. "I am sorry there are not enough females here. That is not our fault. Would you rather we each disappear into our mother's mate's nations, or have a place where you can each have some men from your nations come and meet us in one spot? I suggest you start thinking about who you wish to send to the School of Knowledge to meet us, because that is where we would like to be. Who knows, maybe they will get some actual knowledge or skill you can use at home to make your nations better. It is the *School of Knowledge,* after all." she said and sat down. The room was completely quiet.

After a few moments of quiet, where her heart raced thinking she had screwed up their chances, the nation leaders started debating several different issues with the school's opening. How many men from each region? How was it to be paid for? So many questions and discussions were happening at once that she lost track of the conversation.

Zidicus, who had been standing on the floor the entire time, walked over to her. "You did marvelous," he smiled brightly. "Now would be a good time for you and the others to escape. This is going to run late into the evening, and I know you all were up late last night," he said.

146

With that bit of information, Dani frowned up at him. *"Just how many people did the guards tell?"* she thought.

"Do not worry, little one. Only Aunt Kathy and I know, other than your guards. We are all genuinely concerned for all your wellbeing. I will stay here and continue to guide the regional leaders," Zidicus quietly said.

She smiled and whispered, "thank you," to him, then motioned for the other girls to follow her. The moms all squeezed their hands as they passed them. When she reached the end of their row she looked back to the row with her mom, Aunt Kathy, the other moms, and their men. They all turned and looked over to them. She got a little choked up as they each smiled to her. The moms were a force to be sure, but the unexpected overwhelming support from the men had surprised her. She mouthed another thank you to them and left the hall. Who knows what the future would bring them? Dani only knew that in this moment she felt some hope for their future. Hope she had not had since the beginning of their odyssey, and coming to this new world.

Chapter 19

Eirenic

Unable to stay in bed any longer Dani got up and planned on hanging out with the other girls until they got word of how the council voted last night. She knew they all had tossed and turned most of the night partly due to the amount of capulus drink and the other nervous energy. She walked straight to the door leading into the hallway, having decided to ask whoever was on guard duty if they had heard anything. Just sitting and waiting was driving her nuts. She stuck her head out and found Ladon and Veles on guard duty.

"Morning Ladon, morning Veles," she said.

"Good morning to you, Lady Dani," both said, slightly bowing.

"Come on, none of that," Dani waved her hand at them to stop. "Have either of you heard anything about how the meeting concluded last night? We are kind of dying to know in here," she said.

Both guards looked alarmed, so Dani quickly added. "No, no one is really hurt. It is a slang saying for us. It means we are very anxious to hear what happened. That's all. Like the saying 'sitting on pins and needles,'" she said, watching for understanding. When both guards looked at her with surprised expression, so she gave up. "Never mind, I will try and not use phrases like that."

"My apologies for not understanding your meaning. The image of you sitting on pins and needles did not come across as I think you intended," Ladon chuckled. "I only know that the meeting you speak of concluded sometime in the early hours of the morning. Fraener and Herodion are going to be meeting with Zidicus once he has had a few hours of rest," Ladon said.

"Okay, thanks for the info," Dani said and headed back into their suite, passing on the information to the other girls who were now all sprawled around the living room.

Not wanting to risk going anywhere and miss seeing anyone who would come and give them news, they all waited around nervously. They all seemed to take turns walking aimlessly around the suite. She was going stir crazy inside, so Dani headed out onto the balcony. The other girls followed. The sun was bright, and she thought she might as well work on her tan. The others followed her rolling up their flowing pants and tucked up their shirts as much as they could.

"I wouldn't get too carried away with tucking up part. You never know what or who is going to fly by and get a bird's eye view of us," Dani said, trying to cut some of the tension.

They lasted only about an hour on the balcony. Trying to sit still was torture but none of them could think of anything else to do. All too soon, Dani headed back inside to try and find something to occupy her mind. Zidicus and Aunt Kathy had brought them books on Eirenic. She tried to immerse her restless mind in one. Brooke and the others had wandered back in and were throwing around ideas about what they could do. Brooke, being Brooke had offered to do hair and what passed for makeup on everyone. Dani tried to shrink into the couch. By lunch time she and the others had a bad case of cabin fever.

Dani was about to head back to the guards when the hallway door opened and Aunt Kathy and Zidicus walked in.

"Thank you for showing up now. Brooke was about to start doing a mass hair makeover," Dani shuddered.

"So glad we could save you," Aunt Kathy chuckled and walked into the suite with a tired-looking Zidicus.

"Have you eaten lunch yet?" Aunt Kathy asked.

"Nope, we were getting around to it," Dani said a little too excitedly.

"Hey, is that Aunt Kathy we hear?" Brooke called from the living room.

Dani, Aunt Kathy and Zidicus walked into the living room.

"Please tell us you have good news," Brooke pleaded.

"Yes, we do," Aunt Kathy said, and all the girls squealed in delight.

Zidicus spoke over the noise, "Before we get into too many details, shall we order lunch and eat outside today? It is a beautiful day. I thought after that we could take a tour of the School of Knowledge so you all know the amount of work it will take to get it up and going again."

"We don't need a big meal," Dani excitedly said.

"Sandwiches to go works fine too," Heather said.

"Or a picnic over at the school sounds sweet," Brandi said.

Zidicus smiled and said, "I see we will be heading there sooner rather than later. I shall order our lunches to go and assemble the guards." Zidicus walked back to the door. The moms decided to stay at the palace with their Chosen Ones and catch up with the girls later.

She couldn't remember exactly what she ate for lunch. She was way too excited about walking around the school. Brooke had not even complained about riding a dragon over. The school was huge and made of the same cream-colored stones as the Palace. The entire school gave off an air of aged prestige. Archways over outside corridors were large enough for the dragons to pass through easily from building to building. Inside the buildings there were long halls with rooms branching off just like a normal school back home. There were several classrooms with theater seating as well. All the furniture was pushed to the center of the rooms and still covered with drop cloths. A dusty stale smell permeated the air. It was clear that the rooms had been closed for a long time.

The grounds were overgrown in some areas and would need to be tended to as well. Dry water channels ran through the school just like the ones at the Palace. The water had been blocked at some point and the channels had filled with debris. Those too would need to be flushed. By the time the tour was through, the sun was setting. The moms came over with their Chosen Ones as the sun set and they decided to have a bonfire cookout.

A large rock fire pit that their group had cleaned away earlier now had a blazing fire going. It cast a warm glow over the group seated around it.

There were several fire pits around the clearing they sat in. It was clearly intended to be an easy open area for people to gather and hang out with their spirit animals. Dani guessed the love of a crackling fire and smell of wood burning was universal. It just set a relaxed tone. She leaned back against the carved stone seat and pulled up her feet. Remarkably, the stone was amazingly comfortable and formed perfectly to the curve of her body.

Glancing at their not-so-little group sitting and lounging around Dani smiled. Her mom, Aunt Kathy and the other moms were there with their prospective other halves. As strange as it was, the girls had started getting used to the men being part of their group. She had never seen her mom as happy as she seemed with Azmer. The other moms looked the same. She thought it a little strange how it had happened so fast for them.

Shrugging her shoulders, Dani thought *"if is right, it is just right."*

Dani leaned towards Aunt Kathy and Zidicus, who were sitting to her right. She wanted to ask some of the millions of questions that had been circling in her mind, but it never seemed to be the right time to ask them.

"Zidicus, how did you guys know to meet us at the portal exit?" Dani had tried to ask it quietly but noticed that the other girls had stopped their conversations to hear the answer.

"I do not know if it is the same for everyone," Zidicus paused, looking around, "But I can tell you how it was for me," he put his arm that he had placed in Aunt Kathy's lap around her shoulders. "It was a calling to my soul and that of my pnēvma synergáti," he said and placed his free hand over his heart. "A deep understanding that the one we are meant to spend our days with is coming, the one who would complete us." He turned and gazed into Aunt Kathy's smiling face.

"Your spirit partner felt it too?" Dani asked in surprise. As if in answer, a large, forked tongue gently caressed her aunt's cheek and Aunt Kathy chuckled.

"I think that might be your answer," Aunt Kathy laughed.

Dani looked up to see the giant head of Gordy lift away.

"Why did so many come with the rest of you?" Dani asked, looking over at the other men seated around the fire.

Azmer spoke next. "As Zidicus said, we all felt the calling. In the days before the Great War, when a male felt the call, he would have come with only a few close family members. The difficulties, as you all know, traversing the Axis Mundi do not always have pleasant endings. With the portals sealed, it was a shock to feel the pull. I notified my Nation Ruler, who insisted on coming and bringing a large guarding party to accompany us. To be blessed with a Chosen One before the Great War was cause for a great celebration, the occurrence happening so infrequently. We had all given up hope of ever finding ours after the sealing. The call took us all by enormous surprise. None of us will ever take for granted what has been gifted to us. You are all so very precious to us all," Azmer said, mostly while looking at Dani's mom. She couldn't help but see the blush rise in her mother's cheeks.

"If the guys get pnévma synergáti, spirit partners, is there anything that the girls get?" Dani asked anxiously.

"Yes, you will have pnévma synergáti of your own. It just takes time for yours to be seen and you will need to learn how to interact with them," Zidicus answered.

"Oh, so we get cool animals too?" Brandi asked excitedly.

"Yes and No. Yours are not in the physical realm. Yours will be in the spirit form," Zidicus replied.

All the girls started to speak at once. Zidicus held his hands up for quiet.

"Hold on, let me explain. Females are connected to the spirit world in a very mystical way that males can never be. You give life and in doing so a spirit must enter your body to grow and be nurtured by you. Your pnévma synergáti will be as real as our physical ones. Yours will be of the spirit though. It will be able to manifest so you can see it and you will be able to communicate with it, in here," he pointed to his head. "Just as males communicate with theirs, depending on what your pnévma synergáti is, will determine what it and you can do. Just like our physical form pnévma synergáti have specialized abilities. I cannot tell you where or when your pnévma synergáti will come to you; it is different for everyone. Just have faith that the Creator has it all planned, and you will receive yours when you are meant to."

Silence filled the gathering.

"Well, that stinks; we have to wait for it to show up whenever?" Brandi groaned.

"Any way to speed up that process? I would really like to meet mine now," Brooke asked with hope laced in her voice.

Zidicus and all the other men laughed. "No, little one, I am afraid there is not. If I had to guess at a time frame, I would think maybe a solar span."

"A year, it's going to take a year?" Brandi mumbled.

"A year is not so long. I am only guessing at this time frame. My guess is it will take you that long for your own soul to settle enough from the trauma of being taken from your homes and placed here with us. You will also need this settling so that you may receive and learn how to appropriately use a sacred crystal. This will greatly help you and your pnêvma synergáti bond and communicate. The School of Knowledge will help with that," Zidicus said.

"You use your sacred crystals to help communicate with your pnêvma synergáti. When do we get ours?" Dani asked.

"When you notice your connection start to form. I was told, and it is my understanding, that it happens within here first," Zidicus placed his hand up to his head. "You will know to speak with one of your Professus or I, if that would make you feel more comfortable, at that time."

"Professus?" Dani asked.

"I do not know what you call them. They are the teachers at the school," Zidicus said.

"Oh, professors," Dani said.

They sat quietly for a few minutes.

"When do your pnêvma synergáti eat and, you know, other things? Why haven't we seen any babies? I have never seen one actually eating a meal," Dani asked.

Zidicus chuckled. "It depends on the pnêvma synergáti and what they eat. Depending on their preferred habitat, they eat lesser evolved animals and or plant life. A water dragon will go hunt fish, a dire wolf, a hooved animal, or large rodent. As to other bodily functions, they are very private. It is my limited understanding that they are called to a sacred place when it is their time to propagate their species. It is all tied to the birth of our children. As for the spirit pnévma synergáti, I am afraid I have no understanding of the way they come to be. It is the Creator's planning, as with most things, not our own that decides these things."

"Can you tell us about the Nephilim?" Dani asked.

Zidicus gave a small smile and said, "The Nephilim were created by the Creator of All to keep the balance between worlds. They are warriors, honed and perfected by battles to do the will of the Creator of All and guard the Axis Mundi and its portals that connected all worlds. Warrior Nephilim, the gatekeepers of the Axis Mundi portals, open and close the portals with the blessing of the Creator with the use of their sacred crystal.When the portals are open, lifeforms and communications can pass through between worlds. The Creator also calls upon Nephilim to battle and restore the balance in times when great evil rises on any world. We do not have a lot of information about the Nephilim. They tend to keep their race private and aloof from ours. What little we do know has been gleaned from brief encounters over the centuries. It is said that we do not even see them when traversing the mists of the Axis Mundi but know they are there, always watching."

The group got quiet again and she thought about what Zidicus had said. She looked at him and watched him intertwine his fingers with Aunt Kathy's. The smile on Aunt Kathy's face was so radiant. It warmed Dani from the inside out.

"Hey, if you are Aunt Kathy's "soul mate", that makes you our uncle, right?Can we start calling you Uncle Zidicus, is that okay with you?" Dani asked.

"It would be my honor to be considered as a family member to you all. Thank you, little one, for your gift," Uncle Zidicus tilted his head slightly down in a sort of bow.

The next couple of weeks flew by. They all got up each morning and headed over to the School of Knowledge to work on cleaning it up. Their guards, parents, Uncle Zidicus and Aunt Kathy must have had a conversation about guarding them while at the school. Each of the girls had at least two guards with them at all times while there. One would stand guard and one would help clean.

The guards tried to keep a professional distance at first but, what can she say, the girls got tired of only talking with each other and the brief one-word answers from the guards who helped clean when they were on duty. So, the girls took it upon themselves to break down the awkwardness and start friendships. It was not strange to see a guard who was off duty accompanying them around now. Everyone seemed to enjoy themselves and relax more. The guards on duty did the guard thing. The ones off duty could answer questions, play tour guide, or just hang out.

Dani had been keeping a close eye on Jamie. Several late-night conversations where Jamie would just sob had her very concerned. Jamie seemed to struggle a little more than everyone else. She was an introvert for sure, but she had the biggest heart. At times Dani could swear she saw a blanket of sadness draped around her. They all missed aspects of their home and family, but Jamie had been very close with her dad. Dani knew it weighed heavily on Jamie and tried to keep reaching out to her, getting her out of herself and interacting with them all.

Dani had always been the one the group went to, to talk things through or just vent. Although she didn't mind speaking in front of people to get answers she wanted, she preferred being behind the scenes when it came to the social interactions. She liked watching the other girls stand out in their own unique ways.

At the end of the third week of working to get the school ready, groups of guys started arriving from different nations. Fraener would pull them aside and speak with them before they could even unload anything they and their spirit animals carried. Dani wasn't sure exactly what the conversation entailed but after seeing the deflated looks on the guys' faces, she got the gist. He was laying down the rules for interactions between the girls and the new guys. There was always a lot of head bobbing of agreement from the new arrivals. It was strange to be surrounded by so many guys.

Aside from their mothers, Dani had seen only a couple other women, beside Eulalios. Dani refused to add the title *Lady* to that woman's name, petty - yes, but she was a snooty witch who barely acknowledged their presence and when she did, it was with a sneer down her nose. Brooke was hot on finding out the story between Eulalios and the Regent Ruler, but just hadn't found the time to "properly snoop" around yet. The guards were not a lot of help and were darn good at evading the questions concerning them. Dani had so many questions still unanswered, but right now they had the School of Knowledge to get operational. The questions would have to wait.

The nighttime fire was something they all looked forward to. It was their way of wrapping up a day of hard work. Dani glanced over the large open field where several other fire pits were blazing now. Each clan tended to pick a pit and did not seem to mingle much with others.

"You guys have done a wonderful job," Theresa said. Agreed murmurs from all the adults followed.

"We didn't do it alone. It took everyone," Dani said, smiling.

"I have good news for you all. A Head Chancellor has been appointed. He will be starting the interviews for Professus in a few days," Zidicus announced.

Cheers went up all around. It was really going to happen. The girls were moving into their dorm rooms tomorrow. Brooke's grumblings as they went back and forth to the Palace each day on the back of a dragon still made her smile, but Dani was sure Brooke wouldn't miss the trips. Brooke at least had stopped looking so green when she got off. Dani looked over at her and saw the wide grin on her face. All the girls wanted to get out of the palace and somewhat on their own as soon as possible even if they did not have professors yet.

"What degrees will be offered and when do the girls get to choose their paths?" Amanda asked. Dani had put some thought into this very question as well. For now, Dani was just hoping to get a better understanding of where they were living and what types of jobs were even out there for them.

Uncle Zidicus spoke up, "For now I think working on basic principles of universal knowledge in math, science, language arts and history of Eirenic as well as Agon is a good start. The need to figure out what the girls know and don't know in each subject will be foremost. Once we know this, we will know where to start with each. It will be easier to proceed with what they want to do in their future once everyone has had a chance to settle in."

The girls all chatted with each other and the adults for the rest of the evening. Dani knew everyone was a little nervous and excited about the next day. They would have another bonfire tomorrow night, but it would be just the girls, the other students, and their guards of course. The moms were leaving in the morning to go to their Chosen Ones' homes in the different clan regions. Aunt Kathy would be staying at the palace.

Turns out, Uncle Zidicus is the younger brother to the Regent Ruler. He had a royal appointed job to do at the Palace. Aunt Kathy and Uncle Zidicus being so close by helped soothe some anxiety for the moms and girls. A lot had happened to them all in such a short amount of time. Dani knew her life would never be the same as she had planned back home. It saddened her to think about all her hard work towards her dreams. Now she and the others would be starting over in so many ways.

They did have healers here, but they used the sacred crystals for most of it. Aunt Kathy was cured of her cancer, as all of them had been healed going through the Axis Mundi. It apparently cleansed a person of all ailments. All the moms and Aunt Kathy looked years younger. Dani wondered if it was the reason for the fabled fountain of youth.

Trying to keep herself positive, she chose to think of her career choice changing as a good thing. She had so much to learn about Eirenic and the worlds around her. She was excited to learn more about how she was going to connect with her very own spirit animal. That part, she couldn't wait for.

Chapter 20

Eirenic

Waking up at dawn Dani laid there feeling excited that she would be staying in her room at the School of Knowledge that night and sad at the same time. Saying goodbye to all the moms was going to be tough. They were leaving for their new homes with their Chosen Ones. As a group, the girls and moms had decided the night before to eat breakfast together before they all took off. Getting up she got dressed and put the last of her things in the bag she was taking with her.

Walking out into the dining room Dani sat in the last available seat around the big table. Looking around she saw there was not a dry eye in the group of moms around the table. Conversations were brief and strained. They finished eating and walked out to the landing field, as the girls called it, next to the palace.

"Promise me you will look out for each other," Lynn said to her and Brooke.

"Of course, Mom, we will be fine," Brooke said while wiping a tear off her cheek.

"I know, I know. It's just hard. When did you two get to be so mature?" Lynn said, wiping at her own tears and looking back and forth between her two daughters.

"I believe it is called puberty, Mom," Dani said, trying to lighten the mood. She had already wiped some tears away from her own cheeks.

"Ha, Ha Daniella," Lynn said and gave her a very tight hug.

Dani tightly squeezed her back, "I know that you know I hate it when you use my full name, but I am going to let it slide this time." Her mom softly chuckled.

"We will send posts with the caravans. Please write to us and let us know how you are doing," Azmer said.

"You know we will," Brooke replied.

It was as if an unseen signal was sent. All the men guided the moms over to their spirit animals. The girls raced back inside and up to their balcony so they could see them off from above. Dani's mom and Azmer would be traveling to his home on the open plains. Amanda and Filtiarn would be heading to a forested area several hours away. Wendy and Barbar would be heading to the dense jungle. The most shocking one was Theresa and Ballene, who were heading to Atlantis.

She shook her head. *"Yep, that Atlantis,"* Dani thought.

Apparently, it had been removed from Terra because some of the Atlantis people were playing the whole "treat me like a God" thing. So, the Nephilim removed them from Terra. The entire city was now on Eirenic, in the middle of the ocean miles from shore. That explained why all the men with water spirit animals wore the wet suit type material.

Aunt Kathy and Zidicus had followed the girls up to the balcony. Dani walked over to them, and gently wiped tears off Aunt Kathy's cheeks.

"I know why you are crying, Aunt Kathy. You are stuck with all of us!" she said lightly.

Aunt Kathy ran her hand over her face. "Don't you know it," Aunt Kathy tried to sound cheerful.

"This is the beginning of things never being the same," Aunt Kathy said.

"What do you mean, Aunt Kathy," Brandi asked.

"When we took the trip, we adults knew it would never be the same when you all headed off to college. It just seems to be even more poignant now. Now you all are growing up in new ways and your moms are all off to their new lives as well," Aunt Kathy stated.

They all stood on the balcony looking out over the large open field and watched in silence until the last of the mom's group was out of sight. The nation's rulers had left earlier, after all the details had been put into place for the school. Guards had been left behind to escort the newly bonded

Chosen Ones home. Dani pondered over the few interactions she had with the nation leaders. It was horrible the amount of distrust they had for one another.

"It is so sad," she thought, *"this beautiful world has been torn apart so badly. Maybe with the school reopening, it would bring the nations back together again."*

"Check everything, be sure you didn't leave anything behind, girls," Aunt Kathy said.

They all took one last look around their suite.

"It's strange how much has changed in such a short amount of time," Jamie said to Dani.

"Yeah, but we are getting to go to school at least," Dani smile brightly to her.

They were all still trying to adjust. On more than one occasion, one of the others would come into Dani's room at night and they would sit and chat. Well, chat wasn't quite right. She would sit and let them talk themselves out. Jamie was still having the hardest time of all. It broke her heart to watch her friend sob. Not knowing what else to do, she figured the best thing she could do was to help her let it all out. It was like being home, in a way. She was still their sounding board.

Dani was the last to leave their suite, excited to be heading off on their new adventure. She never knew which guards she would have, so she just opened the door knowing two would be there to accompany her to the landing field. Herodion and Longwie stepped in beside her as she closed the door with a small bag of her stuff in her hand.

"Here, let me take this," Herodion said, reaching for her bag and slinging it over his shoulder. "Excited to start this next journey in your life?" he asked.

Before she could get her "yes" out, they heard Eulalios shouting at someone down the hall. Running into Eulalios was never desirable. Dani figured with the Regent Ruler so tied up in meetings, she was bored. So, she would find some poor soul to pick on and annoy. For some reason she took particular delight in targeting any of them. She, Herodion and Longwie quickly ducked into a side room to wait for Eulalios to pass.

As they all leaned against the walls in the small workroom, she whispered.

160

"Why is it that the Regent Ruler's tattoo is filled in and Eulalios's isn't?"

It had been bugging her since she noticed the Regent Ruler's tattoo when his robe flapped open as he rushed down the hall with his entourage trying to keep up. Didn't that only happen when you find your Chosen One? She did not feel she could ask the questions she wanted while they were walking down the halls where anyone could hear. Herodion exhaled a long, quiet sigh.

"His true Chosen One, as far as we know, is dead. She was a fierce and loyal fighter, pursuing the Evil One into the Axis Mundi during the final heated battle of the Great War. She has not been seen again. We are told her loud piercing scream could be heard right before the sealing was complete. It is believed that she never made it out," Herodion said.

The sadness in his eyes was unmistakable and Dani wondered if he somehow knew her. They had sat in silence for a few minutes when Eualos's voice came through the door reprimanding a servant for not cleaning a side rail to her liking.

"Poor guy," Dani whispered. "So, Eulalios is not with the Regent Ruler out of love." She didn't phrase it as a question, she knew the answer. "She is after power and prestige," she muttered.

Herodion nodded, as he whispered back, "She wormed her way into her position at the Regent Ruler's side not long after that day. She was raised here in the capital city. As one of the few females born, she was overly indulged and given leeway to have her every whim. She can be cruel and manipulative to those around her. I wholeheartedly agree in keeping any interactions with her as minimal as possible."

When the coast was clear they left the workroom and met the others on the landing field. Excitement was vibrating through the group as they flew over to the school with their guards. Brooke's dislike of flying was known by all. Dani wasn't sure if it was the fear of heights or the motion of the dragon's body as it flapped his wings that got Brooke so much. This time getting up on the dragon taking her Brooke didn't even hesitate to get on. All of them were so excited.

"Let the college experience begin!" Dani shouted as they took flight.

They all landed in the vast open lawn of the school and made their way to their dorm rooms. Their moms and Aunt Kathy had asked if they could decorate the girls' rooms as a parting gift. Dani and the others had all agreed to just to keep them happy. They headed up the wide stairway to their floor, excited to see their rooms for the first time. They all turned right at the top of the stairs. Fraener was pointing out whose room was whose.

"Dani your room is the first door on the left and Heather's is across the hall from yours," Fraener called and pointed to the doors.

The doors were offset so that if she opened her door the same time Heather did, they could not see into each other's rooms. She thought that was a pretty sweet feature. She waved to the others and opened her door as they continued down the hallway to their own rooms.

The room was huge. A king size canopy bed had gauze drapes pulled to the posts. Simple but luxurious bedding and throw pillows in deep reds and gold, her favorite colors, covered the huge bed. She could see the same color in accents all around her room.

"I love it!" Dani shouted out in excitement.

Opening doors on the dressers and closet, she saw all her things neatly put away. A small vase of flowers sat on her dresser. She then walked over to her desk and looked down at the mound of supplies on top of it for her and smiled. Her mom and Aunt Kathy had nailed it; it was perfect.

Dani sat down and started sorting her new supplies into manageable categories. Paper as they knew it was more like a thick parchment. Pens were a little heavier than they had been at home, with actual refillable ink reservoirs in them. Pencils were handmade. Each one was ever so slightly different than the others in the whittling of the wood. A knock on the door had her calling for whomever to come in.

"Wow, your room is just as large as mine," Heather said as she walked over and peeked into the bathroom. "Yep, just like mine. We could swim laps in those tubs."Heather turned and walked over to her as she continued sorting.

"Look at all the amazing stuff they got for us," Dani beamed.

"Ready for a break? I am starving. How about we go down and see what they have for lunch?" Heather said as she turned toward the door.

162

Dani hadn't realized how hungry she was until Heather said something about food. She followed her down the hall, walking on thick plush carpet to the grand staircase that led to the ground floor and into the dining area. The halls here were just as large as in the palace, just not as ornately decorated. As the days had passed during the cleanup, she had noticed more pictures being hung around the buildings.

Entering the dining room that had been designated for the girls, she noticed a buffet had been arranged and she and Heather walked towards it. Tables with chairs were in rows around the room. Fraener and Herodion had recommended they keep it a private space for now. After everyone arrived and things settled in, they could talk about making it open to everyone. No sense having a free-for-all over who got to sit with who, just yet. The girls had agreed, not wanting to have a bunch of guys staring at them while they ate. That would just be too weird.

After filling her plate, Dani walked over to a table where Jamie and Brooke were already seated. Brandi was still at the buffet getting her lunch. She had just managed to put her plate down when she heard the entry doors open and footsteps coming their way. She wondered if they might get to welcome a new female to the school for once, when a group of extravagantly dressed guys came through the door. Looking around she saw all the guards around the room stiffen, and Fraener quickened his steps to head off the group.

"To what do we hold the honor, Vice Regent?" Fraener said formally. It was easy to tell that the guards, whom she now thought of as her group of guys, were not thrilled with the group that entered the room.

"I have come to see the unmated and introduce myself. Step aside," the new guy waved his hand.

Dani couldn't help but take note of the arrogance radiating off the guy.

"Then it is your plan to attend the School of Knowledge?" Fraener asked.

"Clearly, now out of my way," the new guy quipped impatiently.

"If you would be so kind, I have been entrusted with the safety of these ladies by your father the Regent Ruler and I need to speak with you and your companions, privately, first," Fraener said more sternly.

"And I am the Vice Regent, you will move yourself out of my way, or I shall have you removed," the new guy's voice was louder and snobby.

Dani hadn't noticed Brandi working her way around the group of guys by the door, carrying her plate. The Vice jerk quickly stepped in her path and grabbed her free hand, leaning over.

"I am Vice...," was all the jerk got out.

Brandi was not one to take being manhandled. Her plate of food dropped, and she throat punched him as he leaned down over her hand. Dropping her hand and grabbing his throat, gasping. Brandi then swept his legs out from underneath him with a karate move. The arrogant jerk fell on his back and conveniently onto some of the food that had spilled from Brandi's plate.

The men stood frozen in different states of shock. The Vice Regent on the floor was gasping for air as he rubbed his now reddening throat.

"Do not touch me or any friend of mine unless they give you permission! You pompous, arrogant, ass! These men here," she gestured to the guards, "are with us. You will respect them at all times, or you are not welcome here," Brandi barked. She was a force of nature at the best of times. Pissed-off Brandi was a category ten tornado under complete control. Scary, very scary.

The Vice Regent gasped and sputtered. "Give me a hand," he spat to his group. When he stood, still slightly stooped over, he said, "Now see here, it is by the grace of my father that you are here at all."

A loud irritated voice came from the table. "I don't think so, jerk wad. All the nations are pitching in for this. This school may be across the bay from the palace, but I looked it up, it belongs to the people of Eirenic, not to one clan or current Regent Ruler!" Jamie was now standing and yelling across the hall.

Wow, Dani had never heard her speak so forcefully before. She was normally the epitome of the shy quiet type. "Go Jamie!" Dani whispered to her.

"Besides, this is the female dining hall and we the females," Brandi swept her hands toward their group, "did not invite you. So, when you can get the - *I am better than everyone else stick,* out of wherever you have it placed, maybe you can come back if we ever invite you." Brandi turned her back on the guy and stalked away, towards the group of girls now standing around the table muttering, "Now I have to go get another plate of food."

"My father shall hear of this!" the Vice Regent snapped as he turned towards the doors.

"Oh, tell him we said Hi and that *lovely Lady Eulalios as well.*" Brandi called after him in a sappy sarcastic tone. The Vice Regent stiffened at the mention of Eulalios but kept moving out the door.

Brandi sighed, "Yeah I know I shouldn't have baited him with that bit about the witch Eulalios living with his father but jeez, what a jerk!" she irritatingly blew out, turning back to the buffet.

"Well, that was fun. You guys hungry?" Brooke said as she sat back down. "Come on, after that guy, you have to be hungry. He had enough ego to fill an amphitheater. Now that he has left, the air he displaced has returned to the rest of us. That should make anyone breathe deep, smell the coffee and eat the buffet."

Brooke picked up a melon of some sort and took a big bite. The guards looked at each other and then started laughing.

"I hope we didn't get you guys in any trouble," Dani said.

"None that we cannot cope with," Fraener said, laughing.

Brandi walked over to the table with a new plate of food. Dani noticed Brandi sat where a book had been placed at the table and asked about it. "Whatcha got there Brandi?"

Brandi reached over and picked up the book holding it out to her, "With all the commotion I almost forgot to show you all this. I found it in the library on a dusty back shelf. The first thing that caught my eye was the strange lines on the binding that I think looks like Hebrew. Remember in Youth Group how we each learned to spell our names in Greek? Well, it looks like that to me. What do you think Dani?"

Dani reached over and took the old leather-bound book. She looked at it carefully before saying, "You know I think you are right. I think this says Seventy." She then opened the book and started flipping through it when Brandi spoke.

"I thought it was all in Hebrew, but if you go to the middle of the book, you're going to get a shock," Brandi said.

She quickly flipped to a little over halfway in the book and just stared down at the writing. "Oh my gosh, it's English. Old world English but English none the less. This looks to be a first edition. Look there is an ink stain here on the margin," Dani said, holding out the book for the others to see the small ink blot in the margin of the page.

"I think this is the Old Testament, or at least part of it," Brandi excitedly said.

She quickly flipped to the beginning of the chapter. It was titled Genesis. "Oh wow, look," Dani pointed, "Genesis!"

"I know, keep going," Brandi said.

Dani then quickly flipped to the following chapters, Exodus, Leviticus, Numbers and Deuteronomy flashed by. "Wow, you're right, it is the first five chapters of the Old Testament. Were there any other books like this one?" she quickly asked.

Brandi sighed out, "No, and I asked. The guy helping set up the library said it was a book brought back years before the Great War. This part you're never going to believe. He said the story told about this book is that an elemental had gone to Terra and found his chosen one there. She did not want to come back to Eirenic, so he stayed there with her until her death. The elemental claims to have helped translate the original texts of the Terra Holy book. He brought it back with him and died soon after arriving. There are no other Terra Holy books here. Do you all know what that means?" Brandi looked around to them all. Dani shook her head no, as did the others.

"Guys, they don't have Jesus here. They don't know about Jesus," Brandi whispered.

Shocked silence followed for a few minutes. Heather spoke next, "I think we should be sharing Jesus here, but do you think we could all take a book we remember in the New Testament and jot notes down first? Maybe start with Matthew, Mark, Luke and James and John? That at least would be a start."

Dani agreed and said, "I think that's a great idea. Who wants what book?"

They each took a book and agreed to start trying to remember key details about them. She finished her lunch trying to rack her brain about the book of John and knew she needed a mental break.

"After we eat, can we go work on the courtyard area that is covered in leaves?" She asked.

"It would be nice to have another large area with benches around it," Jamie commented.

About thirty minutes later Dani stood with what passed as a rake. Everything was hand made on Eirenic, so no two carved rakes were the same. The courtyard they were working on had a newly restored water channel flowing through part of it. The channel widened in the center to create a sizable area with slow-moving water. A canopy of trees provided cool shady areas where they were working to rake up all the dead leaves from years gone by. The architecture of Eirenic amazed her. Everything was built so that their spirit animals could be with them most of the time.

Dani had noticed that neither the Eirenicians nor their pnĕvma synergáti liked to be apart for long. Watching the interactions between the Eirenicians and their pnĕvma synergáti, Dani could see a real and tangible connection. She had heard several the guards having what she thought were one-sided conversations until she realized the pnĕvma synergáti was communicating, but it had to be telepathic in some way. It seemed that the animals could communicate with each other as well. All their connections she found intriguing.

"Having the ability to communicate telepathically with another intelligent entity is fascinating," Dani thought.

"Hey Herodion," she called out to get his attention. He was only a few feet away from her.

"What may I help you with, Lady Dani," Herodion said.

"I am starting to understand the different powers of the different types of the dragons. Some are no-brainers, water dragons can control all forms of water, fire dragons control fire, and forest or earth dragons control plant life. What exactly do the white dragons do?" she asked.

Herodion smiled, "It all."

"Define, 'it all'," she asked.

Herodion chuckled; she knew he was teasing her. "They can do all of those things and more. White dragons are the...," Herodion paused in his speaking. She thought he was about to say something that he did not want her to know.

"White dragons are?" she prompted.

"Special, they can do it all," Herodion said and turned to a pile of leaves, scooping them up and heading to the now exceptionally large pile they had all created.

Dani was positive he was holding something back. Each of the girls had one guard helping to clean, and one keeping watch. As she looked around, she caught the eyes of Brooke. They shared a wicked smile after Brooke motioned to their arms full of leaves and then to the guys around the pile. Silently they communicated their intentions to the other girls.

Walking up behind the guys, they knew they had no clue. Leaves went flying in a coordinated attack that could not have been as well executed if they had weeks to plan it. The guys yelped in surprise and spun around so fast they looked like blurs. The girls just stared at the startled guys that had their hands on the hilts of their swords as if ready to draw them. She looked around at the other guards posted to see each with a shocked look on their faces.

"Well, that went better in my head," Brooke muttered.

"Sorry guys. It was just a little fun. Didn't mean to scare you so much," Dani said, holding in her chuckle.

Herodion was the first to move, trying to brush leaves off. "You did NOT scare us," enunciating the NOT and quickly added, "startled, yes."

"Umm, so now would not be a good time to tell you that you have several leaves sticking out of your hair?" she said with a broadening smile.

She was trying really, really hard not to laugh, but all of them had leaves everywhere. She failed and the other girls soon followed, laughing so hard they had tears streaming down their faces.

"Oh my gosh, you should have seen your faces," Heather gasped out.

"You spun around so fast I thought you would spin into the ground," Brandi added.

"So, this is fun for you?" Herodion asked, reaching up to wipe his head again but only managing to get a couple of the leaves to stick up more.

Dani burst into laughter. Herodion glared at her.

"Sorry, sorry. Here, let me help you with those," she lifted up her hand and walked towards him. When she was almost within reaching distance of his head, Herodion bent down. She thought it was so she could reach the top of his head. She was wrong. Before she knew what happened, she was flying through the air. Squeals from the other girls reached her ears right before she landed, letting her know they were flying, too. She landed in a great poof of leaves, sinking in and almost losing sight of daylight.

"Now *those* were some delightful faces," Ryuu's voice was heard chuckling.

Brooke's muffled voice was heard somewhere off to Dani's right. "I have leaves in my hair. You will pay for that."

It was on! Leaves went flying everywhere. The girls spent most of their time being thrown back into the pile. It was when Brooke asked Ryuu's dragon for help that the odds turned in their favor.

"A little help here if you don't mind," Brooke called towards the large water dragon. Dani could have sworn it smiled at Brooke.

"Don't even think about asking for his help…" was all Ryuu got out as he was hoisted into the air and thrown into the not-so-tall pile of leaves.

"Why, you double-crosser you," Ryuu sputtered from somewhere under the leaves.

"Who's a good dragon?" Brooke purred as she rubbed the dragon's nose that was now down where she could reach it.

Dani looked over to Herodion's dragon. "Whatcha think, Xad? Want to help us even the odds?"

The words had barely passed her lips when Herodion went sailing through the air, landing with a puff of leaves flying high into the air.

"I will be paying that back," Herodion said from inside the pile. She wasn't sure if the comment was directed at her or Xad. She laughed and winked at the dragon just the same.

In the end, only the two dragons helped the girls. The others stood off and watched. Occasionally she noticed a tail flick to mound up the pile of leaves that kept getting spread out.

"Looks like we missed all the fun," Aunt Kathy said, walking into the courtyard and seeing them all lying or sitting around covered in leaves.

Chapter 21

Kolob

Kerberos looked up from the sacred pool in his private prayer room as it went dark, a small smile playing at his lips. He had found it very entertaining to watch the leaf throwing between the guards and girls. He wondered if Dani noticed the ease in which she was communicated with Herodion's dragon. Not being from Eirenic or Agon, she would not understand the rarity of that. A Chosen One could easily communicate with their soul mate's pnēvma synergáti. It was exceedingly rare that a pnēvma synergáti communicated with someone else.

There were dynamics to the pnēvma synergáti interactions with each other and humans that he did not have a complete understanding of. He knew enough to know that it was uncommon for Dani to be communicating so easily with them. He was also interested to find out more about this Jesus. When the young females spoke of him, it was with reverence, and this intrigued him.

As was true with most mornings now, his guard today was Zopyro. He was the only one who would wait for him on the inner wall next to his prayer room and not at the entrance to his chambers. He no longer had the luxury of true solitude. After the ambush on his life and the poisoning attempt, Zopyro pushed for him to consent to always having a guard present with him; he had relented.

"Good morning, my Liege. I hope your rest was good and your viewing and prayers brought enlightenment," Zopyro said.

"As always, my rest was sufficient and the viewing I am given by the

171

Creator during prayer is always enlightening," he answered.

"As you say," Zopyro acknowledged with a slight bow.

Zopyro fell in line behind him as he made his way to the door. Kerberos did not have much in the way of furnishings to impede his movements. Zopyro had joked long ago that a Nephilim of his standing should have more, as was due his rank as Liege. He had quipped back that he was not of the age that needed soft furnishings to comfort his body as the other two Lieges.

"As you already know, the assassin outside of the Hall of Equality was from Liege Burkhart's unit. I believe that information is widely known. Still a meeting has been called to discuss more information about both the assassination attempts," Zopyro stated.

"A meeting indeed," was all Kerberos said, then asked, "Any more private news on the poisoned juice in the library?"

"I was told that any new information regarding current events and the magic sealing the portals would be discussed at the meeting. I personally have no new information on the poisoning," Zopyro said.

Kerberos had been told the affiliation of the assassin by Dionysius right before the poisoning attempt on his life. How Burkhart handled the knowledge that the assassin was from his Nephilim would be interesting. If he condoned it, there would be bloodshed from both houses. His legionaries were loyal to him and so, they stood behind the understanding that the Creator had guided him in his actions. He, without a shadow of doubt in his mind, was doing as the Creator had willed him to do.

The other houses and their Legionnaires did not hold such faith. There was still animosity regarding his actions. Nephilim were still divided in their opinions. Before his actions, there had been division on what to do. Nothing had changed, other than the subject that divided them. The ripple the Creator had tasked him to make was having far reaching effects. The recent poisoning made that fact very clear to him.

The two made their way through the halls and walked through the doorway into the room where the meeting would take place.

"Right on time, Liege Kerberos," Dionysius said. "Shall we begin?"

Kerberos moved into the room and sat in his chair at the circular table. All three Lieges sat with their seconds at their right sides. He watched as three legionnaire scholars from house Dionysius sat across the table from the rest of them.

"Gerlach, if you would be so kind as to relay the information you have," Dionysius said.

"My Liege," Gerlach said, placing his fisted hand over his heart with a slight bow. He then turned to Kerberos and Burkhart, bowing slightly again, "Lieges."

"The current tampering with the magic that seals the portals, has caused a decline in its strength," Gerlach said.

"In your statement you said the current tampering. Are you saying there have been other attempts at breaking through?" Kerberos asked.

Gerlach looked to Dionysius as if asking for help.

"I asked the question, you will answer it," he bit out.

"Yes, there have been other attempts," Gerlach said.

"Why have we never heard of this before now?" Burkhart bellowed.

"If you would calm yourself," Dionysius said. "There was a measure of doubt as to the credibility of the evidence found. Without 100 percent certainty, I would never come and divulge questionable hypotheses and stir up more trouble than we already have," Dionysius said.

Burkhart was still having difficulty controlling his outburst. Kerberos could understand his outrage. He wanted all the information Dionysius had been withholding from them.

"Gerlach, please go over all information and evidence you and the scholars have found or have heard of," he said in a tight-lipped controlled voice then added, "I do not care how trivial you think it is. We want to know everything. Do not hold back the smallest detail. Am I making myself clear?"

Gerlach paled, looking from Kerberos to Dionysius and back again.

"See here, Kerberos. Do not try to intimidate my scholar," Dionysius said.

"I made no threat to him, Dionysius. After I hear all the data and information you have been withholding from me, I will be having a private meeting with you. I would not push me at this time," he watched as Dionysius broke eye contact and looked back to Gerlach.

"Please continue, Gerlach. Liege Kerberos and I will have a discussion later," Dionysius said.

"Yes, yes we will," he whispered and thought, *"The time for secrets from the scholars has past."*

"Eight months ago, a sacred crystal was found dead near one of the secluded sacred pool chambers," Gerlach said. Kerberos could tell he was still withholding information. The way he kept looking to Dionysius for some sort of indications to continue was obvious. Kerberos felt his legendary control was starting to slip.

"If I must, I will have a private meeting with you, Gerlach, so that you are not distracted by Liege Dionysius in any way," he said. The scholar paled further. "I want all the information and I can tell you are withholding things. Be as transparent as the sacred crystal around your neck. I can tell there must have been other sacred crystals found in this state. How many, where, when? I want all the information you have, NOW!" Kerberos snapped.

"There have been six other times that sacred crystals have been found dead," Gerlach quickly said and then paused. Kerberos raised one of his eyebrows. Gerlach quickly continued. "I will start with the oldest one we know of. One was found soon after the sealing. Another was found a year after that and again another year or so after the second one. I cannot tell you the exact dates, but I can go and look them up for you."

He could tell the scholar would like nothing more than to bolt from the room, but he did not give him the option.

"We can get those later. Please continue. I believe you are up to three with three more events remaining," he said.

Gerlach swallowed, "Yes, another was found two days after your females were ushered through the portal. Another was three days after that."

"Which one was the one eight months ago?" he asked.

"The third one," Gerlach said.

"One is still not accounted for. When was the last sacred crystal found dead?" he questioned.

"Yesterday," Gerlach whispered out.

"YESTERDAY? Why in all that is holy did you not inform us of these events before NOW?" Burkhart bellowed again.

"I informed my Liege," Gerlach whispered, clearly shaken by Burkhart's outburst.

"Again why do you keep information hidden Dionysius!?" Burkhart raged.

"Calm yourself, Burkhart," Dionysius said. Kerberos saw a bead of perspiration run down the side of the older Nephilim's face.

"Perhaps this would be a good time to adjourn and reconvene when everyone has had a moment to calm themselves," Dionysius said.

"I do not think so, Dionysius. I have many questions still to be answered and I do not want the answers conveniently lost with the break in time," Kerberos stated.

"Gerlach, it is clear the crystals were used to do an evil act. That is the only thing that costs a crystal's life. I get the impression you are hypothesizing that the dead crystals were used to try and communicate through the sealed portals?" Kerberos asked.

"See here," Dionysius sputtered, "You are trying to lead my scholar to a hypothesis not based on hard facts. What is the point in forming an opinion on a guess?"

"I'm asking for an educated guess Dionysius. Or are you implying that we should not take the knowledge of your scholars into account and send in our own Legionnaires to do some digging?" Kerberos countered knowing full well that Dionysius would never willingly give up his attempt to control the information discovered by the scholars in his legion.

"I think there should be a joint inquiry regardless of the information provided. How do we know they are telling us everything this time?" Burkhart demanded.

"This is why Dionysius, and his legion scholars, are going to tell us everything now. So that when we do our digging, we find nothing new," Kerberos stated.

"You have some nerve speaking of keeping things from others, Kerberos," Dionysius' controlled politician facade fell from his face.

"What I do, I do with the direction and blessing of the Creator of All. I do not believe you can say the same," he said as his eyes bore into the older Nephilim. A fleeting flash of guilt passed across Dionysus' face before he looked back to Gerlach and gave a slight nod for him to continue.

"After the first sacred crystal was found a few years ago, we started being extra vigilant at keeping measurements of the magic that was sealing the portals. With each sacred crystal found dead, we found a correlated spike of energy being directed at the magic used to seal the portals," Gerlach said.

Kerberos sat for a few moments thinking over the information he was just given. One or more of Erebos' followers had been trying to reach him. Not just once but several times over the years. Now, those attempts had increased due to the diminishing magic after Liege Kerberos sent the females through."

"Do you know if the perpetrator was able to get through the sealing magic?" he asked.

"We cannot say for sure yes or no. As the magic dwindles, we are certain it is just a matter of time before communications through the portals will be possible. For now, all we know is those communication attempts came at the cost of a sacred crystal," Gerlach said.

"What of the poisoning in the Hall of Records?" Burkhart asked.

"I can tell you that the poison is from a rare fish found in the deep oceans. It is fast-acting. One must inject the antidote within moments of consuming it to survive," Gerlach said.

"Are there any indications who it was meant for?" Burkhart asked.

Gerlach swallowed again looking over to Dionysius then back to Burkhart. "If I had to make a hypothesis, I would say it was meant to kill Liege Kerberos."

"What facts are you using to make this hypothesis?" Burkhart asked.

Gerlach answered without hesitation, "Liege Kerberos has been frequenting the Hall of Records for some time. He is known to stay in that area of the hall. There are very few that go to that section and when they do it is only a quick trip in and out. Liege Kerberos has been spending hours in that section at each visit. Due to this fact, a beverage service was recently added to that section. Liege Kerberos has a well-known history of having a fondness for the sweet juice since childhood."Gerlach looked over to Kerberos. He just tilted his head. He had already come to the same conclusion.

"It seems you have a target on your back, Kerberos. Take heed that the assailant's aim does not find its mark," Burkhart advised.

With that advice from Burkhart, it was clear that the meeting was over.

"I will take my leave," Kerberos stated.

He stood and walked towards the door as Burkhart continued to vent his outrage at Dionysus for withholding information from them. Zopyro followed close behind him as he walked to the practice field. Kerberos went off to one side where an area was set up for forms practice. He pulled his sword and started the flow of movement through his body, following forms his muscles knew by heart. The practice allowed his mind to focus.

As of yet, no one knew if it would be a gradual diminishing of magic or if one day it would just completely fade all at once. Currently each of the three legions took turns guarding the last sacred pools that had been active before the sealing. There were not enough Nephilim left to guard every sacred pool located in the Crystal Fortress. The decision had been made to guard the sacred pools that had been the most active and the last sealed. Someone had been taking advantage of the limited number of guards to try and reach the Evil One.

He did not need Burkhart to point out a fact he already knew, someone or ones were trying to kill him. He had recently earned the ire of several Nephilim groups. The scholars were not happy that he was digging into the past. Erebos' followers would want him dead to ease their takeover of Kolob and the worlds beyond.

He said a silent prayer to the Creator of all, "Please my Lord, let Dani and her friends' lives stayed uneventful of evil for a while more. I have no doubts the evil will find them in due time. I just pray they are made ready and better prepared when it does."

Chapter 22

Eirenic

Dani knocked on Aunt Kathy and Uncle Zidicus' suite door at the palace. She was looking forward to her Sunday morning brunch date with Aunt Kathy. As she waited for the door to open she thought about the rest of her day. After their brunch she was going on her favorite hike around the cliff side of the lake. Sitting on the cliff face she felt a little bit of solitude from the world around her.

Sundays were the days the girls spent however they wanted. Brandi most days could be seen either reading the book "Seventy" or writing notes on the New Testament book she had chosen. Sometimes all the girls would join Brandi and share what they had so far in their notes. They would all add to each other's books as they remembered things. Other days they just spent it however they wanted. Like the occasional brunch with Aunt Kathy. Sometimes one or all would come, other times just Dani. Lots of times they would spend the day alone. As alone as they could get with two guards and the guards' pnēvma synergáti following them. The opening door ended her internal thoughts, as she was engulfed in a tight hug.

"You know you don't have to knock, Dani," Aunt Kathy said, stepping back so she could walk in. As she entered, she saw Fraener hesitate in the doorway behind her. Herodion must have already gone somewhere.

"You don't have to stand there the entire time I have brunch. I promise I will send someone to get you when I want to leave. Is that okay?" Dani asked him.

"That is acceptable," Fraener said before turning and walking back down the hall.

She and Aunt Kathy made their way onto their balcony. A table was set and overflowing with food. On the far side of the balcony sat Zidicus' dragon, Gordy.

"Good morning," Dani called over to him and smiled when he bobbed his head in response.

"I hope you're hungry," Aunt Kathy said as she sat. "Zidicus ordered all of this. I hope he is planning on coming back to eat some of it," Aunt Kathy laughed.

"It looks delicious," Dani replied, and they dug in.

"So, how are the other girls doing? Settling in okay?" Aunt Kathy asked.

"Yeah, for the most part," she said, thinking of Jamie.

"I know that look. I am guessing that Jamie is still having a hard time," Aunt Kathy said.

She shrugged. The conversations she had with the others were not something she shared, even with Aunt Kathy. They confided in her and she held their confidence no matter what.

"I am not asking you to divulge their personal secrets, honey," Aunt Kathy said. "I guessed that Jamie is having a hard time. She and her dad were awfully close. Not that this has been easy on any of you," Aunt Kathy said.

"It's okay. We are all adjusting in our own ways, I guess," Dani said.

Just then there was the sound of a door being thrown open and bouncing off a wall from above and to the right of them. The sound of raised male voices followed. She and Aunt Kathy looked up to see if they could identify who was yelling and what was going on.

"Regent Ruler, you have to listen to reason. Please, you cannot try to open the portals and allow the evil to return to Eirenic!" A man's impassioned voice, one Dani did not recognize, spoke in desperation.

"How do we know if Erebos still lives? He is most likely dead, and we have waited all this time for nothing! Do not presume to tell me what is best for Eirenic! I am the Regent Ruler, not you! Now do as you are told!" The Regent Ruler's voice grew to a menacing, arrogant shout by the end of his rant.

"Regent Ruler!" Dani instantly recognized Uncle Zidicus' voice for the first time.

"Zidicus, do not start with me!" the Regent Ruler seethed.

"I would do no such thing," Uncle Zidicus' placating voice stated.

There was silence for quite a while. She and Aunt Kathy sat quietly meeting each other's gaze and then turning back to look up, their meal forgotten. The Regent Ruler's loud sigh floated down to them.

"I suppose you agree with them?" he angrily spat out, but with not as much force as before.

"I think they have a valid point," Uncle Zidicus said.

She heard the sputtering tones of the Regent Ruler trying to say something.

"Let me finish if you please. I also feel you have a valid point. We are cut off and do not know what has happened on Agon. Maybe a compromise could be considered?" Uncle Zidicus said.

"Always the peacekeeper, Zidicus," the Regent Ruler said with disdain in his voice. "Maybe you would be more likely to help me if it was your Kathleen that was torn from you," the Regent Ruler said. She heard Uncle Zidicus sigh.

"Democritus, I do not ever want to know what it is like to be where you are right now. It is unfathomable to me. I too would never give up searching. But I would hope that those around me would help temper my desperation and turmoil," Zidicus said quietly.

Silence ruled again from the balcony above them.

"What do you propose?" the Regent Ruler snapped.

"We all agree that the information supports the conclusion that the magic that sealed the portals has weakened since the passage of the females. I propose that we look for a way to send a message through to Agon to a family that we know was on our side during the Great War. If this can be accomplished, we can get the information we all seek," Uncle Zidicus' voice never rose in his exchange with the mal-tempered Regent Ruler. She was impressed. There was no way she would have held it together that long and not snapped back at him.

"Fine," the Regent Ruler sighed. "Have it done!" A door could be heard slamming.

She and Aunt Kathy sat looking at one another for a few moments.

"Is the Regent Ruler always this cranky and unreasonable?" Dani asked breaking the silence.

Aunt Kathy sat for a few seconds more in silence and then said, "Not from what Zidicus has told me. He said that his brother has always been more of an introvert and was a lot happier when he got to do his own things before becoming the Regent Ruler. The devastating loss of his Chosen One and then having to step into the shoes left by the former king has not been easy for him. Apparently, he has become increasingly erratic even for Zidicus to communicate with. The yelling match we just heard is the new norm, I guess." Aunt Kathy looked down at her plate, moving a piece of fruit around before taking a bite.

They both turned and looked towards the doorway when they heard it opening. Zidicus came through the door and shut it behind him. Dani could see his tense posture and knew he was stressed out. She really felt bad for him, having to deal with his brother. Zidicus walked over and placed a kiss on the top of Aunt Kathy's head. He then looked over at his dragon and they just looked at each other for a few minutes. She easily figured out that they were communicating. When Zidicus spoke, it confirmed what she had just thought.

"Sorry you had to hear all of that," Uncle Zidicus said as he sat at the last place setting at the table. Aunt Kathy reached over and squeezed his hand. He looked at her and smiled a tired smile.

Dani's mind was running. The Regent Ruler had said that they had no control of the portals. Yet, they are going to try and communicate with Agon. Something wasn't adding up in her mind. She knew Uncle Zidicus was stressed but she had to ask.

"Uncle Zidicus, do you mind if I ask you a few things? Just to clear up some things that have been bothering me," Dani said.

"As always, please feel free to ask me anything, Dani. What has been bothering you?" Uncle Ziticus asked.

"Well, we couldn't help but hear the Regent Ruler. I mean anyone within a few miles probably heard all that. When we got here, the Regent Ruler said that you all had no control over the portals because the Nephilim control them exclusively. But you all just agreed to use the portals to communicate with the other world, Agon. So, you must have *some* amount of control over them. I feel we are not being given the entire truth here and some particularly important details are being left out," Dani said.

Uncle Zidicus gave a small smile to her. "You really are as bright as your Aunt Kathy says you are. I have not been intentionally keeping anything from you, but I can see how you could come to that conclusion. We could open the portals for communication with the aid of the Nephilim before the Great War and the sealing. The Nephilim control the access to the Axis Mundi. That is what we physically travel through to get to the other worlds. To physically travel, you must have a portal gate at each end to go through. This takes a tremendous amount of energy and precise planning.

A communication portal is different. It is much smaller and uses significantly less energy and precision in using a sacred crystal. The worlds are still connected through the Axis Mundi, but not in a physical way. Your Aunt Kathy says it sounds like what you would call a video call. The Nephilim can still watch and listen to all things that happen if they choose. They can disconnect a communication completely, or not let it happen at all. Understand that the use of a sacred crystal's power must be for pure reasons. You risk damaging or even killing a sacred crystal if you use it wrong. For this reason, we have a department called Ansible that manages all communications.

We are not trying to keep you from communicating with your loved ones you left behind. I understand this must be extremely hard on you girls. Also try and think about how your loved ones would react when your face appeared out of nowhere in a pool of water close to them, or in a reflective glass. I fear they would think they had lost their grip on reality. I truly wish there was an easier way to proceed and connect you with your loved ones left behind. I cannot imagine the depth of my sorrow if I lost you, and I have been blessed with you for only these past weeks."

She blinked back tears as she thought of her father. *"Yep, it sucks,"* she thought, and looked down at her plate.

"Let's talk of more pleasant things, shall we?"Uncle Zidicus said. "I heard you young ladies got to meet my nephew the Vice Regent Ruler the other day," he said, and then busted out laughing. "I must say, if everything happened the way I heard it did, please give Brandi a hug for me. He has needed his ego checked for a long time, having been spoiled for so long by his father."

The rest of the meal went by pleasantly. She told them about how her classes were going and the path she found leading to a cliff overlooking the lake. Zidicus knew exactly the walk she spoke of, having walked the path many times himself as a student at the school.

They all turned as the doors opened again and Herodion walked out to the balcony with Fraener. She noticed the tight set of Herodion's mouth and new it was something not pleasant he wished to speak about.

"Excuse me for one moment," Uncle Zidicus said, and the three men walked back inside shutting the door behind them.

The sound of dragon wings had Dani and Aunt Kathy looking up to see Herodion's dragon, Xad, looking down at them from the balcony wall above. He started trying to entertain them by blowing smoke rings. She and Aunt Kathy burst out laughing. She laughed even harder when Gordy, snorted, clearly unimpressed by Xad's antics. She felt her mouth fall a little open in amazement as Gordy puffed out a heart shape. She and Aunt Kathy laughed and laughed as the two dragons puffed out shape after shape in a duel of creativity. Several smoke shapes floated in the air as the men came back out onto the balcony. They all stopped and looked around at the smoke shapes that had just started to dissipate.

"I see you two were well entertained," Uncle Zidicus said, chuckling. He walked back over to sit at his spot at the table."Herodion and Fraener, grab yourselves a place setting and please join us," Uncle Zidicus said, motioning with his hand to a cart Dani had not paid attention to that sat just behind her next to the wall.

"You will have to show me the walk you speak of so fondly," Aunt Kathy said.

She smiled as the group around her continued with small chat. It became clear that Herodion and Fraener had known each other for a very long time.

"How long have you two known each other?" Dani asked them.

Uncle Zidicus laughed and said, "Before they could walk. The two of them have caused more mischief around the palace than I could recount in a single setting."

She looked over to Fraener for clarification. "My father was the head of the late King and Queen's guard. My mother and the Queen were also remarkably close friends. I have spent my entire life here at the palace," Fraener said.

Before she could ask Herodion how he grew up at the palace the conversation turned, and she forgot to ask. She guessed that Herodion's dad must have been part of the royal guard as well.

The afternoon flew by, and it was getting to be late afternoon by the time she, Herodion and Fraener left to go back to the School of Knowledge.

Chapter 23

Eirenic

Dani smiled as she made her way around the lake on the small path up to the cliff. It was a beautiful early evening. She really enjoyed her walks around the large lake. There was a dense forested area around three sides of the lake. A low spit of land separating the ocean bay and freshwater lake had some low hills on it. She still marveled at the size and varieties of the different animals, insects, trees, and plant life. At night she would gaze into the forests that ran around the back side of the school. She loved to watch the luminescent colors of the leaves, flickering in and out of view as the wind stirred the plants and trees. The girls had not yet had a chance to explore the forests. That was close to the top of her to-do list here on Eirenic.

Walking up the slope, she thought about how she never felt completely alone. Whether from the guards and their spirit animals always following her, or from something she was starting to understand came from within, she was never alone. When she was dwelling on troubling thoughts, she felt a presence that she could not put her finger on. It made her nervous and a little overwhelmed, not knowing what it could be. It wasn't the same as she felt at the cabin. She absently rubbed over her heart as if that was where the warmth was spreading from.

She often thought of missing home and her dad, to everything she had been through. It had been a week since she had heard the Reagent Rulers rant at the palace and was worried about the situation there as well. She always tried to stay positive but at times it was hard. Maybe the next time she saw

Herodion she could ask him about the Reagent Rulers mental health issues. Trying to shift her depressing thoughts she purposely started thinking about the amazing world she now lived in, and her excited expectation she felt at eventually having her own spirit animal.

Dani's view from the top of the sheer cliff wall that rose vertically from the lake below was breathtaking. She looked across the lake to the large campus of The School of Knowledge and the ocean beyond it. The wind blowing in her face brought smells of the lake, forest, and ocean. Each had its unique aromas that would swirl together around her in different ways depending on what direction the wind came from. If she closed her eyes and held her arms out, she almost felt like she was flying. She loved the sensations and the feelings of peace and calm she experienced in that moment. Funny, she remembered having a slight aversion to heights before coming to Eirenic. Guess flying on the back of a dragon could change a person, she thought smugly.

It still amazed her that she had gotten so comfortable with the presence of at least one guard, normally two, and their dragons following her. For being such big men and animals, they were surprisingly quiet. They always kept a respectful distance and allowed her the semblance of "alone time." Right now, she really needed the space to ponder and reflect. She did a lot of reflecting, sitting on the cliff. Mostly she focused on the things that had happened since they arrived on Eirenic. Her illusion of being alone was interrupted by the sound of someone approaching. Turning she saw Herodion sit down beside her.

"Hey Herodion, how's it going?" Dani asked.

Herodion shrugged and said, "What is the saying Heather uses, you know, same old same old."

Looking into his eyes, she could see dark circles under them. He looked like he wasn't sleeping well. She watched as he pulled a clump of grass up and started shredding it. Clearly, he was a little stressed out as well. They sat for several minutes in silence. She didn't know what was stressing him out so much, but it was taking its toll on him.

"So, what are your thoughts this fine evening?" Herodion asked.

"Oh, you know, life, the universe, the usual stuff," Dani answered.

"Tell me your thoughts, please. It will give me a break from my own for a while," Herodion offered a small smile.

"Sure, okay. Well, I just started thinking about the school and more specifically the students. There are what, about thirty of us now? Five of them are me and my friends. I haven't seen one other female student. That is kind of depressing. Something needs to change soon in the male-to-female ratio. Can't more women be found? And I don't even want to think of what "found" means," Dani added quickly, "not ready for that yet." she stopped when Herodion looked as if he was going to say something.

"Fair enough," Herodion said with a small smile. "What else?" he prompted.

"Well, we have four classes so far: History, Math, Science and Language Arts. We girls sit close to the front of each class. The guys sit at least one complete row away from any of us. We can barely get them to say "Hi" in passing. Even at the bonfires, the others stick to themselves.What are you telling these guys when they first show up?" she prodded.

"First, we take your safety very seriously," Herodion said.

"I get that, but..." she tried to cut in. Herodion raised his hand to quiet her.

"Please let me finish. That is not all. The other nations have a mistrust of anyone outside their nation. The Great War did not kill just Eirenician people. It killed our society in many ways. We used to be so much more than what we have become. There is so much bitterness and paranoia that someone will come and take what you covet most. Imagine, you know the odds of finding your Chosen One, your one perfect mate, the one who completes your very soul, are incalculably miniscule. Now we have a better chance of being struck by a falling rock than of finding your Chosen One.

In addition to that, all crystals are mined on Agon. We are cut off from Agon. With the mistrust issues, we have not had success at dealings with the elementals, or magic users, however you wish to call them. They are being difficult and are the only ones who can recharge sacred crystals. Then there is the Regent Ruler who takes nothing into account as he uses anything and everything at his disposal to attempt to get through the magic that seals the portals. We have found that it is weakening more each day after you and your friends came through. The few elementals we do have at the palace and the scholars cannot determine when it will fail completely. The Regent Ruler is helping none of this with his increasingly erratic behavior," Herodion exclaimed in frustration, rubbing his hand across the back of his neck.

She just sat quietly, waiting for Herodion to speak again. After a few minutes, he turned and looked at her and she gave him a small smile.

"Thank you, Dani. It was not my intention to come here and vent my frustrations on you," Herodion said.

Dani reached over and gave his hand a quick squeeze. "No problem, that is what friends are for," she said.

"So, how is your mother and the others?" Herodion asked. She got the hint he was ready for a change in topic.

"They are doing great according to their letters. I just wish we had some way of paying for our mail ourselves. Kind of gets to me and the other girls that we have to rely on others for everything," Dani said.

"I see your frustration. The barter system with the caravans provides much-needed goods for all. It is one of the few things that keeps our society somewhat connected. It benefits all involved," Herodion said. "In a way I am sorry that you and the other girls did not have Chosen Ones to help with this transition. In a selfish way I am glad you did not."

Not knowing what to say to that, she just looked at him.

Herodion continued, "If you and the others had Chosen Ones, this school would not be open. The nation leaders would not be working somewhat together and I would not have a valued friend with whom to talk," Herodion smiled. Then his tone turned serious, "I believe there are greater forces pushing us in a certain direction. How we choose to deal with the direction is for each of us to decide. The decisions each individual makes, will affect the whole of us all. There are consequences for every action we take. I pray to the Creator of All, that most people make good choices."

They sat quietly again, she was swinging her legs over the cliff, trying to think of something to say. She was not sure whether her next question would improve Herodion's mood.

"Jamie found out that you all used to be able to use smaller portal areas to communicate with others around Eirenic. I guess they look like a large wavy mirror that you can speak through. We asked Uncle Zidicus to find out if we can use those to communicate with our moms. He said the communications official at the palace has flatly refused to open them. When we asked if there was anyone else we could talk to, he said only the Regent Ruler. I got the impression he did not want to ask him. Has he gotten worse since our brunch with Aunt Kathy and Uncle Zidicus?" Dani asked.

"I cannot say that I blame Zidicus for not wanting to speak to him. The Regent Ruler is ..." Herodion paused, "very stressed, erratic in his thinking, and preoccupied."

"Do you think the real king should step up? I mean it is his job, after all," Dani asked.

Herodion got a pained look on his face before answering. "I believe the future king is doing everything that he can. To step forward now might bring about the complete unbalance of an already unstable ruling council."

"You know who he is, don't you?" Dani questioned.

Herodion just shrugged and kept looking across the lake.

She scanned the view in front of her, looking out over the lake towards the bay that led to the open ocean. Off in the distance to the right, the palace's creamy surface shone in the sunlight. Off to the left but much closer, the school's vast campus could be seen. In the lakes on the campus, she could just make out splashes of water from large water pnĕvma synergáti that looked like they were having fun. There were several sections of the school that were still not cleaned up and in use.

The wide expanse of dividing land between the lake and the bay had several large rectangular mounds on it. In the middle of the mounds Dani noticed what appeared to be the hollow areas in the shape of a capital "I". Dani wasn't sure what they were but could tell they had been purposely made and were not naturally occurring. She mentally added it to her ever-growing list of things to check out.

Looking back towards the School of Knowledge, she noticed the light of the bonfires starting up.

"Come on, let's go see if Heather found what passes for the ingredients for s'mores here," Dani said as she stood and reached a handout to help Herodion up.

They walked back down to the school and when they got closer, Herodion spoke.

"I will try and make it back to try some of the dessert you have mentioned. I have something I must attend to first," he said.

"I'll try and save you one if I can," Dani replied and headed over to her regular seat at their fire.

Brandi was talking as she sat down, "Look, I don't know about you guys, but I think we are going to need to do something about this bubble we have been placed in. I tried to talk to one of the male students when we were leaving science. The shocked expression on his face when I said 'Hi, how's it going?' would have been funny if it wasn't so sad. He all but bolted for the door! The guy almost took out another guy going through it," Brandi sighed.

"Yeah, I had one practically run out of a building when I tried to talk to him in the hall," Brooke chimed in.

"We need to do something to break the ice, I think. They need to know we aren't man eaters or something. Especially after Brandi took out that jerk, the Vice Regent Ruler guy in the lunchroom," Jamie said.

"I agree, and I've got just the thing," Brandi said with a grin that made all of them take notice. When she was this animated, it normally signaled muscle strains and pain in their futures. "I asked Uncle Zidicus if he knew of anyone that could make us a soccer ball. He was a little confused about what that was, but after working with him and another guy, I have one that should be here in a couple of days. How about we start playing?" Brandi all but beamed at everyone. A collective groan could be heard from the other girls.

Brandi was a sports phenomenon. With anything sports related, she was a natural at it. Soccer was her passion. She was the epitome of competitive and aggressive on the field. She lived by the motto "if you can't run with the big girls, stay on the porch and enjoy the view." She wasn't mean, by any means. She would teach and help anyone, but she expected them to give as much enthusiasm and drive as she did. More than one "fun game" had turned into Brandi wiping the field of every other opponent.

"How about we find out what they do here on Eirenic for fun, too?" Heather chimed in.

"Oh, okay. I guess we can. I mean I will still be having fun with my new soccer ball when it gets here. So, anyone can come join me," Brandi said, deflating a little.

"I think that is a great idea, Brandi. You can show anyone interested in playing soccer and we can also show interest in what kinds of things the Eirenicians do," Dani quickly said. *"Hopefully that unruffled Brandi's feathers a bit,"* she thought to herself.

The plan was made for each of them to ask the guards around them what they did for fun.

Chapter 24

Eirenic

Dani hurried down the bright corridor, excited to be going to history class with Professus Dubsar. History was one of her favorite subjects. She was fascinated and intrigued by learning about the different worlds, and how they are all connected through the Axis Mundi. It was a review day and she was eager to check if the facts running around in her head were correct.

"Please put your seats in a circle so we may begin our review of knowledge taught and learned," Professus Dubsar said.

As they pulled their chairs into the circle, she asked, "Professus, may I ask you something?"

"Of course, Lady Dani," he said in his tight formal voice.

"I was eating my breakfast early today and saw you come out of the bay on a giant tentacle. I am guessing that was your spirit animal?" Dani asked.

Professus Dubsar wore the leather-like, tight fitting clothing she noted all the water tribes wore, under his puffy-sleeved long Professus robe. His was remarkably close to the color of the tentacle that he had walked out of the water on.

"Yes, my pnĕvma synergáti is a giant octopus," Professus Dubsar said.

She thought back to the size of the tentacle. Yes, giant was a good description. The girth at the largest point she had seen was the size of a small car.

"What did you do before coming here to be our Professus?" Brooke asked.

Dani smirked at how easily Brooke had managed to charm most of the

Professus they had.

Professus Dubsar gave one of his exceedingly rare slight smiles at Brooke as he answered. "I am a priest for a small tribe that lives in the tidal area around the cliffs north of the palace. Thank you for asking, Lady Brooke. If everyone is ready, let us begin." He looked around to be sure they were all seated before talking again.

"As you all know, this class is currently set to bring you young ladies up to speed on the history of Eirenic, mainly. But one cannot discount the overlap of historical information needed to get a well-rounded view. So, we also take a more general look at the events on Agon, our sister world, and Kolob, the world of the Nephilim. You are well versed in the history of Terra, so we will not be spending much time on it," Professus Dubsar said.

He had made it abundantly clear the first day of class that the males, other than their guards, were not welcome. As he put it very bluntly, they should already know all this information and did not need to waste their time or his.

"Yep, that put a big damper on the male attendance," Dani thought.

Still, several of them ignored the Professus and sat in anyway. They had little time, so far, to interact with the guys that were still slowly showing up at the school. After Fraener had his talk, they all gave the girls a very wide berth, something that all the girls were getting tired of.

"Lady Brooke, if you would be so kind as to start us off please with a summary," Professus Dubsar said. Dani chuckled in her head; Brooke had the old priest professor right where she wanted him.

"Absolutely Professus Dubsar, thank you so much for letting me start our discussion," Brooke cooed.

She rolled her eyes at her sister's antics. Her sister just could not help it, she was a natural flirt and men, being men, always seemed to fall for it.

"There are four planets connected through the Axis Mundi," Brooke gestured with her hands. "Terra, Eirenic, Agon and Kolob. Both Eirenic and Agon have several different nations on them and are normally ruled by a royal family. Each also has a congress or parliament of some sort that presides under the royal family. Well, that was until the Great War. No one on Eirenic knows what is going on now in Agon or Kolob. You also have this evil guy, Erebos, who is presumed to be on Agon."

"Well done, Lady Brooke. Lady Jamie, if you would continue with our knowledge review," Professus Dubsar said.

Jamie took a quick breath and continued the discussion in her quiet voice, "The determining factor for how the nations on both Eirenic and Agon are divided is depending on what your pnēvma synergáti is, or if you are a mage, slash, elemental user. A pnēvma synergáti is a man's physical representation of his spirit partner, and an animal that they have with them most of the time. All the physical spirit animals look similar to wild animals from our home, Terra, only on a much larger scale. For us, we picture a tiger, but so large that to mount it, the person riding it would need it to lie flat on the ground, and they still need a large leg up. Well, the guys don't, just us girls. Anyway, there are the dragons that can be found in all geographical areas on Eirenic. The geographical areas the other animals come from are tropical, forest, plains, and water. The pnēvma synergáti seem to have evolved from base animals we can relate to that are found on Terra," Jamie's quiet voice was stopped abruptly by Professus Dubsar's quick interruption.

"Remember, Lady Jamie, we are all as the Creator made us to be. The thought of evolving from a lesser form is still a very heated debate." He looked at her pointedly. "If you will, Lady Brandi, continue our discussion."

Dani noted that Jamie slouched a little in her seat after the curt reprimand. Apparently, she was not the only one who noticed, because the look on Brandi's face did not bode well for the Professus.

"Sure Professus. As we all know, evolution can mean several different things. As I am sure you know due to your vast knowledge," Brandi said with a slightly clipped tone in her voice. "On Terra, another name for evolution is natural selection. Where an environment plays a key role in what specific attribute makes an animal's chances of survival higher than others who may not have that attribute. Hence that trait is passed down through breeding of the life form that survives. This does not take away from the fact that God or the Creator of All created everything. It only states the statistical understanding of survival of the fittest that get to procreate and pass on their unique genes." Brandi looked pointedly at Professus Dubsar as if waiting for him to correct her. He inclined his head slightly as a frustrated flush rose to his face.

"As you say," Professus Dubsar said with a curt tilt of his head. "Lady Heather, please continue."

"There is one nation on Eirenic that does not have physical pnĕvma synergáti. Those are the element users. Not having met one, we," Heather gestured towards the seated girls, "call them the magic users but I guess elementals might be a better word. They can manipulate the natural elements around them. It would be nice if we got to meet one of them. Do you think one will come here?"

It was an innocent enough question. One that Dani had thought of asking tons of times. The sharp intake of breath from those seated in the back of the class revealed the obvious tension that one question brought about for Eirenicians.

"I should certainly hope not," Professus Dubsar stated, looking shocked at the question. The girls had quickly learned that mentioning the magic users tended to have that effect on the Eirenicians. The girls looked at each other. They wanted more info on them, but it did not look like they were going to be given any then.

"Lady Dani, continue," Professus Dubsar stated flatly.

"Okay. The sacred crystals are all mined from Agon. Eirenic is more in touch with nature but in ancient times, its people thought of themselves as the perfect warrior race," she paused. Some of the historical information was not fitting together in her mind. She wanted more details and did not know if the now-flustered Professus would provide them but decided to try anyway. "Professus, I feel I have missed some vital pieces of information that I am sure you can provide," she tried to placate the temperamental male.

Professus Dubsar gave a quick exhale and said, "What is it that you have not learned?"

"Thank you. The world of Agon has crystals that are mined and warriors, to an extent. The people of Agon tend to be larger with heavier musculature and bone structure. Agon developed into more of an industrial world.

Eirenic saw itself as the "refined warrior" race and led in horticulture and the pursuits of what they considered appropriate enlightenment. So, what were Terra and its people in all of this?" she asked and closely watching the play of emotions run across the Professus' face before he controlled them.

"Terran females have always been Chosen Ones. You are the means by which Eirenicians and Agons do not become extinct. As for the males of your world, they were brought over as workers. If they connected with a pnēvma synergáti, they could move up in their workforce in their appropriate nation. If they did not," he paused, "they simply remained workers."

Her mouth fell open at what she thought he was implying, and she quickly said, "You mean slaves, don't you," she said it as a statement, not expecting an answer.

"Really, Lady Dani, I thought more from you. Eirenicians do not own slaves. That would be unethical. The Terran were brought to be enlightened. Work needed to be done. One cannot simply live where others provide for all of one's needs. They needed to work to contribute to the society that they now lived in. We provided enlightenment that they would not have gotten on Terra and a sense of worth in contributing to our society. Enough for today let us begin again tomorrow. You are dismissed." Professus Dubsar waved his hand, grabbed his satchel and was out the door before any of them could take a breath.

The sounds of chairs scooting back made her and the other girls turn to look at the back of the class. Some of the male students and guards could be seen moving about as if trying to leave quietly but getting caught in the act.

"Freeze right there," Brandi said, as she raced to block the door.

The male students froze in place with Brandi now in the middle of the group. The students were staring down at her with shocked expressions. Dani watched as Fraener and a couple of other guards that had been hanging out by the door started to work their way through the small crowd to Brandi. Before they reached her, Brandi held out her hand to the closest male student to her.

"Hi, I am Brandi, and you are?" Brandi questioned the dark-complected guy standing with a group of four more that were dressed similarly to him.

"I am Kumbi, Lady Brandi," he leaned over and kissed the top of her hand. "It would be my pleasure to introduce you to my clan mates," Kumbi said, looking over to the left of Brandi where Fraener now stood.

"I think that would be great," Brandi clearly said, loud enough for everyone in the room to hear. She then turned and gave a look of "don't you even think of saying no to this" to Fraener. Kumbi looked back to Brandi with a raised eyebrow and back to Fraener.

"As you wish, Lady Brandi," Fraener said unhappily, but he did not move from his position right behind her.

Everyone still in the room introduced themselves.

"Finally," she thought, *"I can put names to faces and maybe things could be somewhat normal."* After introductions an awkward silence fell, and she thought of ways to extend the newfound connection. A quick solution came to her as her stomach started to rumble.

"I don't know about you guys, but I am hungry. How about we go have some lunch?" Brandi questioned the group standing in somewhat of a circle.

"Of course," a deeply tanned guy, Taton, said. "We shall see you at our afternoon class." The guys all turned to head to the door again.

"Oh, wait. Uhhh, how about a picnic?" Heather quickly asked.

"A pic—nic?" Kumbi asked, leaving no doubt that none of the guys knew what that was.

"You know, you grab food, put it in a basket and eat outside on a blanket," Heather said.

Looking at the guys' faces Dani could tell they had never heard of it before.

"That sounds lovely," Brooke added in her sweet tone. "Would you, all, like to join us for a picnic outside, say in thirty minutes? The cafeteria we eat in has a large outdoor patio attached. I am sure we could just open the doors and eat from the buffet there. That is, if Fraener would be so kind as to send a guard down and check for us?" Brooke added so much sugar to that one question that Dani swore she could see the words dripping across the room.

Fraener sighed, "As you wish," he stated flatly and waved over Veles.

It was more like forty five minutes to an hour before Dani sat on the blanket she and Heather had laid out. Looking around Dani could tell word had spread like wildfire and all the male students had come, not just the ones that had braved their history class. She smiled at that. Her next thoughts had her smile fading, "Well this is kind of a bummer. Everyone is sitting in the same little groups they do at the bonfires," she whispered to Heather.

The girls had plenty of room on their blankets, as only two of them sat on each. It was planned that way in hopes that some of the other students would join them on theirs.

"Yea and our guards glare at anyone who tries to even walks past them. They haven't stood this close the entire time we have been here," Brooke sighed in frustration from the blanket next to theirs.

"This is not working out like we wanted it to," Dani lamented.

All the girls shook their heads in agreement. She looked to her side and saw Brandi's face light up with a huge smile.

"Yes!" Brandi said and jumped to her feet, racing over to a man who had stepped onto the patio.

"Is he holding a soccer ball?" Jamie asked. A collective groan was heard from them all.

"There is no getting out of this. I hope you didn't eat too much," Dani called out. "We are going to be running our legs off."

She could see Brandi practically vibrating with excitement as she dribbled, kicked, and popped the ball in the air, as she headed back to them. Dani looked around and saw all the guys taking a keen interest in her antics.

"Look what I got!" Brandi said, doing a little happy dance.

"I am not in the right shoes for this," Brooke called out.

"Oh, that's fine. You can run and go change and we will start warming up," Brandi looked around their little circle of less than enthused faces. "Oh, come on guys ... Jeez! This will be fun. I promise!" Brandi cheerfully begged. "There is nothing like a nice friendly game to break the ice." She threw her thumb over her shoulder to where the guys sat watching and raised her eyebrows up and down suggestively.

Brooke groaned and said, "Fine, I'll be right back after I change." She stood up and grabbed her plate. "Don't even think any of you are getting out of this. So, you might as well get up and start getting ready," she threw over her shoulder as she headed into the building.

"That's the spirit!" Brandi called after her.

Brandi excitedly dribbled her brown ball from group to group, giving invitation to play. She had everyone cleaning up from lunch and standing around in a semicircle in no time. There were twenty guys and the five girls. Their guards were standing off to the side just watching.

"I was thinking I could teach you guys how to play soccer," Brandi said and started out with a quick explanation of the rules. There were only five guys from each region attending the School of Knowledge, so dividing into two teams evenly was a little trickier but doable. She smiled when Brandi directed the group of five from each clan to split into three on one team, two on the other. Dani knew she smiled even wider when the boundaries for the field and goals were marked by their guards and their Dragons, much to Fraener's chagrin.

Now standing in a defensive back position, Dani watched the starting kick. It soared through the air and was quickly kicked back to the other side. Foot volleyball was played for a few minutes until Brandi gave more advice. A good-natured pile up ensued as all the guys tried to get the ball at the same time, not staying in their positions on the field. They all laughed, and Brandi had one team do a throw in after more directions.

Surprisingly, the guys, including the Vice Regent Ruler and his group, were doing great at not using their hands. Dani had no idea how they could contort their bodies in such ways. After about forty-five minutes of play all of them had grass stains on their cloths and a few sported small cuts and bruises from tripping and running into each other. No one had scored yet and the ball was continually kicked from one side to the other and good-natured ribbing was included. It was fun to watch them all relaxing and having a good time. Even the "I am better than you all" stick seemed to be out of the Vice Regent Ruler's backside. He was giving well naturedly, as well as receiving, in the ribbing department.

Several of the spirit animals started running up and down the sidelines as the ball moved back and forth. Dani smiled at their antics; there was no doubt in her mind they wanted to play too. Just as she thought it, the ball came over to her side of the field, and a giant hyena-like animal ran out, scooping up the ball into its huge mouth. She was quickly left in the dust as she tried to sprint towards the animal. Brandi, now at a full sprint, cut it off before the goal. Dani couldn't even tell the ball was in its mouth. There wasn't even a bulging cheek. Panting as Dani jogged up, she could finally hear the words that accompanied Brandi's demanding gestures.

"You will drop my ball right this instant and so help me if you popped it there will be heck to pay. You got that?" Brandi was pointing up at the animal that had teeth larger than her arm.

The animal blew out through its nose at Brandi, causing her sweaty hair to blow back. Dani caught sight of one of the players running from the far end of the field over to where they stood, and guessed it was his spirit animal. The guy had almost made it to them when she heard a splat. Dani quickly looked back over to a now shocked Brandi, hugging a drool-covered ball to her chest. The spirit animal snorted and walked off the field.

"Thank you for not popping it," Brandi called after it.

"I am so sorry, Lady Brandi. He misses playing Ulama ball. Would you like me to dry that off for you?" the guy asked.

Dani could not hold it in any longer. She busted up laughing. Brandi's shirt was drenched in wet drool. Long strings of it hung from her arms and the ball. Brandi looked back down at her shirt and arms before trying to sling some of the drool off. This made Dani laugh even harder.

"Come on over here, Dani girl, let me give you a big hug," Brandi said, starting to head in her direction.

Squealing Dani tried to make a run for it. She was no match for Brandi's speed and was soon one-arm hugged from behind. Everyone was laughing at this point as Brandi started chasing some of the other girls around for drool hugs. Already slimed, Dani was bent over, holding her ribs from laughing so hard when Professus Sagsar, the head of the school and language arts, along with Professus Usim, their science teacher, came out on the field.

"I hate to break up all this enjoyment, but it is past time for your afternoon class with Professus Usim," Professus Sagsar said.

They all gathered around Professus Usim. All the students were sweaty, and grass stained. Each of the girls also had some degree of drool added to the mix.

Professus Usim looked at them all and just smiled and said, "I think today would be an excellent day for an outdoor class. We shall discuss physical force and motion."

Chapter 25

Eirenic

It was a Sunday morning and Dani headed down to grab a quick bite before she and Jamie left for a walk to the cliff. She had talked Jamie into the walk hoping it might help her depressed mood. Professus Dubsar had assigned each of them a person of importance to do an end-of-year essay on. He had assigned Jamie the Regent Ruler. Dani tried to swap with her, but the Professus would not allow it. He was really being a jerk about it.

Looking through the windows she was glad to see it was a beautiful crisp morning. It had rained for the past week, and it would be nice for both her and Jamie to get outdoors for a while. Winter, it seemed, at a coastal city brought with it rain and fog. Living in Wyoming her entire life, she was not accustomed to weeks of rain. On the other hand, the temperature didn't drop below zero here with a wind chill in the negative double-digits for weeks on end either.

"I guessed it's a tradeoff," Dani thought, *"layers to keep moisture out are lighter than the layers to keep the heat in and the cold out."*

Walking through the cafeteria doors Dani smiled at the scene that greeted her. All the tables were now mostly full. After the first picnic and soccer game, everyone now ate together in what used to be the girls-only little cafeteria. Even their guards, when not on duty, would sit and eat with everyone. Good-natured ribbing about soccer was still tossed around the room. After getting her food she saw Brandi talking animatedly at a table with an open seat, she headed that way.

"I am just saying if the NSs are playing, then we need to get a tougher ball or something," Brandi said between bites. "Maybe even a bigger one. I would feel horrible if one of them swallowed it or it got stuck in its throat and it choked."

"NS? What is that?" Dani asked as she dug into her own plate of food.

"Oh, hey," Brandi turned to look at her. "It's the pnēvma synergáti. That is such a mouthful to say. So, I gave them an acronym," Brandi said with a smile.

"Oh, okay. But you do know that pnēvma starts with a P, right?" she asked.

Brandi rolled her eyes. "Stop nerding out on me. Yes, I know it starts with a P. But the P is silent. So, NS. It sounds better anyway," Brandi said, turning back to the table and her plate.

"If I may be so bold, the NSs, as you call them, would never swallow or hurt your current ball. We have a game played here that uses a similar sized ball," a Polynesian-looking guy said.

"I'm sorry, but who are you, again?" Brandi asked.

"Forgive me, I am Euclid," he bent over slightly towards Brandi.

"Oh, hi. I am Brandi, it's nice to meet you," Brandi beamed a smile.

"Yes," Euclid smiled. "I know who you are. There are a lot more of us than there are of you," Euclid chuckled.

"Oh, well, yes I guess there are," Brandi laughed.

"So, you were going to tell us about a game you play? Is it Ulama, the one I heard mentioned during our first soccer game?" Dani prompted eagerly.

"Yes Ullamaliztli or Ulama as we call it. The full name is a bit of a mouthful to say as well," Euclid smiled.

"Yeah, we noticed that a lot here," Dani chuckled. The group at the table all joined in laughing.

"Ulama is a game we start playing as soon as we are old enough to truly interact with our NSs. It is played with a ball, such as your soccer ball, only a slight bit larger. Depending on where the game is played, whether it is played on the ground, water or air, the ball is a different weight." Euclid looked to her and Brandi as if checking for understanding.

"Okay. I gotta get used to some of this. We have games on the ground, and a few played in the water, but playing in the air? Sounds way cool! Go on, please," Brandi said, unable to hide her excitement.

"The playing fields we use when playing on the ground are large hills that look as if a capital "I" has been dug into the middle of them. The inner stone walls are exceedingly high and must be supported by mounding up dirt behind them. Those walls need the additional support of the dirt to be able to withstand the force placed on them when our NSs bounce off or collide with them when playing." He paused making sure they were following then continued.

"The playing field is the long body of the letter "I". Stone rings are set mid-field, opposite each other and high on the walls. There are also four one-point targets, one located at each end and opposite of each other on the walls, down next to the ground. The playing field floor is divided into four sections you can see by lines on the ground. There are 4 to 8 players plus their NSs on the field when playing. Each team has the same number of players on each side. The waiting area for extra players is the top or bottom of the letter "I"," Euclid paused again.

"With ya so far, keep going." Brandi pushed.

"You earn one point for hitting the targets next to the ground on the opponent's side. If you are exceptionally good, and few are that good, but if you can get the ball through the small stone hoops, opposite each other high on the wall's midfield, you score 100 points," Euclid said.

"So, why do you get 100 points for getting the ball through a high midfield hoop? Is it small or strangely placed? I mean we have basketball, and you just throw it in. There is skill with it, for sure, but not enough to earn that many points. It sounds similar to soccer in some ways. Even some of the field positions are called the same name." Brandi said.

"I have not gotten to the rules yet," Euclid smiled. "The ball cannot touch the hands, just as in your soccer. It can stay for no more than five seconds on the back of your NS, and only if the NS is in constant motion. The skill is moving and passing the ball from a moving NS to another male located on a moving NS. Once the ball hits the ground, it is up to an NS to kick it exactly right to get it airborne again. I do not know if you have noticed, but they have very large feet," Euclid and the guys around him chuckled.

Dani looked at Brandi's face as she processed the game. It went from shock to oh yeah, so fast she almost missed it.

"So, where are these courts and how do we get started?" Brandi beamed.

Dani groaned inwardly, knowing what was going to happen. The thought of plummeting off the back of a moving dragon or other NS did not appeal to her at all. Knowing Brandi, she figured that was exactly what they were all going to be doing soon.

Euclid laughed out loud this time and the other guys around him joined in. "There are playing fields near here, although they have not been cleaned and readied for use. Also, Ulama was designed to be played with NSs. As you ladies have not connected to yours yet, we will need to make some adjustments for play," Euclid said.

Brandi sighed before saying, "We asked Uncle Zidicus if there was a way to speed that up. He assured us there isn't."

Euclid chuckled again. "I am sure yours will be showing up in no time. Your spirit NS's will be just as alive and willing to play as our physical ones are. You will see in time. In the meantime, we will just have to be creative in our playing," Euclid winked at Brandi.

Dani almost spit the juice in her mouth out on the table. None of the guys had ever come close to flirting with them. She had thought they didn't know how. Guess she was wrong.

Not missing a beat, Brandi replied, "Oh, I am sure. Where there is a will, there is always a way," Brandi winked back.

"The game sounds fascinating. Not sure how we are were going to play without NSs, Dani chuckled, "but I have no doubt that Brandi will find a way. I just hoped the rest of us survive it." She smiled at Brandi.

Just then she saw Jamie stand up from another table and carry her tray towards the drop off.

"You all have fun and please try to plan a way that doesn't involve massive amounts of pain for the rest of us Brandi," Dani said.

"You know what they say....no pain, no gain," Brandi replied. Then asked, "Where are you off to this morning?"

"Jamie and I are going to take a quiet walk to the cliffs and back. You are more than welcome to come if you would like," Dani replied, really hoping that Brandi would hear the "quiet" part and decide to stay. She really thought Jamie could use the serenity she found when she walked the path to help lighten her mood.

Brandi looked over to Jamie and a sad smile touched her face. "Nah, I think I am going to figure out Ulama and the field situation. Then start the ball rolling by setting it up so we can all play. Doesn't that sound like *SOOO* much fun?" Brandi beamed.

"Sure, can't wait," Dani replied and walked away from the table. It did sound like fun in a dangerous, bone-breaking way. If anyone could get a field in shape for play in record time, it was Brandi.

Chapter 26

Eirenic

Jamie and Dani walked out into the crisp morning air after picking up their guards in the hall.

"Looks like we get Longwei, Herodion, Askook and Ormr today," Dani said, looking over at the guys following them. The dragons would be waiting for them right outside the doors. As they started walking across the lawn to the path that led around the lake, the men and their dragons took their usual positions. One guard on either side of them, one in front and the last one walked behind the girls. The trail up ahead would narrow, and the dragons would have to go in single file. Sometimes a couple of them would fly around the lake until they reached the top. For now, everyone was casually walking across the lawn.

"Looks like it," Jamie said quietly. They walked in easy silence, each looking around and taking in the scenery.

"Something has been bugging me," Jamie said. She leaned over and picked up a small stick, looking closely at it before dropping it again. "Every time we try and ask about the elementals we are shut down by the adults. Do you think if we ask one of the guys about them, we will get anything?"

"Only one way to find out," Dani answered, pleased that Jamie was thinking of something other than the crazy Regent Ruler or her dad.

"Hey Herodion, can we chat with you?" Dani called out.

She tried to make a point of talking to all the guards, but she and Herodion seemed to get placed together a lot. They had grown close, and both enjoyed an easy banter and quick wit with each other. He strode over to them easily with his long powerful legs and a smirk on his lips.

"Alright, what do you want to know now?" he poked at Dani while chuckling.

They had reached the point where the path began to narrow and Herodion moved to stand beside her with Xad right behind them. Longwei and his dragon strode ahead of them. The other two guards and their dragons took up the rear. Apparently, no one was going to fly around the lake on the way up today.

"Oh, you know, where are the crown jewels hidden and the code to the royal treasury? Just easy stuff like that," Dani laughed back.

Herodion looked at her confused, "Not sure what code you need but the crowns and royal scepter are in the great library. I can take you to see them the next time we are there. As far as a treasury, what would you consider a treasure?"

Dani laughed, "I might just take you up on the tour. Do I get to try them on?" When he just stared at her, she laughed harder. "Just kidding, it was a joke. You know, like what are the winning lottery ticket numbers?" She searched his face, noting the confusion. She laughed out loud.

"Oh, never mind. Sorry. Two different cultures clashing again, I think," Dani chuckled.

"Sometimes you are the strangest female I know, Dani," Herodion smiled, still looking a bit confused.

Laughing harder Dani said, "Believe it or not, I get that a lot even at home."

"So, was that all you wanted to know?" Herodion questioned, still looking confused.

"No, we were wondering if you could tell us about the elementals," Dani asked, keeping an eye on his face as she said it. She saw the quick intake of his breath and the hold. He slowly let it out as if coming to a decision.

"What is it you would like to know?" he asked, not looking at either one of them but focusing on the path.

"Why are you all so averse to talking about them?" Dani asked.

Herodion sighed, running his left hand through his hair. "It is an uncomfortable subject," he finally said.

"Oh," was all Dani said. She did not want to make him feel uncomfortable, but she really wanted answers.

"If you don't want to talk about them, I understand. Can I find information in the school or palace library?" Dani pressed.

"Some, yes," he said, looking over to her with a small smile lifting his lips. "But somehow I do not think even that will answer all your questions," Herodion smiled wider.

"Hey, it's not my fault the school library isn't all that informative on certain subjects," Dani blurted.

She felt the blush run up her face. She knew he was referring to the time he found her trying to find more information on the NSs.

"The mating habits of pnēvma synergáti are delicate and private information for them," he chuckled, waving his hand towards the dragons.

"You shouldn't have stuck your nose into what I was looking up or been so insistent on helping me when you had no clue what information I was looking for," Dani quipped.

"How was I to know? You kept aimlessly wandering around the entire library pulling odd books down for a moment and then putting them back. I was trying to help." Herodion laughed. She could feel her face flush more with embarrassment.

"I was not looking *only* for that information, you know," Dani grumbled.

Herodion chuckled. "Yes, I know, but you turn this delightful shade of red when I bring it up."

"Whatever," Dani waved dismissively and sped up her pace.

"Do you really want to hear about the elementals?" Herodion called with a serious tone in his voice. They had reached the top of the cliff.

"Yes please," Jamie said, having stayed quiet throughout their verbal sparring session.

"Okay," Herodion sighed. "Let's find a place to sit at the cliff and I will tell you what I know."

Dani sat in the middle with Herodion on her right and Jamie on her left. They all sat with their feet hanging over the edge of the cliff face from their knees down. The guards and the dragons fanned out along the path to their

209

right and left. Xad and one of the other dragons leapt off the cliff face and raced around the lake. They sat like that for a few moments no one talking.

"Why is it that you all let us sit this close to the edge and not freak out?" Dani asked.

Herodion chuckled, "Because if you fell, we could catch you."

She and Jamie bent over at the waist, looking at the several-hundred-foot drop below that ended in the lake. Dani then looked over at Jamie and saw the same expression on her face.

"Sure," she drew out.

"Look," Herodion gestured back to the lake. Just as they both looked down again, Xad erupted from the water, quickly followed by Askook's dragon. Jamie gasped, or was that her? It didn't matter; she could not keep her eyes off the dragons. They flew straight up the cliff face. Their wings had to be millimeters away from touching the rock walls. The gush of wind and water droplets rushed past them at an incredible speed as the dragons continued past them into the sky above.

"Okay, so that answers that question," Jamie said after closing her mouth.

"Yep," Dani replied, laughing a little, brushing water droplets off her jacket.

They sat for a few minutes watching the two dragons' race around them. It was fun to see them enjoying themselves. Askook's dragon traded places with one of the others and a type of tag game started. It truly was amazing to watch these fantastic beings.

"There used to be great harmony between the nations of Eirenic and Agon," Herodion quietly said, "before the rise of the Evil One, Erabos." He paused and then started again.

"You see, Erabos was or is, depending on your point of view, an extremely powerful elemental. They say he was the strongest that has ever been. But his strength in elemental manipulation was nothing compared to his strength in manipulating the beings around him to do his will. The elementals can restore a crystal's power once it starts to dim. They cannot revive a dead crystal, but our crystals die only if used for evil. The ability to rejuvenate our crystals puts the elementals in a very crucial role in our societies," Herodion continued, still watching the dragons in the sky.

"How does the crystal know it is being used for evil?" Dani asked.

"We do not know. It just does. We believe the crystals are a blessing from the Creator. Some think they have a kind of inner intelligence and spirit. We do not know for sure, but that is my thought," Herodion said.

They watched the two dragons plunge back into the lake below. She was surprised that a giant splash did not erupt. Instead, it was like watching an Olympic diving competition. There were just the ripples extending out from where the dragons went in. She was watching the ripples reach the shoreline in mini waves when Herodion started speaking again.

"The Great War pit father against son, brother against brother, mothers against daughters and sons. It was and is the most prolific extinction of life that we know of. It consumed all worlds connected to the Axis Mundi, including yours."

"You mean, it was fought on Earth, or Terra as well?" Dani asked shocked.

"Yes. Do you not have a history of great wars being fought? Not small ones contained in one nation, but ones that seemed to encase the entire world?" Herodion asked, looking over at her.

"Well, yes, but are we talking modern history, or way back?" she questioned.

"This is a good question. Time is different on Terra compared to here. But, if I may hazard a guess, I would think it would be in the distant past. Do you have civilizations that disappeared in a great cataclysmic event? Or are there ancient scrolls that depict battles in the sky and oceans? Fought in ways that seemed to be far beyond the technological abilities for the Terrans of those times?"

Dani thought of several cases that fit that description.

"I can see by the looks on your faces that this is the case," Herodion said and then paused for a moment as if collecting his thoughts before continuing.

"I will tell you what I personally think happened. Please understand it is not the only viewpoint. But I think you will get some of the information you seek." He sighed, "I will give you some background history first to help clarifying why elementals are thought of as not being trustworthy." He took a deep breath and let it out slowly.

"Some people say when the portals were partially closed by the sacred guardians, the Nephilim that was the start of it all. Erabos, unhappy with the stringent limitation, somehow was able to get and use a large sacred crystal called The Light of Amun. This powerful crystal allowed him to travel the Axis Mundi to any destination he chose once a Nephilim guardian opened a portal for him to enter. Anyone else was limited to what portal the Nephilim had opened for them to exit through. The Light of Amun crystal also allows the user to use it in any way that person chooses without causing damage to it. The only way he could have gotten the great Light of Amun crystal was with Nephilim help. With the abilities it provided, staying by the portal gates became dangerous before the Great War even started and most definitely during. You never knew who might come through," Herodion said, keeping his eyes on the water below.

"With the powers of the Light of Amun Crystal Erabos' evil spread quickly throughout the Axis Mundi and all worlds attached to it. He and his followers were now demanding that Terrans worship them as only the Creator should be worshipped. They sought to become gods with greed and corruption of the body, mind, and spirit. They felt that because Terrans do not have the connection with a spirit partner, they are lesser beings and easily exploited.

The Nephilim sought to control and deter Erabos' evil influence even more and deal with those Nephilim that followed his evil thinking on Kolob, the Nephilim home world. So, the ruling Nephilim closed down even more of the access points to try and gain more control over what Nephilim was activating the portals and who could communicate or pass through." Herodion picked a piece of grass next to him and started slowly tearing it apart.

"We are not certain on how the portals are opened by the Nephilim, but we know that only they have control of doing it. When they closed all but a few portals, to gain more control, it fueled Erabos' demented ideas of taking over all worlds. He used the closures to put more fear in the minds of Eirenicians and Agonians. He incited this fear by spreading the belief that the Nephilim were trying to take control of all worlds and doom us all to extinction. Using the now panicked, fear-driven people, he added to those that followed his evil way," a sad chuckle escaped Herodion.

"Funny, that exactly what he predicted would come to pass, did. Only it was not by the Nephilim alone, but by all of us trying to contain Erabos and his evil. It took the combined magic from all worlds to seal the portals. As you now know, our very existence is in jeopardy without access to Terra, and in time Eirenicians will be no more," he sat in silence for a breath or two, then continued.

"Let me get back to the history. Small battles started breaking out as Erabos and his followers sought to take control of the portals and rule all the worlds. All-out war soon broke out on each planet. This is what we refer to as The Great War. The Kings and Queens on both Eirenic and Agon had contact with certain Nephilim and with each other. A battle plan was devised to end the war that was killing so many. It was a desperate attempt to contain Erabos in one world and hopefully destroy him and his followers there. Eirenic is his home world." Herodion threw what was left of the shredded blade of grass into the wind and continued.

"The plan was to confine him here. To do this, the portals had to be sealed while he was here. The war seemed to be going our way as we got closer to the sealing date. The King and Queen fought in every way imaginable to keep him here while the sealing was occurring. Magic had to be poured into the Axis Mundi from all four worlds at the same time in order for the sealing to work," Herodion paused now, looking out across the lake to the ocean beyond. Xad landed next to him and nestled his head next to Herodion's side as if to comfort him. She could tell by the sad look on Herodion's face that he was remembering something that hurt him deeply. She was about to reach over to squeeze his hand when he spoke again.

"A final battle was waged. Erabos and his followers, mostly elementals, were making a desperate push for a portal. They knew they were losing the battle on Eirenic, and they were trying desperately to escape to either Agon or Terra. The King, Queen, Regent Ruler, his mate and several other royal family members were guarding the particular portal he had chosen to go through or were in close proximity to it and joined the battle." Herodion stopped talking.

She could see his hand shaking a little in his lap. She reached over and placed hers on top of his, giving a little squeeze. Herodion stiffened for a moment at the contact and then placed his other hand on top of hers, squeezing back. She lifted her hand away when Herodion let go.

"The King and Queen of Eirenic died in that battle," Herodion said stiffly. "The Regent Ruler's mate, Lady Daphnia, as you know, went into the Axis Mundi, chasing after the Evil One. We are sure she has passed from this plane of existence. The Regent Ruler, it seems, is not as convinced. We have our historical accounts from those who survived the battle. Due to the nature of the confusion and traumatic events in battle we are not 100% sure of how exactly things happened.

We do know that Erabos made it into the Axis Mundi. Magic was being poured into the Axis Mundi from all available portals and worlds to seal it. The Eirenic General Frilin was able to make one last communication to a Nephilim Liege after Erabos and Lady Daphnia went through, and the magic completely took effect. It was in this communication that he alerted a Nephilim Liege of Erabos' escape into the Axis Mundi. I believe it was the Nephilim Liege Kerberos who was then able to change Erabos' destination from Terra to Agon. That was the last communication with any other world before the complete sealing took hold.

If Erabos had made it to Terra, I shudder to think what would have become of your world. There were a few Agonians and Eirenicians that sacrificed their hope of ever being able to return to their home world, by staying on Terra to seal the portals from that direction. They also sought to eliminate any of Erabos' followers that would also be trapped there.

The original plan was to deal with Erabos and his followers here on Eirenic, and then reopens the portals. Here, we were winning the war. Something changed when Erabos made it off Eirenic. I do not think the planners of the sealing knew how effective it would be in blocking all passage and communications.

With the King and Queen dead on Eirenic, and their son too young to take up the throne, the King's middle brother stepped into a position he had never planned on doing. The future King only being a boy himself and just losing both his parents was in no shape to rule," Herodion's last words were barely whispered.

They sat in silence for a while, each person deep in their own thoughts. She could not imagine what it must have been like to live through those times. Herodion had given them so much more information than she had asked for. She could tell it hurt him deeply to talk about it. She proceeded, mindful of his pain.

"Why didn't the Nephilim just come and take them out?" she asked. "I have done some research on it. From what I have read, they are the perfect warrior race. They are referred to as "The Creator's chosen Warriors. Created to go and do his will.""

"Nephilim have come through the Axis Mundi to do The Creator's bidding over the centuries. But they cannot stay long in our worlds. The reason they are referred to as "the perfect warriors" is that they must be. The toll it takes on them to survive, even for a short time, in our worlds is extreme. If they stay too long, they die. As to why the Creator did not send them, does your religion not explain that we are not slaves of the Creator? He has given us all free will. It is up to us to determine how we are going to use it. In the distant past he did unleash his warriors. History tells of the mighty winged warriors coming in and laying waste to entire armies. Why the Creator did not send them now, I have no clue other than to guess we must use our free will for the betterment of all."

They all sat quietly again for a few minutes.

"Were all the Evil One's followers' elementals?" she asked quietly.

"No, not all. Why do you ask?" Herodion looked over to her.

"Well, I mean, I get it that he was an elemental and some of his followers were. Did any of the elementals fight him? Fight on your side?" she asked.

"Yes, lots of elementals valiantly battled against his evil and lost their lives," Herodion said, looking a little unsure about why she was asking.

"I understand this is all still an open wound for everyone here. I am so sorry for everyone's loss. I just don't understand why all the elementals are so looked down upon. Were there no followers of the Evil One from the other nations?" she asked.

"Yes, all nations were represented on both sides," Herodion said.

She raised one eyebrow and gestured with her hand for more, hoping he would connect the dots on his own.

Herodion stared back at her. She could see he was thinking about what she said, and then the light dawned as his expression changed.

"I see your point, Dani, and it is a very valid one indeed. He tilted his head to her in a sort of nod acknowledgement. "Perhaps it is time for our way of thinking to change," Herodion said as he stood up. He held out his hands out to help her and Jamie stand. They then went down the path back towards the school.

Chapter 27

Kolob

Kerberos stepped back from the darkening portal in his room, his thoughts still on all that Herodion had said. So many beings had endured so much grief and pain. His mind circled back to questioning whether their decision to close the portals had been the right choice. At the time, it seemed to be the only way. Normally he found that reflecting on past events, most of the time, gave clarity in the decisions made. This did not seem to be the case when looking back at the events that had unfolded and predated the sealing. Some thought that the war was turning in Erabos' favor. He did not feel this assessment to be true. Based on what he just heard Herodion say, he knew he was missing some vital clues from that point in time.

He was impressed by Dani's ability to see past and through all that had happened. In a single conversation, she was able to plant the seed of change in Herodion's mind. The effects of the ripple she had started would have far reaching effects on Eirenic. Those ripples could bring unification to a world that desperately needs it before evil strikes again.

Leaving his room, he headed down the hall, with the ever-present guard falling into step behind him. All morning he could not shake the growing feeling that something evil was stirring. *"Had that not been the plan, to start the ripple across the worlds and finally bring an end to the Great War? To bring the evil out from its dark hiding places."* he thought.

There was no doubt he had a connection to Dani. He puzzled at the purpose of the connection and her role in what was to come. Letting out a frustrated sigh as he headed out onto the balcony that overlooked the practice field, he looked forward to seeing what his Legionnaires were doing.

"Augh the Grinder," he thought with a smile. Recalling fond memories of his youth spent on the massive field practicing. Depending on who your instructor was, greatly affected your muscle pain for days to come. Maybe it was time to bring some of the grind back onto the practice field. Nephilim had their own version of the Ulama ball game. It had been some time since it had been played.

Everyone could feel the slithering of evil going through their midst. Nerves were on edge. A game of Ulama would allow a release of some of the pent-up energy. Then a much clearer mind and body would prevail. The break from the endless questions lying unanswered in his every seeking mind would be welcomed. He could use the release a hard game of Ulama as much as his Legionnaires could.

Opening his wings, he flew from the balcony and out to where Zopyro worked with a few Legionnaires on their swordsmanship. The group stopped as soon as his feet hit the grass, sheathed their swords, and turned and saluted, pounding their fists once over their hearts. He returned the salute.

"Zopyro, have the hoops raised and the fields and men ready for Ulama," he said.

The men in the group saluted again, but with a little more energy this time. He noted the small upturns of their lips as they flew to do as he ordered.

In what felt like moments, the giant field was sectioned off into rectangular playing fields. Kerberos saw the four goals being placed, facing in towards the center so that if you missed your shot, it would fly out of bounds. Two goals were set close to the ground, on opposite corners and two were placed about 50 feet into the air on the other corners. A Nephilim now stood at the end of each sideline to monitor play for goals and out-of-bounds calls. The ball used was slightly weighted. As in the Eirenic and Agon versions of the game, no hands could be used.

Unlike the Eirenicians' and Agonians' game, this game was not designed to sharpen the bond between man and pnêvma synergáti. It was to hone the body, wings, and mind to work together. To work in ways a Nephilim could not consciously think of doing with their body when sparring or in battle. They learned to spin through the air and strategies to move the ball down field and into a hoop. Their weapon in this case was a ball rather than a sword, or an energy shield provided by their crystal. In actual battle, with their hands tied up in the use of weapons, skilled movements of the body and mind saved lives. Ulama sharpened these skills and in return the Nephilim would bring their newfound skills and confidence to their abilities on to the battlefield.

He walked across the field to join a team with a slight smile, thinking, *"Like the Eirenicians and Agonians, Nephilim greatly enjoy the competitive physical exertion of the game Ulama."*

"My Liege, you are playing for the other team?" Zopyro questioned.

"Yes, Zopyro, prepare to be beaten…badly," he smiled.

"Zopyro, do not goad him. I still have an indent in my shin from our last game where the Liege played against us," said Diokles, a legionnaire he had not spent much time with.

He quietly laughed under his breath, "Are we ready?"

After forty-five minutes of playing, everyone sweating and heaving from the thrilling exertion of the game. He was so caught up in the game; he had not noticed the gathering of spectators around their field until the third quarter break had been called. Each team landed at opposite ends of the fields to rest and strategizes for 15 minutes before the final quarter began.

"They now have at least two if not more guarding you at all times, my Liege," one of his players said, wiping his face with a cloth.

"Yes, it seems they try to box me out of the game. Pity, I was having such a good run of it for a while," Kerberos smirked. The challenge of diving and rolling for the ball, kicking it out of the air and taking it from the opposing team had been thrilling. Learning to analyze your opponent's abilities and taking advantage of their weaknesses, while flying and moving a ball, was exhilarating. Keeping the ball in constant motion over every part of the body and wings to score demanded a level of physical stamina that fatigued even him, and he loved it!

"I believe you lost a few feathers on that last dive," one of his teammates joked. "The dive was so steep I am surprised your wings didn't snap off before you hit the ground," he continued.

Kerberos lifted his right wing and looked noting that indeed, he had lost a few.

"Time," the timekeeper called, and they all rose and flew to their positions on the field. His team still had the lead by a decent sized spread. Perhaps he would hang back and let others play more. Just when the ball was tossed into the air, an alarm horn sounded. All Nephilim stopped as the ball thudded to the ground.

A legionnaire wearing the colors of Dionysius' legion, green and white, yelled over to them, flying from the crystal fortress, "My Lieges, you need to come quickly! A guard posted at an inner portal has been found unconscious."

Kerberos flew to the legionnaire, the ground blurring in his vision as he passed over it. When he got closer, he expected the legionnaire to turn and lead back to the fortress. Instead, the legionnaire was looking over Kerberos' shoulder. As he turned and looked behind him, he discovered that both Dionysius and Burkhart had been watching the game. The two of them were making their way to them as fast as they seemed capable of doing so.

The two older Lieges flew far too slowly for him. It was apparent that they were going as fast as they could, and Dionysius' legionnaire would not leave him behind.

"Tell me what portal and you can catch up with me there," he ordered.

The legionnaire looked over Kerberos' side at Dionysius, who must have given his consent for the information to be passed to him. "Sir, the one located on the east side, outside the Hall of Equality."

Kerberos streaked into the fortress and down the halls at such speed the walls like the ground beneath him blurred in his vision. He used every inch of the hall's width, slightly scraping the walls with his beating wings as they lifted and propelled him down the corridor. As Kerberos reached the door to the portal room, he saw two Legionnaires standing off to the side and one more kneeling next to the unconscious one.

"Report," Kerberos snapped.

"My Liege, should we wait for the other Lieges to arrive?" one Legionnaire asked.

The release of tension from the game had been short-lived. He did not have time to wait for the others who were surely still minutes away. Glaring at the male he watched the color leave the Nephilim's face.

"You will answer my question and respect my authority, or I will personally take over your reprimand," Kerberos gritted out.

"Sir, yes sir," the Nephilim gasped taking a small sideways step away from him.

"He is coming to," the Nephilim kneeling on the ground called out.

Kerberos looked away from the antagonizing legionnaire and was somewhat satisfied to see him slide further away from him, down the hall. He kneeled next to the downed legionnaire as the one kneeling stood to give him room. He kept the other three in his line of sight.

"What happened?" The legionnaire on the ground asked and began rubbing a large bump swelling on the side of his head. The groggy legionnaire shifted his position to get off his wings that were folded awkwardly under him.

"What do you remember?" Kerberos asked quickly. He did not want any of the others to add any information to this Nephilim's memory, thus changing the true facts of his recall. He watched closely as the male's focus seemed to waver in and out. With his shifting, a clunking sound was faintly heard. Kerberos looked to the sound and saw a cup roll out from beneath one of the Legionnaire's wings. The Legionnaire grabbed the cup, looking confused.

"I was given this fruit drink. It is one of my favorites." The legionnaire paused, "I remember drinking it and then... nothing really. It's as if my brain is stuck in a fog."

"Do you remember who gave it to you?" he inquired.

"No, but," the male paused, "I remember getting very tired all of a sudden and not being able to keep my eyes open or move my limbs." The legionnaire paused again as if searching for a lost thought. "I remember hearing voices, not one voice, but mumblings of voices. I couldn't figure out who was talking. It was coming from the portal room. It was like someone was having a conversation with someone through the portal," the downed legionnaire said and rubbed his head again. "But that is crazy. The portals can only show what is happening on the other side. You cannot have a conversation through them since the sealing, can you?"

Kerberos quickly steered the legionnaire's thoughts away from what the portal could and could not do wanting to focus on what he could remember.

"Do you remember what those mumblings sounded like? Could you identify the voice of the Nephilim speaking if you heard him speaking again?" It was a stretch, Kerberos knew, but he had to try.

"No, I don't think so. It sounded so far away," the legionnaire exhaled, trying to sit up straighter and holding the goblet in his hand.

"May I have this?" Kerberos took the cup without waiting for a reply and lifted it to his nose. The smell of Datura Stramonium was faint but unmistakable in the glass. The male was lucky that all it did was knock him out. The plant extract not only caused memory loss but vivid horrific hallucinations when enough of it was consumed. It had bothered him initially when the legionnaire said he could not remember who gave him the drink, but it was a moot point now.

"I do remember two words, girl and power. I am not sure of its context in the discussion or why I remember that. It just seemed out of place to me. Oh, I don't know. I clearly remember the murmurs of voices, maybe that is all," the Nephilim raised an arm, leaning into the wall for support as he slowly stood. Several Legionnaires were crowding the hallway now.

"Take him to the infirmary. Porgisl, you stay here on duty," one of the other guards said.

"Interesting turn of events, may I see the cup?" Dionysius asked. "I want the portal room and hallways searched to see if our assailant can be found or left anything else behind," Dionysius stated to his second.

Kerberos handed over the goblet. He had all the information he needed. It appeared, as he had suspected for some time now that conversations can happen through the portals. Now he just had to figure out why Erabos wanted one of the girls. A legionnaire walked back out of the portal room and handed a dead sacred crystal to Dionysius.

Chapter 28

Eirenic

Dani woke up to someone knocking excitedly on her door.

"Come in already," she called, and her door flew open.

"Come on, Dani, you just have to play!" Brandi had her hands clasped together and was waving them up and down, begging her. "Even Kleitos has a girl on his team. You've got to play so we can even up the teams with three girls on each side. Please, you can even ride with Herodion. You and his dragon seem to get along really well. The dragon helped you dunk Herodion in the leaves and all...right? Actually, you seem to get along with all the NSs but I think you have a special place with Herodion's dragon," Brandi continued in her begging voice.

"Have you convinced her yet?" Brooke asked, looking in through the hallway door. Brooke was tucking a tight long-sleeved shirt into even tighter leather-like pants. She noticed another set folded over Brooke's arms and knew what was coming next.

As if sensing where she was focused, "Oh yeah, these are for you. You know, get dressed already," Brooke said, tossing the clothes to her.

Grabbing the clothes out of the air Dani walked into her bathroom.

"The pants look like they are skintight and restrictive. Can I just wear a pair of my own?" Dani called out.

"Put them on you will be surprised." Brooke said.

Pulling them on, Dani was happy to find that they gave as she moved. She noticed her top was red like Brandi's and Brooke's was white. She wondered if that meant they were on opposite teams. She did not have to wait long to get her answer.

When Dani opened the bathroom door and reentered her room, she found the other girls had piled in. It looked like she, Brandi and Jamie were on the red team and Brooke, Heather, and whoever Kleitos was bringing, were on the white team. She was glad he was turning out not to be such a jerk and was excited to meet the mystery girl. Up to this point they had not met any other girls their age.

On the way out to the field Brandi chatted nonstop. Her excitement was catching, almost. Several of the guards flanked them, but at a healthy distance.

"So, we will be playing the ground version of the game. Remember, you cannot touch the ball with your hands. You will be riding with a guard who will be helping you direct the dragons. I will be riding with Euclid on his ginormous tiger. The dragons can hear you just fine; I don't know why they insist that the guards be with us, but whatever. Maybe it is to be sure you don't fall off and get hurt too badly," Brandi said, tapering off at the end muttering. "I haven't tried to do this either. We are all on the same learning curve here."

"You are not helping win me over with the 'Not too badly hurt' comment," Heather chimed in.

Dani snorted, "When have any of us ever been on the same learning curve when it comes to sports with you, Brandi?"

Brandi ignored her comment, instead addressing Heather's. "Don't worry, Heather. I am sure they will keep us from falling off," Brandi paused, "mostly."

Heather sighed.

"Brandi, are you sure this is a good idea? I mean, most of us are not as athletically inclined as you are, you know," Jamie moaned.

"You will be fine. No pain, no gain. Right?Right. Besides, it is too late now; we are here," Brandi motioned for them to walk through a gap in a small hillside.

Once through the gap Dani looked around in awe at the height of the vertical rock walls surrounding them. Stepping in farther she noticed the shape of the capital letter "I" described to them. She started running over the rest of the details she remembered about the game matching them to what she was seeing. She began to visualize how the game was played.

"That is the hoop way up there? How in the world do you even get the ball that high?" Heather asked.

"With skill and practice," Herodion said, stepping over to them. "You also have the opportunity to score by hitting the ball against those spots," He pointed to the red circles located on the side of the wall near the ground.

"Okay, are we ready to get started? I know I am," Brandi's excited voice was starting to make a dent in her nervousness.

All the rest of the girls were paired with a dragon and guard. This game apparently would be played with all dragons except for the one tiger. Everyone agreed that it was safest if they all stayed on the ground.

"Only until we get the hang of it," Brandi had added. Dani looked at the other girls and was pretty sure they all thought that getting the hang of it would be taking a long, long time.

"Hey there, big guy," Dani said walking over to Xad.

"Nice to see you too, Dani," Herodion said from her side.

"Ha, ha," she chided as she reached up and stroked the nose of the dragon's now lowered head.

"So how is this going to work?" Dani gestured up to Xad's back. "I mean, with all the spikes and stuff." Her mouth dropped open as she saw the spikes on the dragon's back start to shrink until there were only tiny bumps where the two-foot-long spikes had been.

"Well, that is a handy trick, isn't it, Xad? You never cease to amaze me," Dani laughed and patted the dragon's face again. His rough tongue came out and licked her cheek as she dropped her hand. She burst out laughing.

"Yeah, yeah suck up. Just don't let me fall off. You are kind of a long way from the ground up there, you know." She wasn't sure why she was talking to Xad and not Herodion directly, but it seemed to come out easier directing her fears to the dragon and not him.

She felt Herodion place his hand on her shoulder. "Don't worry, little one. We will not let you fall."

"I sure hope not. How in the world I ever let Brandi talk me into this craziness, I do not know," Dani sighed.

"It will be fun. You will see," Herodion said, taking her elbow and leading her over to Xad's crooked leg.

Looking up the side, she was reminded yet again that her legs were not as long as the tree-trunk-legged guys around her.

"How about I jump up and then reach down for you?" Herodion asked, stepping up onto the massive dragon leg. The dragon's leg lifted and pushed upwards as Herodion jumped and landed on the back between the shoulder blades. She just stared at him as he reached down for her. Even with his long arms, that was a long way to lean down for her to jump and reach even if she made it on the leg. As if sensing her debate, she felt Xad nudge her from behind.

"Thank you for asking this time. Yes, please," and she was lifted into the air and placed in Herodion's waiting hands.

"You guys could have brought the ladder out here," Dani mumbled. A ladder had been made, after the girls insisted on it, for them to get on and off the dragons on their own. Except for Brandi, who had mastered the on-and-off in a day.

"I think in all the excitement, it was forgotten. I will try and remember it next time," Herodion smiled.

Herodion walked her around on top of Xad's back while Xad was standing still. She had a death grip on his arm.

"I'm sorry Xad if my shoes are hurting your back," Dani called out.

"I weighed a lot more than you do and wear the same type of shoes. Trust me if anyone was going to cause pain, it would be me. And trust me, he would surely let me know about it." Herodion said to her.

She felt a little better about it and started to relax a little. Then Xad started to walk around the field and Dani grabbed a hold of Herodion's other arm with her free hand and dug in.

Herodion laughed. "My, you have the grip of an octopus holding onto a crustacean meal," he laughed again.

"Be nice or I will ask Fraener to put you on KP duty and Xad and I will sit around eating ice cream," Dani grouched.

Herodion's laughter echoed off the walls. "I am guessing this K.P. duty is not fun," he grinned.

"Nope," Dani said, making a popping noise as it came out. "K.P. is kitchen police. You would get to muck out the kitchen."

Herodion busted out laughing again.

"I like the sound of that, Dani," Fraener said from his dragon in the center of a big red circle located in the middle of the playing field. "I will have to keep that duty in mind," Fraener chuckled.

She looked over the scene before her. Brandi was kicking a ball slightly bigger than her soccer ball along the back of Euclid's monster tiger to Euclid as the tiger slowly walked around. The tiger was looking back at Brandi and Euclid with such concentration that it almost walked into a side wall. A huff from Xad had the tiger coming to an abrupt halt inches from the wall.

The sudden change of motion had Brandi stumbling and doing the windmill with her arms, and almost knocking Euclid off who had raced over to help her. The tiger looked back from the wall to his back and quickly but gently gripped Brandi's shirt from behind, steadying her. Poor Euclid lost his footing and slid halfway down the tiger's side, before gripping a handful of fur to stop himself from falling completely to the ground.

Dani started laughing so hard when the tiger, with Brandi still dangling from its lips, looked from Euclid dangling from his side to Brandi hanging from his mouth, whipping Brandi through the air. She could tell the poor thing was torn between helping Brandi or helping Euclid. Brandi had given up trying to control her movements through the air and just started laughing, which in turn brought about a group laughing session.

"Perhaps, we should have the males play a slowed-down version of Ulama. While the ladies watch, just until they get their bearings about them," Fraener suggested, making a placating motion towards Brandi who had finally managed to get securely on the tiger's back again with Euclid.

"That sounds fantastic," Heather was quick to say.

Chapter 29

Eirenic

Dani stood with the rest of the girls at the top of the I-shaped playing field that was her team's rest area. The decision to watch the guys play for a while had been heaven-sent as far as she was concerned. Walking around on the back of Xad had been nerve-racking, to say the least. If Brandi could fall off, the rest of them had no chance of keeping their footing. Luckily, the massive tiger had caught her. Watching from solid ground was more her speed. Fraener dismounted from his dragon and stood in the middle of the red circle, dead center of the playing field with the ball Brandi and Euclid had been kicking earlier.

The blond girl who had been with Kleitos walked over to the sideline with Fraener's dragon. Dani walked over to great her.

"Hi, I'm Dani," she said, holding out her hand to shake.

"Hello, nice to meet you, Dani. I have heard a lot about you and your friends. I am Ida," she said with a shy smile and quiet voice as she reached out to shake her hand.

"Yeah, well don't believe everything you hear about us," Brandi chimed in. "Unless it is about me decking your man. Then yes, that story is true. I'm glad he has turned out to be much better than the conceited jerk we first met."

Ida's eyes got round, and then she busted out laughing. "I have not heard this story. You must fill me in. Kleitos can come across as very self-centered at times. When we first met several months ago on my family's farm, he was very down-to-earth and kind. I assure you the male underneath the one seen around the palace is much different."

"Do you mind if we ask you some questions? You are the first female our age we have been able to talk to from here," Dani asked.

Ida laughed, "I do not mind at all."

"If it is not too personal, I see that your tattoo has not filled in. Does that mean that Kleitos isn't your chosen one?" Dani asked, touching her own tattoo.

"Oh not necessarily. You see, the older you are when you meet your chosen one, the quicker your marking appears. In some cases, it happens at first sight, as I am sure happened with your mothers and aunt. With us younger females, it doesn't normally happen that way. You can know someone your entire life and develop feelings and attachments to them over time. You can also just make up your mind that no matter what. You decide you want to spend the rest of your life span with that person, regardless of markings. The markings can just show up, sometimes, after that. Occasionally, but not often, they do not show up at all. But people live their lives happily either way. It is always nice to have the markings that the Creator blesses your union, though. There really is no set time frame involved. I think you do get a choice in the matter. Unless, of course, you are entering the relationship for un-pure reasons, then the mark will never appear."

"What you just told us relieves some anxiety for us. You have no idea," Dani said.

Ida smiled. "I am glad to help you in any way I can. I cannot imagine what you all must be going through. You are all doing so much better than I would be."

"Thank you. We are trying," Dani said.

"Is there anything else you want to ask me?" Ida asked.

"Have you connected with your spirit partner?" Dani asked.

"Yes, and no," Ida said, rubbing her chest. "I can feel it inside me. I know it is there. I await a trainer to help me with my connection. I believe there will be one coming here next year. I know there is talk of an incredibly special Professus coming, but I do not know for sure who it is. I believe you all will also be getting the same training if I am not mistaken. That is why I have chosen to attend the School of Knowledge next year. Well, that and of course Kleitos will be here." Ida shyly smiled.

"Do you ever feel overwhelmed by your spirit animal?" Dani asked.

"Hmm, overwhelmed? No, I don't. At times I feel it stronger than other times but never overwhelmed. They say the type of spirit animal greatly affects the feelings you have and share with it. If you have an immensely powerful one, I can see where one might feel that way," Ida answered.

She thought about what Ida said as the other girls started chatting.

"I heard one of the guys saying there used to be seats up at the top. Want to come with me to investigate?" Brooke asked.

"I'll come!" Heather replied. Dani watched as Heather and Brooke walked to the entrance and out of the field.

She stood listening while Jamie, Brandi, and Ida made small talk while watching the guys play. How the guys managed to stay on the dragons while diving and moving to kick the ball was beyond her. It soon became evident that being on the smaller tiger's back was not a handicap at all. The tiger and Euclid bounded up walls and leapt over the dragons' backs with ease. Dragons collided with each other and rebounded off the walls. Guys lost their balance, almost falling off, but the dragon and the guy working together made it look like a well-orchestrated demolition derby. Good banter of opponents and laughter could be heard from the playing field.

All of a sudden, Dani got uneasy feeling that started to creep up on her. Looking around the top of the field, she saw Heather watching the game, but could not see her sister.

"Where are you, Brooke?" Dani questioned in her mind frantically searching for her. When the feeling continued to increase, she decided to go look for her sister. Fraener's dragon for some reason decided to follow her. As she exited the field and was about to start up the dirt side, she heard the blood curdling scream.

"Put me down you jerk!" Brooke yelled, followed by more screaming.

Dani ran as fast as she could around the hill, desperate to get to her sister. She felt the mouth of Fraener's fire dragon grip her shirt and give a jolting tug. Fling through the air she was not sure how she landed perfectly positioned on his riding harness. It happened so fast, and she was so focused on Brooke's screams, she didn't have time to react other than land and hold on. One minute she was running, and the next thing she knew, she was riding. As one, they took to the sky, following the screams. An escalating hot pressure was starting in the middle of her chest. She didn't know what it was, but it scared her a little. She had to think of Brooke first, and not panic about whatever she was feeling.

The dragon followed a dust cloud that was moving toward the thick forest surrounding the end of the lake. The dragon was making up ground quickly. She hoped and prayed it was quick enough to catch up to Brooke before they reached the forest edge. They flew around the lake towards the path that rose like a ramp to the cliff that she loved to hike to. She knew firsthand, having walked that part of the trail many times that the forest was very dense not far from the path.

With her blood pounding in her ears the warmth from within was growing until she felt Dani was going to burst into flames as they drew closer to the racing animal. As they got closer she could start making out details of the animal that looked like a giant hyena. It was ridden by a strangely clothed man that was holding onto Brooke. The burning sensation that seemed to be only in her chest started to radiate outwards down her limbs. She did not have time to dwell on it to figure out what it was. She looked over her shoulder, hoping the others had heard the commotion and were close enough to rescue Brooke. She let out a groan when she could see the others were too far behind and would never catch the rider stealing her sister before they reached the forest. No, if anyone was going to have a shot at saving Brooke it would have to be her and the dragon she rode.

Dani tried to focus her thoughts on a way to save Brooke and ignore the lava flowing through her body. Plans started running through her head. The dragon did not dare use its fire, for fear of injuring Brooke. One of them would have to deal with the man and the gigantic hyena, while the other saved Brooke. To her knowledge, hyenas were not great swimmers. She looked to the lake now far below and back to the hyena. It would avoid the water. She had to get Brooke out of the grip of the man. In a tug of war, the man would win. She could think of only one way to loosen his grip. She said a prayer and spoke her plan out loud over and over. She did not know if the dragon could hear her words, with the gale-force winds ripping by them, but she had to try.

The hyena curved around the end of the lake and was halfway up the ramped path, heading higher up the cliff. The dragon did two deep thrusts of his wings, pushing them upwards, and then dove in from behind the hyena. The hyena swerved to the edge of the cliff to avoid the dragon. She and the dragon were now between the tree line and the hyena, just short of the top of the path. She felt the liquid lava pulse through her veins as she leaped from the dragon's back, throwing her body around Brooke who was being held in front of the man. Wrapping her body as best she could around Brooke, the force of her hitting them propelled them both out of the man's grip and off the Hyena. They fell like two stones down the cliff wall towards the lake below. She could hear Brooke's terrified screaming as they fell. As they flipped through the air, she saw the dragon she had been riding shoot past the hyena and man, unable to stop its forward momentum. The man and hyena quickly shot to the top of the cliff and disappeared into the forest.

At that moment the powerful molten lava flowing from within her converges on her back. She let out a groan of pain as it pulled at her skin and muscles. She felt totally lost and overwhelmed by what was taking over her body. Gradually their descent slowed. Time itself seemed to slow as well, as they fell through the air. Just when she thought too much time had passed and they would be hitting the water at such a speed, there was no way they would make it, a giant white blur engulfed them. Gentle claws wrapped around them, and a slight jerk of motion stopped them from falling the rest of the way into the cold wet depths of the lake. She knew it was Herodion and Xad that saved them. She patted the dragon's claw grip in thanks as she squeezed Brooke, who was now sobbing with her head on Dani's shoulder.

As they flew to a beach area near the school, her mind raced with questions. The molten heat within her subsided.

"What the Heck had just taken over her body?" Dani thought.

Her mind then ran to why someone would try and take Brooke. *"Are the nations so desperate they were going to try and steal one of them? Did they not know that everyone else would come after them?"* Dani shuddered with the thought, looking over at the thick forest.

"If the man and hyena had made it there with Brooke, it could have been a very long time before anyone found her." Dani squeezed her sister again. *"All that matters is Brooke is safe. Everything else could be dealt with later. "*

Brooke pulled her head from Dani's now tear-stained shoulder. Looking her in the eyes and said, "Thank you, Dani for saving me." Brooke's voice broke. "I don't know what would have happened if he had gotten me to the forest."

"Do you know who he was? Have you ever seen him before?" Dani asked.

"No, I have never seen him before in my life. He just grabbed me and threw me on the hyena-like animal. He said that one of us had to be taken and it was my lucky day to be the one to be chosen. I had just gone to find the bathroom. I had to pee really bad. Come to think of it, I still do. Do you think we will be landing anytime soon? I would hate to wet my pants on this sweet dragon's claws," Brooke said with a watery smile.

"Yep, I think we can get you to a restroom in no time," Dani said, hugging a still shaking Brooke tighter.

"Everything is going to be okay," Dani said. She wasn't sure if she was saying it to help calm Brooke or herself. In the end it didn't really matter.

As soon as their feet hit the sandy beach, they were surrounded and rushed inside. No one spoke until they were inside. The other girls rushed towards them as soon as they made it inside the cafeteria doors. Hugs and tears were shared by all. She figured the others must have been quickly taken to the School of Knowledge for their safety. Brooke headed for the bathroom attached to the cafeteria with Heather following, and a couple guards. Guards were posted outside the patio doors and doors from the hallway. The other guys from the school were all inside the room as well. Their spirit animals were slightly farther away from the dragons outside keeping watch as well.

"Another line of defense," Dani thought.

They were safe and very well guarded. The guards that were not on the doors formed a circle around the table she, Brandi and Jamie sat at. The other guys from the school circled closely behind them. Brooke quickly returned with Heather and a warm drink was handed to all the girls now seated at a table.

Aunt Kathy and Uncle Zidicus soon rushed in through the outside doors. Hugs were exchanged again, and everyone sat back down in their seats. Between sips of her drink, Brooke told everyone what had happened.

"Perhaps this would be a good time for the girls to go and rest for a few hours," Uncle Zidicus said. Dani looked over to Brooke and saw her leaning slightly onto Aunt Kathy. The adrenalin rush, now gone, had left her feeling shaky as well. Brooke made eye contact with her, and Dani could see the fear in her eyes.

"Hey Brooke, why don't we go up into my room and have a sleepover like we used to do, only this time let's actually sleep," Dani said with a tired smile.

Brooke let out her breath and said, "That sounds fantastic."

Dani had guessed correctly that her sister did not want to be alone right now.

It turned out that none of the girls wanted to be alone. It was a really good thing that all their beds were so big. All five girls piled onto Dani's bed, hugging one another. Brooke was first to conk out. Dani did not think she would, with her mind racing in several different directions. But cocooned by her friends, she must have dozed off.She woke up some time later. The room was cast in shadows, so she knew the sun had set. The rest of the girls soon started to stir.

"Are you all ready to go get some food? I am starving," Brandi said.

Everyone got up, straightened their sleep-wrinkled clothes, and walked into the hall. Looking around the hallways as they headed to the cafeteria, Dani noticed there were several more guards than their usual number posted around the building.

After everyone had gotten their choice of food off the buffet, they returned to the table they had been at a few short hours ago. Uncle Zidicus and Aunt Kathy showed up quickly after they sat. Someone must have notified them that they were up, and the two had stayed at the school because they got there so quickly.

"Any idea what the crazy guy meant about needing one of us?" Dani asked.

She looked behind Brandi and saw Euclid hanging out a few feet away with a couple of other males from his clan.

"We have come up with nothing," Uncle Zidicus said tiredly. "You will all have a much tighter guard from here on. We will not let anything like this happen again," Uncle Zidicus added vehemently.

Looking over to Fraener and Herodion Dani saw stretched lines of strain across their faces. Looking around at the rest of their guards, she saw the same lines on their faces. They were all blaming themselves for what happened.

"Hey guys. There was no way you could have known what that crazy man was going to do; stop beating yourselves up. Brooke and I are both here and fine," Dani called out to them.

"We should not have had all our attention on playing a silly game. Our lack of focus almost cost you and Brooke your lives," Fraener answered.

"So, you are omnipotent now?" Dani asked.

"Of course not," Fraener quickly said.

"Then unless you hold the power to read minds and can see into the future, there was no way for you to know what that deranged dude had in mind," Dani answered.

"I should not have walked off without my guards. The whole thing is my fault, not any of yours," Brooke said. Fraener was about to say something when Aunt Kathy broke in.

"Dani, how in the world did you know what Fraener's dragon had planned?" Aunt Kathy asked.

She thought about it. "I didn't know, not really. I was thinking and formulating a plan in my head. I kept saying that plan out loud, over and over again. It was the only thing I could think of. I guess he heard me or thought the same thing," Dani looked out the patio doors and over to Fraener's dragon whose was looking in. The dragon turned his eyes from scanning the room and looked directly at her. Everyone else turned to them as well. The dragon cocked his head once, as if to say, "Yep," and went back to scanning.

"Fraener, if you would be so kind?" Uncle Zidicus gestured towards the dragon.

Fraener rubbed his hand over the side of his head. "Yes, about that. I have asked him several times. He only gives vague answers. He said "they" were able to communicate. That is all I am getting, stubborn dragon," Fraener muttered the last part.

Dani got up and walked over to the door that the dragon was looking through. As she approached, he turned his head towards her, watching through the glass. She opened the door, and the dragon lowered his head for her to rub him between his nostrils.

"I haven't properly thanked you, big guy," Dani said and stood there staring at where her hand slightly glowed orangey red as she touched the dragon's scales. The warm lava flow within her had pulsed through her to her hand, and then subsided as quickly as it came. Strange, she didn't remember that happening before when she touched him. The name Jurvam Lord of Fire drifted through her mind.

She smiled at him. She now knew this beautiful creature's name and said, "Thank you Jur, I could not have saved Brooke without you."

She was also pleased the being within her was not taking over this time. Jur's tongue flicked out and licked her hand, causing her to chuckle a little. Jur raised his head, looking back outside towards the lake.

She felt a hand on her shoulder and looked back to see Herodion.

"What was the red glow as you and Brooke were falling?" Herodion asked.

"What glow?" Dani questioned.

"It was centered on your back. Did you feel anything?" Herodion asked.

"Yes, I did. There was a burning, pulling sensation on my back. It hurt but I was straining my muscles not to let go of Brooke, so I just let it do whatever it was going to do. It wasn't like I was in control at that point," Dani said.

"What did it look like to you and your dragon, Herodion?" Uncle Zidicus asked.

"To me it took the shape of wings. My dragon will not say anything about it. He just gives me smugness when I ask him. I know he saw it much better than I did but will not say a thing. I also asked how he knew to fly to the lake and catch Dani and Brooke. He won't answer that question directly either. Frankly, it's a little frustrating how all the pnĕvma synergáti seem to vaguely communicate when it comes to Dani," Herodion said.

"Wait, what? What do you mean?" Dani asked.

"Well, they all seem to be taken with you. It is not uncommon for close-knit groups' of pnĕvma synergáti to listen to another human other than their spirit partner, but they all took to you from the start, which is rare indeed. When asked why, they won't answer, or they will give a vague answer if anything at all.

You also know the names of our dragons, although you have shortened them significantly, that is unheard of," Herodion said.

"Dani has always had a way with animals," Aunt Kathy said from the table.

There was a noise of blown out air behind Dani and she turned to look at Gordy through a now-steamed window.

"Did you just huff at me?" Aunt Kathy asked.

Dani watched Gordy and could have sworn he rolled his eyes at Aunt Kathy.

"I guess that was not the right answer," Aunt Kathy said with a small chuckle.

"I agree, Herodion, with your assessment. It is a puzzle to be sure," Uncle Zidicus said.

Brandi walked over to the group now standing at the window.

"I think it is about time for me to give Brooke, Heather, Jamie and you, self-defense lessons," Brandi said, looking at Dani.

"That is a wonderful idea, Brandi. Kathy has told me much about your accomplishments in karate. I think it would benefit the others greatly. The guards cannot be with you every moment of the day. It is just not physically possible. For you all to be able to defend yourselves even for a short time until help arrives would be a blessing to be sure," Uncle Zidicus said.

Dani watched the spirit animals outside the doors while the others talked behind her. She had always felt a connection with animals. To be truthful she loved almost all animals but not most people. The slight warm sensation started in her again and radiated out. She caught her breath. She was not too sure she liked what was going on within her body. It scared her. Gordy and Xad turned to look at her just then. Each one gave her a slight bow of their heads, she returned the gesture. She thought Brandi's proposal, for them all to learn how to defend themselves, was an exceptionally good idea. It was a scary world they all lived in now.

Chapter 30

Kolob

Kerberos smiled as Dani looked out at the pnĕvma synergáti gathered outside the dining facility. He was still very irritated at her actions. He had no doubt the males around her would find out what had happened and why. He was intrigued that the dragons and other pnĕvma synergáti could sense the presence of Dani's spirit animal. He looked forward to watching when the connection between Dani and her spirit partner was made within her. He knew Dani did not know it now, but she was far more gifted and powerful than anyone around her. The power of her pnĕvma synergáti was not matched by any other and was the only reason she and her sister were still alive.

He again got the feeling that something evil was growing in the darkness. Its coming was inevitable. The Evil One had a plan and it involved one of the young females. He had no doubts that the recent event at the sacred pool was part of the plan. The guard that had been drugged could remember nothing else. Neither Dionysius nor Burkhart put much faith in the guard's recall of hearing something about a female. Kerberos had to figure out what that plan was and if the unstable Regent Ruler fit into it.

Walking from his private room, he went through his plans for the day. Each week he checked the storage vaults holding the sacred crystals. He made it a point to check the vaults himself. The count of sacred crystals killed, that they knew of, was now nine. He had a hunch there were many more that he did not know about. As he walked down the hallway, he felt the evil energy in the air intensify. Evil was stirring close by, and building, about to act, not only on Kolob, but on Eirenic as well. The attempted abduction of Brooke was just the beginning.

"Bless me in my actions that I might stop what evil has thought to do. In all that I do, I do your bidding, Creator of All. I sense the urgency to be somewhere, to be doing something important, right now. Someone I care for needs me. Guide me to where I need to be," Kerberos prayed. He needed to find the evil that was lurking on Kolob.

"My Liege," his current guard called from behind him.

"Where is Zopyro?" he quickly demanded as he rushed down the hall.

"He has weapons training; I believe. Would you like me to send for him?" His guard was jogging to keep up with him.

"There isn't time," he forced out before thinking, *"Where? Where am I going?"* he thought as he flew down the hall. *"Please, if it is your will, Creator, guide me to where I need to be."* Exiting the hallway into a wider corridor, he saw Dionysius headed his way and landed feet from him.

"You feel it, too," Dionysius said.

"Yes," Kerberos sharply replied.

"What plans do you have?" Dionysius asked.

"Seek out the evil and stop it," Kerberos answered, getting short with the other Liege.

"Yes, I know this. What exactly do you have planned?" Dionysius said.

"We need to coordinate our Legionnaires to cover more ground." Kerberos said. It would speed things up but his trust in his own kind was stretched thin. Just then Burkhart came storming in.

"What is the plan!?" Burkhart demanded.

"Team up our Legionnaires and search the entire Crystal Fortress. Leave no room unsearched," Kerberos barked out.

Just then, Zopyro came flying down the corridor.

"My Liege, a dead crystal has been found," he gasped.

Kerberos noticed a wadded-up cloth in Zopyro's hand taking it as soon as he landed. Carefully he pulled back the cloth, finding a lifeless sacred crystal inside.

"Where did you find this?" Kerberos asked.

"It was shoved into the sill of a window in one of the alcoves facing the Temple Mount," Zopyro said.

"Search the area. Bring everyone you find to us. We will wait here." Burkhart barked out the order.

Kerberos knew if anyone was found in the area, they would not have been the one who used the crystal to do the Evil One's bidding. No, that Nephilim was long gone by now. Erabos and his evil followers had a plan that was in motion, and he knew it required one of the girls. Still feeling the evil slithering around them he mentally said a prayer, *"Please Creator of All protect Dani and her friends."*

From Dani's previous actions, there was no doubt in his mind that she would do anything to protect and help those she loved. Dani thought nothing of her own safety or wellbeing. He got an ominous feeling Dani was going to need protection the most.

Standing around and waiting for news was not something he did well. He knew evil was moving and a sense of urgency hit him. Without conscious thought, he was moving down a corridor before he even realized his actions.

"Kerberos, where are you going?" Burkhart yelled after him.

"Let him go Burkhart. You and I both know he does things as he pleases," Dionysius said.

Kerberos prayed, "Please, Creator, guide me to where you need me to be. Let me be in time to save her."

Chapter 31

Eirenic

Dani sat at Aunt Kathy's table, feeling strange. Since Brooke's attempted abduction two days ago, the girls had all been put under high security. Even the weekly bonfires had been tense. The man who had tried to take Brooke had not been found. Dani could not shake the feeling that something bad was coming. In an attempt to distract herself from her thoughts and from the heat within, which would build every time she had a strong emotion, she went to visit Aunt Kathy.

"Dani, you seem a bit distracted. I mean beside the obvious, is everything else alright?" Aunt Kathy asked.

Sighing out a frustrated breath she replied, "Yes, no, I don't know. I just have this feeling that something bad is going to happen. You know that sense of dread when you know in your entire being something really bad is going down? That is how I feel right now. The last time I got this feeling, Brooke was abducted. Sorry for just dropping in on you," Dani went on. "But I just needed to be here. I don't know," she said, "it has been a little stressful at the dorms. Brooke never wants to be alone and poor Jamie has been having a heck of a time with Professus Dubsar and his assignment. He gave her the Regent Ruler to do her end-of-term paper on. This means Jamie has had to spend time interviewing the crazy man. That alone is enough to give me the creeps, and Jamie still just seems kind of lost. She told me this morning that he had summoned her for her last interview this afternoon. I guess I wanted to be here...you know, just in case."

Dani knew she sounded a little off, but she just kept having this horrible feeling. Something was not right. It had something to do with Jamie. She could not sit still. The need to find Jamie was becoming overwhelming, and the lava flow within her began to build.

"You know you are..." Aunt Kathy was saying when Dani interrupted her.

"Aunt Kathy, I am sorry, but I need to get out and run some of the energy off. I will come back when I am in a better frame of mind. I am so sorry," Dani got up and gave her aunt a hug. She had to find Jamie. Something was not right. She didn't know how she knew, but she knew. She ran out of her aunt's suite toward the Regent Ruler's side of the palace.

As she ran down the ornately furnished corridors, she remembered she had told her guards that she would be with her Aunt Kathy for the afternoon and would signal them from the balcony when she was ready to go. As closely as they were guarding the girls, she was surprised one had not already popped up to run with her anyway. Rushing down the corridor alone, she knew she was going to be in so much trouble when they found her. She just hoped that her guards did not get in trouble as well. She saw the palace guards at the entrance to the hall leading to the conference rooms that the Regent Ruler used.

"Jamie is through those doors and I gotta get in," Dani desperately thought.

"May we be of assistance?" one of the guards said.

"Oh, um, I was to bring Jamie some information that she needs for her interview with the Regent Ruler," Dani said, catching her breath.

The guard looked her up and down. "Where is this information, we will deliver it for you. The Regent Ruler gave express instructions that he was not to be disturbed," the guard flatly stated.

"Well crap, now what?" she thought before blurting, "It is in my head. I don't think you taking just my head to her will help. Jamie needs this information to complete her report on the Regent Ruler. That was why I was running." she said, and then thought, *"Think fast, what's your excuse?"*

"But, I guess she will have to come back again. I mean I know he is really busy of late, but I am sure he would appreciate you doing your job so studiously. Surely he won't mind having to give up more of his time to talk with Jamie again, so soon after this conversation," Dani pushed.

The guard sighed. "Why was she not prepared with this information before coming?" He sounded frustrated.

Dani countered, "It wasn't her fault, really. She was set to interview the Regent Ruler on Tuesday. Jamie would have had this information by then and would have been totally prepared. The Regent Ruler summoned her this morning for this meeting. I know that he has been changing and moving the dates of all the interviews she has had with him. He has been really..." she paused, trying to think how to not call the Regent Ruler a self-centered, crazy guy who she thinks has lost his marbles.

"Busy, yes really, really busy. So, Jamie did not want to take the chance that he might change it again. The due dates of our reports are in two weeks, she just couldn't take the chance. Jamie asked me to go get some more historical information she had been working on," Dani frantically said hoping she sounded convincing.

The one guard looked to the other who gave a slight nod. "Do not stay long. As you stated, our Regent Ruler is very busy and does not easily tolerate interruptions to his plans," the guard said gruffly as he opened the door.

"Thank you, I am sure he will appreciate your due diligence in your duty," Dani said, rushing past him and down the long corridor. All the doors she passed were open and her quick peek in showed empty meeting rooms. She continued rushing down the long corridor, checking every door she came to. When she was almost at the end, she heard Jamie's raised, muffled voice coming from behind a little door off to the side. She would have passed it if she had not heard Jamie's muffled "No" through the door. Grabbing the gilded handle, she shoved the door open.

"No, I won't do it. I won't go through it. I have changed my mind. You crazy psycho, I won't go through!" Jamie screamed.

What Dani saw caused her heart to stop in shock. The Regent Ruler had Jamie by the arms and was trying to drag her to, *"was that an open portal? It had to be. The shimmering, watery reflective surface was unmistakable. An active open portal, but to where? Where and to whom was he trying to send Jamie?"*

All these thoughts came to her as she raced across the room. Her building inferno within growing the closer she got to them. Dani could see tears streaming down Jamie's face the closer she got.

"You will go through, and I will have my chosen one back!" the Regent Ruler seethed as he fought to pull Jamie closer to the portal.

"Let Jamie go!" Dani screamed and grabbed the Regent Ruler by the arm that was holding onto Jamie. For a split second everything stopped moving. Then a voice sounded from within the portal. She looked to see who was speaking.

"Her, I want HER!" A male voice rang from within the portal.

Dani froze in place. The voice was coming from the other side, through the portal. With a shove, the Regent Ruler threw Jamie to the floor. He spun, quickly breaking from Dani's grip, and grabbed her arms instead.

"You will go through, then," he snarled in her face.

Dani stared into the eyes of a mad man. There was no doubt in her mind that he was no longer sane. Pure psychosis radiated off him in waves as she started to fight for her life. She heard a second voice coming from within the portal. She vaguely recognized it as the voice she had heard when she and Aunt Kathy were in the Axis Mundi.

"You will not have anyone!" the man shouted, and the sound of metal hitting metal could be heard. Hearing his voice again, she had no doubt it was the guy from the Axis Mundi.

"I will have her, and you will finally meet the Creator yourself, Kerberos!" answered the male voice of the one who demanded her.

Dani saw Jamie quickly get up from the floor and attempt to pull the Regent Ruler away from her. Jamie and Dani tried in vain to use the few moves that Brandi had tried to teach them over the past two days. She heard distant shouting coming from the hall. Jamie started screaming for help. Dani could feel the warmth that had flowed in her veins when she was saving Brooke, now flowing to her limbs again, building painfully. She did not know how much more she could take.

Dani wasn't sure who had come into the room as the door behind her bounced off the wall with a thundering boom. She and Jamie were too busy fighting to keep her from being pushed into the portal. Despite the two of them shoving and pushing against the Regent Ruler with all their effort,

Dani was being moved closer to the active portal. She had just registered the sounds of fighting in the room behind her when the crazed Regent Ruler gave a violent shove and Jamie went flying against a wall with a thud.

"YOU WILL GO THROUGH SO I CAN HAVE MY CHOSEN ONE BACK!" the Regent Ruler yelled again.

"Your chosen one is dead, you fool. Let Dani go!" Herodion yelled from across the room and then added, "Get out of my way or die!"

Dani quickly looked back to the portal and saw a winged man reaching towards her. Behind him, she saw two winged men fighting another larger one. The flow of lava in her veins had her holding her own against her side to the portal. The heat continued building inside her and it was starting to border on painful.

"For an old guy, the Regent Ruler is freaking strong," Dani thought as she continued to struggle.

Dani looked back into the sweating face of the psychotic Regent Ruler and then over her shoulder towards the portal. The arm reaching for her was getting closer. She knew if the winged man got ahold of her, she would be pulled through.

"Please, help me," Dani begged in her mind.

The dam inside her broke, and the lava of power freely flowed. She felt the pulsing, burning power like a blast of pure energy. Having no conscious thought as to her movements, she just sensed what she needed to do. Mentally she acknowledged the flowing energy and let it take over her movements. As she inched closer and closer to the portal, she finally understood.

"Uncle, please do not do this," Herodion's panicked voice yelled.

"Uncle? Did he just say, Uncle?" Dani had little time to consider the question. The Regent Ruler looked across the room at Herodion.

"I will have my chosen one back and then *I, I* will be King, and you will be *NOTHING!*" the Regent Ruler yelled.

A chorus of, NOs, were shouted from both sides of the portal as she was pushed another small step closer to the portal. Dani glanced back through the portal to see that the larger winged man, Kerberos, had defeated the other two, most likely killing them, and was racing to the guy reaching for her.

"You shall not have her!" Kerberos roared, closing the distance between him and the other winged man in a blur, his sword poised to strike.

Dani watched as Kerberos raced around the edge on his side to the one reaching for her. At his quick approach the guy reaching for Dani looked over towards Kerberos. It was the distraction she needed, and she stopped pushing the crazy Regent Ruler away from her.

It seemed that was what the molten fire within her needed to spur her further into action. She now felt like she was on fire. She reversed the pressure from pushing back against the crazed man, to pulling him towards the portal with her. She made sure she kept a tight grip on the crazy Regent Ruler. Her backwards twist toward the portal surprised him, who had also been watching the scene through the portal.

She dropped her weight to the tiled floor as her knees bent, bringing up her feet. The Regent Ruler lost his balance and fell forward toward her. She sank her feet into the Regent Ruler's chest, and she shoved with all her might. The Regent Ruler flew over the top of her and into the portal. The winged man, having been distracted by Kerberos, grabbed him thinking it was her.

The pure lava heat that had overflowed within her quickly subsided to a slow burning sensation. She felt the same warm presence inside her that she had felt more frequently since arriving on Eirenic, and absently rubbed her chest soothingly. She was not sure if it was for her or the other that she now knew shared her body with her.

Laying there she stared through the portal trying to catch her breath. She watched in horror as the Regent Ruler's face drained of all color as he was pulled further into the other world. He was gripping his throat in desperation, trying to breathe. She was relieved when he was finally pulled over a short wall that rimmed the round portal on the other side and was out of her view.

The walls in the background of the room on the other side of the portal were made of a white crystal. Kerberos had made it to the winged man reaching for her, who looked in shock to see the Regent Ruler in his hands. A chain flashing around the reaching man's neck caught Dani's attention. A black crystal hung from it. The conversation she had had with Herodion came to her mind. The crystals could be rejuvenated as long as they were not used for evil. The reaching man recovered quickly from his shock of pulling the Regent Ruler through, dropped him, freeing up his hands. The evil sneer that took over his face as he looked up at Kerberos made her catch her breath and hold it as a chill ran down her spine.

"Erabos will not stop until he has what he wants. You have only delayed what is your inevitable demise, Liege Kerberos, and that of anyone who does not follow him," the bad man said, making brief eye contact with her. He then pulled a long, curved pointed knife from somewhere and thrust it into his own body.

She watched to stunned to move at what the bad man had done and saw him slumped to the floor behind the short wall that rimmed the portal. Kerberos walked over and kneeled where he fell. She was glad she could not see the carnage of the three-winged men and Regent Ruler lying dead within feet of each other in that room. Her thoughts were confirmed when Kerberos stood, sheathing his sword, and looking through the portal to her. They stared at each other for a few seconds. She got a warm sensation, but not like before. This was a warm gentle comforting feeling radiating softly through her.

Kerberos was large with strong, chiseled features. His kaleidoscope-colored eyes sparkled with intelligence. Dani was so caught up watching him, she barely caught a flicker of movement in the far corner of the portal as it slightly shimmered on her side. She saw Kerberos' eyes flicker quickly to the same spot and a small look of surprise flit across his face, then back to her. She was just able to mouth a thank you to him and watch a small smile tilt his lips up, when the portal vanished.

Dani tilted her head and look at a spot where she caught a flicker of movement. She was just in time to see a cape flow behind a tapestry next to the portal ring. She jumped slightly when a hand unexpectedly presses into her arm. Quickly looking she saw Herodion kneeling right beside her.

"Dani, are you all right?" Herodion asked.

Nodding was the best she could do to Herodion, and then back to the gap in the tapestry, where someone still stood. Herodion must have followed her gaze because she heard a sharp intake of his breath and his hand that had been rubbing her arm stopped.

The guy behind a tapestry gave a pleading look to Herodion. She quickly looked to Herodion as he shook his head slightly down and then over to one side. Whatever the communication was when she looked back to the tapestry the guy was gone.

"Who…" she managed to croak out.

"No one of concern, let's take care of you first," Herodion said quietly, looking down at her.

"Yeah, as if I would just let that one drop," Dani smirked up at him.

Leaning forward more, so that only she could hear, Herodion said, "I will explain later, when I know more. For now, for his and our safety, please, let it lie," Herodion whispered pleadingly.

She grumbled quietly, her protest at having to wait. She really was in no shape to argue now. It was as if all the events in the past few moments coalesced on her all at once and she was having a hard time breathing. She closed her eyes, not sure if she could look at anyone without losing the very thin thread of her sanity she was holding on to. She listened to the movements around her. She could hear Jamie sobbing off to one side, and muffled shoes and voices sounded all around her. She focused on her breathing, trying to loosen all her overtaxed muscles.

Then she felt it again. The warmth started to build in the very center of her and her breath hitched. She did not know if this was going to be the all-consuming blaze of heat or the comforting one. Then she felt pure, calm heat radiating out into her limbs, loosening her up, and she took a tentative deep breath. The tidal wave of emotions threatening to consume her had died down. She was being embraced by the warmth from within. She had made it, Jamie was okay, and the crazy Regent Ruler was no more.

"Dani! Someone please tell me my niece is okay," Aunt Kathy said in a shaking voice.

"Herodion, can you please explain to me what has happened here?" Uncle Zidicus asked in a hard voice.

"I will explain all, Uncle..."

"By the Creator, where is the Regent Ruler? I was told he was here," Uncle Zidicus continued.

"Uncle, please. Help me get Dani and Jamie checked over first and I will explain what I know," Herodion pleaded.

Dani sat up with help from Herodion and looked around the room. The guards that had been guarding the doorway when she entered, and four others, were kneeling on the ground with their hands on the tops of their heads, fingers laced. Pachua, Longwei and Askook guarded them.

She looked over and saw Brandi, Heather, and Brooke, disheveled and standing off to one side, glaring daggers at the kneeling guards.

"When had everyone gotten there?" Dani thought.

Looking closer, she saw that Brandi was holding her arm, flexing her fingers, and grimacing slightly. She held a small knife in the other hand. Heather held a long gold pole, absentmindedly rubbing her hand up and down it. Brooke, to her shock, had a long spear. The look she was giving the guards on the ground should have had them quaking.

"Dang, I have never seen my sister that angry," Dani thought.

Pure aggression radiated off the three girls towards the kneeling palace guards. As if sensing her watching them, all three girls turned and looked at her, raising their weapons and nodding at her. It was clear that they, too, had been fighting the palace guards to help her and Jamie.

The love and support she felt from each of them brought tears to her eyes.

"Oh, thank you Heavenly Father, they are all alright!" she breathed a small sigh of relief. *"Now to deal with what Jamie had said. Jamie said she changed her mind and did not want to go through the portal. There must have been a plan between the Regent Ruler and Jamie that I was not aware of. I need to find out what that was."*

251

Chapter 32

Kolob

Kerberos sat at the far end of the table in the Triumvirate meeting room. He stared through the round crystal tabletop and halfheartedly listened to the conversation going on across from him. Dionysius, Burkhart, and their advisors debated the information he had given them about the attempted abduction of Dani. In his hand the three lifeless, blackened sacred crystals that he had confiscated from the dead Nephilim rested. Two of the Nephilim were legionnaire guards, and the other was a scholar. The scholar had been the one trying to pull Dani through the portal. Staring at the lifeless crystals he felt deeply saddened over their loss.

"Can you please walk us through the events that occurred after Zopyro reported the dead sacred crystal," Dionysus asked yet again.

"I have told you this multiple time. This will be my last retelling. Do with it as you will," Kerberos said and then continued, "The feeling of something evil lurking about I have had for several spans was confirmed when Zopyro found yet another dead sacred crystal. That feeling only intensified after the discovery and I knew that a greater evil deed was still being performed. The overwhelming urge to find it could not be ignored," Kerberos paused in his retelling then continued, "I left you waiting for a report back on the dead sacred crystal. Praying for guidance, which I received, was the only way I was able to make it to the small portal room so quickly."

He thought back to the moment he had entered the sacred pool room. He knew his heart had never beat with such force as it had then. In all his battles, none seemed to be as important as winning this one.

He continued, "The two guards protecting the Scholar trying to pull the females through the portal had fought well, but not well enough. I quickly thwarted their evil plan. May the Creator of All have mercy on their evil souls, I showed them none."

Kerberos looked at Dionysus wanting a few of his questions answered as well, "The Scholar would have known it was a death sentence to bring a human to Kolob. A dead human female was of use to anyone. I believe the true intention must have been to send the young female directly to Agon."

He purposely had not mentioned the young male he saw exit the portal on Eirenic. Kerberos surmised there had to have been a portal open on Agon to support the plan to get Dani through to the evil one. That open portal on Agon had to be the way the young royal snuck through and hid in the tapestry on Eirenic right before the portal closed. The Creator of All had to have had a hand in the male making it through before the Axis Mundi was once again sealed. If the young male had been caught in the Axis Mundi, he would have died. The Axis Mundi is only a passageway between worlds. It does not maintain an environment conducive to life once the portals are closed.

"How can that be?" Burkhart questioned. "I know of no way to do what you are saying was planned to be done"

Kerberos stared directly at Dionysus knowing he knew the answer just like he did. An unsteady quiet filled the room as he waited for the older Liege to answer Burkhart's question. Dionysus's second was the one to break under his relentless stare.

"There is no way, well unless the scholar knew the transport secret," he sputtered.

Kerberos gave a slight smirk to Dionysus before the older Liege lowered his gaze.

"Yes, old one, I know some of the secrets you keep," Kerberos thought.

"What is it you speak of? What transport secret are you keeping from us," Burkhart demanded.

Dionysus spoke next trying to dismiss the idea, "What he speaks of is just a theory. One would have to know and be able to control the exact amount of energy, to be able to accomplish the task."

"Tell us of this theory," Kerberos asked.

Dionysus grumbled under his breath as color rose in his face before answering, "The theory is that a Nephilim could pull a physical being from one world and place them on another in moments time span. The being would travel through the Axis Mundi at great speed and not even know they had been through it. The theory is known by very few. For it would take a great deal of strength, concentration, and power to complete the maneuver successfully. If poorly done, the being that was being moved could die from the sudden jolt to their system. I know of very few Nephilim with the ability to do such a maneuver and even those that do are wise enough not to try it. The risk is too great to the one being transported through. What would be the point if the result was a dead human?"

"I would hazard a guess my showing up and killing the two guards, the Scholar lost his concentration and was unable to push the crazed Regent Ruler through to Agon, instead pulling him only as far as Kolob," Kerberos said.

"You are saying it is possible to do such a thing. What other secrets are you keeping from us Dionysus? I grow tired of always asking that question," Burkhart seethed.

Zopyro sifted his weight next to him, and Kerberos looked over at him.

"I await your orders, my Liege," Zopyro spoke formally.

He knew that Zopyro had demoted the guard he had assigned to guard him. The same guard Kerberos had out flown on his way to the sacred pool. Zopyro was taking personal responsibility for Kerberos having to battle alone.

"No one on this plane of existence could have kept up with me. You know this. Be just and fair with your reprimand," he quietly spoke. He did not have the energy to do much more after the hours spent answering and retelling the events from the sacred pool room.

"As you command," was the clipped reply from Zopyro.

"Zopyro, I do not have the energy to battle wits with you this eve. We can discuss this further tomorrow," and rose from his seat.

Burkhart's rumbled objections were soon voiced, "Where do you think you are going? We have yet to decide what to do about those Nephilim still loyal to the Evil One, those still willing to act on what they feel is his will. Not to mention how we are going to handle the sacred pool that is clearly an operational portal. The magic that sealed the Axis Mundi must be weaker than we thought," Burkhart went on.

"We must commission more studies on this at once," Dionysius stated.

"My Lieges, I am going to rest. We do not have the identities of all the Evil One's followers. If we did, it would be easy to apprehend them. Place guards on the portal hallway, so that none may enter. Liege Burkhart, if you need any assistance from my Legionnaires, ask Zopyro. I am going to pray and reflect on the events that have occurred today. Pray for the Creator's guidance on the path that we are now on. We know the portal was opened using the power of three sacred crystals. Pray that no other Nephilim are willing to make such a horrendous sacrifice." He placed the black lifeless crystals on the top of the table for all to see. Then he turned and walked towards the doors.

"The path that YOU started us on when you chose to open the Axis Mundi and allow the females through!" Burkhart snarled.

He twirled around and snarled back. "Yes, and now we have four fewer followers of the Evil One in our midst, three of which came from your Legionnaires. Perhaps you could put the energy you use to throw accusations at me towards looking into your own Legionnaires. We might have had even fewer if you had handled them instead of me!"

"My Lieges, we will accomplish nothing if we battle each other," Dionysius said, moving to stand between them. "Perhaps a night of reflection and prayers is a good idea. We will start fresh and anew in the morning with clearer hearts and minds. Shall we adjourn, Burkhart?" Dionysius gestured towards the door. Burkhart stood and stomped past like a petulant child, with his adviser following closely.

Dionysius watched him leave and turned to Kerberos. "Kerberos, you cannot think that Burkhart has ill intentions towards you. Can you not see that it has affected him deeply that it was his Legionnaires that attacked you, and two more tried to help pull a human female into our world?" Dionysius said from beside him, looking up into his face.

"I have also not forgotten that it was a Scholar who was trying to pull the young female through, Dionysius," Kerberos said as he watched the older Nephilim's face flush red with irritation. "It has been a long day. We shall lay this down tonight and pick it up in the morning," Kerberos said and headed out the door to his chamber.

As he lay in his bed he continued to think over the events of the day. Dani had shown great courage when fighting the much larger Regent Ruler. He did not know the events that had happened in Eirenic that brought her and the other female to the portal.

"Why does the Evil One desire one of the young females? Can it be that with the right amount of energy, any sacred pool could become an operational portal again?" he thought.

So many unanswered questions raced through his mind. Landing on the recent information he had heard that the Evil One was using an ancient prophesy to justify his actions. Kerberos thought, *"I need to find what prophesy the Evil One was using."*

Taking a deep breath, he focused back on the young female Dani. He was pleased and relieved that she and her friend were safe. He prayed he was able to continue to keep them that way. A crucial piece of information was missing. He asked again in his mind, *"why does the Evil One want one of the females?"*

He decided he was going to have to take a more active role in guiding Dani. She now recognized and had started building on the fledgling bond with her powerful pnĕvma synergáti. He would need to be sure she was trained on how to interact and influence the powerful spirit she held within her. Recent events proved that the sealing magic had indeed diminished enough for communication between worlds. His abilities to influence and guide her could now increase further. He drifted to sleep with a small smile, formulating his plans for Dani.

Chapter 33

Eirenic

Dani sat staring into the fire. The weekly bonfires were normally lively and boisterous, but tonight it was quiet and solemn. The occasional whispers and murmurs of low conversations could be heard over the crackle of the burning wood. Since the attempted abduction of Jamie and Dani by the now dead Regent Ruler, things had been quite subdued around the School of Knowledge.

"Several of your moms have expressed concerns and are asking if you would think about visiting them soon," Aunt Kathy broke the silence at their little fire.

"Yeah, my mom sent a freaking huge water bird to tap on my window before the sun came up today. It dropped off a note begging me to stay with her for a while," Brandi sighed running her uninjured hand over her hair.

During the fight at the palace, she fractured a couple of bones in her right hand. Looking at her wrapped hand she mumbled, "Darn guard had a hard jaw."

Brandi looked up at everyone and smiled. "But from what I hear, his jaw is a lot worse off than my hand," she chuckled. "I told my mom I was fine, and she was more than welcome at the palace any time for a visit. The healer was awesome, and I will be good to go in no time. Kind of glad she can't call me," Brandi grinned.

A little laughter was heard around the fire pit.

"Jamie, your mom and Filtiarn will be here in a couple of days. Dani, your mom and Azmer will be here as well, about the same time. I would not be surprised if all of your mothers show up though," Aunt Kathy sighed.

All the girls sat quietly after the news. Dani knew all the girls wanted to see their moms, just like she did. She just wanted some time for everything that had happened in the last few weeks to settle in her own mind first. Her mom would be all over her and Brooke. She needed space and time to reflect on her own. They all loved their moms but had all grown so much since seeing them last. Their relationships with their moms would need to change as well. She didn't know how her mom, or the others, was going to feel about their changes.

Aunt Kathy spoke again, "Girls, you need to understand how they feel, please. They need to see for themselves that you are alright. Give them that, and I am sure they will be on their way back home in no time. You have all changed and grown so much. Give them time to adjust to your growth and new independence. No matter how old you are, you will always be their, and my little girls," Aunt Kathy pleaded. Dani thought it strange sometimes that Aunt Kathy seemed to know what she was thinking.

"Why did you have to tell them in the first place?" Jamie moaned. "We are fine, all is fine… What the heck," Jamie sighed in frustration.

Uncle Zidicus answered, "It was not your Aunt Kathleen that told them, it was me. An event of this magnitude must be addressed with all the rulers. Your mothers will come because that is what good mothers do. They make sure their young are thriving and safe. Much will be happening in the next few weeks. Much understanding and patience will be needed by all. Your mothers showed great restraint when the events of Brooke's abduction were relayed to them. Give them the respect they deserve. They care for and love you all so much," Uncle Zidicus' deep voice quietly chastised them.

"How did you three end up in the chamber?" Dani asked across the fire, trying to change the subject.

"Brandi, Heather and I met up for lunch and I don't know," Brooke waved her hand around. "We just had this feeling that something bad was about to happen. We needed to get to the palace and find you two. So, that was what we did. It was weird," Brooke said, rubbing her chest. "Like something was pushing us to get our butts moving. Or at least that was how it was for me," she added.

Brandi and Heather nodded their heads, rubbing over their hearts as well.

"How did you know to be there?" Brooke asked her.

"I got the same feeling telling me to find Jamie," Dani answered. "Thank you all for saving me. I am so grateful for all of you." Her emotions got the best of her, and her voice choked a little.

Jamie grabbed her hand and squeezed it while looking over at her. "If it hadn't been for me, none of you would have been there. So, me too! If you hadn't come when you did, Dani…" Jamie clearly couldn't finish her statement, so Dani squeezed Jamie's hand back.

"The strange sensation you feel, is it like another giving you guidance?" Uncle Zidicus asked.

"Yeah, I guess you could say that," Brandi said, and Brooke and Jamie nodded their heads as well. Uncle Zidicus turned for Dani's answer.

"I think that my spirit partner has been with me since Aunt Kathy and I were coming through the Axis Mundi," Dani said.

Gasps from the girls came out and Uncle Zidicus gave a small smile.

"Wait, why didn't you tell us?" Brooke asked.

"Because it would have sounded really weird to you if you hadn't been feeling something similar. Admit it, you would have thought I had lost my mind," Dani answered.

"Yeah, you're probably right. But I just started feeling mine when I was taken," Brooke said.

Silence reigned for a few minutes after Brooke spoke.

"You have all started the bonding with your pnévma synergáti," Uncle Zidicus said. "Dani, I have been guessing for some time that that was why the other pnévma synergáti had such a fascination with you."

"Why would my spirit partner be fascinating to the others?" Dani asked.

"I do not know. The other pnévma synergáti can sense each other and communicate. When I asked my pnévma synergáti if he could sense yours and what it might be, he just gave me a smug huff. It recently came to my attention that all of yours might have started bonding with you and coming forth from within. It will be very interesting to see how your pnévma synergáti manifest," Uncle Zidicus smiled. They all sat in silence for a few moments.

"I don't think any of the guards will look at you all the same," Fraener said with a smile. "Your skills in fighting will not be taken for granted." They all chuckled at that.

"Who is going to take the Regent Ruler's place?" Dani asked.

"Dang, do you think it will be his son?" Brandi questioned.

"Oh, I sure hope not. He has come around a bit, but I don't see him as ruler material," Jamie added.

"No, I believe the true king will step forward in some way." Uncle Zidicus stared across the fire to where Herodion and Fraener now sat.

Dani looked over at Herodion. He stared into the fire, lost in his own thoughts. Looking closely, she noticed the dark circles under his eyes. She hadn't seen him since the portal incident and was a little shocked to see him dressed not in full guard regalia, but in a stripped-down version. Xad's head was lying just to his side and Herodion stroked between the dragon's nostrils absentmindedly. She knew his world had just been turned upside down. Ready or not, he was going to have to step up.

"So, what happened to the Regent Ruler's dragon?" Dani asked.

Herodion looked up from the fire and over to her before speaking, "We found out today that his dragon chose to pass from this world a couple of days ago. He knew the Regent Ruler had completely lost his grasp of reality. We suspect he did not know the plans that he had, just that his mind was truly fractured. The strain on his dragon over the years, to help try and keep what was left of the Regent Ruler's mind functioning, must have been immense. The connection between us and our pnévma synergáti is so intertwined that what affects one, affects the other." The strain and sadness on Herodion's voice made her want to reach out and console him. She held his gaze until he turned to look back into the fire.

Dani had started putting the pieces of the puzzle together soon after the portal incident with Jamie. Herodion had called the Regent Ruler "Uncle." This also meant that Uncle Zidicus was his uncle, as he was the brother of the former Regent Ruler. Herodion had a white royal dragon, so he was closely connected to the royal family in some way. She was pretty sure she knew how. Looking down into the fire she watched him from under her lashes. She knew that this was not the time to question him more. She would get her answers at some point. It did not have to be right now.

"Not to change the dark mood and all, but have you all looked at your grades?" Jamie asked, clearly excited. "I got an "excellent job" from Professus Dubsar on my report."

"That's awesome, Jamie!" Dani high fived her as the others called out their congratulations as well.

The change in the conversation seemed to signal the end of the time around the fire. She and Jamie left at the same time headed upstairs to their rooms. Jamie had asked her if she would mind stopping off in her room for a few minutes. Jamie walked into her room and sat on her bed, hugging one of her pillows. She shut the door behind her and sat at the foot of Jamie's bed.

"You heard, didn't you?" Jamie asked her, not looking up from her pillow.

"Heard what?" Dani asked.

Jamie sighed, "You heard me tell the Regent Ruler that I had changed my mind about going through the portal."

She had heard her say it, and she knew they would talk about it when Jamie was ready.

"Yes, I did," Dani replied.

Tears started rolling down Jamie's face. The look she gave her broke Dani's heart.

"He said he could send me back to see my dad," Jamie sobbed. "It's not like I want to leave all of you, I don't, but I miss him so much," she continued sobbing. Dani stood and walked over to Jamie, hugging her tightly. She let her cry it all out for several minutes not say a thing. She knew Jamie had been struggling. She just didn't know that she would take such drastic measures as to believe a crazy man.

"Please don't tell anyone else. My mom would freak and never let me out of her sight again," Jamie pleaded.

"You know I never tell anyone what you tell me. But promise me you will never do something like that again. If some crazy person tells you that you can even phone home or whatever, you will tell me. So that we can make sure it's legit before you almost get yourself killed. Okay?" Dani asked.

"Pinky promise on that one!" Jamie held up her pinky for her to wrap her pinky around it.

"How are you really feeling about everything now?" Dani asked.

Jamie went back to picking at a thread on her pillow, then looked back up to Dani.

"You know, better. You would think after the last few days it wouldn't be that way, but it is. I know I cannot get back to my dad, and for right now I will accept that. Yes, I miss him terribly. But it is what it is. I cannot let my grief over missing him run my life. So, I am going to move forward the best I can. Maybe someday I will get to see him again, maybe not. I am okay with that right now," Jamie said.

Dani smiled at her. "Good. I think you are setting a good example for the rest of us. We all have things we need to let go of. I know it is not as easy as it sounds." Dani gave Jamie a hug and headed for her own room.

Chapter 34

Eirenic

In what felt like no time at all, Dani was amazed to be watching all the commotion going on in the girls' suite of rooms at the palace.

"Oh, for crying out loud, Mom, my hair is fine," Brandi could be heard fussing at her mom.

"A ponytail is not exactly dignified," Theresa said.

"Okay, fine. I guess I can't go," Brandi replied.

"Not so fast, young lady. If I can suffer through this, so can you," Ballene said. "The ponytail is fine, my Theresa. It makes her look so young and youthful. We will not have to work so hard to keep the young males from looking at her," Ballene added.

Dani could not keep from laughing when Brandi came walking by with her hair now out of the ponytail. She was trying to smooth the little bump it left in her hair.

"Don't say it, "D," or I may have to hurt you," Brandi muttered under her breath as she headed towards the bathroom.

No doubt, she would be putting a hot stone on her hair to smooth out the bump even more. Theresa walked past following her daughter. Dani was amazed how Brandi's mom could manipulate her hair. The coarse thick texture gave them an unfair advantage. She was lucky if hers didn't frizz out, so she looked like a clown.

"So, we get to see the crowning of a king! How cool is that?" Brooke said excitedly from behind her.

They had all managed to make it to the entryway of their little apartment after hours of primping. Dani was looking forward to having this done and over with. She still hadn't been able to talk with Herodion about the events of the portal night.

The opening of their suite door had her looking towards it.

"You should not be here. Why are you not in the royal chambers?" Uncle Zidicus asked.

Everyone looked in the direction Uncle Zidicus was speaking, and gasped when Fraener walked in, in full regalia that glittered and glowed. Even its grandeur paled in comparison to the outfit of the guy who stepped through the doorway next. He wore the brightest white she had ever seen. Even the shielding of his breast plate was white, with gold trim. He was breathtaking.

Another collective gasp could be heard throughout the room. The guards around them kneeled, along with the other men. All except Uncle Zidicus, who bowed low at the waist.

"Uncle, I am here," Herodion gestured around, "most likely for the same reason you are. We both hate that little room off the back," Herodion reached out and grasped his Uncle on the forearm, pulling him up from his bow.

"Oh, for the love of all, please rise," Herodion said to the group. "I do not wish for any of you to do that," he groaned.

"Formalities must be kept, your highness," Uncle Zidicus quietly said.

Herodion sighed. "Fine, but when we are alone, just us," he waved his hand encompassing the room. "We do not need such formalities," he stated.

"As you wish, your highness," Uncle Zidicus bent slightly at the waist.

"If you do that one more time, I will make you sit in on that darn trade meeting," Herodion chided.

Uncle Zidicus raised his eyebrow.

"Oh, who am I kidding? You are going to the trade meeting," Herodion said and started laughing.

"So, you are the King?" Brandi piped in.

"Yes," Herodion's smile dimmed slightly.

"You are not going to shut down the school, are you? Because if you do that, I might have to hurt you," Brandi said sweetly. The guards around the room stood stiffly.

"You cannot threaten to hurt his Royal Highness, Brandi," Fraener said with alarm.

"Why not? He puts his skirt on the same way I do. And he knows I could," Brandi stated back at Fraener, who looked to Herodion for help.

"Don't look at me, Fraener. She is scary when she is mad. I for one will not sleep well if that was directed at me. So, I will not be closing the school," Herodion said. All the girls let out their breaths and some even made cheering noises.

"But there are some changes that will need to happen," Herodion went on.

"Don't leave us hanging! What changes?" Dani playfully demanded.

Uncle Zidicus spoke next, "His Royal Highness will be attending the school. So certain changes will be made to accommodate him and the influx of students that are sure to come as soon as the announcement is made that he will be attending."

"I am sure the influx of females that are sure to come will be to your liking as well," Fraener said.

Herodion groaned and slapped Fraener on the shoulder. "Just remember we," Herodion waved his hand around the room, "are friends and you can all help defend me against the females that will no doubt be thrilled to see my crown." Everyone laughed at that.

"It is time," Uncle Zidicus said. Nodding, Herodion and Fraener left.

Dani's mom, Aunt Kathy, and the other moms all made rounds of the girls. They fussed and adjusted their long dresses, so they hung just right. Dani smiled when she saw Brandi's hair now lying flat and hanging loosely around her shoulders. Uncle Zidicus and Aunt Kathy left soon after Herodion and Fraener. The rest of them made their way through the now-crowded corridors to where the coronation would take place.

Dani walked with the others into the enormous throne room. She felt like her head was on a swivel as she looked around in fascination. The pillars spaced along the side had carvings and paintings intermixed on them. The side walls had been removed so that more people could fit in. A three, tiered landings rose from the floor on the far end of the room. On the highest point sat two white marble thrones with gold accents running in swirling designs. A purple carpet ran the entire length of the room, from the double doors they walked in all the way up to the thrones. The ceiling had to be at least four stories up and she squinted, trying to see the ornate paintings and murals on it.

Off to the sides of the main chambers where the walls had been slid open or removed, were more open areas. Looking beyond the gigantic pillars she could see every kind of pnĕvma synergáti imaginable. On the left-hand side, she could hear water splashing and knew that even the water pnĕvma synergáti were present. A hush fell over the room as the two enormous back doors swung closed.

After a brief pause, she saw two smaller doors open at the bottom of the massive black ones. The audience stood facing the doors. A procession the likes of which she could only dream of went by, down the center aisle. The rulers of each region entered with their Chosen Ones if they had one. Each had on a plush looking cape that matched the color of the stones in the chains that held the cape together in the front. They continued walking to the front, and each took their place on the lowest tier of the raised floor, facing the audience.

An official with a purple plush pillow with a crown on it came next. The golden crown had several large spikes coming up on its sides. Within each spike a different colored large crystal was rimmed with gold. The crystals matched the smaller stones she saw holding together the regional rulers' capes, except for the crystal on the very front of the crown. It was slightly larger than the other crystals and was a milky white color that gave off a slight glow.

A scepter was carried in next with its base wrapped in the same plush purple cloth the pillow with the crown had been made of. The official holding the scepter upright had his hands on the purple cloth and did not touch the scepter itself. What caught her eyes was the large clear crystal that shone at the top of the scepter's carved golden staff. The officials with the crown and scepter walked past and now stood on the middle landing.

Everyone turned and looked back at the now closed smaller doors. Dani thought she could have heard a pin drop when the two enormous back doors swung completely open. She could now see Aunt Kathy standing in the opening, with her hand on Uncle Zidicus' arm. They proceeded slowly up the purple carpet, and she smiled as Aunt Kathy gave her a wink on the way by.

Herodion followed, several steps behind them. He was the only one that entered with his pnĕvma synergáti, Xad, with all his glory on display. The dragon she had first seen when she and Aunt Kathy were trapped in the Axis Mundi was spectacularly walking down the aisle. A proud crown of horns rose high, circling the top of his head. He was so majestic and awe-inspiring. Xad took her breath away. Dani reached out, wishing she could touch him, but knew she would have to wait. As if the noble dragon knew what she wanted, his tail flicked over and brushed her foot that stuck partially out in the aisle before flicking back behind him. She smiled so wide her cheeks hurt.

At the front of the room, Aunt Kathy and Uncle Zidicus stood next to the officials with the crown and scepter. Xad had walked around the left side, and now stood behind the thrones. Herodion kneeled in front of Uncle Zidicus. Dani watched in awe as the crown was placed on his head by Uncle Zidicus. Uncle Zidicus then handed him the scepter. As soon as Herodion's hand touched the scepter, the clear crystal on the top burst forth with bright rainbow colors. Dani heard gasps of surprise and awe from around her.

Herodion stood and, without looking back, he ascended to the top level where the thrones sat. He turned toward the room and took his place as the rightful king, seating himself in the throne on the left. Xad's two front feet and head were now just off Herodion's right side. She felt as if she had dropped back in time to some ancient scene played out in Europe. Despite the distance between them, as Herodion sat facing the crowd, she could not help but feel compassion for him. Here he sat, raised high above everyone else but utterly alone, on a throne that once held his father and grandfathers and all the others in his line.

Watching him, Dani noted the determined look he portrayed with the rigid set of his body even through the elaborate clothing he wore. Starting at the first raised platform, a wave of movement washed through the room as everyone kneeled. When the wave ended and the sounds of rustling cloth stopped, there was utter silence. As if everything in this place stopped and held its breath.

Dani looked up just in time to see Xad opening his enormous mouth. She had just enough time to brace herself when a great roar and fire blew out from him, above the audience's heads. A wave of heat quickly followed the flames. Just as fast as it started, the flames ended. She watched the flames race across the hall, and quickly looked back to Xad who still had smoke billowing from around the seams of his lips and nostrils. Xad looked pleased with himself as he had a slight upturn to his lips. Her view of the front of the hall was cut off by everyone in the royal chamber rising, and then yelling at once.

The answering roaring of other pnĕvma synergáti could be heard from the surrounding rooms. The sounds reverberated around the throne room in such force that she felt it in her bones. Between the moving bodies in front of her she caught her next glimpse of Xad and now King Herodion, who both were now smiling.

Everyone then left in reverse order from how they entered: King Herodion and Xad, followed by Uncle Zidicus and Aunt Kathy, the officials and then the nation rulers. When her group left the throne room, they followed the flow of people outside for a giant celebratory feast on the palace grounds. She quickly found a quiet spot off to one side and watched.

It was amazing to see so many pnĕvma synergáti in one place. So many different species were represented. Dani saw her friends and family disperse throughout the crowd. Most of the girls were held onto in some way by their mothers and stepfathers. She had managed to slip away from hers with the help of her sister. Brooke of course knew this type of gathering was not her forte. In fact, she hated them. She was not a schmoozing socialite like her sister, who seemed to not only enjoy it, but thrive in what Dani thought was a controlled chaos environment.

"Are you enjoying yourself?" a male voice asked from behind her.

She jumped and turned around so fast in her seat she sloshed a little of her drink out of her glass.

The soldier bowed, "A thousand apologies, my lady. I didn't mean to frighten you."

"No, it's okay. I just didn't hear you come up behind me. I have been a little jumpy of late. Not your fault, it is mine," Dani said as she rose to stand. Since the portal incident, she had been jumping at every little thing. She really needed to get a grip.

"Very understandable considering what you went through. The fault is mine. I should have announced myself," the guard said.

The strangest feeling that she had seen him before drifted through her, but it was hard to identify faces when they wore the elaborate helmets of the guards.

"Dani, there you are," Aunt Kathy said from off to her left. She turned and looked over at Aunt Kathy and Uncle Zidicus as they quickly approached her.

"Do you have a reason to be speaking with Lady Dani, Guard?" Uncle Zidicus asked.

She had never heard him sound so formal with a guard before. A silence stretched between the two as they looked into each other's eyes.

"None, my Lord," the guard said as he did the salute thing with a fist to the chest.

Uncle Zidicus sighed, "These are troubled times. Forgive my aggressive forwardness."

"I completely understand and approve of your tactics, my Lord. I would have reacted the same in your stead," the guard nodded his head.

She thought it strange for a guard to act this way with Uncle Zidicus. As if he was on the same level or even higher in the hierarchy of the social community here.

"I noticed Lady Dani sitting alone and only wished to provide her company. As you have arrived, I will take my leave." The guard turned to go then paused, turning back slightly. He looked at her and said, "I have been assigned as part of the guard contingency at the School of Knowledge. If I can be of any service, you have but to ask for Diogen." he slightly bowed and left.

"Uncle Zidicus, who is he? I feel like I have seen him somewhere before," she asked.

"I highly doubt that Dani, for he is not from around here," Uncle Zidicus answered.

For the rest of the evening, she could not break away from Aunt Kathy or Uncle Zidicus. Every time she tried, one or the other would box her in. She had seen Herodion only from a crowded distance. He was constantly surrounded by people. She could tell the evening was wearing on him by the slight slump of his shoulders as time drove on into the night.

When she caught up with the other girls and their parents on a side lawn after changing, she was relieved. She was so done with the evening. Still, she could not shake the feeling that she knew Diogen from somewhere. Their guards stood a few feet away with their dragons, ready to take the girls back to the School of Knowledge. Truthfully, she could not wait for the solitude of her room.

Hugs and calls of "I love you" were passed around as they parted ways with their respective parents and then other parents. Crazy how quickly the men seemed to fit right in with their little group. She thought about how settled and happy the moms seemed to be with their "mates." She guessed if you finally met the one person meant for you, it should be that way.

She, on the other hand, was in no hurry to find that person. The warmth in her chest vibrated softly as if chuckling. She knew her spirit partner was doing it. She had come to except it presence in her life. She had a strong, settled feeling inside her. She knew the two of them were going to have some rough road ahead. She was nervous about learning to control and interact with a sentient being that dwelled inside of her and could take her over completely.

The strength that had her throwing herself off a flying dragon, slowing her and Brooke's fall, and then tossing the psychotic Regent Ruler into the portal over her head, had not come from her. She knew that it had come from her spirit partner. As confusing as this was for her logical mind, she accepted it to be what it was. She had a choice to live with it or drive herself crazy with it. Her life events in the last year hadn't exactly been sane. So, she chose to just accept it. Life around here was crazy enough.

Lying in bed later that night, staring through the glass door into the night sky from inside her dorm room, her thoughts drifted like the few clouds on the wind she could see. She was just drifting off when it hit her. Bolting straight up in bed, her eyes flew wide open, and her heart raced.

"It's him! Diogen is the man that came through the portal!" she exclaimed to the quiet of her room.

May the Creator of All Bless You Until Next Time

Authors live and die by you taking a minute, giving us stars, and writing a short review.

Please, if you like The Roda Odyssey, help us stay alive for the next chapters in Dani and Kerberos's lives.

We value your time and honest opinions.

Thank you!

About the Author

Ann Marie and Rob McFall are the co-authors of the new sci-fi fantasy series, *The Roda Odyssey*. Married for over three decades they decided to put their combined skills together to write the epic series. Ann Marie is a certified teacher but has held many jobs over the years following Rob's career all over the United States. She also has a very active storytelling imagination. Rob is an Electronic Systems Analyst. He is the logical processor and bumpers to Ann's creative craziness. Both are avid sci-fi fantasy connoisseurs.

They have two grown sons, three dogs, three cats, two horses, a noisy parrot and an ancient llama. Currently home is in the fresh air and space of the countryside, about an hour and a half south of Kansas City, Missouri. Both love to travel and see the wonders of the world and are hopeful to do more in the future. When not counting their many blessings from The Creator of All, writing, playing with animals and traveling, they love to be out in nature or catching some of the many activities in Kansas City.

You can connect with me on:

🌐 https://mariemcfall.com
🐦 https://twitter.com/mariemcfall11
f https://www.facebook.com/mariemcfal

Printed in Great Britain
by Amazon

24491405R00162